THE FALL
A THRILLER

THE FALL
A THRILLER

Michael Allen Dymmoch

Thomas Dunne Books
St. Martin's Minotaur New York

THOMAS DUNNE BOOKS.
An imprint of St. Martin's Press.

www.minotaurbooks.com

ISBN 0-312-32193-7
EAN 978-0312-32193-2

First Edition: August 2004

0 9 8 7 6 5 4 3 2 1

ACKNOWLEDGMENTS

Many thanks to Deputy Chief of Technical Services Michael Green, for telling me about Northbrook and its police department; James Baker, for explaining the fundamentals of film developing; and Greg Duda, for introducing me to the Canon F1. I have taken liberties with the information given me; any errors are my own.

I am grateful also to my editor, Ruth Cavin, at St. Martin's Press; my agent, Jane Jordan Browne; the reference librarians at the Northbrook Public Library, Northbrook, Illinois; Janis Irvine and her staff at the Book Bin, Northbrook, Illinois; Judy Duhl and her staff, and the Red Herrings of Scotland Yard Books, Winnetka, Illinois.

THE FALL
A THRILLER

ONE

Bloodied by a crimson wash of sunrise, a peaceful army of occupation foraged beneath the naked oaks in Crestwood Park, skirting the abandoned tennis courts and playground. Canada geese. Identical in crisp gray and white uniforms.

Watching them, Joanne Lessing felt joy rise within her like the rush of effervescence when you pop a champagne cork. She sighted on the black-booted cadre and aimed with the reflexes of a sniper. Locating one in her camera's shallow plane of focus, she adjusted the lens until the creature stood in sharp contrast to the fuzzy carpet of grass around it. It paused. Joanne breathed deeply and pressed the trigger. There was a whir, a click. The bird was caught in a net of photons.

November 1st. She had been sent to record the aftermath of Halloween; the geese were serendipity.

The light was serendipity, too—right for November, though the air was too warm and the lawn too green—summer reluctant to loose its hold. Grass that should have been mossy with frost was diamonded with dew, so that the grazing geese seemed to be harvesting jewels. And the breaking sun painted nearby maples radiant yellow and glowing red. The month could have been March but for the warmth, the November light, and the absence of the gray muck snow leaves behind. Everything was still November clean.

Joanne pulled away, looking for a better angle. She noted the time, the f-stop and the shutter speed in the small notebook she carried in her pocket. Before she rewound the roll, she checked the lens for dust, ignoring her reflection—oval face framed by dark hair. She capped the lens and took the film from the camera, numbering the cassette before she dropped it in her camera case. She'd selected another roll and was reopening the camera, a Nikon, when the soft whine of tires signaled an approaching car.

The geese froze at attention.

Instinctively raising the camera, Joanne turned to face the road that separated the park from the neighborhood. A gray car, an expensive import, rounded the corner west of where she stood. Too fast.

The geese scattered and took off.

As his car came even with Joanne, the driver started. Judging by his expression, she might have been pointing a gun instead of a camera. The car veered for less time than it took Joanne to notice, then straightened. Too late! It caromed off a Volkswagen parked on the far side of the street. The VW jerked and screeched a protest. The offending car veered to Joanne's side of the road, scraped the curb, then straightened.

Joanne focused the camera instinctively, then remembered it was out of film. She swung the useless weapon into her camera case and, in the same movement, grabbed her old Canon F-1, removing the lens cover as she raised it to shoot.

Worry about exposure later!

The driver floored it. The car shot forward. Joanne aimed, focused, shot, advanced the film and shot again. But the car was at the end of the block by then. The driver accelerated into the turn and was gone.

"Damn!" Joanne said, "Damn! Damn! Damn!" She advanced the film. "LXV 764. Illinois. LXV 764. LXV 764—" She grabbed for her notebook and wrote the number down. LXV 764. Illinois.

She turned to look at the Volkswagen, muttering, "Must've been drunk." She took shots of the damage from several angles and recorded the black streaks on the pavement. Then she recapped the Canon's lens, dropped the camera in her case and set off running.

Her home was a block from the park. A modest house. Tidy.

Gray-roofed, gray-painted brick with white trim and carport, and a stoplight-red front door. She was breathing hard by the time she got it open.

The living room was near dark. Its only illumination—entering by the high window at the east end of the room—was filtered through luxuriant Boston ferns hung in lieu of drapes. In the dim light, quilts and pillows dumped on the couch and coffee table the previous night made a trolls' kingdom of formless shapes and shadows. The blue light from the VCR glowed through a curtain of pothos leaves from the plant on the shelf above and threw jungle silhouettes against the walls. Joanne blinked to accustom her eyes to the darkness.

Her sprint from front door to telephone was interrupted by the gawky half-man that was her son, Sean. The fourteen-year-old stretched as he crossed her path, stopping just short of collision.

"Aaahhh. Morning, Ma-ahh." He half-covered the yawn with one forearm, and circled Joanne with the other.

She gave him a quick peck on the cheek and slipped out of her coat, draping it over the encircling arm. She opened the camera case and dropped her keys in before setting the case on the dining table by the kitchen door. She took the Canon and her notebook out and backed into the kitchen, pushing the door open with her rump and letting it swing closed on Sean as he followed her. "*Hel*lo!"

Sean caught the door autonomically. "Damn! I overslept!" He was looking out the kitchen window, at the struggle going on between sun and cloud.

Joanne swung the camera onto the center island and put her notebook next to it. "It's only 7:30. You forgot the time change."

As she reached for the wall phone by the door, she said, "Daylight savings strikes again!" She punched 9-1-1 and held up a finger to silence Sean.

A voice at the other end of the line said, "Northbrook Police. Emergency."

"I'd like to report a hit and run."

"Injuries?"

"No. No people hurt." She propped the phone on her shoul-

3

der and began to rewind the film in the Canon. "Somebody side-swiped a parked car."

"Did you get a look at the driver?"

"A man. Older. White. He was heading south on Angle, toward Shermer. He's probably halfway to Chicago by now." She popped the camera open and removed the film.

"Can you describe the suspect's car?"

"Gray—I don't know what kind—something foreign, like a Mercedes or a BMW. New. License number . . ." She put the film roll down and opened her notebook. ". . . LXV 764. Illinois."

"Your name?"

She told him, and her address.

"OK," the cop said. "I'll get this description out and send an officer to make a report. It may be a while. Everyone's tied up right now. Thanks for calling."

As she hung up, Joanne wondered what he meant by 'a while.' She had to get her pictures downtown, and if she didn't leave soon, she'd spend the next hour and a half in traffic.

She tossed the film in the air and caught it. "Sean, do me a favor and straighten the living room a bit before the cops get here."

"What're you gonna be doing?"

"Developing this film. I got at least one shot of a hit-and-run car and a few of the damage he did. I'm sure the police'll want them, but I have some stuff I don't want to lose on the roll. And I don't want them screwed up by—God knows who develops their film."

"Awesome! My ma, ace crime reporter."

"Get going. And get ready for school."

"Shit! Does this mean you're not going to drive me?"

"That's right. If you don't hurry and arrange something soon, you'll have to take the bus."

"Oh no! Not that! Anything but the bus!"

In the darkroom, in the dark, she was able to speculate while she cracked open the canister and put the exposed film in the small stainless steel film tank.

Maybe the driver *was* drunk. But at 7:00 in the morning?

She turned the light back on and punched her work number into the wall phone, testing the developer with a paper strip while the phone rang. It was still good. Barely. She turned on the water and adjusted it to the correct temperature. When the thermometer she'd hung under the stream agreed with her guesstimate, she put it with the bottle of developer in a plastic pail and let the water fill the pail.

May's voice came over the phone line. "Good morning. Rage Photo."

"May, you're in early!" Joanne didn't wait for a reply. "I'm going to be late. There was an accident. . . . No, thank God, but I'm a witness, and the police want a statement. God knows how long it'll take to drive in by the time I'm through. Tell Daniel to stand by. I have Rick's aftermath shots in the can and some great geese that I'd like to get back today."

She hung up the phone and checked the thermometer, then took the developer from the pail and replaced it with the film tank before pouring developer in the top of the tank. After she'd stirred it, she set the timer, checking the time on a faded chart above the sink. It hadn't changed since she'd last developed film, but she always checked.

After the fix, the film had to be rinsed for five minutes. Then she cut the roll into strips of six frames and blotted the corners to hasten the drying. The hair dryer she kept for the purpose quickly readied it for printing.

By the time Sean announced, "Mom! The fuzz's here," she had a proof sheet in the fix and the best negative on the roll in the enlarger. She hit the switch on the enlarger and the timed light glowed, then died.

"Tell him I'll be out in a minute."

The car's image had begun to materialize. It solidified on the paper until it stood out sharply in the red light. It was a commonplace miracle that never failed to astonish and entertain her.

The "fuzz" turned out to be female. "Fizz," Sean corrected himself under his breath when Joanne asked him to come into the darkroom and dry the prints she'd just made.

Joanne thought the officer seemed unnecessarily officious. Or nervous, perhaps. Maybe new to the job. It was, after all, only a car that was hit.

The woman asked for her name, phone number, and driver's license before she asked anything else, and as Joanne described what had happened, she took notes.

"Listen," Joanne said, "You don't have to give my name to the local press, do you. Could you just say 'a witness' saw a car speed away?"

The cop shrugged. "If anybody asks me. Usually, they don't though. . . . What about the driver?"

"A man." The cop waited. "It was so fast. . . . When he saw me, he was startled—that's when he lost control and hit the car."

"Did he slow down or stop?"

"No. After he hit the car, he speeded up."

"You said it was a late model, gray import—like a BMW or a Mercedes?"

"I think so, but I'm not a car buff. I *do* have a picture. . . ."

TWO

Rage Photo was in the Goss Building, occupying the east half of the top floor. It was walking distance from the Rock & Roll McDonald's at Clark and Ontario, where the staff often went for lunch. Joanne entered the building by the delivery door and took the freight elevator up. Riding in it always made her feel a little uneasy. Not that it wasn't ritzy for a freight elevator. It had a wrought iron art deco gate that disappeared overhead when it got to your floor, and it was large enough to accommodate a VW bug if you pushed it in sideways. But it wasn't really enclosed. She'd seen too many suspense movies where someone falls down the elevator shaft or just gets the gate shut before the bad guy grabs her foot. She always felt relieved when she was beyond arm's length from the thing.

She was one of only three Rage employees who had a key to the back door, ten feet from the elevator. She used it to let herself in.

The door opened into a small waiting room that was bisected by a white Formica counter running eastward from the door. Except for Rick, her boss, who was sitting in May's chair behind the counter, the room was empty. Rick had a phone wedged between his left ear and shoulder. He was thirty-one, but could have passed for twenty-four. His straight, dingy blond hair hid his face as he pored over May's appointment calendar. He didn't look up when Joanne closed the door and shrugged out of her jacket. Between comments into the phone, he told her, "Jo, this better be good—at least a fifty car pile up!"

She hung the jacket on one of the half-dozen wooden pegs

along the wall opposite the counter. The room opened into a hall-way that had doors to Rick's office and the little dark room on the right, and Hancock's office, the john and the storeroom on the left.

"My car wouldn't start. I took the train."

Rick finally put the phone down and looked at her. "The train that promises on-time delivery?" He swept the hair back, off his forehead.

"I left late. Didn't May tell you? Where *is* May?"

"I sent her on an errand."

Joanne fished two Ziploc bags of exposed film out of her camera case. "Daniel still here?"

"Eatin' his head off the last hour and a half."

Joanne walked over and patted Rick's cheek, then called, "Daniel!"

"Here." Daniel's voice floated down the hall. Joanne followed it back.

The angular young man backing out of Hancock's office with a mail tray of film envelopes was the company gofer. He had what Joanne called a Botticelli hair cut—a little longer than a Beatles cut and at least five centuries older. It didn't go with his black leather jacket, or the shirt showing beneath it that advertised "Anthrax." Daniel's knees poked through the holes in his jeans, and his untied laces were tucked into his high-tops. He mumbled, "Hi, Jo," through a mouthful of donut.

"See what I mean?" Rick called, with mock disgust.

"Fuck you, Rick," Daniel said.

At this, Hancock came out of his office and leaned against the door jamb with a sour smile. He held another film envelope aloft, staring pointedly at Daniel until the young man brought the tray back for it.

"Well," Hancock said to Joanne, "If it isn't our ten o'clock scholar." His thinning, red-blond hair was parted and combed back from a receding forehead. He had pale brows over faded blue eyes, and a strong jaw. With the conservative suits he habitually wore, he looked more like a Loop attorney than a commercial photographer.

8

Joanne ignored him as she balanced the Ziploc bags on the top of Daniel's tray. She knew better than anyone else that Hancock's misanthropy was a facade. He'd loaned her the down payment for her house—just handed her a check for the amount without a word.

"I need these back yesterday," Joanne told Daniel.

Swallowing, Daniel watched Hancock as he said, "You and the Princess." Hancock was gay, and Daniel—though generally civil—had an adolescent's contempt. He called Hancock "the Princess" whenever the photographer was being especially trying. The deadline for his series must be getting close if he was getting on Daniel's nerves.

Joanne dug a twenty dollar bill out of her camera case and held it out to Daniel. "Get some donuts."

Someone had discovered that if you took donuts in with the film and waited, the lab guys would run the order through immediately—but only if it came without paperwork. Hancock's tray of elaborately labeled envelopes would take their place in the queue and be back in the afternoon at the earliest. Joanne's would return with Daniel.

Daniel nodded as she dropped the money in the tray.

"Get more for us, too." She watched Hancock watch Daniel as he retreated down the hall.

Hancock gave an exaggerated sigh, then turned and demanded, "Tell us about this accident."

Joanne was going over her appointment calendar when Daniel got back. The two plastic Ziploc bags had been exchanged for a paper bag containing boxes of slides. She opened the first, from the geese series, onto her desk and began the tedious task of dating and numbering the transparencies.

When she had all the identifying info on each frame, she put them in the projector cartridge for study. All that were out of focus, and some that were just boring or in which the subject was too far away, went in the trash. She was about to put the rest back in the box when Hancock strolled up.

"Wait."

She hesitated. Hancock's scrutiny made her nervous, but it was also flattering. In private, he often made helpful suggestions. At worst, when an audience was present, he was noncommittal.

He spent as much time looking over the pictures as she had, than said, "OK."

Not particularly helpful.

As she shuffled them back into the box, he fished her discards out of the trash and put them back in the projector tray. He looked them over as carefully as he had the others. He finally stopped at one of the miscellaneous scenery shots with the Crestwood Senior Housing building in the background.

"I'd blow this up more and have another look before I gave up on it," he said. He fast-forwarded through the rest of the discards again and returned all but one to the trash. "Try cropping this." He made a frame with the thumb and index fingers of his hand that cut an almost abstract composition of geese and grass and park fixtures from the jumble projected on the screen.

She gave him a rueful smile. "I know. Back to basics."

THREE

Through the kitchen window, Paul Minorini could see a black-and-white police car, parked outside at the curb, and beyond it, the dark back of the bored patrolman assigned to it. Minorini brought his attention back into the room, to the man who was briefing him. Northbrook detective Doug Gray looked like a plumber. He was Caucasian, five-eight, 280 pounds, with thinning, near-white hair, and gray-blue eyes. He seemed cooperative for a local.

Minorini wasn't fooled. Gray might lack the experience of a big-city homicide detective, but he wouldn't miss much, no matter how well he camouflaged predator instincts behind a bland demeanor. Minorini wouldn't patronize him.

"A neighbor," Gray was saying, "stopped by on his way to work this morning with some mail left at his house by mistake. When he didn't get an answer at the door, he got suspicious because our victim was as predictable as a TV sitcom. Anyway, the neighbor looked through the window and saw feet and called nine-one-one."

Minorini nodded. The feet were no longer on the kitchen floor, the body having been removed to the Cook County morgue for autopsy, but their position had been marked on the white linoleum with strips of black plastic electrical tape. As had the rest of the body except the head. The victim's head had made its own mark—with the blood that seeped from two small caliber bullet holes.

"As near as we can tell," Gray continued, "he opened the door and let the killer in—maybe at gunpoint. The goof shot him through the eye, then put the gun to his head and finished him. Twenty-two or twenty-five caliber, probably silenced."

"The killer locked up on his way out?"

"Yeah. The patrol officer had to kick the door. There were no other signs of forced entry." Gray waited as Minorini looked around.

Apart from its lack of feminine touches, the room was a standard suburban kitchen—white walls and linoleum floor, white-painted cabinets, white appliances and mini-blinds that substituted for curtains. The accessories—dishrags and towels—were the washed out blue-and-lavender-with-geese that had been the rage years earlier. Black fingerprint powder was smudged on any surface that looked like it would hold a print. From the number and distribution of smudges, Minorini judged that the technician knew what he was doing. Why not? They might not have murders in the burbs, but they had plenty of burglaries. He glanced around again, then said, "Let's see the rest of it."

Gray nodded and stepped around the outline on the floor. Minorini followed.

The kitchen was at the front of the house, between the garage and a hall leading from the front door to the back. It wasn't the usual arrangement, but convenient. Across the hall from the kitchen, a living room faced the street north of the house. There was a window on the east wall, and a door to an adjacent office on the south. The room was sparsely furnished with the kind of stuff that looks great in the showroom, but doesn't wear well. An entertainment center beside the office door held a few best-sellers, no electronic equipment, CDs, tapes or videos. A sofa backed up to the street windows, paralleling a glass-topped coffee table and facing the empty shelves. End tables flanked the couch, and chairs faced the coffee table at either end. The room was neat, but the smooth surfaces showed a fine film of dust, disturbed only on the coffee table and the end table nearest the hall.

"You did your interviews in here," Minorini said. He didn't mean it as a question.

"Yeah, not that there were that many. The guy lived alone and didn't have many visitors, didn't socialize with the neighbors."

"We'll want his phone records."

"We're working on that."

"And talk to his mail carrier. See if he got much mail. And from whom."

Gray nodded. He seemed neither eager to please nor offended that the Feds were horning in. A professional. Minorini was relieved. He said, "Did he have a maid service or cleaning lady?"

"We'll know after the canvass." Gray seemed to be waiting for a dismissal. Then he looked behind Minorini, toward the door. Minorini turned to see his partner, Special Agent Wayne Haskel, enter the room. Haskel fit the FBI profile—clean cut, clean-shaven and stone-faced. He was six feet tall and physically fit, with brown hair and hazel eyes. Minorini waited for his report.

Haskel looked pointedly at Gray, obviously waiting for him to leave before speaking. It was the sort of arrogance that had earned the Bureau its bad rep among the locals. Minorini felt a surge of annoyance. There wasn't any reason Gray couldn't hear what Haskel had; Gray *was* the primary on the case. Minorini kept his irritation hidden. "What did you find out, Wayne?"

Haskel looked at Gray again before saying, "As the locals surmised, Mandrel was a protected witness. Real name, Albert Siano. 'Bout eight years ago, he testified against some real heavy hitters on the east coast and . . ." He shrugged. "The mob never forgets."

"We may have a break on this one," Gray said.

Haskel looked surprised—as if he'd thought Gray couldn't talk. Minorini let Haskel ask, "What's that?"

"A woman who lives near here was out taking pictures in the park about the time our victim was shot. She may have seen the killer."

"Well, why didn't you say so?" Haskel said. "Let's get with her."

"We can't right now. She's at work, and we don't know where she works." Before Haskel could say anything sarcastic, Gray added, "She reported a hit-and-run, property damage only. The officer who took her statement didn't have any reason to connect it to this so she didn't press for a full autobiography."

Gray's radio hissed and he said, "Excuse me," and walked to the other side of the room to answer it. When he came back, he told them, "We just got another report on what we think was the getaway car—a woman who lives in the Crestwood Senior Housing seems to have seen the same hit-and-run as our photographer."

"And she's just now gotten round to reporting it?" Haskel demanded.

Gray shrugged. "I'll ask her. You coming?"

Mrs. Harriette Cronin seemed to Minorini like a larger, wrinkled version of the girl she must have been before puberty—straight-figured as a two-by-four. And she had an oddly childlike voice, though, mercifully, no tendency to talk childishly.

She hadn't been going to call at all—she told them—there was a witness who'd surely seen enough for the police to catch the driver. But then Doris—Doris Davis, Mrs. Cronin's next-door neighbor—had made such a fuss that Mrs. Cronin had had second thoughts.

They followed her up to her room, a brightly lit space on the third floor facing the park. The walls were covered alternately by bookshelves and Audubon posters. Though most of the furniture was new, the armchair by the window was well worn.

After he'd inspected her view, Detective Gray asked, "How is it you happened to be looking out when this accident occurred?"

"No happened about it," Mrs. Cronin said. "I was watching the geese. There was a flock grazing in the park and the young woman was taking pictures of them."

"Then what happened?" Haskel demanded.

Mrs. Cronin looked at him sharply, and seemed about to say

something she must have had second thoughts about. Then she said, "Some idiot came screeching down the street in a gray car and scared them off."

"Did you get a look at the idiot?" Gray asked.

"No. He was too far away. And I didn't have my field glasses. I don't need them for watching geese."

"What did the photographer do?" Minorini asked.

Mrs. Cronin turned to face him. "Well, when the car came down the street, she turned and pointed her camera at it—that's when it hit the other car. Then she put down *that* camera and picked up another camera. I'm sure she got pictures. And she *must've* seen the license plate. It never occurred to me that she wouldn't report it—until I mentioned it to Doris. *She* said I should've called the police."

"And we appreciate that you did, ma'am," Gray said. "And just to be on the safe side, you probably shouldn't mention it to anyone else until we catch the guy."

FOUR

Three men were sitting in a car in front of her house when Joanne got home. As she walked up the drive, they got out and strolled over to meet her. She felt a sudden apprehension. Two of them were tall, tanned and fit, with conservative suits and haircuts, and impeccably pressed shirts. One of these was dark complected and handsome—Hispanic or Italian—the second lighter and coarsely featured. The third man was older and heavy. He wore a sport jacket over a shirt that looked like he'd served hard time in it. He'd unbuttoned the top button, and loosened his tie. As the group met her at the top of the drive, he said, "Mrs. Lessing?"

They were between her and the door. Joanne felt her apprehension swell to near panic. Irrational.

Then the older man pulled aside the front of his jacket to show a badge on his belt. "Detective Gray," he said, "Northbrook police."

Joanne's relief was profound but short-lived. The vague threat the three strangers had posed suddenly became specific. "What happened? Is Sean all right?"

Gray looked puzzled, briefly, then seemed to realize what she was asking. "Your son? He's in the house. He told us you'd be home soon, so we waited."

The other men didn't speak, and Gray didn't introduce them. They must be police, too, but they didn't seem as friendly.

Joanne said, "What's this about?"

"The hit-and-run you witnessed this morning," Gray said. "Can we come in for a minute?"

· · ·

Before they started, the dark-haired man introduced himself as Special Agent Minorini and his partner as Special Agent Haskel. Something her ex-husband, Howie, once said flashed into her head—*government suits*. He'd been referring to FBI agents. These two fit the part. *FBI!* Minorini asked Joanne if she minded them taping the interview.

She remembered Howie telling her once that cops interview subjects and interrogate suspects. She wondered why the FBI was involved. "Was the car stolen?" It was.

The cops had printed all her negatives and blown up details of a few—the rear window and rearview mirrors of the car—presumably to get a likeness of the driver. But no such luck. The single disconnected eye and eyebrow visible in the center mirror were too grainy to be of any use. She'd have discarded the whole roll. The shots were focused and balanced, but boring as calculus.

They'd also brought a large map of the park and nearby streets. They asked her to mark where she'd stood when she spotted the car, where it had been when the geese took flight, and where *she'd* been when she snapped the first picture.

She wondered how they knew about the geese.

Their questions were just like the cop's who'd taken her report earlier: "You were taking pictures. Were you trying to shoot the hit-and-run driver? Might he have thought you were taking his picture? Did you point the camera at him? You weren't trying to photograph him, but he may have thought you were? Was he going fast initially? Did he slow down after he hit the car? Could you see him clearly? Could he see *you* clearly? Would you recognize him if you saw him again?"

They were obviously trying to determine why the driver swerved. She didn't know. They seemed to be making a Federal case out of a simple hit-and-run, even if it *was* a stolen car.

Agent Haskel asked, "Why didn't you shoot him when he hit the car? You *were* pointing the camera at him at that point?"

"I couldn't." She shook her head. "I'd used up all the film,

17

and since I didn't have time to reload, I had to change cameras. By the time I got the other camera out, he was where I caught him in the picture."

"You always carry two cameras?"

"Nearly always. I'm a professional photographer."

"You didn't tell the officer that."

"She didn't ask."

"Where'd you get it processed?"

Joanne hooked a thumb towards her darkroom. "I developed it myself. In my darkroom."

The others looked sharply at Gray. The officer hadn't told them that, either, she guessed.

"What was on the rest of the roll?" Minorini asked. His voice was neutral—not accusing, just curious.

Joanne shrugged. "Pictures of my son." She let her tone imply 'nothing of interest to the police.'

Haskel said, "Mind if we have a look?" His tone said he didn't quite believe her, and that it wouldn't matter much if she *did* mind. Joanne looked at him more closely, as she would at a portrait that didn't quite flatter its sitter. She decided that he appeared ugly because of his expression rather than because the collection of features making up his face was unattractive.

He asked, "So why did this guy swerve? A squirrel run in front of him or something?"

"No, there was nothing I could see." They waited again. "My guess is he wasn't expecting anyone to see him—or, at least not anyone with a camera."

Her questioner exchanged glances with his partner.

Suddenly, the whole situation seemed absurd. Joanne was tired and hungry and she resented these people inviting themselves into her house to ask for information without reciprocating. She said, "What's this about?"

Detective Gray said, "You didn't listen to the news." It wasn't a question.

The younger men gave him a sharp look.

Gray seemed annoyed, but Joanne couldn't tell if it was with her or the others. She shook her head and waited. He continued, "A man who lived a couple blocks from here was murdered. . . ."

"And I may have seen the killer!" Joanne finished.

She turned to the pressed-and-prim tag team. Mutt and Jeff—the good cop, bad cop routine—was something else she'd learned about from Howie. "Why is the FBI involved?"

Haskel started to say, "We'll ask—" but Minorini cut him off. "We have reason to believe organized crime may enter into it."

Joanne shivered in spite of herself. It seemed so melodramatic—thriller movie stuff—but here they were.

"Would you mind coming with us," Minorini continued, "to look at some mug shots?" His tone implied it wasn't a request. "If this individual has a record, we'll have his picture on file."

Mentally, Joanne ran through the list of things she'd planned for the evening. She shrugged. "I guess not."

"We'll drive you down and bring you back afterwards." He made it sound, at least, as if he gave her credit for appreciating the urgency.

"I'd like to change and make arrangements for my son, if you don't mind."

Gray said, "Sure. And we'll have your statement typed up so you can come in tomorrow to sign it."

She nodded, her mind already revising her schedule. Sean could go to Jane's for the evening . . .

FIVE

They took her to 219 South Dearborn, downtown Chicago, because the Feds had a more extensive gallery of mob portraits than the local law. Detective Gray followed in his own car. Inside the ninth-floor FBI headquarters, they were issued visitors' IDs and followed agents Haskel and Minorini through the building. Detective Gray seemed as out of place as she.

When they reached the picture room, Haskel disappeared, leaving Minorini to explain that Joanne should study the faces carefully and let him know if she spotted the hit and run driver.

The mug shots were on computer, many black and white, most color. None of the faces looked familiar. Joanne found herself mentally criticizing the photographers' technique. Most of the pictures looked as if they'd been taken by the same person, with harsh light that flattened the faces and created unflattering shadows. Some of the subjects looked dead, but of course if they were, she wouldn't be looking at their pictures.

She lost track of time. After a while, the faces looked the same. She began to feel dazed. She became aware of being hungry. When the computer operator finally said, "That's the lot," Joanne felt as if she'd been given a reprieve. But it was only temporary. Minorini asked if she would like to take a break before they started on the Identisketch computer.

"What's that?"

"The electronic equivalent of a sketch artist."

"Maybe I'd better check the plumbing."

He escorted her to the door of the ladies' room and asked if she'd like coffee. She would.

"With?"

"Just cream, thanks."

He was standing outside the door with three coffees when she came out. He handed her one and offered one to Gray, who was waiting in the room with the computer. The woman in charge of it sat her in front of the screen and began to question her about the shape of the suspect's face, his eyes, his ears, the contour of his nose. To Joanne's disgust, she discovered she couldn't quite picture the driver's face. Nevertheless, the operator gradually constructed a portrait on the screen. It seemed to Joanne that the composite looked more like a generic bad guy than the real thing, but apart from knowing that it wasn't a good likeness, she couldn't say what was wrong.

"I've gotten lazy," she said, finally. "I have this photographic memory . . ." She patted her camera case. ". . . if I get enough shots. So I often don't bother remembering—or even noticing—details." Life moved too fast, sometimes. Sometimes you had to catch it on film, stopping the action, to get a look at what was happening.

The operator printed out copies of the final composite, which she gave to both Gray and Minorini. They walked back to the reception desk in silence. When they turned in the borrowed IDs, Gray said, "I've got to be going. I'll take Ms. Lessing home."

"That's okay," Minorini said. "I'll take her."

Gray thrust out his hand and Minorini shook it. "Tomorrow, then."

Minorini nodded. Joanne watched with him as the Northbrook detective disappeared. Then Minorini said, "Since I've screwed up your evening, let me buy you dinner."

It wasn't like being asked on a date, Joanne thought. It was purely quid pro quo. She'd been cooperative, if not particularly helpful; he'd feed her, probably at the taxpayers' expense. She was hungry and tired, and the thought of the half hour—or more at this time of day—drive home on an empty stomach was more painful than the thought of having to make small talk with this stranger. She said, "Sure. Thanks."

He took her to Cavanaugh's, sandwiched between the John Marshall Law school and a city parking garage south of Jackson. He parked in a no-parking zone. The restaurant was noisy and crowded with lawyer types.

They found seats in a corner where they could easily see the door but wouldn't be obvious to everyone who came in. Minorini pulled out a chair for her that faced the wall, then sat opposite, with his back to it. The waiter appeared and stood by attentively.

"Drink?" Minorini asked.

"Yes. Chardonnay?" The waiter nodded.

Minorini said, "Guinness. Thanks." When the waiter went away he asked, "How long have you been a photographer?" She could barely hear him above the noise.

"Five years." He waited. "I only turned pro three years ago, when we moved here."

"Where did you live before?"

"California."

"What made you decide on Chicago?"

"I wanted to get away from my ex." She'd told him earlier she was divorced, during the Q and A of his initial interview. "And I have family in the area." Before he could ask something else, she said, "Are you from around here?"

"Philadelphia." He didn't have an accent she could detect.

"Did you choose Chicago?"

"It was the best of the options I was offered."

She watched him studying the menu. He seemed all impervious surface—gorgeous, smooth as polished granite. The waiter brought their drinks and took their dinner order—a Reuben sandwich for Joanne, a burger for Minorini. While they waited for the food, he answered the questions she put to him about the Bureau and his career. His responses seemed straightforward, but he managed to keep his recital as impersonal as a resume, no feeling for the work, no delight or boredom. If he felt any disappointment over her failure to identify the hit-and-run driver, who—she was convinced—had murdered her anonymous neighbor, he gave no sign.

The food was good and plentiful. It came and went while they made further conversation. When Joanne tried to get any information of substance—about his work, the mob or the current investigation—he put her off with tact and skill. He was the perfect host, courteous and attentive, but as interesting as tax law. She accepted coffee but declined dessert and found herself studying the contours of his face as if for a portrait. In the dim light, he looked like the romantic lead in a movie—tall, dark, exquisitely masculine. But was he the hero or the antihero? Or worse, was he a polished version of Howie?

"What were you saying to Jones about a photographic memory?" he asked.

Jones must be the Identisketch operator.

"In one of his books, Rollo May accused people of using cameras to store up the events of their lives, like treasures, without really experiencing them. I'm afraid I'm guilty of that. Film 're-members' detail so much more accurately than memory, I don't often bother to notice details of what I'm shooting—I just concentrate on getting the perfect composition and exposure, and the proper focus."

He was staring intently at her as she spoke. Howie used to stare just so when he wasn't paying attention because he was concentrating on how to get in her pants.

She felt a vague disappointment. Agent Minorini was just making listening noises.

Then he seemed to come back to the present. "Bottom line," he said, "would you recognize him if you saw him again?"

"I don't know."

The small talk had petered out and an uncomfortable silence settled in. This was the point at which—in the romances and the movies—there was a cut to later action.

"How did you get into this line of work?" she asked to fill the void.

"I majored in English. While I was bouncing from job to job after college, the Bureau seduced me with promises of adventure and romance. Besides, someone's got to do it."

"*Someone's got to do it?* Didn't they warn you, in English, about clichés?"

"The *real* stuff dreams are made of." He laughed without apparent amusement. "Back in those days we were the Good Guys. Remember *I Spy?*"

"*Our hearts are pure because our cause is just?*"

He smiled. "Just, but not innocent."

"There are no innocents."

"*You,* my dear lady, are an innocent."

SIX

He as good as said that I'm totally naive!" Joanne told her friend Jane Kendall. "He called me an innocent!"

"Not everyone would find that insulting," Jane said.

They were sitting cross-legged on Joanne's couch, drinking Chablis. Since Joanne's car still wouldn't start, Jane had brought Sean home and had stayed for a drink. Sean was installed in his room, insulated from the world by a cocoon of music. At least what *he* called music.

"There must be some correlation between being a jerk and being a gorgeous male," Joanne said. "He's certainly gorgeous."

"Yeah, well," Jane said. "Remember that reggae song about marrying an ugly woman? It goes twice for ugly men. You're better off with some guy who doesn't think he's God's gift."

"It's moot anyway. They'll never get the killer, so I'll never see Special Agent Minorini again."

"What's special about him?"

"He's very photogenic." Jane laughed. "But as far as I can tell, all FBI agents are called special agents. Who knows why?" Joanne finished her wine and said, "Want another?"

Jane thought about it and said, "Oh, why not?"

Joanne gathered the glasses and walked to the kitchen.

When she came back, Jane waved a copy of the latest *Chicago Magazine* at her. "You didn't tell me about this." She sounded hurt.

Joanne didn't have to look to know what she meant. "I didn't really believe it till I got my copy."

Rick had sent her to get pictures to accompany a feature on

shoplifting. He was charging for a week of her services and he more or less gave her carte blanche. It had taken her nearly the whole week to master the technique of indoor hunting, two days to actually capture the suspects.

She'd gotten the first sequence—a series of shots before, during and after a theft—by setting her camera on a tripod in the camera department and becoming part of the display. When she noticed a man watching the sales clerk, she'd focused her camera at an f-stop that would allow sufficient depth of field, and waited with remote in hand.

Her quarry turned his back to the store's security camera and watched the clerk, watched Joanne, too, though not as carefully. She must have seemed to be a customer or an employee occupied with setting up a display. Joanne dropped out of his sight and watched him in the mirror of a display case glass. She could see him well enough. After the camera he'd been inspecting disappeared beneath his coat, she'd stepped casually behind the service counter to call security.

The thief considered other purchases. Joanne had readied her F1, uncapped its telephoto lens and calculated the exposure for the indoor light. The man gave her plenty of time. While he bought film for the camera he'd just boosted, she substituted one of the store's Nikons for her own Minolta that she'd put on the tripod. She'd slung the Minolta under her arm and put her coat on over it while the sales clerk packaged the thief's film. By the time the shoplifter was ready to leave, Joanne had the F1 around her neck, over her coat, and was ready to follow him.

She'd caught the climax in the parking lot, as the security guards arrested the man getting into his car, and the finale when the Northbrook Police bundled him into a squad car.

There were two other sequences, similarly shot, identical except that one included the expression of despair on the face of the shoplifter's accomplice when she realized her partner had been caught. And there was an individual shot, captioned "Booster!", showing a woman slipping imported champagne into a false-bottomed box. The Booster's look of triumph was priceless.

Joanne's name and copyright notice appeared below that picture. She'd snapped it at her local Osco, a year before the shoplifting assignment.

"And I haven't seen you since it came," Joanne told her friend.

"These are fabulous. You're too good to be true."

"Howie had me brainwashed forever into thinking I was lucky just to be his wife." She'd gone along with him, taking whatever he dished out. And then she'd discovered photography.

The camera had saved her sanity during the breakup. Learning to use it was like getting glasses for the first time when you've been nearsighted all your life. Photography had taught her control, had taught her she had choices and that art is about choosing what to control. Camera and lens, whether to use a flash or filters, aperture, shutter speed, even when to hold the camera vertically or horizontally. To quote Feininger, *Good photographers rely on choice, not chance.*

The problem of how to live with Howie or live without him had been forgotten as she focused on the problems of fixing line and form and color. One day she'd discovered that Howie mattered not at all. She smiled, remembering. "I keep waiting for the other shoe to drop." She knocked wood on the coffee table.

Jane laughed and held up her glass. "To independence!"

Joanne touched her glass to her friend's. "And choice."

SEVEN

In the year and a half that Minorini had been assigned to Chicago, he'd had occasion to attend three autopsies at the Robert J. Stein Institute of Forensic Medicine—Cook County Morgue. He parked west of the modern white stone facility, next to a Chicago PD squadrol, in the Official-Business-Only lot. He entered through the intake door on the loading dock. The two Chicago cops assigned to the wagon were kibitzing with the morgue employee on intake duty as he weighed and photographed his latest customer.

The body—young, male, black—was laid out on a man-sized stainless-steel tray topping a gurney parked on a scale built into the floor. The cops and the morgue guy were wearing latex gloves. Like the victim, they were black. The morgue guy looked up just long enough to take in Minorini's ID and to nod. No one seemed the least concerned about the dead man. So much for racial solidarity. But maybe they didn't see the deceased as one of them. Maybe he was just a dead lowlife. Gangbanger or not, Minorini thought, he'd been family to someone. Minorini was suddenly glad he didn't have any kids.

The morgue guy began undressing the body. "Who you s'posed to see?" he asked.

"Whoever's doing the post on Albert Siano."

"That'd pro'ly be Doc Cutler. He do all the biggies. Know where ta go?"

Minorini nodded, realized the man wasn't watching him, and said, "Yeah," but didn't move. The spectacle of the preparation held him. There was a large-caliber hole below the victim's left cheek bone and one through the lower, fleshy part of the right side of his nose.

The younger cop, who looked a lot like Walter Payton, said, "They say bangers favor Tech Nines cause they don't get much practice in, an' they're all lousy shots."

The older cop laughed. "Like our shooter, here?"

Minorini turned away.

There were three autopsies underway when he entered the post-mortem room. Detective Gray, gowned in blue like the ME and his assistant, was standing at the naked feet of Albert Siano, chewing gum as he watched them examine Siano's remains. Gray said, "Minorini."

"Detective Gray," Minorini said. "Doctor."

The medical examiner nodded at Minorini and told his assistant, "They're going to make a Federal case out of this one."

The assistant didn't get it. Cutler shook his head. Gray chuckled without smiling.

They watched as the ME's photographer pushed a wheeled ladder to the foot of the gurney and climbed the ladder to get a full body photo of Siano. She advanced the film and repositioned her perch for close-ups, first without, then with a ruler to show scale. Like the young gang member, Siano had taken two shots to the head, but in Siano's case, they were small caliber and close range, the work of a professional killer.

The ME gave the word, and his assistant rolled Siano over and began to open his head. Once the skull was cracked, so to speak, the ME took over. And the photographer worked with him, recording the damage.

"I brought you what we've got on Siano," Minorini told Gray. Gray nodded.

Judging by the tiny amount of gunshot residue on the face, a right-handed gunman had ended Siano's career with a bullet through his left eye. The contact wound to the temple, with its

29

star-patterned tears and characteristic circular burn mark, was just insurance. Ever since Ken Ito, the pros didn't take chances.

The rest of the autopsy was anticlimax. Siano had been sixty-two, with a failing heart and iffy liver, but he'd been robbed of the few years he'd had left, and Minorini was sworn to make someone pay for that. He'd do his best. He looked at Gray and decided that the grim-faced detective probably felt the same way.

EIGHT

Joanne," May said, dropping a pile of notebooks on the counter in front of her. "Be a lifesaver and take these in to Rick. If I go in there I'm gonna kill one of 'em."

She frowned, and Joanne thought again, as she had many times, that May should have been a model. She was as tall, slender, and poised as the best. She had a perfect oval face, flawless skin—just darker than coffee with cream, huge obsidian eyes, tiny nose, and a sensuous mouth. Her hair, today, was braided in tight cornrows, each ending in a gold bead, and she wore gold Laurel Burch earrings. Her taste in clothes ran from flamboyant African-inspired to tight jeans and sweaters. Today she was dressed up.

"Who's he with?" Joanne asked.

"Rita. Who else?"

Rita was Rick's ex-wife. She'd been named, or perhaps she'd changed her name—Joanne wasn't sure—for Rita Hayworth, and Joanne secretly believed that Rita had married Rick for his name. From what Rick said, rage had been the dominant emotion while they were married. The excitement their fights created seemed to have become a drug they both still craved. Rita owned forty percent of the company—not a deciding percentage, but enough to give her some rights that she used as an excuse to pick fights when she was bored.

"Why didn't she ever come around to bother us when she was married to him?" Joanne asked.

May sniffed. "Too busy spendin' his money. Guess now she can't do *that,* she figures to stop him making any."

Hancock stuck his into the room to add, "Yeah, and us, too."

"He's got to do something about her," May said. "This's getting to be a real drag."

"What's he s'posed to do," Hancock said, "put out a contract on her?" Joanne knew she'd reacted badly to that suggestion when he added, "Oh. Sorry, Joanne."

Joanne knocked lightly, then opened the door before Rick could tell her to go away. "Excuse me," she said, and walked over to put May's notebooks on the desk. She looked Rick in the eye and said, "You'd better go talk to Hancock."

"Oh, Jesus! Just what I need now." Rick got up and hurried out, the better to head off the storm she'd just conjured in his mind's eye.

As Joanne started to follow him, Rita said, "You're Joanne Lessing, aren't you?"

Joanne stopped and nodded.

"*The* Joanne Lessing? The one who did the bikers on the *Tribune Magazine* cover?"

"Yes."

"You know, I'd kill to have someone do something that flattering of me. I don't suppose that's possible."

Joanne shook her head. "I'm sorry."

"Rick's orders?"

"No. It's just that—I'm not afraid of you."

"What?"

What made the pictures unique, Joanne explained, was that she'd been terrified of the bikers. Getting close enough to make their portraits had given her a high that was like what she imagined for cocaine. It was reflected in the results.

"You're putting me on!"

"No. Really. It's how I deal with anything I'm afraid of. I'm not sure why. Maybe it's like whistling a happy tune, or maybe I just get used to whatever it is—like getting desensitized to a phobia. I don't know."

Rita shook her head. "That's the damnedest thing I ever heard. You're as crazy as Rick. You fit right in here." She made a dismissive gesture with her hand, and Joanne escaped into the hall.

Rick was just coming out of Hancock's office. "Cute, Joanne."

"Don't start on her!" May popped her head out of the dark-room doorway and gave him a mock scowl. "I *axed* her to get you outta there. You got clients waiting."

Rick rolled his eyes, shook his head and muttered, "Damned conspiracy," but headed off in the direction of the conference room.

May laughed. "Guess I'll jus' go tell *Ms.* Rage it'll be a minute."

NINE

The neighborhood canvass had turned up zilch on Siano's killer, and the autopsy hadn't told them anything new. Since nobody'd recognized the generic bad guy in Joanne Lessing's composite, Minorini turned his lens on her. Maybe, now that she knew that the mob was involved, she had a good reason to not remember what the hit man looked like. Or maybe, now that she knew the Bureau was involved, she wanted out for some other reason.

He started with the Secretary of State's Office, Driver Services Department. Lessing had traded a California license for one from Illinois three years earlier; she'd had a clean driving record since. No changes of address, either.

Using her DOB and social security number, he was able to determine that she had Visa and Discover cards as well as Sears, Kohl's, and J.C. Penney's. All had what seemed to him to be unhealthy balances. She was paying a little more than the minimum on each card every month and seemed to be late with a payment on one or another almost every month. Probably par for a single mother with problems collecting child support. He checked on that next. California records showed a Lessing divorce roughly three years earlier, and several filings since to collect back child support. From the looks of it, Howard Lessing never paid until his ex-wife's lawyer hauled him back into court—four times in three years.

Lessing claimed to be a professional photographer, so Minorini checked the membership roster on the Professional Photographers of America website. She wasn't a member, but when he queried Rage Photo, he got a hit. Richard Rage, the owner, was. Just for kicks—and because he didn't have any hot leads—he ran all the usual checks on both of them. No arrests, no wants or warrants, no bankruptcies, lawsuits or judgements against either, no complaints to the Better Business Bureau—a pair of regular citizens.

He sat back at his desk and laced his fingers behind his head. There was something about Joanne Lessing that made her stick in his head—the little show of gumption, maybe, when she'd demanded to know what was going on, or maybe the metaphor she'd used—her photographic memory. She wasn't flashy, but she wasn't bad looking. He wondered what she'd look like dressed up. Or undressed. On a whim, he got on the phone to the photography section and asked if anybody there had heard of a Joanne Lessing.

Somebody had. "Check the current *Chicago Magazine* feature on shoplifting, and the *Chicago Tribune Magazine*'s April 11th issue on motorcycle gangs."

Minorini rang off and called *Chicago Magazine*. By the time he'd finished talking to the *Tribune,* his fax was spitting out the shoplifting article. He put his feet on the desk while he studied the photos, which could easily have told the story without a word of text. His estimation of Joanne rose with each picture. Funny, as professional as the feature was, she hadn't apologized for the amateur quality of the shots she'd taken of the fleeing hit man.

When the *Tribune* editor emailed the biker article, Minorini's puzzlement grew. She'd managed to get close enough to the gang, figuratively speaking, to get candid pictures of the members' mundane activities—changing a baby's diaper, mending a tire, waterproofing boots. But more than ordinary human events, the pictures captured emotions—pride, dismay, delight—and demonstrated an awesome mastery of the camera.

Minorini wasn't sure what instinct made him hide the articles when he heard Haskel approach.

"You wanna go grab a bite?" Haskel asked.

"Yeah, sure." Minorini shuffled his notes and reports into a neat pile and wrapped a file folder around it. He put the file in a drawer and locked it out of habit.

"So d'you get to first base with our star witness last night?"

"Grow up, will you?"

"Touchy, aren't we. It's been how long since you got any?—I saw the way you were looking at her."

"Yeah, right."

"She's gotta be every man's dream—a virgin, figuratively speaking."

"Virgins are highly overrated. I'm holding out for a woman who can watch my back."

TEN

The murder was the lead in Thursday's local news. The reporter for the *Northbrook Star* took two and a half columns to give the paragraph's worth of information the police were willing to part with. Her coverage added nothing to what Doug Cummings had said in thirty seconds on the radio. The Police Blotter section added that a resident at 1000 Waukegan Road had seen a gray car hit a car parked in the 1800 block of Milton before speeding away. There weren't any details. The reporter hadn't, apparently, made the connection between that item and the lead story. And, thank God, no one mentioned her.

Joanne put the paper down to answer the phone.

"Jo!" Howie's voice came whining over the line from La-La Land, like a switch turning on all her old feelings of rage and depression. What had she ever seen in the jerk?

"What do you want, Howie?" She imagined him lounging next to the pool with the phone, letting the sun worship him.

He laughed. "You used to be such a nice girl, Joanne."

"Girl is the operative word, Howie. I've grown up. Now that I'm a woman, I won't put up with your shit."

"Don't start . . ."

"Get to the point."

"I want to talk to my son."

"He isn't home. You'll have to leave a message or call back."

There was silence while he considered the alternatives, then he said, "I want Sean to spend the holidays with me."

"Fine.

"Here." He was beginning to sound irritated.

"No.

"*He* can choose."

There was anger in the statement. She could still recognize his patent effort to be cool, to be reasonable, and the implication that *she* was somehow the cause of whatever disagreement they were having. She wondered if she would ever be able to be indifferent, to feel nothing—no annoyance, no inadequacy or regret. She felt herself slipping into her old way of responding. "You're right, Howie." Her irritation with herself made her add, "He's old enough to tell you where to go himself."

Howie had kept her insecure and dependent. When he discovered that he couldn't snow her family, he'd put them down and moved her to Los Angeles. Isolation had come to seem normal, but it had not been freely chosen.

"God dammit, Joanne. I pay support. I've got rights."

Joanne raised the handset overhead but stopped it aloft. Then she carefully replaced it in its cradle and unplugged the phone.

It wasn't fair. It wasn't enough that she'd paid for the mistake of marrying Howie with all the years of living with him. She was still paying. It wasn't his fault entirely. He was two thousand miles away and she could always hang up the phone. Why did she still feel so bad? Even now, when she stood up to him and gave as good as she got, she felt depressed.

Sean had left the mail piled on the counter with the paper. She could see it was all bills. People didn't have time to write letters anymore, at least the people she knew. Not that she'd have had time to answer if they did. She opened everything and put the envelopes and inserts in the recycling bin. She made a quick estimate of how short her paycheck would be and stuffed the bills into her paperwork drawer. Well, they weren't due for two weeks and something would come up by then. If not, she could pay a little on each and keep them all off her back till next month.

· · ·

Twenty minutes later the swinging door flew open as Sean barged in. He tended to be dramatic at times for no reason that she could see, but it went with the shocking T-shirt slogans and the extreme hair style.

"Ma! Can we go to McDonalds?"

"*May* we go to McDonalds," she said, quietly.

"That's what I said."

She lowered her head and raised her eyebrows.

Sean said, "May we go to McDonald's?"

"If you're buying. I'm broke."

"What do you do with all the wads of money you're always getting paid?" He punctuated his question with mock hits to her upper arm as if it were a punching bag.

"Oh, I spend it at the salon. . . ." She held her hand up at eye-level with her wrist bent to show off an imaginary manicure, then fluffed a make-believe hair style. "And the boutique." She curtsied, holding out an imaginary skirt.

He giggled. He opened the refrigerator and peered inside. "There's nothing to eat in the house!"

"I'm sure that can't be true. I spent a hundred dollars at the Jewel last time. There must be *something* left."

He fanned the air with the fridge door. "Nah, look. Nothing. Not a cracker or a crumb even."

Joanne pulled out the carton of eggs and said, "We could have scrambled eggs."

"For dinner?"

She grabbed a block of cheddar. "We'll put cheese on them and call it an omelet. And we have potatoes we can bake."

"No butter."

"We'll just have to put cheese on the potatoes, too." She opened the freezer and took out a package of frozen spinach.

Sean said, "Yech!" He looked in and added, "No ice cream."

"Deprivation!" She opened cabinets until she spotted a bag of marshmallows. "We can have crispy treats for dessert."

"No Rice Krispies."

"Then we'll have corn flake crispy treats."

"You *are* relentless."

"Who told you that?"

"I heard dad tell his lawyer. I looked it up 'cause I thought it was something bad."

"I prefer to think of myself as inventive. As in—"

"I know—Necessity is the mother. Or is it *a* mother?"

She gave him a mock frown, then said, "To get back to dinner, where there's a will there's a way."

"I thought it was an attorney."

"What?"

"Where there's a will there's an attorney. Gotcha!" His grin faded suddenly and he seemed wistful as he added, "Too bad dad's such a dickhead. He's missing a lot of fun."

"Not to mention some really bad puns. Speaking of your dad, he called."

"So?"

"He wants you to come out for Thanksgiving."

When he didn't respond, she said, "How do you feel about that?"

"It sucks. I don't want to go."

"Well, don't then."

"You mean I have a choice?"

"Everyone has choices."

ELEVEN

Veteran's Day dawned slate gray and lemon yellow before crimson light burst below the overcast like a muzzle-flare fixed by fast film. The red faded. The slate-colored clouds thinned and blued.

Joanne resisted the urge to grab her camera. She could have run off a roll every morning, but her portfolio contained enough sunrises. And anyway, they were a cliché. Everyone with a camera had a dozen. All beautiful.

She walked the few blocks to Cherry Lane for the parade that would wind around the shopping center, burrow under the Metra tracks, and peter out somewhere near the Methodist church. Her assignment was to try to find something fresh about the day or the event. Failing that, she was expected to come up with acceptable variations of the stock photos—tears on the cheeks of a crusty Korean War vet, the defiant pose of a man left paraplegic by Vietnam, or the heart-tugging flag-waving of a child, à la John-John Kennedy.

She hated war. The Civil War. World Wars I and II. Korea. Vietnam. The Gulf. The latest War. War games. War and Peace. All the millions of words—or for that matter, photographs—hadn't stopped a single bullet.

The crowd was sparse, few willing—apparently—to stand out in the damp cold. She snapped off a few shots out of habit as the parade drummed past, nothing worth the film. And then she saw an old man—in his sixties or early seventies—arguing with another who appeared to be his son, while the third generation—in the person of a boy ten or eleven—watched in dismay. She grabbed her F1 and began to earn her pay.

She noticed Special Agent Minorini when she had half a roll left in the camera. She kept track of him while she finished off the parade. It would have been an easy event to satirize, especially since she lost interest in her assignment as soon as she spotted the FBI agent. He'd seen her, she was sure, but he was acting as if he hadn't. She used her last two shots to catch him as he looked her way.

She changed the film in the F1 and exchanged the Canon for her Hasselblad. As the spectators straggled away, she adjusted the camera and plotted her course, cutting off the agent's escape route near the Walgreen's.

"Special Agent Minorini!" She snapped his surprised look and added, "What brings you back to our friendly little town?"

"I was in the area. I figured I'd stop and see if you remembered anything else."

Joanne shook her head. "How did you know I was here?"

"Your son told me. I stopped at your house."

"You've been spying on me."

"I didn't want to interrupt you. Your son said you were working."

"I'm finished. I'm on my way home."

"Mind if I walk with you? I left my car . . ."

She shrugged and shook her head.

He said, "I hear you're pretty good. Will you show me your work sometime?"

"If you'll let me shoot you."

She could see he was surprised, but whether it was because of her request or her choice of the word 'shoot' she couldn't tell. She clicked the shutter, then clicked it again to get his startled response to being photographed.

"Why?" he asked.

"You're very photogenic." All impervious surface, she thought. This time he shrugged. "Why not?"

She set up the lights and the umbrella reflectors in the living room and let him page through some of her scrapbooks while she walked around and shot him from every angle. The old pictures were a good distraction.

"How on earth did you get this?" He held up a photo of a school bus with a line of Canada geese apparently waiting at the open door to board. The front bird was stretching its wings, seeming to converse with the bus driver.

"When I got the assignment, I found out what geese like to eat and started carrying a bucket of it in my car. Whenever I got the chance, I bribed them to cooperate." She tapped the photo. "These guys were hanging around Wolters Field, in Highland Park, where they park the busses. I just left a trail of bread crumbs—so to speak—for them to follow. The driver was serendipity."

He shook his head and held up another photo. "What about this one?" The picture showed a goose perched on top of the green interstate sign, above a highway overpass. "You climb up and put birdseed on the sign?"

"No. I just noticed the goose up there. The crazy things'll go anyplace. The only thing surprising about *that* picture is that the bird waited while I turned the car around and came back."

He pointed to the picture of an enraged tiger. "This is great. It's almost as if you caught the essence. How'd you get close enough?"

"With a 200-millimeter lens and fast film." She didn't bother to add, "and with a week of hanging around the cat house, feeding donuts to the keepers." Eventually she'd had her chance. The cat was irritated and distracted by a veterinarian's attempts to tranquilize it. Joanne passed up several chances to shoot while the cat was snarling at the vet. Then the cat turned his head and noticed her and growled. And she had his soul neatly trapped in the Minolta.

As Lessing was putting her equipment away, Minorini pulled out the picture of a man caught by the camera like a deer transfixed by headlight beams.

"Who's this?"

She laughed. "He was someone I went out with when I was first divorced. He used to call me every night and ask how my day was, but I never felt he was letting me get close or letting me get to know what he was really like. He was always pleasant, never obviously evasive but he'd never let me take his picture. He said it made him feel uncomfortable.

"But taking pictures is how I relate to people. Photographs help me work out how I feel, so it was hard not to shoot him. It got to be a challenge—to get him without his knowing. He didn't like it. Once he even took the lens off my camera and wouldn't give it back until I promised no more pictures. I eventually gave up on him. I'm still not sure what his problem was, I just knew we'd never work it out."

Minorini looked at the photo. It was flattering—like the portrait of a movie star. It could also have been a surveillance photo.

At that point, Lessing's son walked through the room. There was obvious pleasure in her face, and Minorini could see that the kid picked up on it.

He'd never thought about the difficulties of raising a kid alone—or even with help, for that matter. His ex hadn't been keen on the idea of kids. "You're not home enough to help with 'em," she'd said. Lessing seemed to be doing well enough with Sean.

"Did you ever wish you'd had more kids?" he asked her.

"Sometimes."

TWELVE

Agent Minorini," his secretary said. "There's a package here for you. A messenger dropped it off."

Minorini glanced at the Tyvek envelope from Rage Photo but he waited until he was at his desk to open it. It contained the pictures Joanne Lessing had taken the day before. Along with those he knew she'd taken were two surveillance photos. They were very good, sharply in focus and clearly showing that the object of the surveillance was unaware of the camera.

Her message was clear enough; the pictures made her point exactly. She didn't like to be stalked and she wanted him to know how it felt.

The shots she'd taken with the Hasselblad were also in focus, though he hadn't seen her make any adjustments. He thought the expression she'd captured pretty much summed up what he'd been feeling.

With one exception the rest of the pictures looked like the pretty-boy stuff you see in men's clothing ads, flattering, but impersonal. The exception looked like a Calvin Klein commercial.

"Whatcha got there?" Coming in without knocking, Haskel startled him.

Minorini shoved the parade site pictures back in the envelope. He handed the rest to Haskel, who looked at them and asked, "You planning a career change?"

"No, why?"

"These look like the things actors hand around. Why are they all black and white?"

Minorini had wondered that himself.

Haskel returned the pictures. "You got a great second career in front of you."

The guy in the photography section who'd put him onto Lessing's magazine spread had a number of things to say about the photos, mostly technical, in a tone that sounded envious. The first was "Joanne Lessing," even before he turned the pictures over to read the copyright notice on the backs.

"How the hell do you rate?"

THIRTEEN

Stalking the wild judge, Joanne thought. It sounded like *Stalking the Wild Asparagus,* whose odd title stuck in her head though she'd never read the book. She gathered that his honor had agreed to an interview for political reasons and couldn't refuse to sit for a portrait to accompany it, but he wasn't really cooperating. Rick had made the appointment with the judge for Tuesday, but he told Joanne to take as long as she needed. "If you can get a decent shot," he told her, "we can get more of these assignments." Accordingly, Joanne had asked the reporter who'd done the interview for background information, and was at the Daley Center at 8:30 Monday morning.

They wouldn't let her in with her cameras. When she protested that she had an appointment, the cop on metal-detector duty called upstairs to confirm it and told her, "Tomorrow, lady. Your appointment's tomorrow." When it was obvious he wasn't going to budge, she took the cameras back to her car and locked them in the trunk. On her way back, she stopped in a drugstore and bought a FunSaver. By three P.M., Joanne had a roll of underexposed shots of the judge and his court, and an idea of the man and his schedule.

Tuesday morning, she had her camera set up on a tripod in the Daley Center Plaza to catch the judge as he passed the Picasso on his way to work. A strategically thrown donut got the resident pigeons aloft at the precise moment his honor passed, Starbucks coffee in hand. The sudden flight startled him, and Joanne caught her elusive quarry looking interested. If he realized he was the object of a photographer, he gave no sign. Once he was safely inside the center, Joanne packed up her equipment and followed.

This time the cops let her in, and she went directly to the judge's court room. Instead of her Canon, she'd brought the Hasselblad, though she hadn't used it enough lately to be entirely comfortable with it. But she knew the best pictures would be candids. After loading her Nikon with fast film, she checked the light level. Cameras were forbidden in court, so she set it carefully atop the rail separating the court from spectators and attached the remote. After focusing on the bench with a depth of field wide enough to catch whatever the judge did there, she camouflaged the camera with her coat and waited for the court to come to order.

By the time the judge announced recess for lunch, she had exposed almost the whole roll of film.

The appointment for the judge's portrait was from 1:00 to 1:30 P.M. in his chambers. It took five minutes to set up the Hasselblad and lights, during which time the judge drummed on his desk with the eraser end of an unsharpened pencil. "Could I have a smile, your honor?" she asked, when she was ready.

He made a face suggestive of intestinal discomfort. Joanne snapped the picture, then captured his satisfied smile as he thought he'd sabotaged her shot. A third shot caught his surprise at being caught smiling. Before he had a chance to think about her tactics, she handed him the 4×6 prints of yesterday's shoot and caught his initial reaction to them.

"How . . . ?"

"They're just test shots," she reassured him. "So I wouldn't waste any time today." He seemed mollified when she added, "None of them turned out well enough for the feature." She asked him to look left and right and recorded his unenthusiastic compliance. She asked him about the family pictures on his desk, and about his feeling for the law, and recorded pride, affection and respect. At 1:28, she folded up the tripods, dropped her flash into the camera case, and offered her hand to the judge. "Thank you for your time and cooperation, your honor." He hesitated briefly, then shook with her. "I'd like to take a few more shots around the building," she added. "I should have the proofs for you by the end of the week."

Out in the hall, she reloaded the Nikon with fast black-and-white film and changed to the 200-mm lens. She wasn't sure what made her look out the window at the street below—maybe her hunter's instincts—but when she did, she instantly recognized the older of the two men strolling across the Daley Center Plaza to a waiting limousine. It was the hit-and-run driver; she was sure—dark eyes under saturnine brows, prominent nose, and thin-lipped mouth set in an angry line. He appeared to be about sixty, but he held himself erect and looked fit. Neither age nor easy living had softened him or diminished his vigilance as he scanned the surrounding street and sidewalks.

But he never looked up.

FOURTEEN

Joanne found Paul Minorini waiting in front of the Goss building. He followed her inside and up in the Gothic elevator. In the office, she felt the familiar sensation of home that made even the deserted entryway seem comforting. She hung her coat on one of the pegs along the left wall and stopped at May's counter to sort through her exposed film. She held up two rolls. "This," she said of the first, "you'll probably want *your* lab to develop. Color." She handed it to him and held the other up. "I could develop this now, if you've got time. I'd prefer to, so I can see how I did. I assume once you take possession, I won't see the pictures unless it goes to court."

He nodded. "Go ahead—I've got all night." He took off his coat and hung it next to hers. When he put the color roll in an inside suit pocket, she got a glimpse of steel and leather. His gun.

He was a Federal agent. Of course he carried a gun.

She said, "Make yourself at home."

She sorted through the film of the judge, scribbling "J" and the roll and job numbers for each before dropping it in an envelope for developing. Minorini—Paul, as she was starting to think of him—watched without showing impatience.

When she'd put the negatives in the dryer, she wandered out to report that they looked good. "As soon as they're dry I'll print up a proof sheet, and we can see for sure."

"How long'll that take?"

"Twenty minutes."

"I took the liberty of making a reservation for dinner. I owe you that much at least."

A reservation!

"I'll have to let my son know."

He wandered through Hancock's open office door while she was dialing. Sean wasn't home, so she left a message on the machine, then went after Paul.

"Hancock's office," she told him.

"*The* Hancock?"

"Yes."

Suddenly he said, "Jesus!" He was staring at the poster-sized blowup of an internationally famous face, hideous in its absolute rage.

"Hancock calls it 'Kabuki,'" she said dryly. "I think 'Hancock as Kali' would be more appropriate."

He nodded. Either he was familiar with the goddess of destruction or he was good at covering his ignorance. How odd to think of an FBI agent familiar with Hindu mythology. He said, "He ever sell these?"

"Sometimes. When he can get his subject to sign a release."

"Did she?"

Joanne grinned. "What do you think?"

"Doesn't like women much, does he?"

"Not that woman." She closed the door and pointed to another portrait behind it, a loving, very flattering portrait of herself.

FIFTEEN

As Minorini looked over the glossy black-and-white prints, the adrenaline high made him dizzy.

Joanne pointed to one of the head shots. "That's him," she said. No question about who she meant, and there was absolute certainty in her voice.

He didn't recognize the man she pointed out. He hated that he'd have to wait until morning to follow through on an ID, but he had promised her dinner. And he was reluctant to part company, though proximity—considering his growing attraction—crackled with danger.

Except for a bit of fuzz here and there—from dirt on the Daley Center windows—the photos were clear enough to show the license-plate numbers on the two cars. They were amazing, and he said so. The compliment made her blush, and he had to squelch his own arousal.

"Can you blow up some of these?" he asked.

"Sure."

He pointed out which details he wanted, then grabbed the phone to call and have the plates run while she worked. He had names by the time she came out to say the enlargements were in the dryer. One of the cars belonged to a small time member of the Chicago outfit. The other owner, Maria Dossi, was a cipher. No matter. They'd get to the bottom of things eventually.

And in the meantime, he deserved the rest of the evening off.

SIXTEEN

The restaurant had a real maître d', who greeted the FBI agent by name and seated them at a good table. When he'd gone away with their wine order, Joanne resisted the urge to ask Minorini about his more interesting cases and said, instead, "How did your family react to your becoming a G-man?"

"I was born to be either a cop or a mobster." She raised her eyebrows. "I grew up in a very tough neighborhood. It's probably just luck I'm not Paul 'the Minnow' Minorini."

"Was that your nickname in school?"

"Grade school." She waited. "In high school, they called me 'Barracuda.'"

"Why?"

"Because I devoured the first guy who called me 'Minnow.'"

She couldn't help the smile. Whatever he'd been in high school, he seemed to have become a nice man. And well educated. He'd said "devoured," not demolished.

He smiled slightly, sending a pleasant shiver through her. "What did they call *you* in high school?"

She wasn't imagining it. He was interested. "Jo," she said. "I've always been Jo."

"Where did you learn to use a camera?" he asked.

"From a very nice man in California."

"A lover?"

"No. I was too burned, and he was too eager. He scared me, he was so eager. I wasn't ready."

"What happened?"

"I didn't know how to break it off but I couldn't. . . . Eventually, he got frustrated and stopped calling."

He pointed at the menu. "Have anything you like—it's on the Fed. Escargot?"

"Thanks, but I don't eat anything I can't spell."

"Lobster?"

"Is that spelled c-r-u-e-l?"

He shook his head and said, "No veal." He didn't seem offended. She shrugged apologetically, lifting her eyebrows. "You're a vegetarian." He wasn't asking, not after the corned beef last time.

"Nothing so radical."

The waiter came with a bottle and Joanne watched him and Paul perform the opening ritual. The wine was excellent. Her surprise must have showed because Paul looked amused but pleased.

"Do they teach you to be wine connoisseurs at FBI school?"

"Also not to wipe our noses on our sleeves." He pointed to the array of silver flanking their plates. "And which fork to use. How did you get into photography?"

" 'I started out as a child,' " she said, quoting Bill Cosby. He ignored her attempt at humor, or he wasn't familiar with the reference. He waited. She wondered if this was how he got his suspects to confess. She started again, filling the silence.

"I didn't date much in school. I was shy. Howie—my ex-husband—took advantage of that to convince me he was saving me from life as an old maid. He used to 'let' me type his papers and, sometimes, do his research. Before I took up photography, I didn't appreciate my talents. I was like most people, I guess. What was easy for me seemed like no great thing. I've always been pretty good at spelling and grammar, but Howie used to accuse me of pretending to be better than he when I corrected his papers without being asked. That would have never occurred to me."

"Some guys just don't get it."

"When I was a kid I used to wish I had some magic that would preserve everything—you know—special moments, favorite people I didn't often see." She realized how inadequate that was as an explanation and tried again. "I wanted to save the specialness or the newness—like my bike, before it was all scratched up, or tiny baby kittens—things that don't last forever. And everyday things, like my Dad's overalls hanging by the back door, with his gloves and all his regular tools sticking out of the pockets."

Paul nodded as if he understood.

"Then I discovered photography. It *was* magic, an ordinary sort but, in a sense, what I'd always been looking for. Once I started peering at the world through the lens of a camera, everything looked different. Howie seemed so much smaller, I could scarcely see him sometimes. And I stopped listening to his lies."

"How long ago was that?"

"Six years." He waited; she went on. "I was living in California." As she said it, it sounded to her like *once upon a time,* or *long ago, in a galaxy far away.* "I was still married. Sort of. Getting therapy—that's what you do in California when your marriage goes *sort of.*"

Paul made a gesture that reminded her of someone lighting a cigarette, and she said, "Do you smoke?"

"I quit. Go on."

"Good for you. Where was I?"

"*Sort of* married in California."

"My therapist suggested that I take up a hobby. Something I could do for me. Or something I could do *not for Howie.* I saw this photography course being offered—it was one of the few things Howie hadn't gotten into—so I took it."

"And discovered you had talent?"

"I was told I had talent. Even now I sometimes have to look at what I've done to believe it."

"I take it Howie wasn't supportive?"

"Howie's one of those people who tries something and becomes an instant expert. He reads a book on the subject—usually by the foremost authority—then knows *every*thing about it. While we were married he took up hang gliding, investing, scuba diving, water skiing, running and sailing and racquet ball. Oh, yeah, and wine. He must've spent five thousand dollars trying to become a wine snob. He still can't tell cabernet from Chianti.

"Anyway, after I'd been at it a while, I spent two days sneaking up on a condor, calculating the best angle and the perfect exposure. I caught it in mid-flight. Howie's comment was 'it isn't centered.'" She laughed. "That was the first picture I ever sold. A conservation group bought it to put in one of their calendars."

"What did Howie say to that?"

"I don't know. Maybe he's never found out. After he made that comment, I realized I'd never please him so I might as well please myself. I got a lawyer the next day."

"Why did you move here?"

She shrugged. "My brothers live in Gurnee and Oak Park. Northbrook's sort of in between. The clincher was that my best friend's husband was transferred to Chicago, and they moved to Glenview. What about you? Do you have a family?"

He seemed to be thinking about whether to answer that while he signaled the waiter. He let the question float between them until the man had come and gone with their orders. Then he said, "A sister who lives in New York."

A sister. No wife?

He added, "No wife *or* kids."

"Ever married?"

"Once. Once upon a time." Joanne waited. "She made it *me or the job*."

The statement fell between them, and silence glassed over the distance it put between them.

The waiter ended the awkward pause with more wine.

"What are you thinking?" she asked when the waiter had left with their dessert order.

"Heart of Darkness."

"The Conrad story?" She thought, odd subject.

"Mm-hmm."

"What about it?"

"It's the perfect metaphor for certain jobs."

She waited. When he didn't elaborate, she said, "Yours?"

He took another sip of his wine and ignored the question.

She pressed. "What made you think of it?"

"Going after corruption can be very corrupting." He looked at his glass, as if it represented what he meant. Then he seemed to realize how much he'd revealed of himself because he changed the subject abruptly. "I didn't like the movie. Did you see it?"

"*Apocalypse Now?*" she asked, not sure how she knew he was referring to that particular version of Conrad's tale. He nodded. "What didn't you like about it?"

"I don't think Coppola understood the purpose of the frame. If you don't establish your witness's credibility," he went on, "his whole testimony becomes meaningless."

She wondered if he was saying something about what was going on between them, or about his job, or if he was simply expounding a favorite theory. She said, "Maybe that's what he intended. It was a meaningless war."

He shrugged. "How much did the film cost to make? A pretty major expense to restate the obvious."

Much later, when Paul pulled his car onto her street, she was feeling aglow from the wine and the camaraderie, and his sheer, glorious masculinity.

He put the gearshift in park and turned off the engine. He didn't seem in any hurry to escort her to the door.

In her earlier life, she would've waited for him to make a move, fearful of encroaching on his male prerogative. Tonight emboldened by the wine and lust, she shifted closer on the seat. She could tell he was aroused. His breath was faster, and when she pushed against him, he pulled back—as if he didn't want her aware of the hard evidence. She said, "You said you weren't married."

He drew a breath in between his teeth and turned his head from side to side as if it wasn't working well enough to shake.

"You have HIV?" she continued.

He let the breath out, slowly, between his teeth. "No."

"Don't you find me attractive?"

"Jesus!" he said. "You're a witness. Stop it!"

The hurt she felt suddenly was an echo of what she'd felt so often with Howie. She threw the car door open. She was at her front door before he could get out of the car.

SEVENTEEN

Joanne was still stinging the next afternoon when the doorbell rang. She opened the door to find Paul Minorini.

"On my way home," he said. "I wanted to update you."

"Stopped by? On your way home from downtown?"

He grinned. "Can't get anything past you, can I?"

She waited, making no effort to relieve his discomfort or invite him in.

Finally, he said, "We have to talk."

She crossed her arms and leaned against the door jamb.

"Can I come in?"

She shrugged and backed through the doorway, leaving the door open for him.

He followed her in, looking grim.

She didn't want to hear his troubles. She waved to the couch and said, "Have a seat and I'll be with you in a minute. I'm developing."

He blinked, then apparently realized she meant film. He nodded and walked over to sit on the couch. Joanne went back to work.

She was surprised at how angry she was feeling. If she'd had any idea how involved this whole thing would get, she'd never have reported the hit-and-run. Under other circumstances, she would have given anything to have a man like Minorini showing up at her door—but as it was, she knew he didn't give a damn about her. She resented his invasions of her time and the reminder that her hard-earned new life could be so easily disrupted. She took her time in the dark room, studying the negatives she would otherwise just have printed to study later. Maybe he'd get tired of waiting and leave. When the prints were all hanging to dry, she straightened up before going back to the living room.

He didn't blame her for being mad, and he had a feeling she'd be even more angry when she heard what he'd come to say. He'd been too open last night, too cordial. Distance was supposed to be the rule in dealing with witnesses. He'd forgotten himself and let things get out of hand. Not that he hadn't wanted her. But he'd never compromised his job for self-gratification and he wasn't about to start now, no matter how badly he might want—What? Just where did he think he could go with Joanne Lessing? She was an innocent about to be destroyed by the bad luck that made her a witness. He'd only exacerbated the situation by letting his infatuation show.

That was it—infatuation. A situational accident caused by a chance meeting with an interesting woman at a time in his life when he'd been celibate longer than he'd ever admit. Much better for him that she was angry. It would keep her at a distance.

He'd let her vent. If it took the pleasure from his evening, so what. He had a lifetime of evenings to make up for it. She only had until they put the case together for the grand jury.

He sat back on the couch to wait. She had a right to know—not that Haskel and the others would agree—and he'd tell her if it took all night. He owed her that.

He spotted the album and wondered if she'd put his picture in it along with the camera-shy suitor. A piece of paper fluttered out as he picked up the book, on it a poem titled *Photographs*. Poetry wasn't something he usually bothered with, but he read it:

> *They are saved for posterity like pressed flowers,*
> *Their petal faces flattened by private emotions.*

Tragedy cut them,
And they were dried by the camera's eye,
And they have color, still,
Wedding white,
Funeral purple,
Red blood splashed forever . . .

Unsettling. He flipped through the album to the end and found his least favorite of the pictures she'd taken of him, the one that made him look like a Calvin Klein model—cool and untouchable, completely self-absorbed.

Agent Minorini—Paul—hadn't left. He was sitting on her couch as if he had nothing to do for the rest of his life. He stood up when she came in, then sat back down.

She sat on a chair opposite. "Well?" To hell with him if he was offend by her rudeness. She didn't need this.

"Your pictures have turned the office inside-out. We identified your hit-and-run driver as Gianni Dossi, the brother-in-law of a mob heavyweight. We think he's a professional killer who's been Teflon up to now."

"How nice for you. What's the catch?"

"They want to convene a grand jury."

"So I'll be asked to testify?"

"I'm afraid so."

"If he's what you claim, he'll kill me!"

"No! We'll protect you. And after the trial we'll set you up with a new identity."

She jumped up. "You can go to hell! I've worked too hard for the life I've got!"

"I'm sorry. Dossi lives in Highland Park. His house is titled in his wife's name, but there's no question it's his. He's not gonna give that up. And once he knows we have a witness, he's not gonna sit around and wait for an indictment. You don't have a choice."

"The hell I don't. I'm not gonna testify unless you're charging him with murder. And you can't, can you."

"We'll do our best."

Joanne laughed, sounding to herself like she had when Howie insisted they could make things work—after she'd served the papers. "You don't have enough evidence for an indictment."

"You're an attorney now?"

"No, but I typed all my ex's notes for his criminal law courses. And he always said *civil* law is easier because you don't need as high a standard of evidence. It doesn't take a law degree to see that you don't have enough for a criminal indictment." She walked to the front door and opened it. "Please leave. You're not gonna shoot craps with my life."

EIGHTEEN

Joanne was matting the 8×10 print of a horse jumping a fence when she became aware of Rita standing behind her.

"I want *you* to take my picture," Rita said, her eyes on the print, which documented the owner's daughter riding in her first show last summer in Lake County.

"Portraits really aren't my thing. Why don't you ask Hancock?"

"Are you kidding? I've seen that *thing* he has hanging in his office. Besides, Rick showed me your pictures of the judge."

Joanne sighed. "What do you do for a living?"

Rita grinned, showing her teeth. "My sole raison d'être is to complicate Rick's life."

"Have you ever thought of modeling?"

She gave Joanne a sly smile. "Why do you think I want my picture taken?"

"What if I could get Hancock to promise he'll make you look gorgeous?"

"How would you do that?"

"Tell him the story of the lion and the mouse."

"What? Oh, Aesop. Tell me, have I got bad breath or something that you're so anxious to pawn me off on someone else?"

"No. Of course not. It's just that I hate portraits, so I'm not at my best doing them."

"Yeah. Sure."

. . .

Hancock's reaction was predictable: "Surely you jest!"

"Look," Joanne told him, "If we put together a decent portfolio, she might just land a job. And be out of *our* hair."

"A model? Are you out of your mind? She'd be here *all* the time. She may be a bitch but—in case you hadn't noticed—she's a knockout."

"What if I promise to get her an audition with a theater company?"

"Can you promise they'll hire her?" Joanne gave him a *don't mess with me* look, and he said, grudgingly, "Only if you get Jan to make her over. She looks like the Bride of Frankenstein with that makeup."

"Deal. When?"

He shrugged. "Set it up with May."

"Promise me you won't do a Kabuki on her."

"Oh, really." Joanne waited. Hancock finally said, "You can be a real pain." She gave him a Rita grin. "All right, I promise."

"Thanks. You won't regret it."

"I have already. Send Adonis in, if you see him."

Jan's reaction was like Hancock's, but in the end she agreed to make Rita up for the same reason Hancock had. She was tired of the firestorms and didn't have any better ideas.

May set them both up for the following Tuesday, and scheduled Joanne to be on hand as well. "You gonna start fires, girlfriend," she said, "you gonna stay around to fight 'em."

Next, Joanne called Harold Willis, director and producer of a small repertory company on the edge of Lakeview. "Harry, are you still looking for the next Maureen O'Hara?"

"Sure," he said, "but then, I still buy lottery tickets."

"I think I found her for you."

"What's the catch?"

"She's only had one gig since high school." As Rick's wife, Joanne thought, but she wasn't going to say so.

"And that was in the sixties, right?"

64

"No. She's only twenty-nine. Hancock's doing her portrait."

"Hancock does portraits of kitchen appliances. This beauty have a name?"

"Rita Rage."

"Rick's ex? No way! I've heard about her."

"You don't have to date her, just audition her. If she's awful, tell her 'sorry,' and I'll get someone else to hire her."

"What's in it for me?"

"She may turn out to be sensational."

"Not good enough."

Joanne sighed. "How about free publicity candids for your next three plays?"

"I love her already."

NINETEEN

Minorini, the Northbrook cops sent this over—thought it might be connected to the Siano hit." Haskel handed him a fax, the copy of a police report on a hit-and-run killing of a sixty-three-year-old woman, DOA at Glenbrook Hospital. Someone had highlighted the phrases "no witnesses," and "unable to locate any skid marks or other evidence that the driver made an attempt to avoid the collision."

Minorini read the report twice and gave it back. "So?"

Haskel handed him more faxes. "Takes on significance when you connect 'em with these."

The subsequent pages were the photocopy of a newspaper interview, some weeks earlier, in which the DOA claimed to have witnessed the property damage hit and run that Joanne Lessing had reported. The DOA wasn't Hariette Cronin, their witness from the senior housing, and hadn't mentioned Mrs. Cronin to the reporter or said anything at all about seeing Lessing. The third fax was a stolen car report—a Northbrook resident had left his Cadillac running out front while he ran into the downtown post office to pick up his mail. When he came out "just a second later," the car was gone.

"What do you think?" Haskel asked.

"I think if the DOA had seen what she claimed, she'd have mentioned Joanne Lessing."

"And if she'd kept her mouth shut, she'd still be breathing."

"No doubt. I'd better go see what Mrs. Cronin knows about this."

"You don't think that might put whoever did this onto her before we can get her into the protection program?"

"If the cops haven't interviewed the other residents yet, I can sit in. If they have, maybe Mrs. Cronin will show up at the DOA's wake and I can talk to her along with everybody else."

The Northbrook cops had interviewed all the Crestwood residents—Detective Gray told Minorini—with no results. According to her neighbors, Doris Davis had acted as if she were meeting someone special, coyly inviting questions they hadn't asked. She'd been crossing Angle Avenue when she was struck.

Minorini didn't bother to go to the postmortem. The medical examiner's findings were as expected. Cause of death was multiple injuries inflicted by a motor vehicle. Manner of death—homicide. By the time the body was released to the funeral home, the Northbrook police had found the stolen car that was presumed to be the murder weapon. Preliminary indications were that their presumption was correct. Like the Siano hit, there were no prints, and no physical evidence other than the damage to the car and to Mrs. Davis. There were no witnesses. Everything pointed to a pro. Déjà vu.

The wake was held at Hanekamps in Deerfield, a small red brick building with a white columned carport, flanked on the west by blue spruces and bushy pines. It was just north of Edens/I-294 spur, only a mile from the senior housing where Doris Davis lived. Joanne parked in the lot behind the building and went in. She'd been there once before, to take pictures for a *Northbrook Star* article on funeral homes. There was only one visitation parlor in use—barely—just half a dozen mourners. And Paul Minorini!

Joanne ignored him as she pretended to sign the guest book. If someone had run over Mrs. Davis on purpose, no use giving him a clue to finding her. She walked slowly up to the casket and knelt to study the old woman's face. To the best of her knowledge,

Joanne had never seen her before. She looked to have been in her seventies and couldn't have been a threat to anyone.

Joanne got up and went over to the dazed-looking young man in the front row of the chairs facing the casket. She put her hand on his arm and said, "Mr. Davis?" A guess, but the obituary said "survived by a son, Edger. . . ."

He looked up. "I'm afraid . . ."

"Your mother was a neighbor. I can't tell you how sorry I was to hear of her death." The truth, if not all of it.

He nodded. "I just talked to her the other day. . . ."

She listened and made sympathetic noises, but she was distracted by the FBI agent in the back of the room. As soon as decently possible, she excused herself.

Minorini had slipped out ahead of her and was standing between the building and her car. "Did you know Mrs. Davis?" he asked.

"I could ask you the same thing." He waited for her answer. "No. I just thought it was funny we happened to have two hit-and-run accidents so close together in time and place."

"It's a coincidence."

"That's why *you're* here? I saw the write-up in the *Northbrook Star*. It said Mrs. Davis witnessed the hit-and-run car *I* photographed. Now she's dead. The driver probably thought she was me and ran her over to eliminate the witness who saw him get away after he killed Mr. Mandrel."

"If we can find out who killed Mrs. Davis, they're going to serve you with a subpoena to testify about it."

"That's crazy. There's nothing I can add."

He shrugged.

"You don't understand," Joanne said. "Maybe there's no way you could. All the years I was married to Howie, I might've been asleep—my brain was dead. It wasn't that I was stupid, but I thought I was—which is the same thing. All those years, Howie never missed a chance to tell me I was incompetent, that I was nothing without him, that I couldn't make it on my own. And I believed him. I guess it's like advertisements—if you hear something often enough . . ."

She stopped and swallowed back tears of anger and frustration. "Howie told me what to do. Howie told me what to wear. Howie told me what to think. Howie took care of everything. If he'd gotten caught cheating on our taxes, I could've gone to jail. I didn't have a clue about what I was signing. I clipped coupons and shopped sales and stretched the pittance he gave me for an allowance so *he* could go out and party. It took catching him in bed with another woman to finally wake me up. And then I had to start from scratch. I had all the problems of a new high-school graduate—all the insecurities and lack of experience—only I wasn't cute any more."

"So why did you keep his name?"

"By the time the divorce was final, I'd made a name for myself—as Joanne Lessing. I just tell anyone who asks that Howie and I are *not* related.

"But I've finally found my vocation. I've worked hard to get where I am. Do you understand how it feels to finally discover your thing? To find, after years of believing you were good for nothing, that there's something you can shine at?"

She watched his face closely for amusement or disdain, or a sign, however subtle, that he understood. His expression was unreadable.

"I won't start over with something else," she added. "I'd rather be dead!"

"Would you rather your son was dead, too?"

She thought she detected sadness in his eyes, but it wasn't enough. He was still standing between her and her car. She said, "Get out of my way," and strode forward as if she meant to run him over.

He stepped aside and let her pass.

TWENTY

The vague fears that had beset Joanne during her breakup with Howie returned, but more specific now. The pervasive anxiety coalesced into images of a faceless attacker. She thought frequently of getting a gun, of carrying it strapped to her ankle or in her camera case. Fear made her want to blow the head off her anonymous stalker. And her aggressive thoughts disturbed her as much as her unseen nemesis. What was she becoming, she who had never hunted with a gun, who'd bought Have-a-Heart traps to rid the house of mice, and routinely transported spiders out of doors? She was horrified to realize that—in her mind—she'd crossed the line already.

If I could, I'd kill the son of a bitch!

What have I let him do to me?

At work, she looked up gun stores in the yellow pages. When she put the book back, it occurred to her that her fingerprints would be on the pages listing gun stores. She felt guilty already— as if having the idea of buying a gun for protection was enough for a conviction if Gianni Dossi turned up dead. As if the police would invariably discover her guilty intention.

The store seemed shabby. It was U-shaped, with the upper arms of the U ending in twin store fronts, only one of which opened to the street. The two arms connected near the back of the store where a service desk sported a hand-lettered sign: "72 hour waiting period for handguns; 24 hours for long guns." A jar of money on the counter was labeled "Help keep guns legal." Merchandise filled bins and large cardboard boxes on the floor. Behind and under old-fashioned plate glass counters lay a mind-boggling selection of holsters—labeled "right-handed" or "left-handed"—and handcuffs, nightsticks and guns, gun grips, and uniform accessories. *Street Weapons,* book and video, was available "for law enforcement only." There were racks of jackets, belts and shoes. A poster advertising the movie *Homicide* was autographed by Joe Mantegna. There were mountainous displays of ammunition and gun cases and rifle stocks, as well as scopes, and how-to books. The patrons all looked like security guards or Chicago cops—big men, mostly, with ponderous guts, and a few women in uniforms that fit poorly. A clean-cut clerk alternated between watching the customers and the news on small black-and-white TV.

Joanne felt like a sheep at a trade show for wolves. She must have looked out of place to the other, long-haired man who stepped over to wait on her.

"Yes, ma'am?"

"What if I want to buy a gun?"

"Do you have your firearms card with you?"

"I don't have one."

The salesman seemed to lose interest. "Sorry, you have to have a Firearms Owner's ID card."

"Where do I get one?"

He pointed to the service counter. "You fill out a form and pay fifteen dollars. It takes one to three months."

One to three months! In a *week* I could be dead. I *don't have three months*! She said, "Forget it."

"If you're looking for protection, why don't you get yourself some pepper spray?"

TWENTY-ONE

If naming a thing gives you power over it—as ancient people believed—then making its likeness might really capture its soul. Joanne had first felt something like that power when she'd discovered she could neutralize the things she feared by catching them on film. Perhaps the close proximity necessary to get the picture caused habituation.

Once she'd decided to neutralize Dossi, it took her only fifteen minutes to find the real-estate tax-index number for the only Dossi listed in Highland Park—Angela, although she had to go to the County building in Waukegan to look it up without attracting attention. She called the county assessor's office from a pay phone before she left there, and a clerk who sounded like a six-year-old gave her the street address.

Her next stop was the building department at the Highland Park Public Works. She waited outside the two-story brick-and-glass edifice until the parking spaces were completely filled. Then she followed the driver of one of the pickups inside and upstairs where the permits were issued.

As she'd expected, all the clerks were occupied. She watched and listened for a while, then followed a man who was directed to the office of the building inspectors—beyond the service counter, at the end of the hall. No one paid her any attention.

Beyond the restrooms and the coffee setup, just past the water fountains, the green, 2-foot by 3-foot plat books lay on a counter in a messy pile. The shelves below the counter held a bonus—books showing sewer and water easements. It didn't take long to find the property she was looking for, less time to photograph the page and put away her camera.

She was restoring the water/sewer book to its place when one of the clerks came up behind her. "May I help you?"

Joanne turned around. "Could you explain how to get a building permit?"

The property was huge, bordered by equally large estates on two sides, and the Heller nature preserve on a third. The surrounding high brick wall was topped by iron pikes, and marked at intervals by a security system logo and signs warning "Beware of Dogs." She drove past slowly. The wrought iron gate was closed, probably operated like a garage door by a remote device.

The neighbors on either side looked equally impregnable. Joanne spotted an infrared sensor guarding the drive of one. The other had gates that were open, but had an unimpeded sight line from the front of the house. After she'd memorized the salient features of all three houses, so she would recognize them from another angle, she drove on.

She was back the next morning in camouflage pants, an olive-drab jacket, and navy knit hat—hunting garb. It was overcast and cold, so her upturned collar wasn't conspicuous—not that there was anyone around to notice. She'd brought her field tote and the old Canon loaded with black and white film. She left her car in the lot at the Heller Nature Center.

She took her time. She was used to long hunts. Sometimes it took her a week to get the shot she wanted. The trick was to seem innocuous or be beneath notice, to hang around long enough to become as invisible as the ever-present cable installers or the FedEx guys. In a forest preserve, carrying a camera was good camouflage. She hammed it up, pointing at crows and cardinals, and winter-drab finches, stopping to set it on the field tripod to "snap" stands of winter-bare trees. It was almost two hours before she made her way around to where the 54-inch storm drain marked on the plat emptied into the nearby branch of the Skokie River—what would have been called a creek where she'd grown up. The mouth of the outfall was protected by a heavy metal grill so old the bolts holding it in place were crumbling to rust. According to the plat book, this was lower end of a channel that ran under Dossi's property.

Where there were storm drains, there were manholes, and were there were manholes, there were manhole covers. She stowed the camera and got out her flashlight and the crowbar she'd brought. The manhole was fifteen yards from Dossi's brick wall, surrounded by a thicket. A piece of cake.

To her surprise, the drain was almost dry—thin shelves of ice a third of the way up the sides marked the water level when the weather had turned cold, but the stream had since receded to a trickle along the floor of the passage. The tunnel angled southeastward and, she estimated, another twenty yards beyond Dossi's boundary wall before it turned. She had to walk bent over in the center of the stream holding the duffel out in front. She hoped any footprints would eventually be washed away.

Instead of getting smaller, as she'd expected, the passage ended at another outfall-mouth set in the side of a berm topped by a line of spruce trees, and guarded by a metal grate. The grating was shiny and new but bolted to old brackets that clung to the passage wall more out of habit than anything. Beyond the grate, the outfall fed from a detention pond surrounded by the berm and landscaping designed to mimic a natural area. Dossi's house was two hundred yards beyond that. Not a mansion by Highland Park standards, it was still three or four times the size of her own house.

By prying the brackets loose on one side of the grate, she was able to swing it outward like a door and squeeze her duffel past. She took her time, watching for the promised dogs.

An hour passed as she moved from cover to cover, studying

the house and garage, watching for security devices. She didn't expect Dossi to be home on a weekday morning, but there should be someone there—the wife or a housekeeper. She found a spot among the spruces on the berm that was a perfect natural blind from which she could see the entire rear of the house. She used her 200-mm lens to peer in the windows of the few rooms lit against the gloom of the season. Inside, a dark-haired woman, Hispanic-looking, pushed a vacuum cleaner into view and moved around the room, setting things straight and dusting.

Following the action was difficult with the heavy camera lens. Joanne decided that next time she'd bring binoculars. Next time! What was she doing here even once? She had only Minorini's word that Dossi was as claimed. After all, Highland Park wasn't a hotbed of mob activity. In fact, Michael Jordan was the town's most notorious citizen.

She was about to end her voyeuristic trespass when a limousine pulled past the house and up to one of the three garage doors. The door opened. The limo pulled inside and the door closed. The adjacent door opened and a gray Volvo pulled out.

Joanne put her eye to the camera and, through the lens, was able to see a young man at the wheel in a dark suit or uniform coat and chauffeur's cap. Not Dossi. Not the man she'd seen driving away from Crestwood Park. Maybe it was Dossi's chauffeur leaving for the day. Or changing cars. She couldn't see the driveway from where she was—only the garage and its approach. She couldn't see if the Volvo left the property. For all she knew, it was parked at the front door. She debated working her way around to get a better view, but decided against it. Better call her surveillance off for the day. Better find a less conspicuous place to park her car.

She came again at dusk. A park district service road guarded by a padlocked chain was the perfect place to leave the car. The padlock had long since rusted open but had been left on the chain for show. She pulled far enough up the road to hide the car from casual glances, then replaced the chain. As she worked her way around to the manhole access to Dossi's property, she pondered her motives. Did she hope to confirm what Agent Minorini told her? Or gather evidence of a crime? Or reassure herself Dossi was human and vulnerable as anyone?

Her first glimpse of him in his lair surprised her. He was an old man, sitting in a chair in his bathrobe, reading the news, sipping something from a china cup. He was wearing reading glasses that he rotated forward on his nose to look through—must be an old prescription. Framed by her binoculars, his face was familiar. She'd seen it in the park and at the Daley Center. She tried to conjure up *Goodfellas* or Don Corleone, but she was reminded of Robert Loggia in *Big*. Familiarity didn't necessarily breed contempt, but it did tend to exterminate her fear.

After four evenings and two afternoons, she had a picture, figuratively, of the Dossi household, and half a dozen exposures of the man himself. He seemed to live alone with the housekeeper and two German shepherds that were let out from time to time to do their business. Maybe his wife had died or was away. The housekeeper served him meals in what appeared to be a family room at the rear of the house. Later he would watch TV, or go up to the room above and pace, or stare out at the yard. Joanne couldn't see his face then, just a silhouette, but she'd caught him with her long lens when he half-turned and the room light lit his features.

Sometime he spoke on the phone. Once he had a visitor, a hard-looking man who dressed like the FBI. The man was ushered in by the chauffeur and led out afterward. The chauffeur seemed to stay in the house, too, on the first floor, next to the housekeeper's room.

In her darkroom, Joanne watched the last of the pictures materialize—surely that was how one would describe the gradual assembly of the image. By some trick of light and shade, or accident of distortion—or maybe a bad batch of solution—she seemed to have caught the essence of the man—his soul—and it was demonic.

She took the prints into her kitchen and laughed at her imaginings. In the clear light, she saw not the portrait of Dorian Gray, but the man himself. The photos were nothing more than interesting studies, the face of a strong personality with a sardonic expression.

She wasn't sure what she would do with the pictures. For the time being, she put them in glassine envelopes with their negatives and tucked them in the back of a notebook she kept in the dark room. One day, when the whole Dossi business was far enough in the past to seem like an old B-movie plot, she'd destroy them. In the meantime, she'd use them to remind herself that—mobster or not—Dossi ate his meals alone. And was as vulnerable to a stalker as she.

TWENTY-TWO

Minorini's immediate supervisor was Robert Butler, who—to hear him tell it—had been in Chicago since Ness and Capone had gone head to head. After Minorini brought him up to speed on the latest development in the Siano murder case, Butler said, "You checked this Dossi out?"

"Yeah. He's the brother-in-law of a known outfit guy. We've never looked at him closely because he's got a successful investment business and a modest lifestyle."

"Why would he personally do a hit?"

"I think because he's the million-dollar man."

"The hit man we've never been able to ID?" Butler's expression betrayed his skepticism. "You're telling me this guy would risk everything for a hit? Why?"

Minorini shrugged. "It's what he does. Probably not much of a risk. If I'm right and he's our killer, he could do a simple hit in his sleep. It may even be a matter of professional pride. Siano's had a price on his head for a long time. Lessing being on Dossi's escape route was just his bad luck—nobody can control all the variables. He's been seen before. He just blends into the scenery so well no one ever remembers him. My guess is the camera freaked him. A photo would do him in, even if Lessing were an amateur. A defense attorney would never be able to get around a picture."

The Friday before Thanksgiving, Haskel sauntered into Minorini's office and dropped an envelope on the desk.

Minorini opened it and unfolded the paper it contained. The words "Subpoena" and "Jane Doe" jumped out from the array of words on its surface. "What's this?"

"A judge is willing to entertain our request for a wiretap on Dossi," Haskel told him. "*If* we can convince him we're not just on a fishing expedition. He wants to question our witness himself."

"Our word's not good enough?

"Guess not. Anyway, I figured you'd probably like to do the honors. And maybe you could bring the locals up to speed—as much as they need to know."

"Tell me again. Why are we doing this, Haskel?"

Haskel gave him a gimme-a-break look. "You're the one that ID'ed Dossi for our million-dollar hitter."

"Lessing won't testify. She knows she won't have any healthy alternative but the witness protection program if she does."

"We got the bitch in a vise," Haskel said. "If she doesn't co-operate, we just take her into custody as a material witness."

"You think of them all as just mopes, don't you?"

"That's what they are."

"Then what's the point?"

Haskel just laughed and walked out. Minorini resisted the urge to put the subpoena through his shredder.

Detective Gray put the two large Starbucks cups on the table of the Major Case conference room and pushed one toward Minorini. "Black." He sat down and waited.

Minorini took the top off his coffee and tried it. Too hot. He put the cup on the table. In spite of all the recent seminars, task forces, and memos on interagency cooperation, talking frankly with a local cop went against all his training and experience. Nevertheless, Gray was the primary on an open homicide. Minorini told him about Dossi and his suspicions that Dossi might be the mysterious hitter no one had ever lived to ID.

"But you have nothing really definite?" Gray said.

Minorini shook his head. "But unless you're a real sucker for coincidence, you've got to admit it's a fair circumstantial case. Lessing's sure she saw him leaving the area. The car he was driving was stolen. And Doris Davis, who claimed to have seen him hit the parked car, was run down by a similarly stolen car not long after she went public with her claim."

"Why would he do the hit himself? If you're right about him, he could afford to subcontract the job. Why risk it?" Gray took a sip of his coffee and made a face. Must also be too hot.

"Because he's the best," Minorini said. "And the mob's wanted Siano for so long they'd willingly pay his fee."

"And the Feds want Siano's killer so bad you're willing to try anything to nail him."

"Siano's just the last in a series of hits going back thirty years. This is the closest we've ever gotten."

Gray shook his head. "So you're gonna ruin this poor woman's life on the outside chance it'll give you a lead?"

"It's not my call."

"Why are you bothering to tell me?"

"We don't want to call attention to our witness by putting her into the system before we have to, especially considering what happened to Siano and Mrs. Davis—this guy's a wizard. But, since a subpoena's been issued, there's a chance somebody's looking . . ."

"And you could kill a number of birds with one stone if *we* kept an eye on your star witness."

"In a word."

Gray shook his head again. "I think you're just setting her up as bait." He stood and began pacing his side of the table. His heavy face was mottled with rage. "And if she gets hit, we get the heat."

"To the best of my knowledge, that's not true."

"To the best of *your* knowledge. Isn't *that* comforting." He stopped and leaned over the table into Minorini's space. "We'll watch her because she's one of our citizens. But nobody's buying your little farce. I personally think it's a crock!"

Interview over.

Minorini walked out without another word. What was there to say? He hadn't been told of any plans beyond getting a wiretap on Dossi, but Haskel was panting on this one like a drug dog at the airport. And Haskel was always a whole lot more interested in where he was going than how he got there.

With a rap sheet as long as most of the creeps his testimony had put away, Siano hadn't been anyone you'd bring home to meet the family. But the Bureau toadies, with the eager help of the U.S. attorney, wouldn't hesitate to sacrifice an innocent bystander to get his killer. And it was a fact that they didn't have enough yet for a grand jury presentation. So Gray's charge—that they were using Joanne Lessing for bait—looked more accurate the more he thought about it.

Minorini got in his car and slammed the door. There were times, like when Showers's exhaustive work put Alton Coleman away, that Minorini was proud to be with the Bureau. But at times like now, he wished he'd gone into banking.

TWENTY-THREE

Joanne took her time coming back from lunch. Just enough snow had fallen to wet the streets, the air was warm—around freezing—and misty, making the city look like a grainy, low-contrast photograph. It was the sort of day where the vapors from car exhaust hung in the air like ghosts, long after the cars were out of sight.

A shiny clean, dark green car, the kind she'd come to recognize as government issue, was parked facing the wrong way in front of the Goss building. As she approached, Paul Minorini got out and came toward her. Condensation made him seem to breathe fire and the look on his face reinforced the impression. He pulled an envelope from an inner pocket and thrust it at her.

Joanne resisted the impulse to take it. "For what?"

He said, "I'm sorry." With his left hand he took her right and shoved the envelope into it. "A subpoena. You've been served." He closed her hand around the envelope. "If you ignore it, we'll issue another—with your real name on it. Don't make it come to that." He let go of her hand and stepped back. "Once your name is out there you'll be in danger."

"Damn you!"

He shrugged. "It wasn't my idea . . ." He retreated to his car.

"You fucking coward!" Joanne shouted at him.

He opened the door and got in. Before closing it, he glanced up briefly. For a moment his government façade slipped and she glimpsed something else—apology or regret.

. . .

She was shaking by the time she got upstairs. Rick was in the hall, hanging up his overcoat. When he looked at her, his face went blank. "Jo—What is it?"

She couldn't tell him, couldn't speak yet. She held the envelope up and waited while he opened it and read the contents. "It says 'Jane Doe.'"

"He told me—Special Agent Minorini said—that was for my protection. If I don't show up, they'll go back to the judge and have him issue one with my name on it. Which'll make it more likely the mob could find me."

"This is crap! Let me take it. I know a lawyer. . . . If he can't get this thrown out, he'll know someone who can. Just forget it. Go spend Thanksgiving with your family and don't even think about this again. I'll take care of it."

"Rick, I don't want to get you—"

"Forget it!" He put the subpoena in his inside jacket pocket. "I'll take on the whole damn FBI if I have to." He put a hand on her shoulder and squeezed it. "They're not gonna cost me my best shot."

She could feel tears wetting her cheeks.

Rick used his thumb to rub the tears away. "We'll get through this." He took her arm and steered her down the hallway. "May's got an assignment for you. Why don't you talk to her about it?" He patted his jacket over the pocket with the paper. "And let me take care of this."

TWENTY-FOUR

Two days before Thanksgiving, Joanne and Sean piled their things in the car and headed south on I-294. She brought along all her cameras and a case of oil because the car was leaking almost as much as it was burning, nearly a quart a week. Sean brought his Game Boy and Walkman and a case of CDs. They left around 5:00 A.M. and were on Interstate 80, well past I-55, before sunup.

I-80 ran west through mile after mile of wheat-yellow grasses alternating with fields of stubble poking through skimpy snow and open fields and horizons that seemed endless after the forested suburbs of Chicago. Joanne switched on the radio, and all the stations seemed to be playing country music—"How Long Are You Gonna Be?", "Easy on the Eyes, Hard on the Heart," "Black Eyes, Blue Tears." There was a difference, though. You didn't hear Johnny Cash much any more, or Kenny Rogers or even Reba. And she missed Dolly and Conrad.

After trying all the stations, Sean demanded, "What *is* this?"

"Farm country," Joanne said. "Country music country."

Slouching on his spine, he put on his headphones and popped a disk in the Walkman. He folded his arms across his chest and tuned the country out. Joanne turned the radio up and sang along.

Here and there she saw cows or a horse, even a herd of Poland China pigs sunning themselves on the south side of a hill. Occasionally a corn field would be unharvested, and she'd wonder if the cost to bring it in had gotten above the crop's worth. The country odors—hogs and wood smoke—brought her back twenty years to her high school days.

When she saw the signs for Galva, 110 miles west of Joliet, she that knew she was almost home. Then she spotted the faded TRUST JESUS on the bridge spanning Small Creek. Three hundred yards further was the exit, and two miles down County C, the family mailbox with its line of naked black walnuts and brown-leafed oaks marking the drive.

Graveled and graded recently, the long driveway widened at the end to a yard between the house, with its surrounding grove of volunteer catalpas, and the barn. A dark blue van and a white SUV flanked the red Ford Ranger parked at the kitchen door. Joanne pulled in next to the van. Sean took off his headphones and sighed.

She forgot, from trip to trip, the familiar security—or maybe predictability masquerading as safety. From the porch swing to the chrysanthemums freeze-drying in the hollow of an old stump, from sparrows flocking in the yard to the fat orange tabby watching them from the top porch step—the sameness had ceased to be boring. Home.

"Same old farm," Sean said like an echo. He sounded happy.

The door opened, and a pack of canines poured out, led by her mother's black-and-white border collie. Joanne's brothers, Ken and Allen, were right behind the dogs, coatless in the cold, laughing and joking. Their collective breaths rose like a slow shout.

Dropping down to hug Kip, the collie, Sean seemed to forget he was fourteen and sophisticated. He pushed away his cousin's Golden and his uncle's Labrador retrievers, and wrestled happily with his grandmother's mutt.

Allen dragged the other dogs off Joanne as Ken hugged her and took her bags. They ushered her into the house, into the warm cavern of the kitchen and a chorus of "Hi, Jo"s.

Joanne's mother, Elizabeth, and her sisters-in-law, Kate and Mary, were crowded into the space between the sink and the stove. Kate was kneading bread dough, the others making salad. It got more crowded as Joanne squeezed in to hug each of them in turn. The welcome and the aroma of roasting meat brought a déjà vu of childhood suppers.

Amy, Ken and Mary's twelve-year-old, was perched on a chair next to the table, painting her nails with an electric shade of violet as she feigned indifference to the adults around her. But she said, "Hi, Aunt Jo," without taking her eyes off her work.

"I'll take your stuff up," Ken said. He favored their father most and was beginning to show the same early signs of wear and tear.

Joanne said, "Thanks," as she relinquished her coat to Allen. "Oh, but leave the cameras."

"Cameras?" Amy yelped. "No pictures!" She grabbed her polish bottle and limped out of the room with her toes crooked upward to keep from getting polish on her grandmother's floor.

Joanne laughed and put her camera case out of the way under the table. "I can't use the camera till it warms up, Amy," she said to the girl's retreating back. Amy kept retreating.

"She's just looking for an excuse to split," her mother told Joanne. "You can have her chair and tell us what you've been up to."

As a child, Joanne had gravitated to the company of the men. She'd found their talk of hunting and machinery more interesting than the recipes and gossip her mother and aunts exchanged. Elizabeth had always been there, silent, taken for granted like the earth or the horizon. It wasn't fair, Joanne thought, but her father's work had seemed more important. In retrospect, it had just been more interesting.

After dinner, when the kids were in bed and while the men watched sports highlights on the late news, Joanne found herself poring over the family albums with Kate and Mary. They'd traced the family history from her great grandparents' formal wedding portrait to Kate and Allen's write-your-own-vows nuptials, when Sean was three.

Joanne and Howie had stayed to the very end, hours after the bride and groom took off. Howie had been drinking, pestering every attractive woman for a dance. Out of boredom, Joanne borrowed someone's camera to record the professional photographer packing up to leave, and she'd snapped a couple shots of Howie while she was at it.

She closed the album with a snap. "I can't stand it!"

"I know how you feel," Kate said. "My sister says that anything that even *reminds* her of her ex makes her want to slit her wrists."

"It's not that. It's these pictures. I can't believe I took them. They're awful!" She handed the book to Kate, and reached under the coffee table for her Nikon. No flash. She'd splurged and loaded fast film, hoping to get some candids.

Kate immediately reopened the album.

"Oh come on. You were pretty good even then. Look at this one of Howard."

"Completely overexposed." Joanne removed the lens cap and checked the internal light meter.

"Joanne!" Mary said. "Is that all you can see? The man you married!"

"And divorced. Give it up, Mary. Howie and I aren't even prehistory. I think we were finished before we went west. I just didn't know it."

Mary shook her head, and Kate laughed. "You've met someone new. I can tell."

Joanne thought about Paul Minorini and said, "He's married." No point in explaining that it was to his job.

Kate nodded. "Sis told me, recently, she hadn't let herself feel anything forever, because what's the point? *All* the good guys are taken."

"She's right." Joanne shrugged. "But I have to admit, I haven't felt this way about a man since before marriage turned Howie back into a frog." She looked up and caught her mother's eye. Elizabeth had just come into the room with a tray of mugs. Irish coffee; Joanne could smell it. She thought she detected sadness in her mother's look, perhaps because of what her daughter had just confessed—a crush on a married man. Gone from bad to worse.

But Elizabeth would never say so. She had tried to tell her daughter that Howie was a poor choice, had asked Joanne to hold off on marriage until she'd finished college. And when Joanne told her to butt out, she'd promised never to offer her advice again. She put the tray down, just as she always had. She wiped her hands on her apron and said, "Can I get anyone anything?"

Joanne snapped her picture, then her slightly annoyed look at being photographed.

Allen switched off the television and walked over to sit on the arm of the couch next to Kate. Joanne caught the look Kate gave him as he helped himself to coffee and handed her one.

Ken got up and swiveled his chair around to face the group. "C'mon an' sit down, ma."

She smiled at him, her firstborn. Joanne clicked the shutter again. This time Elizabeth didn't seem to notice. "Thanks," she said, "but I've had a day. Lock up before you turn in."

There was a chorus of "Good nights," then a long silence. Amy materialized from somewhere, hanging over her mother, retreating into the dark edges of the room whenever Joanne pointed the camera her way. Joanne got up to take several more pictures of the others; Ken squeezed into her place beside Mary. He started poring over the albums. Joanne remembered that she'd brought copies of Sean's school portrait. The pictures were in her camera case, so she dug them out and gave copies to Mary and Kate.

"I can't believe how much he's grown," Mary said.

"God!" Ken said. "When I was his age, I was praying the war wouldn't end till I was old enough to join."

Joanne sat cross-legged on the floor across the table from them. "You weren't ever that dumb, were you, Ken?"

"Yeah. I'll tell you how dumb I was. I supported the war just because you and Dash were against it." Dash was an old friend of the family, a local hippie and like a third brother.

Joanne shook her head.

Ken said, "One question you never did answer for me, Jo."

"What?"

"What would you have done if we were invaded?"

"Joined the resistance."

"Remember how the old man always swore he'd get you hunting?"

"Well, he did. Sort of. I'm a pretty fair shot with a camera." She stood up, suddenly, and shot her reticent niece with a finesse that would have done credit to Hemingway.

During her exile in California, she hadn't let herself think of family—too painful, too apt to remind her of the void in her relationship with Howie. Now that she was home, she couldn't imagine leaving them again.

TWENTY-FIVE

Minorini lowered his binoculars and slouched back in his seat. Trailing Lessing on the interstate had been easy; she drove a conservative five miles over the limit and signaled her turns and lane changes well in advance. He'd been able to hang back almost out of sight without danger of losing her. Trailing her through open farm land was quite another thing.

After she turned into a drive marked by a mailbox labeled SCHROEDER, he scouted the "neighborhood." He found a "driveway"—actually a turn-in over a culvert in a ditch separating the road from a fenced field of timber. The turn-in was just below the crest of a hill overlooking the Schroeder farm. It didn't appear to have been used for months. The gate was a tricky arrangement of barbed wire and two-by-fours that had been dragged to one side and left, tangled in the weeds stretching between the fence and the shoulder. He backed his gray rental in and got out to see how it looked from the road. Between its nondescript color and the coat of salt dust it had picked up on the trip, the car faded nicely into the background.

He'd brought binoculars, a thermos of coffee and sandwiches. He'd made a name for himself in the Bureau for his patience. Not even the longest stakeouts fazed him. But now he was restless, impatient to get the weekend over, the holiday. He had too much time to think.

It seemed that he'd spent a large percentage of his life on stakeout. It had become as automatic as driving. He didn't question the necessity of the job or the time it soaked up. What was problematic here was his motive. Keeping an eye on a witness, he told himself. Lessing was a witness of sorts, but in a case they had yet to make against a criminal they'd only tentatively identified. She wasn't a flight risk. And at this stage of the investigation, she was only theoretically in danger. One day she'd be called to testify, then ushered into the witness protection program. After which, he'd never see her again. That would be a relief because she was starting to get to him, starting to disturb his concentration. It had gone way beyond wondering how she'd look naked, gotten into how she would look in a wedding dress. She was so far out of the loop she was a different species. It was nuts.

Even so, he envied her, especially the kid. He was tired of one-night stands with desperate women. At forty-five he had no wife and no kids, no fixed address. The only family he *did* have was his sister, with whom he had nothing in common, whose feelings for him seemed more theoretical than real. He was tired of coming home to an empty apartment, not that it was a bad place—state-of-the-art stereo and 47-inch TV—but he had no one to listen or watch with. No one to share his bed. He needed a woman. And maybe he needed a shrink to help him figure out why he didn't have one.

The car was much less comfortable than his office but there were fewer interruptions. He'd brought files with him, transcripts of the various wiretap sessions in which a mysterious hit man was mentioned. He was almost certainly the mysterious shooter who took out Circone. The million-dollar man, who for a million dollars deposited in a Cayman Island bank account—never the same one—would take care of anyone. No one had ever seen him. No one knew his name. No one knew how to contact him.

There was nothing but Lessing's ID to connect Dossi to Siano. Even that just put him in the neighborhood—nothing definitive. There were 33,000 other people in the neighborhood of North-brook at any given time.

Minorini went over what they'd gleaned on Dossi. He'd been a successful investment manager before he retired at age sixty-three. What was suspicious was that all his assets were in his wife's name. And she was in Italy visiting relatives. Dossi'd been at the Daley Center to back up his daughter in a divorce hearing. The Bureau'd dropped the ball on that one. They knew the Dossi girl was married to a made man; they just hadn't picked up on her father. And they hadn't expected him to testify in her divorce.

That connection and Lessing's ID were enough to get a wiretap. And that would be enough to get Lessing killed if Dossi was their guy. It was something he was willing to bet his Thanksgiving weekend on.

Except for a trip into the timber to relieve himself, Minorini kept at it, restarting his car when the windshield got too frosted up to see through. It was late when the last light went out in the farmhouse—after two A.M. His gas tank was close to empty and he felt as if *he* were running on fumes. He went back to the highway for gas and food, then found a small motel where he could get a shower and a few hours sleep. He was back on duty by seven A.M.

The Schroeders came and went, ice skating and shopping— judging by what they took out and brought back.

Thanksgiving day, Minorini knocked off early and had dinner at a truck stop. It wasn't a real surveillance. A real surveillance required authorization and someone to spell you. For the first time in years, he felt like a voyeur.

TWENTY-SIX

They were nearly through Thanksgiving dinner, into pie and coffee, when Elizabeth held her hands up for silence. "I want you all to take your stuff out of the attic. Anything left here by spring, I'm going to sell at a yard sale."

"What's up?"

"I'm selling the farm. I found a man to buy it and I'm selling it."

"What?"

"You can't!"

"I can and I am."

"Why not just rent it out?"

"You gonna come back and run it?"

"No."

"Well, then . . ." She held a hand up, forestalling further argument. "It was different when your father was alive. It was lonely, but I had suppertime to look forward to, and someone to share a bed with afterwards. Now I'm alone. Now it's just phone calls and holidays. And that's not enough. I need a life."

"What will you do?" Joanne asked.

"I don't know. Travel, maybe. I always wanted to go to China. And when I get back, maybe I'll get one of those Amtrak passes and see the country."

"By yourself?" Allen demanded.

"If I have to. But maybe I'll get lucky."

"Maybe some gigolo will latch onto you," Ken said.

"Humph."

"What's the time frame on this?" Allen asked.

"We hope to close in February. But I won't have to be out until after Easter."

There was a long silence that made Joanne think of the mood the day her father was buried, and the dinner they'd had following the funeral.

Allen finally broke the spell. "It's a good thing Jo brought her cameras. She can take pictures of everything for us. You can let us know what it costs, Jo."

She hadn't said anything to Sean about the FBI's threat to their future. It was magical thinking to imagine that it would all just go away, but since there was nothing to be done, there was no point in spoiling everyone's holiday by mentioning it. Still, she felt as if she had some terminal illness. And because it might be the last holiday with all of them together, she listened more carefully. And snapped more rolls of film than any time since she'd gotten the camera.

Sunday morning, sun turned the frozen landscape into glass. The cold pressed ice crystals from the air like a flurry of diamonds materializing from another dimension.

Joanne had forgotten how, in the country, Sunday marked the passing of the week and enforced rest. In the city, Sunday was just the last chance to get ready for Monday. When all the others—even Sean—piled into the van and SUV to go to church, she opted to stay.

The attic had been dusted and swept in the not-too-distant past, but there was a closeness to the air, and it was cold. Elizabeth obviously saw no reason to heat a room she never used. Joanne had to go back downstairs for her jacket. When she returned, she raised the shade on the dormer window to augment the single working light bulb. Dust motes materialized as the sun laid down a yellow rectangle on the scarred pine floor. Elizabeth had cleared a space next to the stairs and hung a large, hand-lettered cardboard sign over it: GARAGE SALE ITEMS. There was also a fiber barrel labeled TRASH. Clutter surrounded the cleared area. It was wedged under the rafters and piled, in places, to shoulder height. An orphan kitchen chair, a child's sled with peeling paint and rusted runners, an old balloon-tire bike. And behind the backboard from Ken's blue-ribbon science fair project was Joanne's hope chest. It was solid black walnut, about four feet by two feet by two feet. Her father had built it for her one Christmas when he'd had more time than money.

She'd left it when she moved to California. Some part of her had known already that there was nothing much to hope for with Howie. Someone—probably her mother—had buried the chest under a pile of things left over from Joanne's childhood: her Nancy Drew series, roller skates, the collar from a dog flattened on County C by a truck, a mirror framed by a horse collar. . . .

Joanne moved the board and put all but the dog collar and books in the Garage Sale area. The collar went in the trash; the books she piled near the stairs. If Amy didn't want them, maybe she could sell them to an out-of-print book dealer.

She found a rag and dusted off the chest, then lifted the lid. The interior was faced with cedar and its fragrance wafted upward, bringing back the after-school sessions she'd shared with her close friends, daze-dreaming of Cinderella beaus disguised as doctors or lawyers or airline pilots. Twin trays of solid 5/8ths cedar board, six inches deep, were set into the top of the body, finger holes drilled through the sides so the trays could be removed if the wood swelled in humid weather. The trays were full of memories: all four high school yearbooks, blue ribbons from 4-H, family photos and the picture, with Dash, from her senior prom, the little trophy she'd won at a turkey shoot. . . . The target she'd won it with was scrolled inside a toilet paper tube. She pulled it out and flattened it on the floor, fingered the small hole in the turkey's paper breast. She let go of the edges and the target rolled itself back up. Might as well pitch it. She twisted and folded it and shoved it back in the t.p. roll, then tossed it in the trash. The rest of it could wait, she decided. She'd sort through it at home. She lifted the trays out, onto the floor. Underneath was a bundle wrapped in what looked like her father's old hunting jacket, red plaid wool, covering everything beneath the trays. She didn't remember putting whatever it was in there. When she pulled the cloth, something heavy that was wrapped in it fell against the inside of the chest. She tugged it free.

Lying diagonally atop her own things was her father's .3006. Blued barrel and black walnut stock gleamed in the poor light. In the corners of the chest not occupied by the gun were a paper grocery bag and the small fishing tackle box he'd kept his cleaning kit in. Joanne lifted them out before she dared touch the gun. The bag held her father's galoshes that he'd worn on every hunt as long as she could remember. The case held extra ammunition and cleaning supplies and a letter addressed to her.

Serendipity! She had something to defend herself against Dossi with.

She laughed inwardly. Right! A thirty-ought-six was hardly a defensive weapon. A hunting gun, it was long range and deadly accurate. She caressed the silken stock her father had carved himself and sanded and polished, feeling the care he'd lavished on it.

The gun brought back the memory of the last time she'd held it. September, the year before he died. He'd cleaned it and readied it for hunting season, practicing so he could make a clean kill. Killing was the only thing she'd disagreed with him about. For him, it was a way of keeping score as well as of keeping food in the freezer.

He hadn't lasted long enough to see her become her own sort of hunter.

The letter began: *Daughter, May be a mistake giving this to you, but I don't want the boys fighting over it and you were always the best shot. Pity. Never mind . . .*"

Sometimes song birds chased the crows . . .

TWENTY-SEVEN

Monday morning Minorini met Haskel in the elevator at 219 South Dearborn.

Haskel looked as fresh and sharp as a new graduate. "You look like you had something to be thankful about," he said. "Where were you? I tried to get you all weekend."

"None of your business," Minorini told him.

Haskel laughed. "FYI, the judge gave us another subpoena for Lessing. I got somebody serving it as we speak."

The air was crisp and cloudless when Joanne cracked open the front door to see what the day was like. The neighborhood was a snapshot taken with the focus set on infinity, lines drawn so precisely that even in the distance the tiniest detail could be seen, and nothing was at all ambiguous. Least of all the government issue car parked across the street.

She closed the door and went to the window, peeking between the drapes to watch the car while she tried to think what it could mean. The driver must have seen her because he got out and crossed to ring the bell.

What to do? Sean must've left for school already. Joanne confirmed that he was gone and found the note he'd left her in the kitchen: "Mom, Staying after to record a set with Brian. Have a great day! Love, Sean."

That took care of one worry. And just left her with the problem of evading the guy on the front porch who was now leaning on the door bell.

She grabbed her coat, keys and camera case. She made sure she had a hat and gloves, and plenty of change in her pockets. Then she went to the back door. She opened it, then slammed it shut. She ran back to the living room and looked out to see the FBI man disappear into the side yard, at the west end of the house. She was out the door and had it locked in a second. She sprinted east, the half block to the corner, and dodged around her neighbors' six-foot hedge. Hidden from sight if her pursuer had figured out the ruse, she slowed and dug into her camera case for a bus schedule. The Pace 212 bus came through town at half hour intervals and, as luck would have it, the bus was due in five minutes. She started walking toward Waukegan Road.

She got two blocks up Waukegan, almost to Dundee Road, before the bus came. She paid for her fare and a transfer and sat behind the driver, wondering, as the bus retraced her route, how long the Fed would wait before looking for her elsewhere. She got her answer as they passed the Metra station. The car was idling in the station fire lane as its driver scanned the crowded platform. He never noticed the bus stopping on Shermer to pick up passengers. Joanne watched him until the bus moved her out of view.

She had a long time to think. In Glenview, she transferred to the 210 bus that zigzagged through the suburbs and the North Side to the Outer Drive. The Feds would probably meet that train and the next, thinking she'd given them the slip in the crowd. But they'd also send someone to Rage Photo to intercept her as Minorini had a week ago. He knew about the service elevator, so he'd probably watch that, too. Today. And tomorrow.

She thought, briefly, of giving up—they'd get her in the end. There were too many of them. But why make it easy? Maybe the subpoena would expire—did they do that? Or maybe the judge would get tired of them coming back and back. Or maybe she'd get lucky and terrorists would blow something up and draw them all away. Not!

By the time she got off on Michigan Avenue, she'd decided to approach slowly and watch for her chance to slip past them. Leaving to go home would be easy. They wouldn't be watching for someone coming out.

Four blocks from the Goss building, she spotted a window display that gave her an idea. "Hospital supplies—buy or rent." Among other things, they had wheelchairs. And they took Visa. When she finally wheeled herself up to the Goss Building's front door, the Special Agent on surveillance duty held it open for her. He didn't give the fat, gray-haired woman in the chair a second glance, but kept scanning ambulatory females passing by. It was all Joanne could do to keep from looking back at him while she waited in the lobby for the elevator. When the door closed behind her, she felt as if she'd survived some great disaster. She pushed the button for the floor below Rage's and held the door open for a while—long enough for a crippled woman to deplane—before she pushed it again for her real destination. When she wheeled herself into Rage Photo's reception room, May said, "Can I help you?"

Joanne wished she had her camera ready. May's face took on an expression of confusion, then of amazement before she finally said, "Joanne? What the hell's goin' on?"

"Process server."

"Ahh. What can I do?"

"Nothing. You didn't see Joanne today. She didn't call in."

"Gotcha. Meantime, whoever you are, Rick's got somethin' he needs done."

"Thanks, May." Just for the hell of it, Joanne wheeled herself into the back.

Lessing surprised Minorini—not just that she'd evaded the three agents sent to serve her, but she'd demonstrated nerve as well as ingenuity. He wasn't sure if he'd misjudged her or if she'd grown stronger under pressure—like the 110-pound woman who lifted the car off her husband when the jack failed.

Once he'd gotten the report, it took him half the day to reconstruct what happened. Part of it was logic. He knew Lessing had been at home last night—he'd followed her and Sean back from the farm, saw them pull into the carport, and go inside. He'd seen the lights go on and, later, off. Bergman, the agent who'd been sent to serve the subpoena, had seen Sean leave for school and Joanne peer out the front door later. When he realized she'd given him the slip, Bergman had let the air out of Joanne's tires. He'd checked after he saw the train off—the car was still disabled.

The local cab companies confirmed that Lessing hadn't called them. Which left the bus. The bus driver remembered her—not a regular. He'd thought she was a spotter—someone sent to pose as a passenger and report on his performance. Transferred to the 210 she had. The 212 driver had given his 210 counterpart a heads-up, so *he* was able to say where Lessing got off.

When Minorini told him, Haskel started swearing. "We're going over there and arrest the lot of them for obstruction!"

Minorini went along to the extent of walking in the door and asking for Joanne.

Joanne was in the darkroom when the Feds came in. She recognized Agent Haskel's sneer, even through the door. The other man spoke more softly, his voice only a murmur.

May told them she hadn't seen Joanne, and when they asked to have a look around for themselves, she said, "Sure, go ahead— if you got a search warrant."

Haskel did a creditable Terminator imitation when he told May, "I'll be back."

They were able to see for themselves that the receptionist was covering for her.

"We have no probable cause," Minorini told Haskel after the woman told them they'd need a warrant. "Let's go."

Haskel hesitated; Minorini didn't back down.

Out in the hall, waiting for the elevator, Minorini said, "Leave it to me."

. . .

By quitting time, the surveillance operation seemed to have moved elsewhere. They'd probably watch her house and maybe the Metra station. If they hadn't figured out about the bus yet, she could get home all right, and maybe cut through the neighbor's yard to get in the back way. By the time she got home, Sean would be there with lights on. Maybe the Feds would think she was staying at a motel or somewhere.

Maybe pigs would fly.

Joanne was the last to leave. Before she let herself out the back door, she went out on the fire escape to look for government cars or agents parked nearby. The air was twenty degrees warmer than when she'd come to work, and the relative humidity was so high that the tallest buildings disappeared in the orange haze of fog-reflected sodium-vapor light. Traffic poured west on Ontario, honking and blinking. Further south, it streamed east at a more sluggish pace as people getting off work slogged into the city to shop. Beyond Ohio street, the Merchandise Mart shouldered above the intervening buildings decorated for Christmas with floods of red and green. Christmas. Would she and Sean spend it in some anonymous Federal hideout, phoning their holiday wishes to the family?

She shivered and hurried back inside. Before putting on her coat, she put a note on the wheelchair asking Daniel to return it to the rental place.

The hall was empty. The antique indicator above the service elevator pointed to the second floor. She pushed the "down" button and listened nervously for human sounds as the old contraption clanged and rattled its way upward. She was sighing with relief by the time it stopped and the service gate clattered up.

Then Paul Minorini stepped out of the shadows and shoved a paper at her.

"I'm sorry, but you've been served."

101

TWENTY-EIGHT

Minorini stood in the lobby of the Dirksen building and watched Haskel studying his watch. From his vantage point, Minorini could see traffic on Jackson Boulevard and Randolph Street, and Alexander Calder's red "Flamingo" sculpture across Randolph in the Kluczynski plaza. He also had an excellent view of three of the building's entrances and the metal detectors.

Haskel scowled and stalked over to say, "She's not coming."

"Did Bergman report that?"

"No. He hasn't called in. That's a crock too!"

Minorini took out his cell phone and asked for Bergman's number. He tapped it in as Haskel rattled it off.

"Bergman." The agent's voice sounded fuzzy.

"Report," Minorini ordered.

"Lessing got on the 7:34 train. She ought to be there by now. But you wouldn't be calling if she was. What's with her?"

"Why?"

"I offered to drive her to the train and she told me to drive myself to Hell."

"Maybe she's just pissed about her car."

"Yeah. She told me if it's not fixed by the time she gets home she's gonna call the local cops, then invite channels 2, 5, 7, 9 and 32 to come take pictures. Think she's kidding?"

"One way to find out."

. . .

About three minutes after nine, an eastbound CTA bus stopped on Jackson. Minorini noticed it because he was still watching for Lessing. When the bus pulled away, she was among the passengers at the stop. He watched her look both ways, then angle across the street. He could tell the moment she spotted him by the change to furious in her body language. He walked over to the revolving door to wait for her.

She pushed through it without acknowledging his existence. She didn't look at Haskel, either, as she blew past him. In fact, she didn't slow down until she got to the end of the metal detector line.

Haskel flashed his badge at the marshals and went around the queue. When Minorini got in line behind Lessing, he noticed she wasn't carrying her camera case.

She ignored him. When her turn came to step through the arch, she dropped a handful of keys and coins in the basket and charged through, holding her hands out for her property as soon as she cleared the detector. She headed for the elevators, ignored the car Haskel was holding for her, and stepped into the next one. Minorini followed, bypassing the detector.

Lessing had moved to the back of the car facing the door, as etiquette required. He couldn't bring himself to face her; in her place he'd be homicidal. So he turned his back and pushed the button for the fourteenth floor.

By the time the elevator door opened, Joanne was light-headed with rage. She stepped around Paul Minorini without making eye contact, and out into the hall. A stainless steel plaque on the wall told her where to go to report in, and she turned toward the courtroom with the FBI agent following.

Three men in charcoal-gray suits and power ties blocked the doorway. One of them, a man who looked about forty, detached himself from the knot and came toward her. "Mrs. Lessing?"

"*Ms.* Lessing."

"Ms. Lessing. Sorry. I'm US Attorney Aaron Mercer. I'll be taking you through your testimony." He held his hand out to shake.

Joanne ignored it. Mercer seemed startled. After a long moment he dropped the hand and looked pointedly at Paul Minorini who was standing on the elevator side of the group. The agent shrugged.

A fourth man, older than the others, had been hidden by the group. He stepped close to Joanne and said, "Ms. Lessing? I'm Carl Norman. Mr. Rage asked me to represent your interests. Could we—" He jerked his head toward the far end of the corridor. "Talk?"

Joanne followed him down the hall, where she told him the whole story.

"Mercer will ask you questions," Norman told her. "Or he'll ask you to tell the judge your story."

"Do I have to tell it?"

"The only grounds on which you could refuse to testify is to avoid self-incrimination. And since you haven't committed any crime, you can't plead the Fifth."

"What if I refuse on the grounds that the mob will kill me if I talk?"

"The judge will order you to talk and offer to put you in the witness protection program. You said you won't consider that. Why on earth?"

"I have a life, Mr. Norman."

"Well, if this man they want to wiretap really is connected, you won't for long."

"It's not fair!"

"But it's the law."

"What if I just refuse to talk?"

"The judge will jail you for contempt until you testify. And I doubt the mob would trust you to accept an indefinite stay in County. Even in solitary you wouldn't be safe."

"Then I have no choice?" In her head she heard her own voice telling Sean, "You always have a choice," mocking her.

Norman shook his head.

"Why did you bother to come?"

"If they ask you anything irrelevant or anything of a personal nature, I'll object. And the judge will probably sustain me. He's known for being scrupulously fair."

The courtroom reminded her of a chapel—dark, paneled walls, subdued lighting with spots on the main altar, but with a US flag and the seal of the Northern District Court instead of a cross. The sanctuary was divided from the spectators by the first row of pews, and the acolytes positioned themselves between two marble-topped tables within it. A man in a suit sat behind a dark wood partition before the bench, paying no attention to the federal lawyers. And on the bench, the judge was already seated.

If the room resembled a chapel, the judge was an inquisitor in his black robes. He was a big man, old and heavyset, with a stern expression. He moved only his mouth and his eyes.

Mercer and his cronies put their files on one of the two tables. Norman led Joanne to the other and held a chair for her to sit in, then took a seat himself. Agents Minorini and Haskel stood at attention, like sentries, by the door behind the jury box.

After a few moments, Mercer asked the judge if he'd like to "do this in chambers."

"No," the judge said. "Just lock the doors." They waited while one of Mercer's junior partners walked back and complied. Then the judge said, "Are you ready to proceed, Mr. Mercer?"

"Yes, Your Honor."

Mercer called Joanne to the witness stand and swore her in. He started a series of stilted questions: "Were you, on the morning of November 1, in the area of . . ." etc. They seemed silly to Joanne, and must have to the judge as well because he finally said, "Just let the lady tell her story, Mercer."

Joanne looked up at him and thought she saw him wink. What she saw for sure was that the judge had one hand gripped tightly in the other and both were trembling slightly. He must have thought she was staring because he frowned, then said, "Just tell me what you saw."

. . .

When Lessing had finished testifying, there was a long, uncomfortable silence, broken when she asked, "Your Honor, may I go?"

"If there are no further questions, certainly."

Lessing looked at Mercer. He shook his head. She got off the stand and walked over to confer with her lawyer, seated at the defendant's table.

Minorini would've stayed where he was—the back of the jury box—if Haskel hadn't followed her when she went out.

Minorini entered the hall in time to hear him say, "Ms. Lessing."

Joanne stopped. Haskel held out an 8×10 of Albert Siano, one of the autopsy photos taken from an angle that showed off the bullet holes.

"Just so we're on the same page, this is what this guy does to people!"

Joanne reacted as if someone had handed her a snake. Then she seemed to recover. "If you had proof of that, you wouldn't need my testimony."

"These people don't go to trial," Haskel said. "One way or another, nobody testifies against them."

"Because they kill people?"

"Not just that. The way things are, if you go to court and testify you lose. Even if we win, you lose."

TWENTY-NINE

Hancock was setting up his lights by the time Joanne arrived. Jan had finished Rita's makeup, and Rita was glowing.

She seemed curiously nervous, Joanne thought. This must be more important to her than she cared to let on. When she spotted Joanne, she brightened and relaxed. "You changed your mind?"

"No. I'm just here to watch."

"Watch and learn," Hancock said.

Joanne laughed.

Hancock removed his suit jacket and tie and rolled his sleeves to the elbows. Like a symphony conductor, he began to direct Rita's every movement without ever touching her, all the time stooping or stretching, walking backward, or pushing invasively close to get his shots.

"Relax, darling. These are stills, not videos. Let's have a smile. Very nice. Now the one you make when you've got Rick tied in knots."

Rita gave him a murderous glare; he snapped it and said, "My God, don't smile. You'll crack your face!"

Hancock recorded surprise, a laugh, then irritation as she processed his suggestion and tried to foil his intention by not smiling.

Joanne only half-paid attention as Hancock shot off three more rolls. Rita followed his instructions tentatively at first, then with greater and greater enthusiasm until they both seemed to have forgotten Joanne.

When he had used up the film in all four of his cameras, Hancock told Rita to take a break.

She came over to where Joanne was sitting. "You set this up!" Joanne didn't bother to deny it. "Why?" Rita answered for herself. "To get rid of me!"

Joanne grinned. "Let's say we thought your energy might be more productively directed."

Hancock rolled his eyes.

"When will the pictures be ready?" Rita asked him.

"Two weeks."

"Two weeks! You haven't heard of One Hour Photo?"

Hancock stopped. "If that's what you want, why don't you go to one of those snapshot kiosks and take a strip of passport photos? You could blow them up yourself at Walgreens."

Rita flushed.

"Hancock!" Joanne found herself close to shouting. He turned and stared at her. She ignored him. "Rita," she said. "We have other clients. And contracts with deadlines. And when you're paying for your portraits—I'm sure you understand. . . ."

"I understand Mr. Hancock's forte is photography, not diplomacy."

Touché!

"Shall we continue?" Hancock asked. "Give me a look like a cat watching a bird."

Rita looked at him and widened her eyes.

"Very good. Now, imagine I'm from the IRS, here to see your books. Now I'm the man you love most in the world. Turn. Now your fantasy lover is coming through the door."

At this point, May entered, and Rita guffawed. Hancock said, "Whoops!" and blushed.

In confusion, May looked from Rita to Hancock to Joanne, which caused Rita to laugh more heartily.

Hancock recorded everything.

"Joanne," May finally said, with annoyance in her tone. "Rick wants you."

. . .

"How's it going with the Bitch Goddess?" Rick asked.

"Rita's sensational. And you'd better watch your mouth or we'll be back to square one."

He held his hands up in an 'I surrender' gesture. Then he put them down and asked seriously, "How did it go with the Feds?"

She shrugged. She felt like the heroine in one of those woman-in-danger thrillers. Bad melodrama. Only she wasn't Julia Roberts and her nemesis hadn't presented her with an overt threat.

"Mr. Norman seems to think that we'll have to go into the witness protection program if they bring Dossi to trial."

She remembered how *up* Sean had been when they came home from the farm. "Does Grandma *have* to sell it?" he'd asked. After today, it was denial not to break the news. Maybe she should just give up and start planning. . . .

No! Then she'd have to give up photography. And Sean would have to start over in a new school, and abandon the extended family he'd finally come to appreciate. No way! She'd shoot Dossi first!

Rick said, "Shit!"

"Yeah. I've got to get back. I'll keep you posted."

On the train, on her way home, Joanne thought about the day. The anger that had propelled her from the courtroom in a white heat still made it hard for her to think straight. She had to go to Naperville in the morning to set up a shoot for an advertising layout. She should have asked Rick to cancel. She hoped the Feds had fixed her car. If not, *she* would have to cancel.

She remembered the rifle in her hope chest. Hope.

When it was her father's, she'd ignored the gun. But now that it was hers, she could feel it exerting a subtle pressure to settle her differences with Dossi permanently. Why not use the definitive solution?

My God! What am I thinking? ...

That was the trouble with guns, why private citizens shouldn't have them. The knowledge that it was there stopped you from thinking of a better way to solve things. And if you didn't plan to use it, you wouldn't be ready if you needed to. And only the police were trained to plan.

She wished she could ask Paul Minorini about it, but then he might suspect about the gun. Then she would have to stop fantasizing that it would save her life.

THIRTY

She was already ten minutes late when she and Sean flew out of the house. Ten minutes late, ten to drop Sean, twenty-five or thirty to get to the shoot, twenty more to get set up. Damn! And the car was furry with frost.

Her gloved fingers fumbled for the right key, and the key slid off the lock twice before it found the keyhole. Upside down. Damn. Damn.

"Hurry up, Mom. I'm freezing!"

Joanne suppressed a retort as she opened the door and dropped her camera bag on the middle of the seat. She reached over and unlocked Sean's door. She had the key in the ignition before she remembered her promise not to drive another foot without first checking the oil. This time she said "Damn!" aloud. "I forgot to check the oil."

"Can't you check it after work?"

"Like I was going to do yesterday? Anyway, we can't go till the windows are scraped, so you can do that while I check." She flipped open the camera bag and grabbed the package of lens papers, then pulled the hood release. Sean reluctantly took up the scraper. He started working with a haste spurred by cold.

The hood hinges *groaned.* Nothing in the engine compartment was distinguishable in the half-light. Cold seeped through Joanne's pants, prickling the skin of her thighs. She shivered and hurried to get the flashlight from her camera case. She had to do a little dance to avoid colliding with Sean as he rounded the car to get the driver's side window. He finished the window by the time she'd located the dipstick. "Come here, Sean. I want you to learn how to do this."

"Can't I learn in the summer?"

She paused long enough to give him a daggers-look, and he shut his mouth tight and joined her. She handed him the light. "Keep it there, please." She guided his hand until the light was where she needed it. "On the hole where the dipstick goes."

Sean shifted his weight from foot to foot but managed to keep the light steady. She didn't tell him to hold still. Her own feet were burning with cold, and she jigged up and down, in place, as she pulled the dipstick out. She didn't bother to wipe it; "add oil" could be read clearly above the black, congealed oil. Threading the stick back into place took a freezing eternity.

She said, "Take off the filler cap, while I get the oil."

She started to point, but Sean said, "I know, I know, just hurry."

She almost gave it up. It was too cold to be fucking around with the stupid car, too early in the morning. But that's what she'd said last time she drove it, when she'd only suspected the car needed oil. Tomorrow morning probably wouldn't be any warmer. And she couldn't afford a new motor.

When she had the stuff out of the trunk, she put the keys back in the ignition so she wouldn't lose them, and fumbled with the cap on the container.

Sean was playing the flashlight beam around the engine compartment. "What's that?" he asked. He pointed at an off-white mass of what appeared to be glazier's putty stuck with wires on the back of the engine.

Jesus Christ! A bomb!

"Sean, get away from the car!"

"What?"

"Just get away! Now!" She looked up and down the street, as if whoever did this might be waiting around to watch the fireworks. No one.

Sean said, "That looks like a bomb or something. What's going on?"

Joanne stepped around to lift her camera case from the seat and to reach for the keys. Better not! There must be a limit to how far their luck would hold. "Sean, have you got your keys?"

"Sure."

"Then let's go." She half-ran towards the house, forcing Sean to turn and run ahead of her. The terror she was feeling must have been apparent, because Sean began to move with the urgency of near-panic, fumbling with haste. He got the key in the lock and said, "Mom, what is it?!"

"Just go! Get inside!" When the door was safely closed behind them, she said, "Get away from the windows. In fact, come in the kitchen." The adrenaline rushing through her made her feel light-headed. She grabbed the phone and punched in 9-1-1. She held her hand up when Sean looked ready to interrupt. One minute.

"Nine-one-one. Emergency."

"Good morning." Why did she say that? "I think I found a bomb."

The squad car pulled up without the fanfare of red, white and blue lights she'd been expecting, and she walked out to meet it, giving her car a wide berth.

The officer got out and put on his hat. "You the lady with the bomb?" He wasn't successfully hiding his amusement.

She pointed towards the car. "Yes. On the motor."

"You'd better stay back." He almost sniggered. He walked over to the car and began a perfunctory examination. She could tell when he spotted the bomb—his whole body expressed his surprise—and he hurried back to grab his radio mike. "Guess what?" he told the dispatcher. "The lady's got a real bomb!"

"I'm Sergeant Amis. Maybe you'd better tell me what happened."

"I told the other officer . . ."

"I know. We like to get it more than once."

She told him.

"You got any enemies?" he asked.

She shook her head. None that she could name.

"You owe anybody?"

"Just the bank."

"They usually just repossess things. How about work? Any trouble there?"

"The sort of people I deal with would probably just kill me on the spot if they were that mad."

"What about your husband?"

"I don't have a husband."

"You got an ex?"

"Yeah, but we're on good terms."

"Maybe you'd better give me his name and address. Maybe *he's* got someone trying to kill him."

"It couldn't just be a mistake? The wrong address or something?"

"It looks like a professional job." he said. "Pros don't make that kind of mistake."

She couldn't resist. "Are you sure? I mean, who'd know?"

"Good point, but are you willing to take the chance?"

When Detective Gray arrived, he was furious that he hadn't been notified immediately, and brusque to the point of rudeness. "It never occurred to you that this might be connected with that mob hit you witnessed?"

It had, but she said, "I didn't witness anything but a hit-and-run fender-bender."

"Yeah." He turned to the man with him, another detective, Joanne surmised. "Get that Fed on the phone—Minorini."

"I called him already," Joanne said, "while we were waiting for the bomb squad."

"I *don't* hate to say I told you so," Special Agent Haskel said. "*I told you so!* These people don't kid around."

He was standing in her kitchen with Paul Minorini, facing her across the counter. Detective Gray and Sergeant Amis stood at either end of the counter and let Haskel do the talking. The bomb squad had disposed of the bomb and hauled her car away. Sean was in his room.

"How did they find out about me?" Joanne demanded.

"What're you talkin' about?"

"I was told my testimony was going to be sealed. How did they get my name?"

"They paid someone off or intimidated someone," Haskel said. "What's the difference? They found you, and now you're a sittin' duck."

She looked from one to the other and thought Haskel seemed uncomfortable.

Paul seemed only interested. "She's got a point," he said. "Maybe we can find the leak and trace it."

THIRTY-ONE

They had a half hour to gather their possessions and pack. Joanne brought her cameras, tripod, photo albums, and boxes of negatives. Sean took his walkman and CDs, his laptop and a couple of handheld video games. Both of them threw clothes into suitcases, but it was hard to think what they would need on such short notice. The Feds—Paul Minorini and a man named Carver—drove them to the Loop. In the parking garage beneath Federal Plaza, Minorini had them get out of the car and enter the building in a scene straight out of a James Bond movie.

Upstairs, in the heart of FBI territory, Joanne and Sean were separated for "debriefing." Agent Minorini left Joanne alone in a small beige room—furnished with only two wire-frame, leather-seated chairs and industrial carpeting. No clock. No magazines or table to put them on. There wasn't even a two-way mirror. Maybe there were hidden video cameras, she couldn't tell. Being "debriefed" consisted of telling her story over and over to the half dozen different agents who came into the room over the next several hours. Each one had questions—many she'd already answered. By noon she felt like a TV sitcom that's been rerun so often everyone knows the words.

Shortly after noon, Paul Minorini came back and asked what she'd like for lunch.

"Sean. What have you done with him?"

"Nothing. Agent Jones is showing him the Etch-a-Sketch."

"Oh."

. . .

They ate in a conference room, Joanne and Sean, agents Minorini and Haskel, and John Carver, who turned out to be a US Marshal. One of the secretaries brought in a pot of coffee and a bag of Italian beef sandwiches. Agent Minorini went out and returned with soft drinks in cans.

When they were finished, Sean asked to be excused "to check the plumbing," and Carver volunteered to escort him.

Joanne waited until the door closed on them, then told the agents, "If I'm going to be a target, let me be bait."

"You're crazy!" Haskel told her. He was smiling like a crocodile.

"Being desperate does that to you."

"What about your son?" Minorini asked.

"We can send him to stay with friends—in Florida. They have a place in the Keys, one of those gated communities that's high-security and secluded. And they have lots of kids. Their neighbors probably wouldn't notice one more."

"Then what?" Haskel said. "Even if we could nail this guy without getting you killed, then what?"

"Then you send him to jail and I go back to my life."

"You got more guts than brains." He shook his head. "Even if your idea worked, you think you'd be safe with this guy locked up? He'd have all the more reason to blow you away. No way. We're gonna stash you in a safe place while we see what we can turn up and whether you'll be needed to testify any time soon. And soon as we can arrange it, you and the kid are going into the Witness Protection Program."

They had to sit on the floor of the new car before Agent Minorini pulled it out of the garage. The day had warmed and clouded over while they'd been inside, and a light drizzle coated the car within minutes.

It seemed as though they drove around forever. She knew they got onto the Dan Ryan, I-55, and I-294 from the overhead highway signs. But there were dozens of lesser streets she couldn't identify since she couldn't look out. Even Sean was getting tired of the cloak-and-dagger routine. By the time they pulled up to a nondescript building in a nearly deserted industrial area, Joanne had no idea where they were.

After the overhead door closed, Minorini invited them to wait in the office. They seemed to be in a government service facility. There were vehicles of every vintage and description, from luxury cars to a mail truck, in every state of repair.

The "office" was separated from the service area by a glass door and from the rest of the facility by a metal one labeled RE-STRICTED ENTRY. Like the customer waiting room of a high-end car dealership, the room had a coffee service, couch and chairs, and a TV mounted near the ceiling. Several TV remotes were lying around on end tables, along with copies of *Time* and *Newsweek, The Wall Street Journal*, a two-day-old *Trib* and today's *Sun-Times*. The walls were fabric-textured and decorated with travel posters—someone had a sense of humor. Between the ad for Fiji and one for the "Emerald City," an institutional electric clock announced that it was three P.M.

Agent Minorini invited them to "make themselves comfortable," before he disappeared into the restricted area. Sean grabbed a remote and started channel surfing.

Ordinarily, Minorini would have handed the Lessings off to the US Marshals and forgotten them until they were hauled out of hiding to testify. But in this case, he was providing the safe house. Until something more permanent could be arranged, they were stashing the chickens right under the fox's nose—in one of the most exclusive northern suburbs, in a house belonging to Minorini's great aunt. The elderly woman spent her winters in Florida, southern California, or southern Italy while Minorini kept an eye on her affairs. The neighbors were used to his coming and going, and since his sister and her family usually stayed there on trips to Chicago, his having a few visitors for a couple days wouldn't occasion any talk. Best of all, the rental wouldn't appear on any vouchers, so there was one less chance for a leak.

At 4:00 P.M., they got to watch the Channel 7 version of their story on TV: "Authorities are not saying who they think planted a bomb in this quiet North Shore neighborhood. The home-owner, Joanne Lessing, thirty-eight, found the bomb under the hood of her car early this morning while checking the oil. Agents from the Bureau of Alcohol Tobacco and Firearms defused the bomb. Local authorities are investigating. Lessing told police she has no enemies."

When the reporter started announcing details of the latest po-litical scandal, Sean changed channels.

At 4:30. he was channel surfing again when a minicam re-porter standing in front of their house got their attention.

"Neighbors in this quiet Northbrook neighborhood are at a loss . . ."

"It's like a movie!" Sean said.

In a pre-recorded interview, one of their neighbors expressed disbelief that anyone would want to hurt "such a nice woman."

The scene flashed back to the "live-on-the-scene" reporter. "Police are also looking into the possibility that this was a bizarre case of mistaken identity. They aren't saying where the Lessings are at this moment. Back to you . . ."

Sean changed to a cable station after that.

They left at the peak of rush hour. Minorini stowed his charges in the back seat of one of three identical Lincoln limousines that had dark tinted windows and the same license plate.

As they'd arranged, Carver got into one of the limos and

pulled out. His orders were to drive to Midway and take a turn around Departures, circle the airport and stop at Arrivals. Then look for a tail. One of the mechanics had orders to leave ten minutes later and perform the same charade at O'Hare.

Minorini pulled out fifteen minutes after that and took a roundabout route to Kenilworth.

THIRTY-TWO

It was raining just hard enough to snarl traffic, so the trip took nearly two hours. At least with the tinted windows, they could sit up and look out. Street lights and Christmas lights glistened off the wet streets.

Paul Minorini drove like an android, like Mr. Data might, with no apparent impatience. Joanne was surprised when he turned onto the Edens, amazed when, finally, he pulled into the driveway of a house in Kenilworth. He'd called ahead on his cell phone, and a light went on at the back door as the car pulled past the house into the rear yard. As much as Joanne could see in the gloom beyond the circle of illumination, the yard was surrounded by a hedge of columnar junipers. The drive ended at a two-car garage. Paul stopped the car with the passenger door as near the back door as possible and said, "Wait until I open the car door for you, then go straight into the house. Don't look around. I'll bring your things. Okay?"

Sean said, "Yeah, sure."

Joanne nodded.

When they got to the door, a blond woman opened it for them and closed it behind them. She gestured at the room behind her and said, "Make yourselves at home. But stay away from the windows."

Sean nodded and started looking around, eventually wandering out of the room. Joanne took a few steps away from the door and turned to watch the woman open it for Minorini, who'd put on a baseball cap and was carrying their luggage. He put it just inside and went back for the rest of their things. When he had everything in the house, he introduced the blond.

Megan Reilly was a US Marshal, Witness Protection division. She'd be staying at the house with them while Minorini hunted the bomber, and the Marshal's Service made more permanent arrangements for their future.

There it was again. Their future—her future—in the hands of others. "What does that mean?" she demanded.

"Megan will explain," Minorini told her. "I'll be back in a few days, and I'll fill you in on developments. Meanwhile, let Megan know if there's anything you need." He tipped his cap and let himself out.

Megan locked the door behind him. "Let me show you around," she said.

The house was huge, with real fireplaces, high ceilings and tall windows. Your tax dollars working overtime, Joanne translated to herself. The crown moldings, doors, and door and window frames looked like dark-stained oak or walnut. The living room walls and wall-to-wall carpets were ivory. The couch and chairs were covered with a creamy pink material patterned with antique roses in a darker pink; the drapes were the same material. A pale green oriental rug was laid over the carpet in the center of the room, and matching runners covered the high traffic areas. The fireplace had a mantel of green marble.

"Whose house is this?" Joanne demanded.

Megan gave a twisted half-smile. "It belongs to a private citizen. The Federal government is house-sitting in return for using it rent free as a safe house."

The dining room was as rich as the front room, though the drapes were a deep blue that was repeated in the pattern of the 9×12 oriental. Joanne recognized Winifred Godfrey as the painter of the huge exquisite oil on the wall opposite the window—back-lit white tulips. She'd seen a similar treatment of red tulips for $6200 at an exhibition. There was a crazed glass globe of white silk peonies on the polished table.

Sean appeared while they were inspecting the pseudo-traditional kitchen that seemed equipped with every modern gadget.

"I'm Sean," he told Megan, shoving his hand toward her.

She took it as she said, "Megan Reilly."

"What do I call you?"

"How about Megan?"

"Cool. Are you a Special Agent too?"

"A US Marshal. Your bodyguard as a matter of fact."

"You're a whole lot prettier than Ricky Linderman."

Megan smiled. Joanne wondered if she'd seen *My Bodyguard*.

Sean said, "May I have a pop?"

"Fine with me but it's up to your mother."

Megan helped carry their luggage upstairs, and let Sean choose one of the three rooms across the back of the house. Naturally, he took the one with the TV and cable hookup.

Joanne took the room next to his. As downstairs, lovely wood and fabric predominated in classic designs. The prints on the walls looked more like the originals of some unknown artist than reproductions of established ones. It was all rather like what Joanne would have chosen if she'd had an unlimited budget.

Megan put Joanne's suitcase down inside the door and opened the closet. Above the clothes rod was a shelf piled with smoothly folded sheets and fluffy towels and washcloths. "If you need anything else, holler."

"Thank you."

Megan walked toward the door.

"Wait."

She stopped and turned to face Joanne.

"What's going to happen to us?"

"We'll give you new identities and set you up in another part of the country. We'll help you find another job. As long as you don't come back here or contact anyone from here you'll be safe."

As long as!

"No! I can't accept that! Our family's here!"

"Exactly. And these people will be watching them, waiting for you to make contact. I know it's hard. And it's not fair. But you're alive. Your son's alive."

"We just spent three years putting ourselves back together. We can't just start over."

"If you want to live, you'll have to. Look. I'm not sure it's sunk in yet, but someone tried to kill you. They'll keep at it until they succeed—if they can find you."

"Why can't you just catch them?"

"We're trying. But this is a mob thing. Even in prison they have influence.

"Look, you've had a hell of a day. Let's get you settled in and get something to eat. Come downstairs when you're unpacked and we'll arrange supper. Things may look less bleak after you've had a night's sleep.

"And if you take it a day at a time, you'll get through it."

Joanne felt a little flash of insight. Megan was like the dog-handlers at the pound. She'd take good care of them, but not let herself get attached. When their time was up, she'd hand them off and never think of them again. Joanne couldn't blame her. You couldn't take them all home.

But what happens to the ones no one claims?

After they'd cleared the remains of the pizza they'd ordered and put the dishes in the washer, they moved into the living room. Megan had laid out a fire earlier. Now she lit it. Joanne sat at one end of the couch, Sean at the other. For a while they watched the flames in silence. Then Megan excused herself. When she came back, she said, "I'm turning in. Don't answer the phone or the door, or make any calls. If anyone comes, wake me. If you open an outside door or first floor window, the burglar alarm will go off. Goodnight."

Joanne felt her insides knotting as Megan spoke.

Sean didn't say anything until the marshal had had time to get out of earshot, then he stretched to drape himself across Joanne's lap. For a moment, he rested his forehead on the couch arm. Then he rolled sideways to face her and worked his arms between her and the couch back. He looked up at her.

"Why does someone want to kill us?"

A simple, direct question. And it deserved a straight answer.

"I'm pretty sure it has to do with the hit-and-run I witnessed."

"But no one would—Oh. He might have killed the guy down the street. Duh!"

Joanne nodded.

"And all this time I thought Agent Minorini was coming around because he wanted to go out with you."

"FBI agents aren't allowed to go out with witnesses. And anyway, I doubt he'd be interested.

"Don't sell yourself short." He shrugged as if it were moot anyway. "We gonna hafta be here for Christmas?"

"I don't know, Sean."

She put her arms around him. She could feel his fear as he clung to her like a much younger child.

THIRTY-THREE

At least we ought to check her out," Minorini told Haskel. "We'd look really stupid if it turns out her ex-husband is trying to kill her."

"I leave that in your capable hands, pal. And she's got family around here, hasn't she?" Minorini nodded. "Track 'em down too. Maybe someone's trying to get to a relative through her. Or maybe she said something to one of them that she forgot to mention to us."

One of the credit applications Joanne had filled out listed a Ken Schroeder as her "nearest relative not living with you." As he picked up the phone to arrange a meeting, Minorini wondered how she interpreted nearest—closest in age or physical proximity, or just closest?

Ken Schroeder was the founder and president of his own computer consulting firm, one of the new breed of businessmen who'd gotten his start in a video arcade and graduated to giving advice to his grandfather's cohort.

His office bridged the generation gap—enough plush and gloss to reassure the money, enough electronic gadgetry for most technophiles. He had a kinetic sculpture on his burled maple credenza and traditional photos in Lucite frames on the matching burled maple desk. Because of their placement, Minorini could see the subjects of all the photos except one eight-by-ten. The ones he could see were family portraits.

The requisite computer was hidden within the desk, but its flat screen monitor rose out of the desk top. As Minorini crossed the room, Schroeder made the screen and keyboard disappear into recesses so cleverly engineered that the surface looked solid to the casual glance.

Schroeder had blue eyes in a tanned face. There was a little new-moon scar beneath his right eye. He was dressed to impress by understatement. He rose and offered Minorini his hand, a firm handshake, and a soft, leather reclining chair. "What can I do for you Mr. Minorini? Or is it Agent Minorini? Someone hacking into your systems?"

"You know anyone who'd want to harm your sister?"

The question got to him. "Joanne?"

Minorini nodded. He figured Schroeder's shock was genuine.

"No, of course not." But as Minorini waited, his certainty seemed to falter. "Well. She *did* do those photo essays on bikers and shoplifters. Maybe one of them? What do you mean by harm?" He must've missed the local news.

"Someone tried to bomb her car."

Schroeder paled. "Is she all right?"

"We have her in protective custody. Along with your nephew."

"What can I do?"

"We need to find out who's got it in for her."

"Yeah. Ah . . . Jesus! I don't know. Joanne's the last person . . . You sure it's not a mistake—maybe someone trying to get her neighbor and went to the wrong address?"

Minorini shook his head. "Do you have any enemies who might hurt your sister to get back at you?"

"No, of course not. My enemies might try biological warfare—er—computer viruses—or sic their lawyers on me, not— Jesus! Can you protect her?"

"We'll do our best," Minorini said. What if someone up the chain of command had decided to use Joanne Lessing for bait?

"*She* doesn't know who?"

"We asked her, and she said she doesn't have any enemies. But women sometimes lie to shield abusive partners."

"Not Joanne. And I don't think Howie . . . I mean, he's a jerk

127

but—" He gestured, knocking over the framed 8×10 photo Minorini had been staring at the back of, allowing Minorini to get a glimpse—a group with guns. He beat Schroeder to the pick up by a heartbeat, backing away far enough so that Schroeder would have to come over the desk or around it to get possession. Plain view—sort of. But he'd bet it would hold up in court.

The picture showed Schroeder and Joanne as young adults with a younger man and an older one. "My dad," Schroeder said. "With Joanne and my brother Allen and me. The only time he ever got us all to go hunting with him."

Minorini handed the picture back, then gave Shroeder his card. "If you think of anything that might help us, however improbable, call me."

Schroeder nodded. "Just take care of my sister."

"I will."

Allen Schroeder was a house painter, North Shore style. That is, he and his wife ran a decorating business out of their Oak Park home. Neither of them could imagine Joanne with an enemy. Nor did they have any enemies of their own. After conducting a brief telephone credit check, Minorini believed them.

L.A. was hot, even in December. Minorini had forgotten how hot. He wished he'd worn a lighter jacket. He wished he could take his jacket off, but then he'd have had to carry his gun in his briefcase, and that wouldn't do.

He recognized Tagmier immediately, though he hadn't seen him in years. Even at 45, Tagmier *looked* like a special agent. After they shook hands, Tagmier handed him a folder with the neatly typed label LESSING, HOWARD. "You can look it over on the way," he said. "Lessing ought to be at the office by the time we get there."

"You had him picked up?"

"We *asked* him to assist us. Guy in his position can't afford to piss us off."

Minorini didn't have a problem with that. After Tagmier filled him in, he was even less inclined to worry about Howard Lessing.

"If you want, I can get you a transcript of his divorce proceedings," Tagmier said.

"Just summarize for me."

"He moved here from Chicago with his wife, Joanne, right after law school. I guess she basically put him through. He wasn't exactly a Rhodes scholar. He went to work for the Public Defender's office after he passed the bar—on his second try. Soon as he got some trial experience and made a few contacts, he went solo. The wife went to work for him as secretary and clerk until he got successful enough to afford paid help."

"What *about* the wife?"

"Nobody seems to know much. Apparently she was quiet, mousy, always deferred to him. Till one day she must've had enough. Went out and hired a divorce lawyer."

"Messy divorce?"

Tagmier shrugged. "Not very. Either she had a hell of a lawyer or she threatened to tell where the bodies were buried. He let her take the kid and leave the state. Most guys fight that even if they don't give a damn about the kid."

"What else did she get?"

"Two years of maintenance while she finished her BFA, nominal child support till the kid turns twenty-one. And he pays for the kid's education through graduate school."

"Not overly generous considering what he probably makes."

Tagmier shook his head. "He's mortgaged to the hilt. And don't forget, he's got an image to maintain."

"He a player?"

Tagmier laughed. "In his dreams. He makes most of his money from real estate commissions."

"Tell me about your ex-wife, Mr. Lessing," Minorini said.

Lessing laughed nervously. "What, she rob a bank or something?"

"Her life's been threatened."

Lessing gestured *time out*. "Hey, that was a long time ago!"

"What was?"

"If you don't know . . . Nothing. When people get divorced they say things. . . ."

"Why did you let her move out of state?"

"Are you kidding? I wanted as much space between me and the bitch as I could get. Europe would have been even better."

"And your son?"

Lessing softened briefly, then shrugged. He didn't answer the question.

"Did Joanne have something on you? Or threaten you?"

"Yeah. She said if I didn't let them go, I'd end up like that asshole, Bobbit—with parts missing."

"Cut the crap, Lessing! Unless maybe you'd like *me* to start looking for whatever she has on you."

That got to him. "Nothing! She threatened to turn me into the IRS for tax evasion. Nothing to it, but I didn't need the hassle. And frankly, at the time I couldn't afford to hire another lawyer. You met my son?"

"Yeah. Nice kid. Hard to believe you're really his old man."

THIRTY-FOUR

Joanne didn't see Paul Minorini again for three days. She was reading in the living room after watching the 10:00 P.M. news when she heard the back door open. The alarm didn't sound, and she'd watched Megan set it before turning in, so she went to investigate.

Paul put down a gym bag and reset the alarm as if he lived there. Then he noticed her and said hello. He looked hung over, but still asked, "How're you doing?"

She felt an overwhelming awkwardness—like a high school wallflower suddenly asked "How's it going?" by the varsity quarterback. She shrugged. "Have you? . . ."

"Found anything?" He shook his head. "Not for want of trying. I even interviewed your ex."

"Howie? In L.A.?" He nodded. She couldn't resist laughing. The thought of Howie on the receiving end was delicious.

She looked for Paul's reaction—he wasn't amused. She realized he must be tired. "I'm sorry, but you should've asked."

"We have to check out everyone."

"You look beat. Have you eaten?"

"Just airline food. Hours ago."

"There's some lasagna left. And salad."

He brightened. He picked up his bag and led the way to the kitchen, where he dropped the bag on a chair and pulled another out for her. "Sean asleep?"

"Are you kidding? Teenagers are nocturnal. He's upstairs OD-ing on cable."

"Megan?"

"She may be asleep. She went upstairs an hour ago. I don't think she's feeling well."

He nodded. "An abscessed tooth. She asked to have someone spell her so she can go to the dentist tomorrow. I'm it."

"Funny she didn't mention it."

"She wouldn't." He opened the fridge and took out the covered dishes they'd stored the leftovers in. "Ordinarily, they have female marshals guard women, but things are really tight this week—lots going down. And one of the women is out on maternity leave."

"Do they ordinarily put witnesses up in mansions?"

He grinned, and she was struck again by how attractive he was. If only . . .

"This isn't a mansion. By North Shore standards, it's practically low-income housing."

She watched as he loaded a plate, then helped himself to salad while he nuked the pasta. He took out a Killian's when he put the salad bowl back. It was clear he knew his way around a kitchen. This kitchen.

"Get you something?" he asked.

She pointed to the lager. "One of those?"

She waited until he was nearly finished before asking, "How's Howie?"

"If he had anything to do with planting your bomb, he's the best actor in Tinseltown."

"If Howie had the nerve to commit violence, he'd have killed me during the divorce."

"So I gathered. What ever possessed you to marry him?"

"Didn't you ever make a dumb mistake when you were young?"

He took a long pull of the Killian's and gave her a dazzling smile. "A few."

. . .

Megan didn't come back. She was so feverish the next morning Minorini sent her off in a cab and phoned her office to call her in sick. They told him they couldn't replace her until next Thursday when Carver would be free. Three calls later, Minorini was on loan to the Marshals' Service.

He spent the next few days making follow-up calls and reading reports, and a lot of time playing video games with Sean. The kid didn't complain about their situation, but in his place, Minorini would've gone nuts.

As far as the games went, Sean was a fair shot and a mean strategist. And he had the advantage of familiarity.

When they got tired of *Quake* and *Seventh Guest,* they played *Monopoly* and *Scrabble* and *Trivial Pursuit* with Joanne. She made Sean watch the Discovery and History channels while Minorini was working, insisting that "If he can't be in school, at least he can do *something* educational."

In his salad days—the phrase made Minorini think of Dylan Thomas—*The force that through the green fuse drives the flower.* He'd wanted children. He'd envied his sister's stable relationship. Then his wife had left him and his sister's marriage began to seem like a life term, or at least an indeterminate sentence. Sour grapes. Cognitive dissonance, the shrinks called it. Your mind turned what you couldn't have into something you didn't want. Now he found himself wondering again what it would be like to have kids. His sister's life didn't seem any more appealing, but it would be nice to try for something, nice to share something with someone.

Enough mind-fucking! He must be really horny if a witness could get his thinking so screwed up. A witness for Christ's sake!

If he'd met her twenty years ago, when he was so-to-speak a virgin— But twenty years ago he'd never have noticed her—not flashy enough, too quiet.

He sighed. That was life. Sometimes your timing sucked.

. . .

Sean slept in on Minorini's third morning. After breakfast, Minorini lingered over coffee with Joanne. She'd been doing most of the cooking and had helped when he insisted on taking his turn. She'd explained it as "I'm not too good at doing nothing."

"You know," she said suddenly, "Salman Rushdie never went into the witness protection program. I can't imagine the mob being more ruthless and relentless than those Islamic terrorists."

"True, but Rushdie dropped out of sight for quite a while. And besides, he has the money to buy a lot of security. The Marshal's Service isn't going to foot the bill, and I haven't heard that you've written any international best-sellers."

"Then I return to my original suggestion—let's send Sean to my friend's and set a trap for these creeps. I'll be bait."

"Even if I were willing to entertain the idea, I'd never sell my boss or Haskel on it."

"You think I'm crazy, but you're too polite to say so."

"I don't think hope is crazy, but you're too optimistic."

"You're not as cynical as agent Haskel, are you?"

"Oh, I'm every bit as cynical. I just wasn't raised to believe rudeness is ever justified."

She took a sip of her coffee and looked out the window.

He had a sudden urge to hold her—which he resisted. He said, "What made you finally decide to leave your husband?"

"I noticed the horrible example he was setting for our son. Sean was getting too old for me to keep pretending he wouldn't notice."

"What sort of bad example?"

"Oh, bragging about how he inflated his hours and underreported his income, and pulled off insider trading deals."

"So he's a crook."

"They're going to screw him in the ground when he dies. But if I'd turned him in, he'd have gone to jail and I wouldn't even have child support."

"How do you stand that? I'd have shot him."

134

"I didn't have a gun."

"Seriously."

"I *am* serious."

Minorini gave her a look.

"Seriously, *I* got Sean. Howie thinks the one who dies with the most toys wins. He saw *Citizen Kane* but he still doesn't get it."

"*Burning Daylight*," Minorini said. She raised her eyebrows. "A Jack London story about a Citizen Kane type who finally *does* get it."

The next morning, Minorini took inventory. They were low on milk and beer, fruit and Classico. He'd asked Joanne to make a list of what she needed, and she'd dutifully noted laundry soap, toothpaste and tampons. Then she'd gone to get Sean's list.

He took his coffee into the dining room and sat facing the window that overlooked the backyard. It was a typical Chicago winter day—overcast, gray, and cold. Not raining or snowing. Waiting. As they were.

It was the easiest surveillance he'd ever done. And the hardest. The more time he spent with her, the more impressed he was with Joanne's guts, and good humor, and ability to make the best of things. More than that, he could feel a mutual attraction intensifying between them.

Proximity, he told himself. She was theoretically available and embodied everything he was starving for. But he had no illusions. Any feelings she had for him were due purely to Stockholm syndrome.

She appeared in the doorway as if conjured by his thoughts. She'd put on one of Sean's sweaters, a size too large, with big front pockets. She pulled a paper from one and handed it to him with a smile. "Sean made me promise I wouldn't look at this. 'Guy stuff,' he said."

Minorini glanced at Sean's list. The magazine title sandwiched between *Thrasher* and *Wired* probably explained the secrecy.

"You let him read *Playboy?*"

She reached for the paper. "Let me see that."

He snatched it away. "Didn't you promise?" He put the list in his pocket. "You think of anything else you need?"

"I did, as a matter of fact." She took a paper from the other pocket and sat down at the far end of the table, facing the same way. "If I had black-and-white film and some supplies, I could take pictures and develop them in the bathroom."

She was looking out at the yard, but he didn't think she was seeing it. He reached for the list.

Joanne held it out, then withdrew it before he could take it. "I guess that would be silly. There's no point. I couldn't print the negatives without an enlarger. I suppose I might as well ask for my darkroom." She crumpled the paper and lobbed it at the wastebasket, made it in with a rim shot.

"I promised Sean a game of *Quake,*" she said, getting up. She didn't seem angry or resentful, just resigned as she walked away.

She didn't deserve this! He suppressed a flash of rage, then resisted the urge to go after her, to offer the comfort of the lie—that everything would turn out well.

He couldn't remember feeling so strongly about his ex-wife. He'd met Carrie in a bar ten years earlier, an upwardly mobile professional with a good line and a great figure. She could be dynamite in bed when she wanted to be—which got to be less and less often as time went by. She'd been attracted to the FBI mystique originally, and ultimately repelled by the steel-jacketed control that was its genesis. When she decided she didn't want the man behind the façade, she'd dumped him.

John Carver arrived Wednesday night while Joanne was helping Minorini load the dishes in the washer. With his newspaper, laptop and suitcase, Carter looked more like a jet-lagged businessman than a marshal. Before he would let Minorini show him to a room, he asked to use the kitchen table.

He spread his newspaper out over one end and got a small plastic container from his suitcase. Opening the case, he took out rags, small bottle brushes and a bottle of gun oil. He removed the 9-mm Smith & Wesson from his shoulder holster, dropped the magazine, and stripped the round from the chamber. As he started breaking the gun down, he said, "I'm so jammed up today I didn't have time to clean it."

"Did you get a chance to eat?" Joanne asked. She'd leaned back against the counter and crossed her hands over her chest, tucking her fingers in her armpits.

Recalling his own arrival, Minorini felt a stab of jealousy. Stupid. Joanne was hopelessly domestic about some things. Like feeding people.

Carver smiled. "I ate at the hospital with my wife."

"Is she sick?" Joanne asked.

"No, expecting. We have a weekly Lamaze class at Evanston Hospital, and I don't have time to go home after work so we eat in the hospital cafeteria."

"When's she due?"

"Any day. But it's our first. The doctor said it may be late."

There was a long silence. Carver cleaned his gun; Minorini and Joanne watched.

Finally Joanne said, "Did you ever have to shoot anyone?"

"No thank God. . . . It changes you."

Minorini said, "*You've* never killed anyone?"

Carver shook his head. "I had a buddy when I first joined the service, a real macho type. He killed a man. A righteous shooting, but he couldn't forgive himself. He was killed when he hesitated during a subsequent incident. It's not like most people think from seeing assholes mow 'em down on TV and just walk away."

"And if you *do* learn you can do it," Minorini added, "you're on the slippery slope. You're willing to entertain the possibility of killing as an option."

Joanne seemed to have a startling thought. She froze for a minute. Then she said, "Are you speaking from experience?"

THIRTY-FIVE

Minorini was glad to be back to work the next day, though he felt as if he'd never get caught up. When Haskel came in to shoot the shit, Minorini asked him, "We get anything interesting from our wiretap yet?"

"Nada. Either Dossi's not our boy or somebody tipped him off. Maybe your girl fingered the wrong guy."

"Maybe pigs can fly."

Haskel laughed. "How you been makin' out with her?"

"She's a *witness*."

"Don't tell me you wouldn't like to get in her pants."

"I'd *like* to get a raise. What's your point?"

Haskel laughed. He spotted the video games on the desk that Minorini had bought for Sean. "Having trouble qualifying?"

"What?"

"Playing these is a hell of lot more fun than banging away at the range. Cheaper, too."

"I don't know what you're talking about."

"That kid in Paducah. Never shot a gun before, then he walks into his school and nails eight out of eight. All head shots."

"Get out of here."

Haskel chuckled. "Butler wants to see you sometime this morning."

. . .

Butler leaned back in his chair and made a steeple with his fingers. Minorini had seen him do it often, hadn't figured out if he was bored or trying to project some obscure image.

Butler said, "I need a favor."

Minorini raised he eyebrows.

"I need someone to stand in for me at the State's Attorney's Christmas Party. You just have to show up with a date so there're no empty places at my table."

Minorini shrugged. "Okay."

Butler seemed more relieved than the "favor" warranted. He could have simply ordered Minorini to go. "My secretary'll give you the details."

Minorini nodded.

"On this other thing— We got any chance of finding our car bomber?"

"Not unless someone decides to talk."

"Or of tying it to Dossi?"

"Doubtful."

"Okay. Give it another week. That should give the marshals time to make their arrangements. Then you can get on with something more productive."

Minorini nodded. "They're still shorthanded. I'd like to keep spelling the guy who's guarding Lessing until his relief is back from sick leave."

"That's not in our budget."

"I'll do it on my own time. It wouldn't hurt to have them owe us."

"I guess what you do on your time is your business." He didn't say "Should you screw up, the Bureau will disavow any . . ." but the implication was unmistakable.

As Minorini turned to go, he remembered something else and stopped. "There is one other thing—a long shot."

Butler put on his mildly interested face.

"Lessing's expressed her willingness to help us nail this guy."

"How does that work?"

"She's got friends she could send her son to stay with, then she'd put herself at our disposal—as bait."

"Nah. Too risky."

When Minorini took over for Carver that evening, Sean was restless as a caged coyote. Even the new video game Minorini'd brought didn't seem to settle him.

"What's wrong, Sean?"

"You gonna erase us?"

"I beg your pardon?"

"You know, like in that Arnold Schwarzenegger movie where he made people the mob was after disappear—erased them."

Minorini nodded. "Something like that."

"I miss my friends. It's funny. I was fine before we moved here. I never had a really good friend in L.A. Then we came here. I miss 'em."

There was no good response to that. Minorini nodded sympathetically.

"And there's nothing to do here. I'd like to kill whoever's doing this to us."

"That might solve one problem, but you'd end up with a worse one."

"I know." He stopped pacing and shook his fists. "I'm just bummed!"

"I might have something that will help with that. Come with me."

He led the way to the basement, to a door at the far end secured with a combination lock. He unlocked it, opened the latch and snapped the lock shut on the staple, locking the door open. As he reached in and flipped the light switch, he felt a sense of déjà vu.

The room was an oversized walk-in closet furnished as a gym. It had an old-fashioned bench press with barbells, a wall-rack of dumbbells—from two pounds to twenty-five—a stationary bike, and mats for floor exercises. A heavy bag and a punching bag hung from the ceiling joists.

Sean followed him across the threshold and stood just inside, taking it in. "Cool!"

"When I was a kid I'd come down here and take it out on the equipment if I felt like beating someone up."

Damn! He hadn't meant to let that slip. The trouble with losing your objectivity.

"Is this your house?"

"No, but I used to come here when I was your age." He pointed to the bench press. "This you gotta be careful with. You drop this on your throat or chest, you could strangle or suffocate. You need to get someone to spot you."

"Did you?"

"Always."

Sean was polite enough to keep his "Yeah, sure" to himself.

Minorini showed him how to use the punching bag, to set up and maintain a cadence. The kid was bright. It didn't take him long to build a mesmerizing rhythm. After he'd done enough reps with the barbells to tire himself out, Minorini left him working up a sweat on the bike.

He didn't try to soft-pedal it when he broke the news to Joanne. "I mentioned your offer to be bait—no dice."

"Could Sean spend a few weeks with my friends anyway?"

"You seem pretty intent on getting rid of him."

"I want him out of danger." She sighed and blew her breath out upward, so it stirred her bangs. "And I guess I secretly hope you'll change your minds and try to trap these bastards so we can go back to our lives."

He didn't dignify *that* pipe dream with a response.

Joanne felt isolated and restless. This was what they meant by stir-crazy.

Eventually, purely from boredom, she loaded her F1 with fast black-and-white film and started snapping candids. Because she

141

had only two rolls left, she waited for the best shots—the ones she'd have selected from a roll of okay pictures. She tried to catch the others in poses or activities that suggested the inner man. Sean, who was used to having her record his every activity, ignored her. Carver seemed oblivious. She wondered how much experience he'd had as a marshal. He seemed to resonate between the deadpan of an FBI agent and the enthusiasm of a kid playing cops and robbers. Joanne thought the picture of him showing Paul Minorini photos of his very pregnant wife would probably be something Mrs. Carver would like.

Minorini seemed annoyed when she told him what she was doing: "Practicing."

He didn't ask her what. "Aren't you almost out of film?"

"Yes."

"What's the point?"

"It's what I do."

THIRTY-SIX

Haskel was waiting in Minorini's office the next morning. "Butler's had second thoughts about your long shot. Wants to talk."

Haskel invited himself to join the party, trailing Minorini into Butler's office, parking himself in Butler's other chair.

Butler got right to the point. "I've decided your little trap idea wasn't bad at all—just needs a few adjustments."

"No, you had it right when you said it's too dangerous."

"It would be if we really used Lessing. But we don't have to involve her at all. We'll do a bait and switch. The Marshal's Office told me Reilly's coming back to work tomorrow. She's about the same size and build as Lessing. We'll let it leak that we're sending our witness off somewhere secluded. We have the Marshals pick up Reilly instead of Lessing and when Dossi sends someone in to kill her, we've got him."

"Supposing it works and we nail him. How does that help Lessing?" Haskel asked.

"It doesn't. But it'll help us plug our leak. And that'll make it safer for the next confidential source we're forced to put on the stand."

"Meanwhile, what do we do with Lessing?"

"Nothing. We leave her right where she is. If Dossi hasn't found her there by now, she's probably safe enough." Butler pointed at Minorini. "Paul, find out where she was proposing to send the kid. I'll have somebody check the place out, and if it looks safe, we'll send him there and plant someone to keep an eye on him. Just for insurance."

"Who's gonna guard our decoy?" Haskel asked. "I'm game."

"Okay. And check with the Marshals. I think they got some new guy coming in. Maybe he could join you and Reilly."

"Isn't this all pretty labor-intensive?" Minorini asked.

Butler gave a mirthless laugh. "So's investigating dead protected witnesses."

"Who's gonna deliver the kid?"

"You seem to enjoy volunteer work, Minorini. I thought you'd like to do it."

"Who guards his mother while I'm gone?"

"She's got a marshal guarding her," Haskel said. "Carver'll just have to tell his wife to put a cork in it and work 24-7 until we nail this thing."

Minorini agreed to baby-sit the kid all the way to Florida so he could check out the security at the friends' "gated community."

They checked in early and took seats in the waiting area where Minorini could eyeball the other passengers. When they started boarding, he had an attendant seat Sean first, then watched everyone else board. *He* got on just before they closed the door.

They were on American with the 2/3 seating. He had them put Sean by the window; he took the aisle. The boy was excited. He actually listened to the preflight safety lecture, then sat with his hand shading the cabin-light glare so he could watch the rollout and takeoff.

"Wow!" he said as the plane banked over the city and climbed above the lake.

"You ever flown before?" Minorini asked.

"Not at night. We flew from L.A. a few times to visit my grandparents, but always during the day. When we moved here, we drove. The lights are awesome!"

Minorini nodded. He envied the kid the experience. He himself had flown so much it had lost its luster.

The flight was blessedly uneventful. Minorini used the quiet time to go over the whole business in his mind, from the first call after Siano's death to Butler's peculiar change of mind.

Sean alternated between dozing and peering out at the lights. They were somewhere over Kentucky when he asked, "You gonna marry my ma?"

Minorini shook his head. "Can't. She's a witness."

"But would you if she wasn't?"

"If my aunt was a man she'd be my uncle."

Sean gave him a look of annoyance. "But do you like her?"

"You're not shy about asking questions, are you?"

"Ma always says, 'If you want to know something, ask.'"

"Does *she* always answer your questions?"

"No, but when she doesn't, she at least tells me it's none of my business."

"Ah. Well, I guess a straight question deserves a straight answer." Sean waited. "I like your mom. If she weren't a witness, I'd probably ask her out. As for marrying, that's something it's best not to think about until you know a person really well."

Sean thought about that and nodded. "That's cool." Then he put his headset back on and retreated into his music.

THIRTY-SEVEN

Joanne regretted sending Sean away as soon as the door closed behind them. Odd how someone who hadn't even existed fifteen years ago had become the center of her life. She didn't know how she would survive if he came to harm. She spent the next two hours cleaning, interrupting John Carver's work to demand he help her move a couch or reposition rugs.

After his third trip to the garage with trash and recyclables, Carver put his hands on her shoulders and said, "He'll be all right. He's probably safer in a plane than at his school. And Paul's the best. He won't let anything happen."

"I know. It's just—"

She was cut off by the beeping of his cell phone. He said, "Excuse me," and flipped it open. He walked across the room to talk.

She could tell by his body language the news wasn't good. She waited until he returned the phone to his pocket before asking, "What is it, John?"

"Ellie's gone into labor—contractions ten minutes apart. I told her to call a cab and go straight to the hospital."

"You'll meet her there?"

"No. They've got no one to relieve me."

"You have to go! You can't let her go through this alone."

"She won't be alone. Her doctor's meeting her at the hospital and there're plenty of competent people on staff. Ellie understands."

Howie had been off on a fishing trip beyond Catalina Island when Sean was born. Unable to reach him and with no family in the area, Joanne had called her Lamaze teacher. The woman dropped everything and came, but it had still been a terrifying experience, and Joanne had had to be medicated for the ensuing depression. Sean had been exclusively hers after that. She'd borne him; she'd birthed him. Howie had been as relevant as a sperm donor. It was one reason she'd encouraged Sean to have a healthy disrespect for lawyers.

"NO!" she told Carver. "No, no, no, no, no! None of them is her husband. Trust me on this. She needs *you.*"

"I can't leave *you* alone. Even if nothing happened, I could lose my job."

"Not if no one finds out. And *I'm* not going to tell. I'll be fine. As soon as you're out the door, I'll set the alarm and go to bed. No one will suspect there's anyone here. You can come right back as soon as you're sure Ellie and the baby are okay; no one'll be the wiser."

"Unless something happens."

"If anyone comes near the house, I'll call you. If someone tries to break in, I'll dial 9-1-1. As long as you don't have an accident coming or going, everything will be fine."

"It goes against all my training and good judgment."

"It's your first child. You have to be there."

He held out for another half hour. Then a near-frantic call from Ellie did it, coupled with Joanne's insistence that nothing would be different from the last two boring weeks. Ellie was at Evanston Hospital—not too distant—dilated to five centimeters when Joanne finally pushed John out the door.

Paul called to say they'd taken off safely from O'Hare and had been forced to land in Atlanta. He'd call when they finally got to Ft. Lauderdale, but it would probably be late.

She got angrier as she prowled the empty house, even the rooms used by Paul and Carver. She felt as if she were looking for something—she'd recognize what when she found it—then decided what it was she needed—film. She opened drawers, found

Carver's spare cartridges in a suitcase in his closet, Paul's spare gun in a locked aluminum case in a dresser drawer. She found a pocket calculator, a bunch of keys, the homeowner's—Elizabeth Cross's—checkbook. But no camera equipment. She was out of options as well as out of film.

At six, she turned the news on.

Tom Skilling eventually came on to say it would start snowing between 7:00 and 9:00 P.M. "There ought to be a good accumulation."

When they started to report the sports, she shut the TV off and resumed her stalking.

In the back hall, she turned off the house alarm and the back porch lights, and stepped out on the porch. The air seemed warm—as usual before a storm—and she could smell snow coming. There was a luminescence in the air, probably reflection off the cloud cover, that kept the night from being truly dark. She checked the yard for signs of prowlers, then walked to the garage. Both the side and overhead doors were locked. And Carver must've taken the keys with him.

But what about the set she'd found with the checkbook? She could try them, though the probability of finding film in the garage when there was none in the house was remote at least.

She went back and got her coat and the keys. On the porch, she tried them until she found one that locked the back door. Another let her in the side door of the garage. Inside she found a silver-blue Mercedes. She walked around to the driver's side and opened the door.

What if she borrowed the car? As long as she didn't damage it, who'd notice? And even if they did, what could they do about it?

She sorted through the bunch of keys and found one for the car. She could go get film and be back before anyone noticed. Better yet, she could take her exposed film home to develop it. And get more from the stash she kept in her freezer.

But what if the car-bomber was staking out the place?

Surely after two weeks he'd have gotten tired and gone away.

To be safe, she could park some distance away and sneak up to the house. If anything looked odd she could turn around and run.

She went back in the house and filled her pockets with exposed film, then went out to start the car. The engine turned over on the first try. She raised the overhead door and let the car warm up a while. Before she backed out, she familiarized herself with the vehicle and turned off the dome light so it wouldn't give her away when she opened the doors.

There was an electric door opener tucked over the sun-visor, and after she pulled the car out, she closed the garage door.

By the time she got to her neighborhood, the few flakes that were falling hadn't yet affected traffic. It took only twenty minutes. She parked one street over from her house, in a spot where two tall spruces cut off the glow from the streetlight. She stayed on the sidewalk as she rounded the block, walking like someone in a hurry to get home. When she turned onto *her* street, she searched the houses on either side for a bomber or any neighbors looking out. Fortunately, not enough snow had accumulated to bring out the shovelers. She left the walk and slipped along the hedge that marked the west boundary of her property.

She paused at the back door. Had the Feds alarmed her house? Or booby-trapped it? Or set up surveillance cameras? She was almost beyond caring. Her key still worked, and there were no sirens or klaxons as the door swung inward. She left her boots on the mat and made her way to the darkroom without turning lights on.

She lay her film out on the counter, and set the water running, adjusting the temperature. Before she started to free the first film roll from its metal jacket, she tested the developer. Habit. From habit she glanced at the test strip. It must have been five full seconds before the results registered. The developer was worn out. The trip had been for nothing! Damn! Damn! Damn!

Furiously she searched through the shelves and cabinets for fresh developer, moving bottles and boxes. There was none. When she moved one of her notebooks, the glassine envelope of Dossi's pictures came tumbling out. Her attempt to catch it sent it whirling toward the floor, scattering its contents.

Dossi smiled up at her from the pictures, from the comfort of his home, as if gloating over their respective fates.

It was too much!

She felt a dizzying surge of rage. She shuffled photos and negatives together and shoved them back in the envelope. She crammed the envelope in her pocket.

Her brother's question pounded in her ears: "What would you do if we were invaded?" And her own flip response: "Join the resistance!"

This was war! And so far the enemy had taken her home and family, her job, her very identity. What she had left was the gun. She wondered if the Feds had found it yet.

The tiny flash on her keychain was enough to light the way to her room, where the hope chest stood undisturbed. Inside it, under the bag with his boots, the rifle lay nested where her father left it, wrapped in his red flannel coat.

But how to take it safely from the house? The dull gleam of gun metal would be amplified by the streetlights. It needed a cover. She gathered it up and wrapped it in the jacket. She grabbed the bag with her father's boots and the cleaning kit. She removed a box of cartridges from the kit, and put the kit in with the boots. She put the cartridges in her pocket. Passing the hall closet, she remembered the bundled leaf-recycling bags she'd bought in August. It took only a moment to slip gun, jacket, and boot-bag into one of them. Then she fled back to the kitchen.

She'd slipped into her boots and was out in the yard before she could think what she was doing.

There was snow enough on the street to mark her path as she pulled away from the curb, enough to build traffic at the intersections. The borrowed car went well.

She took Dundee Road to Skokie Boulevard, then backtracked

on Lake-Cook Road to Ridge. She was surprised it only took five minutes to get past the Highland Park police station. Five minutes later, she put on the four-way flashers while she got out to drop the chain, then pulled the Mercedes onto the side-road and shut it off.

She stood next to the open driver's door while she pulled her father's coat on over hers, her father's boots over her own. She loaded three cartridges—one for a clean kill, one for backup, one for luck—and put the box on the floor of the back seat, and the envelope of photos next to it. Then she was ready.

There were obstacles she scarcely noticed—the snow that was coming down fairly fast now, underbrush and burrs that snagged her clothing, the frozen manhole cover. She'd forgotten that. She left the rifle next to it while she returned to the car. The trunk light flashed when the trunk opened; may as well set off a car alarm. She grabbed the bulb, removed it. She lay the bulb on the trunk floor and used her keychain flashlight to find the tire iron.

She thought only about the job. *Close the trunk. Retrace your steps. Pry open the manhole cover without dropping it on your foot or fingers.*

The half-foot of water in the storm drain was crusted over with ice; she slogged through it. Ice held the grating in place at the mouth of the storm drain. She used the tire iron to break it free, trusting the thickening snowfall to muffle the sound. A hundred or so yards from the outlet mouth, she found a spot with an unobstructed view of Dossi's windows.

She took a sitting stance, not quite as steady as the prone position, but better—in her limited hunting experience—for hitting a target situated overhead.

Through the scope, she could easily see Dossi, could see every cruel line of his face. Definitely the face she'd seen speeding away from the park that century-long month ago. What could make the man do what he did for a living?

She took several deep breaths, then let them out slowly, watching the crosshairs wobble across her target as she did so. The trigger was cold against her finger tip. What was making this so hard?

I can't do it.

Think of plastique!

Think of Sean, crying himself to sleep, trying to start life over again.

Think of Dossi's victims in the morgue drawers, white and cold as fish-flesh. Cold as the trigger.

Rage ignited her hesitation like flash powder, burned her red, then white-hot.

No!

The rage shook her.

No! No! No!

She counted ten. The shaking subsided slightly. Twenty. She took two deep breaths and peered back through the scope. Dossi had moved away from the window. Thank God!

Then he moved back into her line of sight and stopped, facing someone standing near the window.

The someone turned, and she could see his face, familiar, though it took a moment to recall from where.

The Federal court! He was the one who demanded her appearance! Dossi hadn't known who she was before the hearing. She lined the crosshairs up on his chest. She heard her father's voice say, "Kicks a little to the left."

But she would only have one shot. Then the others in the room would take cover. Shooting the judge wouldn't free her of the threat Dossi posed.

She moved the crosshairs to center on Dossi's left breast pocket. She moved her head so the scope wouldn't strike her face when the gun discharged.

Her mind was saying, he's far too far away. Nobody can . . .

Dossi stepped to the window and looked out.

Joanne fixed on his pocket button. She heard her father's voice say, "Breathe in. Let your breath halfway out. *Squeeze* the trigger. Don't anticipate. Let it surprise you when it finally fires."

Just what she did as she was waiting for the perfect picture. . . .

BLAM!

Her ears were slammed by a concussion like an M-8O exploding near her head. And the flash from the muzzle flare burned her eyes.

THIRTY-EIGHT

A cloud of powder-smoke materialized between the muzzle and the target, mingling with the flying snowflakes. The odor, and the crack echoing in her eardrums, brought a memory fragment—too brief to be identified—from childhood, then an overwhelming feeling of disaster. She felt a sharp pain in her right shoulder from the rifle's kick. She closed her eyes.

What have I done!

She opened them. The window was too small to see clearly, let alone hit.

I must have missed.

She put her eye to the scope again and saw—clearly—a man rushing to the window. With a gun. Awareness hit her like the recoil of the rifle and, for a moment, she felt ill.

Oh, God!

But she must get away—for Sean and Rick and Hancock. For all those who thought well of her, perhaps even Paul.

Pull yourself together! Deal with it!

Oh, God!

What had been a satisfying fantasy, like blowing Howie's head off during their divorce, was suddenly premeditated murder. "Malice aforethought." And no sane jury would accept that her carefully thought out plan was self-defense—against what theoretical threat?

What's done is past.

There was a pop of distant gunfire. Unreal. Uncanny. Toy soldiers fighting a TV war. Dossi's bodyguard trying to make amends. At this distance, he couldn't hope to come close, but it wouldn't take him long to figure where the shot came from. And come looking. Or send the dogs.

A frantic voice whispered, "Get out of here!" Her own voice. *Think!*

She thought she heard the dogs bark. A snowflake moistened her cheek where tears should have been. She felt strung out, but some rational part of her mind said, *Back up and get going!*

She reached down and felt the reassuring lump of the car keys in her pocket.

Nothing else to lose. Nothing important. Grab the gun and go.

She backed away carefully, slowly, dragging the rifle behind her in the snow. She would have to dispose of it. Pity. She wouldn't leave it behind.

The snow was falling furiously. Big soft flakes had already obscured the tracks she'd made coming. She walked like an automaton, stumbling—in the oversized boots—over every weed and exposed tree root. The gun had slipped into the cradle of her arm as if by its own volition. She was scarcely aware of the culvert when she got to it, squeezing around the rusted grill, cracking and splashing through the shallow water with its crust of ice like movie-set window glass that shattered without causing damage.

Once out of the storm drain, she concentrated on getting back to the car without tripping or dropping the rifle or the tire iron. The snow muffled every sound, like a white noise, except the soft galumph of her feet in her father's boots. She had no idea how long she was taking. Forever.

She almost missed the car in the dense fog of snow. Her quaking hand couldn't, at first, make the key enter the lock. How long did it take the police to get a helicopter in the air? Then she forced herself to take a deep breath. This was nonsense. They couldn't fly close enough in this mess to see her. All she had to do was keep the car on the road until she got it home. No one would connect her to the shooting unless they caught her with the gun.

Think! What next?

Hide the gun. Get out of these clothes. Get back before some-one misses you!

Her hand trembled less violently as she unlocked the trunk. It must be true, what they say about getting used to anything. She replaced the tire iron. She took off the hunting jacket and turned it inside out to prevent any burrs and dirt she might have collected from getting on the floor mat. She lay the gun on the jacket and folded it around the weapon, then got the photos and cleaning kit from behind the front seat and put them in the trunk, in the leaf bag.

Before she got in the car, she cleaned the snow off the windows. She kept the boots on until she was sitting sideways in the driver's seat, taking off the right boot first, putting her right foot on the car floor, then shaking off the boot and dropping it on the floor behind the seat. She repeated the procedure for the left. She was careful to keep her mind on business, not to think *why* she was doing it. She started the car, reversed it. She backed slowly down the drive. Only when she was on the road did she turn on the lights. She left the car running on the street while she raised the barrier chain back in place. Maybe it would be a while before anyone thought to check it, to see if it was really locked. Maybe that would slow down the pursuit.

Don't count on it.

The fastest way home would be back the way she came, but something made her turn the other way. Towards Dossi's drive. There was maybe a half inch of fluffy, slippery snow on the black-top. She had to go slowly. She looked at the dash clock and was surprised to see it wasn't even eight o'clock. She'd been away from the house just over an hour. She concentrated on keeping the car on the road.

Panic nearly paralyzed her as red and white lights flashed from the fog of whirling snowflakes. Police! She was caught! Might as well surrender. Can't outrun radio.

Stop it! Think! Of course the cops are coming. Someone's just been shot. She slowed even more, preparing to stop like a good citizen. The cop car blazed past, its lights amplified by the surrounding snow. Joanne kept going. As she approached Route 41, cars materialized on the road ahead. She slowed and left an interval when the line in front stopped. She sat breathing deeply, telling herself *que será, será.* The line inched forward.

THIRTY-NINE

The drive had been plowed when Joanne finally pulled into it, the near inch of snow pulled away from the garage door and pushed into neat piles on either side of the parkway. She wouldn't have to shovel to remove the evidence that she'd been out. In another half an hour, there wouldn't be a trace. The back walk and porch had been cleared, too. The homeowner must have a service contact for snow removal.

She activated the garage door opener, but stopped the car short of the door. She got out and brushed as much of the snow off as she could—no use soaking the floor and calling attention to her trip. She parked inside and turned off the garage light, but left the door up while she went to get rags from the house to clean off the snow and road salt. There wasn't anything she could do about the water on the floor. With luck it would dry before anyone noticed. She gathered her father's boots, the leaf-recycling bag, and the shrouded rifle, and hurried into the house.

She wanted a drink desperately, but it would have to wait until after she cleaned up.

She wondered about the gunshot residue—that's what it was called, not gunpowder. Trace evidence along with hair and fibers. She could remember Howie pontificating. "That's what trips up most clever murderers." *Me* now, she thought. How could she have guessed her unpaid service as a typist for a personal injury lawyer would prepare her for a life of crime. Bless Howie. Or curse him. Well, she would wash the clothes before disposing of them. She wouldn't dump them from the car—too likely to arouse the notice, and the wrath, of the anti-litter crusaders—or put them in the trash—too obvious.

She lay newspapers out on the table and put the rifle on them. She put the plaid jacket on the kitchen counter and combed the burrs out of it, discarding them in the disposal. The jacket and her father's boots she took downstairs and dumped into the washer. She set the temperature on hot, added detergent and, when the agitator started, bleach. So much for residue. And if they found fibers, maybe they wouldn't match. She remembered the Dirt Devil in the broom closet. She got it and ran back to the car with it. She spent five minutes vacuuming each seat, ten on the trunk. She locked the garage and put the keys back where she'd found them.

In the kitchen, the gun lay on the table like an accusation.

After a hunt, her father had always cleaned his guns. He'd made a ritual of it, laying the materials out just so on the kitchen table.

She took out the cleaning kit and opened it. Her father's letter lay inside. She got as far as "Daughter, May be a mistake . . ." before the tears pouring onto the page started to blur the text. She wiped her eyes on her shirt sleeves and took the letter to the stove, lit one of the burners and held the page to the flame. When it was all but consumed, she threw the curled ash in the sink and washed it into the disposal.

She cleaned the gun before dismantling it. The metal parts she wrapped in newspaper and slipped into the garbage. She took the stock into the living room and laid it against the pyramid of kindling Carver had built that afternoon.

After scouring the kitchen she took a long, hot shower, poured herself a double shot of whiskey, and started the fire. The kindling caught from the first match. When the flames were tall enough to reach into the chimney, she fed them Dossi's pictures. She watched the emulsion turn brown and bubbly like a toasting marshmallow, then blacken and curl. The negatives contracted and twisted, morphing into matte black cinders around the burning gunstock. She settled down to watch the fire consume her father's work.

The stock was a glowing ember, and Joanne was feeling strung out but nearly sleepy when the phone rang.

She picked it up on the third ring. "Hello?"

"Joanne?"

"Hmm. Paul?"

"Were you asleep?"

"Yeah."

"Just called to say we made it. Sean was dead on his feet. I told him he could talk to you tomorrow. Where's Carver?"

"I don't know. At this hour, probably sleeping. Shall I wake him?"

"Nah. Don't bother. I'll talk to him in the morning."

FORTY

Haskel was waiting for him at the gate. Minorini felt a stab of panic and maintaining his Bureau facade was hard. "What's up?"

Haskel drew out the suspense. Bastard!

"Something happen to Joanne?" Minorini demanded.

"It's Joanne, is it?" The laugh-lines at the corners of Haskel's eyes grew marginally deeper—the closest he would come to "gotcha!" "Nah, she's okay. *Dossi* bought it."

"Dossi? How . . . ?"

"Wouldn't we all like to know that. Sniper took him out."

"Jesus! When?"

"Just about seven last night."

"Where?"

"In the privacy and comfort of his own living room."

"That why you're not guarding Reilly?"

"Nah. Our trap worked like a charm; Reilly and I had a nibble. A mouse went for our cheesecake and got blasted into oblivion. We spent most of the night filing reports."

"That's why you look like shit this morning."

"Yeah. Butler wants us to get on this Dossi thing, *pronto.*"

Joanne awoke cramped and stiff, curled into the fetal position. Symbolic. She wondered if she would spend the rest of her life fighting the urge to regress.

The act she'd thought would save her life had changed it irrevocably. She felt vaguely ill, the way she imagined it would feel to have AIDS or some other disastrous social disease, something you couldn't tell people about, dread-filled. It was a rerun, amplified unimaginably, of how she'd felt when she divorced Howie.

She knew if she'd just carry on, the feeling would fade. It had before. But the in-the-meantime stretched before her like an indeterminate sentence. The cops might never get her, but she would do time. She'd do life. It would always be there. No statute of limitations on murder.

She got up and stared at herself in the mirror. She looked as washed out as an overexposed print. When the adrenaline wore off and the rage subsided, you were left with depression. She remembered reading Dante's *Inferno* in school. Significant that the center of Hell was portrayed not as everlasting fire, but as a frozen wasteland, the absence of all warmth and love.

She found, when she looked outside, the world was like a negative of itself, with a total reversal of figure and ground. The uniform, off-white sky was a pale suggestion of its usual depth. Snow brought out every branch and tree trunk. Objects and buildings that formerly were white revealed themselves in hues of pink and blue and amber. The trees looked taller and, where there were no trees, the land was wider and more forbidding. She couldn't tell if this wasn't just guilty awareness of her vanished innocence.

And then the sun came out.

Carver was still asleep. Joanne decided not to wake him, but she wanted to be sure they didn't miss the garbage pick up.

The door opened just as she was putting on her coat, and Paul walked in. She looked at him apprehensively, seeing him for the first time as a felon would.

He didn't seem to notice any change in her, though he seemed excited. "You're all right!"

It was not what she'd expected, and her surprise was genuine. "Of course. Why wouldn't I be?"

"Dossi was killed last night. Somebody shot him."

The news—though it was hardly that—caused her to gasp inwardly and freeze outwardly. Confirmation of her worst fear. And fondest hope. "Thank God!" The words burst out before she even thought. His astonishment made her add, simply, matter-of-factly, "I'm free."

"Ah. Yes."

She felt an irrational annoyance at the disappointment his tone implied. Perhaps her candor had knocked her from whatever pedestal he'd had her on. But even to herself, she sounded defensive as she said, "I'd be a damn liar if I said I was sorry."

"Yeah."

He seemed to finally notice that she was wearing her coat. "You weren't planning to go out?"

"I didn't think it would hurt anything if I just put out the garbage. Today's pickup day and besides this, there's tons of stuff Carver put in the garage. And I haven't been out of this house since we got here."

He looked angry. "Where *is* Carver?"

"Still sleeping, I guess. I didn't see any reason to wake him."

"What did you and he do last night?"

"I turned in early. I have no idea what he did."

"The noise didn't wake you when they shoveled the drive?"

"Neither time."

"They shoveled it twice?" She nodded. "How do you know they did it twice?"

"When you called the second time, I got up to use the bathroom." And looked out, she thought, to see if John was back yet. "The drive had been shoveled. I remember thinking it was silly because it would have to be done again when it stopped snowing."

She looked pointedly at her watch. "If we don't get this out, we'll miss the garbage man." She tugged at the trash bag.

He took it from her, and lifted it with surprise. "What've you got in here?"

She felt a flush of panic. Her mind stumbled for an answer, for a stall. "He'll be here any minute!"

"OK. OK." He picked up the garbage bag and opened the door. "You throwing out an anvil?"

"It's just some old canned stuff I found in the back of a cabinet. The cans were bulging. They didn't look safe . . ."

She could hear the garbage truck backing down the drive. She looked out and saw the driver get out, looking for the garbage can still inside the garage. He shrugged and climbed back in his truck.

Paul ran out the door. "Driver, wait!"

Her heart stopped as the truck jerked forward, restarted as it screeched to a stop.

Paul half-trotted towards the truck and made a free throw at the back of it. The bag hit the edge of the hopper and teetered like a rim shot for a heart-stopping instant, then disappeared.

Paul stepped to the driver's side of the truck to yell, "We got more. Can you wait a sec?" He hurried toward the garage, digging in his pocket.

The truck driver jumped out, looking annoyed, but helped Paul drag the garbage bags to the truck and throw them in.

Then Paul told the man, "Thanks," and he took off with a clash of gears.

Joanne's relief made her feel light-headed.

When Paul came back in the house, he said, "The marshals have orders to stay a few more days—just to be sure Dossi didn't take out a contract on you before he bought it. Then you'll be on your own."

FORTY-ONE

There was yellow police line tape across Dossi's drive when Minorini and Haskel drove up. Minorini showed his ID to the young cop on duty, and they waited while he conferred with a superior over the radio. Finally he told them, "You can go in. Detective Anslie will be here any minute." The cop stayed where he was.

The crime scene technicians had finished with the house; it had that tossed and abandoned look—everything out of place, everything smudged with black fingerprint powder.

It didn't take them long to find the room where Dossi bought it. The only one without an oriental rug, it had a dried blood smear in the center of the floor. Two windows were missing on the north side. The room was freezing. They walked over and looked out one of the empty sockets at a snow field crisscrossed with tracks. Probably a team with a metal detector and a dog had searched it for shell casings or anything else the shooter might have left.

"Pretty decent shooting," Haskel said.

"Piece of cake for a sniper."

"Yeah. Well, don't forget it was dark out and snowing like a son of a bitch."

About a hundred yards from the window was a small clump of bushes festooned with yellow crime scene tape. The shooter's stand.

"You figure he was standing or kneeling?" Minorini asked.

"Dossi was close to six feet. And judging by where he landed . . ." Haskel pointed to the blood smear. "He must have been standing a foot or so from the window. A through-and-through." He pointed to a foot square hole in the back wall of the room where the evidence team had removed the wall board. "According to the report, the slug came halfway through the drywall in the next room. I'd say our shooter was either kneeling or prone."

Minorini nodded, then pointed beyond the shooter's stand, to another part of the yard also cordoned off with tape. "What's that?"

It looked like a small detention pond with surrounding pines.

Detective Anslie's voice answered him from the doorway. "That's where the shooter got in."

The Highland Park police station was on the ground floor of an ugly, flat-roofed building, a two-story brown brick core flanked by single-story wings. There were a lot of windows, but the view didn't seem like much from either side of the glass—the Solo Cup factory and a small forest of bare trees outside, Spartan offices within.

They had Dossi's housekeeper in the break room with a policewoman. The cop was reading a paperback novel, the witness pacing. The young Hispanic's eyes were red-rimmed. Her clothes looked slept in.

Minorini asked her to sit down at the table, and she did, anxiously. He asked her for her name and repeated the question, "¿Cómo te llamas?" when she didn't answer right away.

"Manuela Gutierez," she told him.

"¿De dónde eres?"

"De Honduras."

"Go on, Manuela. What happened? ¿Qué pasó?"

In Spanglish—and with many gestures—she told him.

She had been sent to bed early. Señor Dossi had a visitor Manuela had not seen, a woman perhaps. Not his wife. He had let the visitor in himself.

Manuela was nearly asleep when she heard a loud noise—like

a firecracker—and Carlo, Señor Dossi's chauffeur, had come to her door demanding to know what had happened.

"*Pero yo no sabía.*"

She followed after Carlo when he raced to the parlor where Señor Dossi had been entertaining his guest. The visitor was gone. Señor Dossi was lying on the carpet. Señor Dossi was dead. Carlo said so. Manuela thought the visitor had killed him, but Carlo pointed to the window and said something—a word Manuela didn't know—had shot Señor Dossi through the window. She saw that there was a small hole in the glass. Then Carlo pulled a gun out of his jacket and turned off the room light. He went to another window and broke it out and began shooting. She couldn't see at what.

"What did you do?" Minorini asked. He noticed that the policewoman had put down her book.

"Nothing, señor. I was too afraid. I did not know what to do. Then I heard pounding on the door and the police came."

Minorini glanced at the policewoman who seemed to have no response to that.

The police had made Manuela lie down on the floor while they searched the house. Then one of them—a woman—searched her, and they made her sit in the living room for a very long time. Later, the policewoman took her into her room and ordered her to get dressed and they brought her here. They offered her food and water, and access to the toilet, but they would not let her leave, or make a phone call, or know what was going on. They would not even tell her what happened to Señor Dossi. And different people kept coming in to ask her questions.

What had she done?

"Nothing," Minorini told her. "You did nothing. But the police need your help to catch whoever killed your boss."

Manuela nodded. "*Por supuesto. ¿Cómo puedo ayudarle?*"

Minorini had her start with how she got the job. . . .

Carlo hadn't seen the visitor's face, but did notice he had badly shaking hands. He didn't see the license plate but got a fair look at the car. On the advice of a court-appointed attorney, Carlo was quite willing to cooperate. They would not be charging him with any weapons violations, in return for which, he would tell them what he knew.

Minorini had him start at the beginning.

"How long did you work for Mr. Dossi? And who might want to see him dead?"

FORTY-TWO

The safe house was in Wisconsin. Minorini didn't bother going to see the scene because Butler—mindful of the flap surrounding Waco—had let the Wisconsin State Police handle the investigation. Butler was having them fax their reports, so Minorini was able to get the official version before he queried Haskel and Reilly about it.

Basically, while waiting for someone to spring the trap set for Lessing's would-be killer, the decoy team—US Marshal Reilly and Special Agent Haskel—had observed a vehicle approach their location, slow down for a look, and move on.

The driver apparently parked some distance away and sneaked up on their position. When he kicked in the door, they'd identified themselves as federal agents, whereupon he'd opened fire. They returned fire and shot him to death.

A fingerprint check identified the shooter as Armand Wilson, 37, recently migrated from Michigan, with an arrest record going back to his juvenile days. He had never been convicted, however, because witnesses either changed their stories or didn't show up to testify in court.

The state police lab matched the bullets that killed Wilson to Haskel's and Reilly's weapons. Reilly's shot would've stopped him—a center body-mass hit—but Haskel had nailed him through the heart and head, dead center. Either bullet would've done the job.

The Wisconsin pathologist who'd done the autopsy for the state police hadn't been able to add anything to what he'd put in the autopsy report. Wilson had been in relatively good shape ante mortem. Cause of death—GSWs to brain and heart; manner of death—homicide, apparently justifiable.

The investigating officers had found the gunman's vehicle, an SUV with a plow attached, parked a quarter mile down the road. Wilson apparently hijacked it several hours earlier after shooting the owner.

Minorini questioned Reilly and Haskel separately.

Haskel refused to be specific. "The son of a bitch drew on us, so we drilled him. Period."

Reilly's story was more detailed.

"We told the shooter to drop his weapon. He opened his eyes wider, as if he'd just seen the devil, and he screamed, 'Fuckin' double cross.' There was an exchange of fire. We both shot at him. According to the lab, Haskel's the one who got lucky."

"Then what happened?"

"He fell. We closed in and disarmed him, but he was obviously dead."

"Who else was there?"

"Just Haskel and me."

So Haskel had killed him.

Minorini spent the next twenty-four hours checking all his sources, trying to find someone—anyone—with the motive and opportunity—or bankroll—to kill Dossi. Nothing.

Dossi, sixty-three had been a retired investment counselor living off the interest and dividends from his portfolio. His bank was a conservative establishment and squeaky clean, and while declining to give specifics, the bank manager assured Minorini that Dossi had acquired his wealth over a period of forty years.

But that's how organized crime did it, laundering the proceeds from drugs or vice or gambling by running the cash through profitable, "legitimate" businesses. It was only if you noticed that a Rogers Park pizza joint was selling more food than the Hard Rock Cafe, or the million-dollar car wash was located in a neighborhood where most of the cars were abandoned, that you'd have a clue. As long as they paid their taxes, no one was going to notice.

Now that Dossi was dead, several informants were willing to venture that the mobster had been responsible for no fewer than nine hits—but they knew of none recently. Nobody'd ever heard of him botching a job or failing to fulfill his part of a contract. It was eerie, Haskel remarked, how quiet everybody was, really.

Wilson was from Detroit, so Minorini called a detective he knew there.

"Tell me about Armand Wilson."

Jake Splinter said, "What's he up to these days?"

"You know, there's a whole country here, outside Detroit. All kinds of things happening." Splinter laughed. "Wilson opened fire on a couple of Federal employees and got himself killed for his efforts."

"I always figured he'd come to a bad end. He was one of our more interesting lowlifes. Shoot his own mother if the price was right. You ever meet him?"

"Just in the postmortem pictures."

"He was actually black—passing. Father must've been white. His mother was from Jamaica. Grew up in a very nasty neighborhood."

"Bottom line, what was his deal?"

"Got into a lot of trouble as a youth. I'm sure you've seen his rap sheet."

"Yup."

"Somewhere along the line he got smart or got a handler. He's rumored . . . *was* rumored to be an enforcer, but no one would go on record. . . . He had one peculiarity, though. He'd never shoot a kid, or kill anyone in front of their kid."

"He have a preferred MO?"

"Liked to gain entry by posing as a delivery guy, or landscaper, or repair man, then blast away with a 9-millimeter at close range."

"Thanks, Splinter."

What landscapers did in the winter was plow snow.

Minorini was getting ready to call it a day when Haskel ambled in and parked his butt on the desk.

"You been awfully quiet all day, Paul. You POed 'cause someone did you out of the pleasure of nailing Dossi?"

"No. Just thought I'd have a better chance of solving this thing if I put some time in on it."

"Well, maybe this'll help." He handed Minorini a fax. "Highland Park just sent us this list of motorists that were seen in the area at the time. You'll never guess who's on it."

"Tell me."

"The very judge who gave us the wiretap!"

"No shit!"

"He's not our shooter, though." Minorini waited for him to elaborate. "He has Parkinson's. Which explains his waiving of the 'all rise' bit in his courtroom. He couldn't hit a barn door with a shotgun—hands shake too much. The cops checked with his doctor."

"So what was he doing there?"

"Wouldn't say. Won't talk to us. We're checking his prints against the unidentified latents they found at Dossi's."

"He went along with that?"

"Not exactly. We had him look at a photo lineup to see if he'd noticed any of the subjects hanging around his neighborhood. They were very clean photos."

And the judge left his prints all over them.

Haskel grinned. "If we get a hit, we'll let him explain to a grand jury."

By the time the fingerprint report came back—a match—Minorini had asked Butler to let him interview the judge without Haskel.

"Why?" Butler demanded.

"He's aggressive and sarcastic, and I don't think that'll get us anywhere with His Honor. He's too used to dealing with lawyers.

The Marshal's Office will want in on this anyway. Let me see if I can arrange for one of them to do this with me, maybe Reilly. I know she can keep her claws sheathed."

The cases the judge had been scheduled to hear that day had all been reassigned to another judge without explanation, the reassignments posted on his courtroom door. Minorini and Reilly tracked him to his office suite, where Minorini showed his identification to the clerk guarding the door to the judge's chambers, and she buzzed them in.

"We need to talk to the judge," he told her.

When she reached for the phone, Reilly put a hand on it, preventing her from picking it up. Minorini walked over and tapped on the judge's door. When he heard, "Who is it?" he pushed the door open and stepped into the room. Reilly followed.

The judge was standing at the window, back to the door. His right hand, resting on the window sill, was trembling; his left, hanging at his side, shook so violently he seemed to be tapping a beat against his leg.

He turned and growled, "How dare you?"

Reilly stepped in front of Minorini and said, "We're investigating a murder, sir, and you're a material witness at the very least. If you won't talk to us here, we'll have to take you downstairs."

"Why should I talk to you?"

"You shouldn't," Minorini said, "if you had anything to do with Dossi's murder."

The old man snorted and trembled his way to the chair behind his desk. The chair rattled from the vibration as he pulled it out. He fell into it with a thud and leaned his elbows on the desk, grasping one hand in the other until the tremors seemed controlled. He nodded jerkily at the chairs on the other side of the desk.

"What were you doing at Dossi's house?" Reilly asked.

"What makes you think I was there?"

"Your fingerprints."

"Ah. Well, I was invited. I knew him, you see. His wife's a dis-

173

tant cousin of mine. I didn't make the connection at the wiretap hearing or I would've recused myself. But when he called—he called me himself—and asked as a family favor if I would come see him . . ." The judge shrugged.

Minorini said, "What did he want?"

"He wanted to know on what legal grounds I could rescind the wiretap order. At least that's what he *said*. He hinted that if I didn't reverse myself, he'd arrange to destroy my reputation, then get another judge to do it. Either way, he'd be off the hook."

"What did you tell him?" Reilly said.

"As soon as he made his demand, I put in my request for senior status and left it with the chief judge's secretary."

"Why?"

"The public's perception of a court's integrity is more important that a judge's impartiality, or legal expertise, or intelligence. I'm sixty-seven years old—not ready to die yet, but I'm not about to let anybody blackmail me."

"You went to see him, though," Minorini said. "Why?"

"Out of curiosity, mainly. One of the reasons our system requires direct testimony is so that the triers of fact can judge a witness's veracity for themselves. I've been on the bench a long time. I wanted to see what Mr. Dossi had to say for himself."

"Why go to the trouble of getting a federal judge involved? What was he really after?"

"I've been thinking about that. Maybe an alibi."

"How's that?"

"I understand an attempt was made on Ms. Lessing's life. Maybe Mr. Dossi wanted an unimpeachable alibi witness to his whereabouts when the assassin struck."

"And someone killed him instead. Why, do you suppose?"

"I'm sure he had enemies. . . . When he was shot, I had just looked out the very window the bullet came through.

"I suppose I didn't really expect to avoid getting involved. . . ."

"There wasn't anything I could do for him. I called the police, but apart from what I told the 9-1-1 operator, there wasn't anything I could tell them. So I left."

By that time, Minorini knew, the cops already had a car on the way. Something—either the sniper or the fatal bullet—set off the security alarm.

"Your chauffeur hasn't accounted for his whereabouts when the shooting occurred."

"I didn't tell my chauffeur not to talk to the police."

"But he didn't," Megan said. She was leaning forward in her chair.

"He's worked for me for years. I'm sure he feels— Out of loyalty . . ."

Reilly persisted. "He loyal enough to shoot Dossi for you?"

"Of course not!"

"We'll be asking him."

The judge nodded. "I'll have him drive me to the police station to make my statement. I'll ask him to tell them what he knows."

Minorini believed him, but he checked the story anyway. The judge was an old man with a distinguished career. He'd been married to the same woman forty-seven years, had children—none with obvious financial or legal problems—and grandchildren. No one had anything bad or even mildly scandalous to say about him. His credit was good, his bank balance healthy. The Parkinson's might have suggested financial problems ahead, but the judge had a great insurance policy.

The more digging Minorini did, the more he was inclined to believe the judge had guessed right when he said Dossi wanted him for an alibi.

So Dossi had sent the hit man. No surprise there. Too bad they couldn't question *him*. Convenient for someone that he was dead. Who had they leaked the fake safe house location to? Who in the Bureau knew about the trap? Who in the Marshal's office? And who killed Dossi?

FORTY-THREE

As soon as the Marshals let her, Joanne called Sean with the news that they'd been reprieved. He was ecstatic, then very quiet.

"What's wrong, Sean?"

"I was wondering— Would you mind if I stayed a while longer? I mean— Will you be okay?"

"Having fun in spite of yourself?"

"Well, yeah."

"I'll be fine. The Marshals said they'd arrange to fly you back. We'll just ask them to make it a week later."

"Thanks, mom. Are you at home?"

"Not yet. This afternoon."

The Feds had been diverting her mail so, on the way home, Carver took her to the post office to get it redirected. And since ATF still had her car, he drove her to the grocery store to stock up.

When they got to her house, Carver insisted on going through it and the carport to check for booby traps or bad guys. Feeling guilty, she supposed, for leaving her alone. If he only knew!

Before she sent him on his way, she made him coffee and asked to see his pictures.

When he left, the house seemed empty. And it was dirty— three weeks accumulation of dust. She swept and vacuumed and mopped. She took down the drapes and walked them to the cleaners to be dry cleaned. One room at a time, she washed the curtains and, while they were drying, the ceilings, walls and floors. When she'd emptied the refrigerator, defrosted the freezer, and cleaned the oven, she tackled the darkroom, moving everything out to scrub the walls and sink.

She kept it up for three days, falling into the dreamless sleep of exhaustion each night until the whole house was spotless, the attic and carport neat, even the crawl space inspected. In all of this—she was aware—there was an element of Lady Macbeth.

When there was nothing more to clean, she took a cab to Helix and maxed her Visa on film and darkroom supplies. Back home, she replenished the spent developer and fix, then developed all the black-and-white film she'd exposed in exile. She took her time printing the resultant negatives, playing with the timing, blowing some up until they looked like grainy abstracts, cropping others, until she was satisfied she couldn't improve on any of them.

Then she called Rick.

"Do I still have a job?"

"Is the Pope still Catholic? When can you start?"

"Tomorrow. Sean's out of town, so I'll take everything you've got for me. I don't have a car, though."

"No problem. You can use mine."

Her friend Jane stopped by that evening and they shared a bottle of chablis while Joanne filled Jane in on the last three awful weeks and—the version she'd told the FBI—on the night Dossi was shot. "Murdered," she told herself. She found it hard to say the word. Harder than pulling the trigger. For all the fantasizing she'd done before the fact, she'd never imagined the aftermath.

"This whole thing's changed you," Jane told her. "You seem depressed. Maybe you should see someone."

"It's just that it's brought back all the bad feelings from my divorce—anger and frustration and helplessness. I'll get over it."

What alternative did she have?

FORTY-FOUR

In the conference room of the Highland Park Police Station, the city's Chief of Detectives introduced Minorini to cops from Waukegan, Deerfield and Lake Forest, Lake and Cook Counties, and the State Police. Gray had also been invited, as a courtesy to Northbrook and on the outside chance he knew something.

Highland Park got things going by summarizing what they had so far: Dossi had been killed with a 30.06 slug. The bullet entered the front of his chest, to the left of his sternum, and exited at the rear, tearing through his heart and leaving a hand-sized hole in his back. Death had been instantaneous. They'd been able to calculate the position of the shooter—inside the property fence, one hundred yards away, and they were pretty sure he'd gotten on and off the property through a storm drain. Other than that—cutting through the BS—they had nothing, no shell casings, no trace evidence, not even any tracks, thanks to the snow. They were fairly certain they'd found where the shooter had parked his car, but they hadn't found anyone who'd noticed it. Basically, they had zip. The whole thing had been well planned or lucky as hell. But it had more of the feel of a political assassination or a SWAT operation than a mob hit.

The Highland Park detectives were following up on everyone Dossi's staff could think of who'd contacted him in the last month. And they were going over his phone records.

The state cop wanted to know what Minorini could add. He told them about his visit to the judge and what Haskel had said about the quiet.

"What do we know about the victim?"

Minorini shrugged. "Now that he can't hurt them, there's all kinds of vermin coming out of the woodwork to rat on him. He was a top-of-the-line hit man; his investment business just a way to hide his earnings. In light of what's being said, it's pretty amazing his name's never come up in all the years we've been watching his associates."

The Highland Park detective's skeptical expression gave Minorini the feeling that he suspected him of knowing more than he was telling. Minorini didn't try to correct the impression. The Bureau's reputation with local law enforcement wasn't undeserved.

When they'd wrapped things up, Detective Gray made a point to walk out with him. On the sidewalk in front, he said, "Meetings like this make me ready to kill for a cigarette." He pulled out a pack of gum and offered Minorini a stick. Minorini shook his head. Gray unwrapped a piece and put the wrapper in one pocket, the rest of the pack in another. Before he put the bare stick in his mouth, he added, "Seems to me, Lessing is the one who benefits most from Dossi's death."

Minorini found himself thinking of how sexy Joanne had seemed when she'd said, "I'd be a damned hypocrite if I said I was sorry." He hadn't suspected her capable of aggression before that, but as he thought about it, he realized she'd stalked the animals she'd caught on film, from the Canada geese to Dossi himself. She'd stood up on the third floor of the Daley Center with her camera, like a hunter in a blind, and coolly nailed him.

"Nobody ever considers the possibility of the hit man being a woman," Gray said. "But have you seen her pictures? She has the killer instinct. If I thought she could handle a thirty-ought-six, I'd be showing her picture around at gun stores and gun shows."

An uncanny echo of his own thoughts. It was the moment to share his own doubts or forever hold his peace. "We're talking someone who's been under twenty-four-seven surveillance for weeks, someone who won't eat lobster because of how it's killed. And I spoke to her on the phone twice the night of the murder." He shook his head. "I could buy a female killer, just not this female."

Gray shrugged. "Well, no statute of limitations on murder. Sooner or later, somebody'll come forward with something."

Minorini was halfway back to his office when he remembered that Joanne had spent Thanksgiving at her mother's farm. And there was that photograph in Schroeder's office. If not the rifle in the photograph, maybe another. . . .

He would have to check it out.

FORTY-FIVE

Ken Schroeder offered Minorini the same soft, leather chair as on his first visit and said, "What can I do for you today, Agent Minorini?"

"Have you talked to your sister recently?"

"Yeah. She called to say she was okay and that someone killed the creep that tried to bomb her car. So she's off the hook."

The scar under Schroeder's right eye stood out on his face like an accusation. Minorini had seen such scars before, on the faces of hunters who were careless with their scopes. He shifted in his seat. "She say why he tried to kill her?"

"Something to do with her being a witness in a mob killing."

"And?"

"That's all."

Minorini picked up the group photo with gun from Schroeder's desk and said, "Thirty-ought-six?"

"Hey, you're good if you can tell from that far away." He must've meant from the point of view of the photographer.

"Lucky guess. Who got the gun when your dad passed away?"

"No idea. After he died we looked for it—we were going to bury it with him—but we never found it. He probably gave it to someone he thought would use it."

"You're not a hunter?"

"I never could hit anything unless I was right on top of it. And my brother Allen's the same. Joanne was the only decent shot but she could never bring herself to kill anything. Maybe that's why she's so great with a camera—she can bag her limit without hurting a fly. The lot of us must've been a great disappointment to my dad. He loved hunting."

"So you don't hunt?"

Schroeder grinned. "Only in the boardroom and the stock exchange." He seemed too relaxed to be involved.

"Do you own a gun?"

"God, no. I've got kids. And my wife's a city girl. She's terrified of guns."

"Where were you the night before last?"

"Why?" Minorini let the question hang until Schroeder answered it himself. "You're looking for whoever killed the guy who was after Joanne. It wasn't me. After I left work, I was stuck in traffic until about 8:30. Then I was home the rest of the night."

"Stuck in traffic'd be pretty hard to prove."

"No, as a matter of fact. There was an accident on the Kennedy. The police took my name as a witness."

"What time?"

"I don't know exactly. Around seven?"

"What department?"

"State Police."

Allen Schroeder had been having dinner with his in-laws when Dossi was shot. Minorini called on them to confirm, and they were incensed that the FBI would even ask about Allen. Schroeder also confirmed his older brother's story about the gun. The family Schroeder looked like a genuine dead end. Thank God.

The Marshals had taken Joanne home and given her the green light to go back to work. They hadn't returned her car. Minorini met her as she was leaving Rage Photo and offered to drive her to the train. He waited until she'd put her seat belt on before he asked her about the gun.

She looked terrified for about seven tenths of a second, then relieved. "Lost, thank God."

"Thank God?"

"After my dad died, we couldn't find it."

"Thank God?"

"If we still had it, my brothers would be on your suspect list, wouldn't they?"

"Possibly."

"That's absurd anyway. I'm the only one who could ever hit anything."

There was something challenging about the way she said it that brought Minorini's radar on line. But she had the best alibi in the world, didn't she, this woman who loved lobsters?

They made small talk for the rest of the ten minutes it took to get to Union Station. He let her out in front and watched until she disappeared inside.

He hadn't had all that much experience with witnesses suddenly reprieved from banishment, but something about her behavior didn't ring true. She seemed too depressed and edgy, or not relieved enough—something. He didn't have a clue about what it meant.

But there wasn't a hint from any of his sources of there being a contract out on Dossi. And if there had been, Joanne wouldn't be someone with the money or connections to arrange it. She was the only one he knew of with a motive. But then, he knew so little about Dossi that he really had no idea who else would want to kill him.

Still, Joanne's photos of Dossi, and her curious depression, and the amazing lack of other suspects kept coming back to mind. Maybe she *had* done it!

The idea materialized like a movie ghost, then solidified until he began to feel he'd been poleaxed. It was too out of sync with his image of Joanne, the soft touch who wouldn't eat veal. Impossible! How could a lone female outwit the mob, the cops, and one of the best security systems out there? The more he thought about it, though, the more he realized that anti-female prejudice was the chief obstacle to making a case. Her sex was irrelevant. He knew plenty of female cops who'd have had the guts and the ruthlessness to do it, given the provocation she had. She had motive. That left means and opportunity. She'd gone home to her mother's farm for Thanksgiving. It was conceivable she'd picked a gun up there. Lots of farms had guns, sometimes so many that one wouldn't be missed. But, of course, even if she'd had the nerve and the gun, she had the best alibi in the world. Carver was with her the whole time. Wasn't he?

FORTY-SIX

John Carver was at his desk in the Marshal's office, on the twenty-sixth floor of 219 South Dearborn. He waived Minorini to a chair and offered coffee before he said, "What's up?"

"Just trying to clear up a few odd points. Got a couple questions."

"Shoot."

"You get any odd calls the night Dossi was killed, or hangups? Anything like that?"

He thought Carver hesitated before he said, "No."

"What time did Lessing go to bed?"

"Early I think, but I didn't take notes. Why is it important?"

Minorini shrugged and shook his head. "What time did they shovel the drive?"

"About 4:15 A.M."

"That exact?"

"Yeah. The guy knocked on the door to ask me to move my car."

The first time or the second, Minorini wanted to ask; he knew what time he'd called Joanne. There was no reason he could see for Joanne to make up an extra plow pass, or to even think of it if it hadn't happened.

"I figured you had a service and I checked," Carver said. "The name on the truck was the same as the name on your sheet. Was something wrong?"

"No. Just checking to see they didn't do it too early."

He went back down to his office and called the plow service.

What time had they plowed the drive? They didn't know offhand. Was there a problem? Maybe. Maybe not. Could they find out for sure and call him back?

Eventually their driver called him. He sounded groggy and admitted to having been roused from a sound sleep to answer Minorini's questions.

He gave the man the address. "You remember what time you plowed there?"

There was a loud yawn, then "As close as I can remember, mid-morning—that's sometime between four and five o'clock your time.

"Did you plow it earlier?"

"Are you kidding? I'm lucky if I get to it once before the owner bitches."

"Had it been plowed earlier?"

"Yeah, now that you bring it up. I didn't think of it before, but it *had* been done earlier."

"You know who might have done it?"

"Nah. But you know these homeowners. They see their neighbor's drive gettin' done, they can't wait. They offer the guy twenty or thirty bucks to do theirs, too, while he's at it. And—you know—it's easy money for five minutes work, so he does it. . . . Or sometimes a guy'll plow the wrong drive by mistake. He won't bother trying to collect from the homeowner, 'cause he wasn't supposed to do it. And he won't mention it to his boss for obvious reasons."

"Were any of the other drives plowed?"

"No."

"You notice any other trucks around while you were there?"

"No. I got six houses on that street. I did notice one guy doing his own drive with an industrial-sized blower. Probably the only time he's ever had to use it."

"Thanks."

"All part of our friendly service."

Minorini hung up the phone and decided—just long enough for his adrenaline to surge and make him light-headed—that Carver must've nailed Dossi.

He abandoned the idea as quickly as he'd considered it. Even if Joanne was a cipher, Minorini knew John Carver wasn't a killer. He wasn't the sort to abandon his post, either, unless—

Minorini reached for the phone and called information.

"What city and state?"

"Evanston, Illinois."

"Yes?"

"Evanston Hospital."

The operator said, "Thank you," and a computer voice instantly took over. "The number you have requested, 847-570-2000, can be immediately connected for no charge. If you press one . . ."

When SBC had connected him, he asked for the Maternity Department, then asked whether a Mrs. John Carver, or a Gloria Carver, had just delivered a baby there.

"I'm sorry, sir. We're not at liberty—"

"I'm Agent Paul Minorini with the FBI, Chicago office at 219 South Dearborn. Get the number from directory assistance and call me back." He gave her his extension and hung up. When the woman called back, Minorini repeated his original question.

Yes, there was a Mrs. John Carver there. Would Agent Minorini like to speak with her?

"No. I just need to know when she delivered, is it a boy or a girl, and are Mrs. C and the baby all right."

When Minorini hung up, he immediately called Carver.

Carver said, "Hello."

Minorini said, "Congratulations, John. Why didn't you mention your good news?"

"With all the excitement, it must've slipped my mind that I hadn't."

"Wife and daughter okay?"

"Yeah, sure. Or I would've taken off."

"I'd love to see your pictures. Why don't you stop by my office on your way out this afternoon?"

. . .

Carver didn't have any pictures with him when he walked into Minorini's office five minutes later. Minorini greeted him with, "How long was Lessing alone?"

"How did you know?"

"Literally overnight you went from being paranoid that you'd be stuck on duty when Gloria went into labor to being totally unconcerned."

Carver nodded. "Eight hours. . . . I guess I better go back up and make a report." He looked pale enough to be in shock.

"That's up to you. I won't lie for you, but as far as I'm concerned, no harm, no foul. And I'm not about to say anything if nobody asks."

"You could get in major trouble."

Minorini shook his head. "It's not as if you were out screwing around."

Carver said, "Thanks," as he held out his hand.

Minorini shook it. "What're you calling her?"

"We're thinking maybe Joy."

So Carver hadn't done it.

When he'd left, Minorini spread the papers out on his desk in roughly chronological order. Obviously, they'd all missed something. He read until he came to the Highland Park police reports, to one of their canvass reports. What jumped off the list of cars seen in the vicinity when Dossi was shot was a silver-blue Mercedes that one of the cops had noticed as he was racing to respond. The Mercedes was also traveling towards the scene, so he hadn't noted the license plate number. And with the snow and all, he hadn't been able to see the driver. Minorini didn't blame him for that. Highland Park didn't get all that many shootings. And besides, the car was going the wrong way for a getaway.

Maybe.

Or maybe the driver was just more clever than the cops.

It was too crazy, but it nagged him. So at eight P.M., when he finally admitted to himself that they weren't going to solve anything today, he hit the Kennedy northbound instead of going home.

The silver-blue Mercedes seemed to be just as he'd left it. He'd had it washed on the way back from driving his aunt to O'Hare; there was no trace of salt or road dirt. Not trusting the weak overhead light, he got the Maglite from his trunk and gave it the once-over—the garage floor underneath, too. Nothing.

Inside, the upholstery looked as if it had been detailed—no dust or fingerprints. Fingerprints. He didn't have a kit and didn't want to expose this line of inquiry by asking for one, so he put on gloves and improvised with graphite lock-lubricant. He wasn't too surprised to find there were no prints on the driver's door handle, outside or in. Nor anywhere else, not even where smudges from his own prints should have been. The trunk was unhelpful. It was as clean as the rest. He couldn't remember noticing the arrangement of its contents when he'd last had it open, so he couldn't tell if anything was moved.

He closed the trunk and got a roll of paper towels with which to clean up the graphite. Just to be thorough, he put on a clean pair of gloves and carefully felt beneath the seats.

Under the driver's side, where it must have fallen when Joanne took the car out, he found a 3×5 black-and-white photo of Dossi, wearing the same dressing gown he'd had on when the sniper took him out. In the picture, Dossi was reading the news, totally relaxed—judging by his expression, completely unaware he was being watched.

It wasn't a great photo—too grainy. It had probably been taken at night with a telephoto lens and fast film. But its existence was a tribute to the photographer's stalking skills. The style was unmistakably Joanne's, her quarry caught au naturel. The picture was snapped or cropped to be artistically balanced. Even without her fingerprints, it could convict her.

He got a poly bag out of his trunk and put the photo in it. He'd check for prints later with the proper stuff.

Maybe.

He could hear Haskel's "No! You're putting me on! Not the mope!"

They're all just mopes to you aren't they?

And wasn't it still purely circumstantial? There was a universe of difference between shooting someone with a camera and with a .3006. Wouldn't a jury assume that?

Minorini didn't know. He wasn't altogether certain why he wrote his find up on his personal computer, encrypted the report, and saved it in a hidden file. He told himself he wanted to be sure.

He thought of Joanne's picture of her ex-boyfriend, and her skill with a gun and camera.

Where would she get a gun? What happened to her old man's gun? Maybe *she* had it. Maybe she'd had enough trouble from the Feds.

He slept fitfully. He dreamed he was the sniper and when he looked through the scope, Lessing was in his crosshairs.

When he got to the office next morning, he asked Butler, "We still got Dossi's body?"

"I think so. Although his lawyer's been screaming about that. Why?"

"It occurred to me we never had Lessing ID him."

"Kinda moot now."

"It may have some bearing on who killed him—I mean, we ought to be sure he was the one who killed Siano."

"You may be right. It can't hurt anyhow. But if you're gonna do it, get a move on. We can't hold the remains much longer."

The woman with the red hair must be one of the agency models, gorgeous, blasé. In another lifetime, Minorini would've been interested. In his life before Joanne.

"I'm looking for Joanne Lessing," he said.

"Who are you, the FBI?"

"I am, as a matter of fact."

She was only momentarily nonplussed. "She rob a bank?"

"Not to my knowledge."

She gave him a smile that was pure Mae West and said, "Well, I'm sure if she's shot someone it was just with a camera."

He started to laugh, but the word "shot" stuck in his craw and Detective Gray's comment echoed in his head. Who was the last person in the world they'd suspect of shooting Dossi? And who had the most to gain? The thought was interrupted by a man's voice.

"Something I can help you with?" The speaker was five-ten and fit-looking, with blue eyes and thinning, red-blond hair. His tone was more sarcastic than helpful.

Minorini said, "You must be Hancock."

"I'm afraid you have the advantage."

"Special Agent Minorini, FBI." Minorini didn't offer to shake.

Hancock didn't seem impressed. "I thought you boys had your own photographers."

Before Minorini could reply, Joanne came out of Hancock's office and slipped her arm into Hancock's. "Don't be defensive, darling. Paul's not going to arrest me."

Hancock looked startled. "Paul is it?"

"And I need all the work I can get."

Joanne's voice sounded too bright, Minorini thought, too stagey. She was trying to cover some strong emotion. Jealously, perhaps? Maybe she'd been eavesdropping on his conversation with Red.

Hancock pulled his arm free and patted her hand. "Don't let me interfere with commerce." He turned into his office, then stopped and turned back. "Rita, would you like to see your proofs?"

"Does a bear sleep in the woods?" She gave Joanne and Minorini a knowing smile which only Joanne returned, and followed Hancock into his office.

191

FORTY-SEVEN

The drive north was slow and tense. Paul hadn't told her where they were going, just that he needed her to make an ID. She figured it out when he pulled into a parking space on the north side of a newer, two-story building on Utica in Waukegan. A sign next to the door proclaimed it an after-hours entrance. To the Lake County Morgue.

Paul rang the bell, and the door was opened by a smiling black man with bad teeth. The man stepped back. Paul took her elbow, and she found herself in a hallway that seemed to parallel the north wall of the facility and stretch from front to back. The man led them to a curtained window in the south wall. "You wait here," he told them. "I'll open the screen. When you're ready, tap on the glass."

They waited. After a few moments, the curtain opened, revealing a small space—maybe three feet by six—surrounded and separated from the rest of the room by another curtain that hung from a track on the ceiling. The attendant pushed a shrouded gurney into the viewing space. He didn't seem in any hurry. Joanne wondered if he'd been trained to be patient or chosen for the trait. She wasn't in a hurry either. She could tell by the shape beneath the sheet she was about to see a body. And she knew without doubt whose body. The only question was—

"Why?"

Paul turned from his own silent contemplation of the "view" to say, "I beg your pardon?"

"Who is it?"

"His name's Gianni Dossi. Ready?"

"No!"

As if he hadn't heard, he rapped on the glass. The attendant pulled the cover back, exposing Dossi's face. Joanne stared.

In death, he seemed small and shrunken—gray as clay, with sagging flesh and wrinkled, scrape-marked skin. His eyes were slitted, the whites dried black. His watchfulness was gone, his predatory animation. The remains were to the man she'd stalked and photographed as road kill was to a fox or coyote. It was hard to imagine him a threat to anyone.

You couldn't weigh a soul, she reminded herself, though it had substantial presence. Dossi's soul was decades gone. Not her fault. Now the life force that had made him more than the sum of his biochemical reactions was gone too.

She said, "How did he die?"

"Heart shot, through and through. A Bureau sniper couldn't have done a neater job—except they go for the head."

"Who do you think did it?"

"The Bureau doesn't have a clue. Maybe we were wrong thinking he was the one who shot your neighbor. Maybe he was a victim just like Siano."

"But he's the one I saw in my neighborhood. I'm sure! What else would he be doing there?"

"Maybe he had business with Siano. Or maybe he saw the shooter—that would make him a marked man."

She felt slightly dizzy. She'd never considered that Dossi might be guiltless. Then she noticed Paul hadn't answered her question. "Who do *you* think did it?"

"You don't like my theory?"

The bomb hadn't been planted in her car after the Jane Doe subpoena was issued, only after her name got out.

"If he wasn't a hit man, why would anyone come after me?"

If Dossi were an innocent, why would anyone care if she saw him in her neighborhood. And . . . "Why would he be driving a stolen car?"

Minorini shrugged.

"The man Dossi killed— How did he do it?"

Awkwardly put, but Paul must have understood because he said, "Dossi put a gun to his head and blew his brains out."

"And the man who shot Dossi?"

"What makes you think it was a man?"

She felt a stab of panic. How did he *know*?

Relax! He's just being argumentative. *He can't know.*

"I just assumed— Most violent crimes are committed by men. Aren't they?"

His face was passive but she was sure he was laughing at her.

"Mmm-hmm. Dossi was killed with a rifle. Care to venture what kind?" She shook her head. He continued. "At least Dossi had the guts to face his victims."

The implication was "not like a sniper."

"Funny," she said, "how when someone goes after a dangerous animal with a rifle it's called hunting, but if the animal happens to have two legs, they change the name."

He grinned. "Touché."

She walked away from the window and stopped at the door, then turned to take a last look. Without benefit of the undertaker's art, Dossi looked nothing like the guest of honor at a wake, nothing like Doris Davis.

The memory of Mrs. Davis and her bewildered son bludgeoned Joanne's fledgling remorse. Dossi had *forced* her to kill. He was no more deserving of her sympathy than the foxes and coyotes her father had hunted.

When they stepped outside, the sun was setting, breaking through fluffy clouds that were dropping ice diamonds of snow. The flakes seemed to evaporate as they hit the traffic-warmed pavement.

In the car Minorini said, "You know how to shoot a rifle, don't you?"

Her startled response was so fleeting, he almost missed it. She said, "Why do you ask?"

He had her! He only had to push a little and he could present

194

the Bureau with an easy conviction. He'd have another notch in his gun handle, but what else? The glory would fade. The Bureau would soon ask what have you done for us lately? In ten years he'd be pensioned out; Joanne would just be getting out of prison. But what about Sean? If Joanne were arrested, Howard Lessing would no doubt ask for custody. And without Joanne's influence, how would Sean turn out?

Minorini wondered what would happen if he just didn't connect the dots. Failure to solve one more mob-connected hit wouldn't ruin his career. Why fuck up the kid's life to nail a murderer's killer?

"Just making conversation," he told Joanne.

Joanne had taken the train that morning, and since she'd agreed to help Paul with the ID, he offered to drive her home. He took Route 41 south. Traffic was jammed, and Paul turned west on Old Elm Road, then headed south on Ridge. The route took them past the Heller Center. She was aware of him watching her as they jogged east on Half Day—past Dossi's house—to pick up Ridge where it continued south again. She kept her eyes on the road ahead.

Someone had thrown away a can of rust-colored paint, and it had splashed out on the faded asphalt as the garbage truck went down the street. It looked like a half-dried blood stain on the pavement. Joanne had noticed it before, but it had just been paint then. It was blood in hindsight, a foreshadow of the blood she'd spilled.

She felt unclean, as if she'd just been diagnosed with AIDS or cancer. Would the feeling ever fade? With AIDS, you died. With cancer, you died or you got better. No one died of guilt unless he got caught. Lots of guilty Nazis died peacefully of old age after committing unspeakable atrocities. All she'd committed was a desperate necessity. But how long before the feelings faded?

"A penny for your thoughts," he said.

"Not worth a cent." He waited. "Just wondering how to film that paint splashed on the pavement."

"What paint?" he said, but she knew he'd seen it. She doubted that he missed much of anything.

Minorini remembered the rush he'd felt when he first saw *Bonnie and Clyde*. *Sex and violence*. Absurd as it was, the idea that Joanne killed Dossi sent an echo of that excitement through him.

As they approached Lake-Cook Road, she interrupted his reverie, her face pale and flat in the deepening dusk. "Does anyone ever confess?" she said.

"You mean come forward and say, 'I did it and I can't live with myself'?"

She nodded.

"No. The people who commit murders usually don't feel remorse. Or much of anything else, apparently."

Navigating the intersection was like driving in snow. It took constant vigilance to avoid disaster and the constancy was exhausting.

He was suddenly afraid she was going to say she did it. "It seems to me the killer can't afford to indulge in remorse. If the mob gets him, they'll make a horrible example of him. If we get him, he'll go to prison where the mob'll make a horrible example of him. If he's smart, he'll keep his urge to confess to himself. Or find an old-fashioned priest who'll give him absolution and take his secret to the grave."

He knew! No, he was fishing, but she wouldn't take the lure. Or was he warning her that in this case, confession would *not* be good for the soul?

How many times had Howie come home from visiting clients at the jail, seething with frustration—Why can't they just keep their mouths shut?

Paul turned off the wipers. Snowflakes landing on the heated windshield liquefied. She watched the drops run down. Traffic streaming past seemed to be in a parallel universe.

"Do you still think I'm innocent?" She felt her face redden and her scalp prickle as she recognized her Freudian slip. Thank God it was dark and he was driving.

The lights from oncoming traffic reflected from his eyes as he glanced at her without turning his head. He looked back at the traffic. "I underestimated you."

"What made you decide that?"

"Your pictures."

"Ah."

"You can get away with acting dumb, but your work gives you away."

"I don't act dumb."

"Okay. All right. Say you don't constantly show off— What?"

"I didn't say anything."

"But you were thinking *Where does this guy get off? He doesn't even know me.*"

"Yeah?" She couldn't keep from smiling, and even though he wasn't looking at her, she knew he'd heard the amusement she was feeling.

"I'm trying," he said.

"Why?"

He shrugged and glanced from side to side as the car approached a cross street, then he looked at her. "Your pictures of the shoplifters were like trophies. And the shots you got of the bikers made them look like wild animals in their native habitat—fierce."

"That's how I saw them initially. But when I got close enough I realized that, like lions and tigers, they were only dangerous when they were threatened or hunting."

"When I first met you, I thought you were a typical divorcée with kid."

"What do you mean by typical?"

He hesitated.

"Think I can't take the truth?"

"No."

"Well?"

"Financially strapped, a poor judge of men, a little desperate . . ."

"Well the first two are right on. And now?"

"You've got a lot more guts and brains than I suspected."

"Just what every man looks for in a woman."

He gave her a look she couldn't read. "Some of us." They traveled two blocks without speaking, then he said, "Have you made any adjustments to *your* first impression?"

"I was afraid you'd turn out to be like Howie."

"Have I?"

"You remind me of one of those fast cars with the tinted windows—impossible to see inside. But you're not anything like Howie."

Paul turned onto her street and stopped the car in front of her house. It was dark except for the front porch light. He put the car in park. "Sean's not home yet!"

"Once he decided I was really out of danger, he asked to stay and visit. He's flying in the twenty-first. Would you like to stay for dinner? I could throw a pizza in the oven."

She thought he drew his breath in rather fast.

She wondered when she'd begun to think of him as Paul.

"Why not?" He unbuckled his seat belt, then turned off the ignition and removed the key.

After they'd finished the pizza and a bottle of Chianti, Joanne invited him into the living room. She turned the stereo on low as he made himself comfortable on the couch.

"You any good in bed?" she asked. She was gratified to note that, for the first time since she'd met him, he seemed unnerved.

She'd been a virgin when she met Howie. She'd supposed her lack of satisfaction with him to be her own fault, so she'd researched sex with the same naïve enthusiasm she'd employed in

"Phone records," the woman said as she walked out of the room.

Haskel said, "Dossi's phone." He dropped the sheet back on the pile. "Waste of time and paper. We got transcripts of all those, along with the dossiers of everyone he talked to."

"And now we have the phone records," Minorini told him. He let his tone say, Go away and let me do my job.

Haskel laughed. "Job security, I guess."

As soon as the door closed behind him, Minorini paged through the sheets. Only the top four or five were from Dossi's home phone. The rest were from all the pay phones at the Harold Washington Library on the days Carlo had driven Dossi there. Minorini took them out to the secretary's station and made duplicates. Back in his office, he put the originals in an old file—where no one would think to look for them—and reached for his phone.

Half an hour later, he had a long list of names—the individuals whose numbers had been called from Dossi's phone and from the library phones. By cross checking the surveillance records compiled since the wiretap was put in place, Minorini was able to eliminate as irrelevant most of the names on Dossi's phone call list—his daughter, his wife in Italy, his health club, restaurant reservations, golf courses, pizza delivery. . . . As Haskel said, the Feds had transcripts of all those conversations, and all were innocent or at least not incriminating.

The lists from the library phones were much longer, and many of the numbers were unpublished. To save time and aggravation, he marked off the calls made an hour before and after the time Carlo recalled Dossi's being there and concentrated on those. And on the theory that the unpublished numbers were more likely to belong to someone up to no good, he called his source at the phone company to get names to go with them. He was halfway down the list, writing the name and address next to each number as his informant gave him the information, when one number seemed to jump off the page. He forgot for a moment what he was doing. He knew the number! He'd called it more than once—to get Haskel!

"You still there, Minorini?"

"What? Yeah, sorry. What did you say?"

"I said, I can't get you the out-of-state number."

"Okay. How 'bout the next one . . . ?" He skipped Haskel's and read off the next few. When they got to the end of the list, he said, "Thanks. I'm gonna put you in for a commendation."

"A pair of playoff tickets would be better—any game."

"I'll see what I can do."

Minorini rang off and called the Detroit FBI office.

Detroit called him back an hour later. "Got an ID on your unpublished caller—Armand Wilson."

Bingo!

"You get an address?" The agent gave it to him and said, "Isn't Wilson the lowlife you guys just nailed?"

"Yup. Thanks."

"Any time."

Minorini hung up and called the State's Attorney's office. "We subpoenaed Armand Wilson's phone records yet?" They had. "Mind faxing me a copy?"

He told the secretary to watch for the fax. He'd just made up his mind to worry about Haskel tomorrow when the phone rang. He picked it up; Butler's voice announced, "ATF got your bomb setter."

"Where? When?"

"Caught him red-handed putting a device in a Cadillac. They've got him over at the MCC. Why don't you meander on down and see what he's got to say for himself?"

Minorini left his gun locked in his desk and walked the block and a half to the Metropolitan Correctional Center. The federal jail looked like a twenty-seven-story monument to the computer punch card, from the stone age of data entry.

The bomber told them he was Milo Jaxx, a plumber from Beverly, and he wasn't in the NCIC computer. But there was something a little off about his south side accent, so one of the marshals sent his prints to INTERPOL. His real name was Terrence T. Finn, wanted for an impressive number of offenses in his native Belfast. He'd been in the US for nearly thirty years, had established his alias back in the days before identity theft became a growth industry, back when notarized photocopies were all you needed to get a driver's license.

The bullshit required for Minorini to get in to see Finn seemed to take forever. And for the first half hour of the interview, Finn refused to talk. He was tired, he said, of the Mutt and Jeff routine the marshals had been playing him all morning. He was tired of the smell of Feds. Minorini finally asked to speak to him alone.

"We need some help, here," Minorini told him. "You're up to your crotch in this; you could use someone to put in a good word. How 'bout it?"

"Yeah right."

"We think a certain mob guy hired you to eliminate a witness, but then dis-hired you when the bomb didn't go off."

"You can think what you like."

"This guy was pretty big, and you didn't deliver," Minorini said. "*Was*. That's got us thinking maybe you had something to do with his currently being past tense." He could see Finn thinking. He added, "We'd be willing to overlook the murder attempt—since the witness wasn't harmed—if you cooperate."

"You'll put that in writing?"

Minorini shrugged. "Why not."

"I'll wait while you get it made official."

An hour later, Minorini sat across from Finn, with Finn's lawyer and a US Attorney parked at right angles. The paperwork lay on the table like a centerpiece.

Minorini said, "When did Dossi first call?"

Finn looked at his counsel, got a discreet nod, and said, "About two in the afternoon, the Tuesday after Thanksgiving."

About an hour after Carlo claimed he had the meeting in the forest preserve.

"Just what did he say?"

"He said he had a little pest problem he wanted me to solve. Told me it was worth a hundred bucks to know that I'd take care of it immediately."

"A hundred dollars?"

"Yeah. That meant a hundred grand—in case anyone was listening."

"I see. And you knew the caller?"

"Not by name. I couldn't a picked him outta a lineup—that's how it works—but I recognized his voice. We done business before."

"What did you call him?"

"Mr. Million. Cause if he did a job for you, it would cost that."

"So why did you work for him for less?"

Finn frowned. "He was the only one I ever heard of getting that kind of change." He shrugged. "His money was good. And he always paid within twenty-four hours. He used to recommend me for the stuff that was beneath him, and I think sometimes for stuff when he needed an alibi. Anyway, I fucked up. I got no idea why that one didn't go off."

Minorini let him wonder.

But Finn came close to guessing. "That broad must have the luck of a narrowback."

"So what happened next?"

"I get another call from Mr. Million—check the Chicago news. I say, Just tell me. 'You screwed up,' he says, 'I'm gonna overlook this one, 'cause this broad's charmed or something, but you're out of it.' I'm lucky he just canceled my contract and didn't take one out on me."

"Did he say what he was going to do about his problem?"

"Told me to forget he ever called. I wasn't about to ask."

During the postmortem the marshals held after they took Finn back to his cell, they laid out what they had so far. A rumor. Someone high up in the US Marshal's Office had been seen dining with a mob-connected union boss. No names. No definitive details or even any provocative ones. Obviously the absence of data was creating a vacuum that rumor and speculation were rushing in to fill.

FORTY-NINE

Joanne," Rick said when she walked in the door, "Fitz pulled a no-show and he's supposed to be shooting a wedding in forty-five minutes. You gotta do it for me!"

Rick didn't often ask for big, last-minute favors but . . .

"I can't go dressed like this. And if I go home to change—"

He whipped out his wallet and pulled out a credit card that he shoved at her. "Here. Stop at Fields and get yourself something. May, you called a cab?"

"You asked me that three times already," May said. "It should be down there waiting."

Rick took a handful of bills out of his wallet and handed them to Joanne. "Have the cabby wait while you go in Fields."

"Okay, just let me get my stuff together."

"It's all ready—film, backup cameras, tripod, reflectors, background screen, battery packs—Just go!"

"Rick, chill!"

"This is too close! That son of a bitch is never getting another assignment from me. C'mon. I'll carry this stuff down to the cab for you."

Joanne shrugged and gave up. She could check the plumbing at Fields. . . .

The sales lady looked Joanne over and gave her a cool reception—until Joanne hinted that she had an unlimited expense account and no time to make use of it. Twenty minutes later—after taking a whole ninety seconds to admire a striking, midnight blue evening dress—Joanne was on her way in a conservative navy pantsuit, with her jeans rolled up in her camera case. The saleslady even sold her a lint roller—for twice what she'd have paid at Walgreens—to make her black car coat look presentable.

The family was angry because the photographer they got wasn't the one they thought they'd been promised. And she wasn't a man. They were getting a deal—she was much better than Fitz—but she was depressed and tired and didn't feel like selling herself. Without anger or emphasis, she told the father, "You can sue, if you can find a lawyer to take your case."

"We *won't* have any trouble finding a lawyer."

She shrugged. "Maybe, but you haven't got a case."

"The hell I haven't. My daughter's getting married in twenty minutes and the photographer I hired hasn't showed!"

Joanne felt exhausted. There was nothing she'd have liked better than to just go home. But she owed it to Rick to give the guy a last chance. "Your contract with Rage Photo states that you'd be provided with a professional photographer, not necessarily a *male* professional photographer. I'm a professional and I'm here to fulfill Rage's commitment. However, if you prefer, I'm authorized to refund your deposit. All you have to do is sign a release stating that your contract with Rage is dissolved by mutual agreement."

"Are you outta your mind? The wedding's in twenty minutes!"

"Then I presume you're withdrawing your objection to my doing this job?"

She thought he might have an attack of some sort as he tried to think of an alternative. "Are you any good?"

Better than you deserve, she thought.

Finally, he said, "Go ahead. But if your pictures aren't terrific, I'll see you never work in this town again."

Bad dialog, recycled from a soap opera. Joanne just stared at him. If it was an indicator of his taste, she could do the job half asleep. She looked around. The church was old and photogenic. The bride and groom presentable. There shouldn't be any difficulty in creating the illusion of happily ever after. For a minute, she was tempted to do a Fitzharris job of it—barely adequate. As soon as she had the thought, she was ashamed of it. She'd do the job for the happy couple. To hell with the old man. And with any luck, she'd get him back later. She'd catch him on film making a fool of himself when he'd had too much to drink and started feeling up the bridesmaids.

FIFTY

Minorini was sitting in Haskel's chair, with his feet on Haskel's desk, the next morning when Haskel came in.

Haskel had a Starbuck's coffee cup in his hand and a *Sun-Times* under his arm. He put the coffee on the desk and dropped the paper next to it. "What's up?"

"You tell me."

"Nothing *I* know of."

"We still have a leak."

"Kinda moot now, wouldn't you say?"

"Not till it's plugged." Minorini thought that made Haskel squirm a little.

"Shit! It could be anyone, it could be a clerk, or anyone in the US Attorney's office. It's probably Judge Hollander. That story he gave you about visiting Dossi was a load of crap."

This last idea seemed to have stiffened Haskel's backbone. Maybe he thought he'd distracted Minorini from his original line of inquiry. Now he took the offensive. "Get outta my chair. What is this? ATF got our bomber. I got our hit man, and Dossi undoubtedly got what he deserved. Who cares who did it? Or if you care, *you* go chase your tail trying to solve it. And see if you can find out who did Hoffa while you're at it. Get out of my chair!"

Minorini got up slowly and walked around the desk.

Haskel sat down behind it. "Get out of here and let me read my paper." As Minorini got to the door, Haskel said, "This is personal with you, isn't it? Why? You got something going with Lessing? You pissed because someone put her in the line of fire?"

"Maybe I am. Maybe I'm sick of the civilian body count and having to have a score card to tell who the good guys are."

"No, I think you let Lessing get close to you at your little safe house—maybe close enough to ring your chimes. If that's the case you ought to just bang the bitch and stop trying to cover up with this leak crap."

"Is that what you'd do?"

"I'd fuck her brains out. But that's not your style is it, Paulie? Maybe you ought to marry her!"

"Maybe I would if she'd have me!"

Haskel sat back in his chair and laughed. "Meantime, you got a little plumbing job to do. Better get to it."

Minorini just looked at him.

Haskel laughed again and said, "Drip, drip, drip."

There was a pink message slip on Minorini's desk: "Call Mr. Butler." He picked up the phone and hit the button for Butler's number.

"Butler."

"It's Paul."

"Yeah. You got a date for that State's Attorney's Party?"

"Not yet."

"What the hell—It's tonight, you know!"

"I'll get someone. If worse comes to worst I can call an escort service."

"Cute."

"I'd like to talk to you about the Dossi case."

"Tomorrow afternoon. Right after you report on your State's Attorney gig."

As soon as he disconnected, Minorini rang up Rage Photo and asked for Joanne. When she said hello, he said, "Come with me to a party tonight. It's a political thing. I have to attend, but all I have to do is show up in a tux and bring a presentable date."

"It might be worth it to see you in a tux. What time?"

"About seven?"

"Shall I bring my camera?"

"Your call. But I'm sure there'll be photographers."

"Why don't you pick me up at work? We have a dressing room for the models. I could change there, and you won't have to drive so far."

FIFTY-ONE

Fields still had the dress. Midnight blue silk, classic lines, a neckline suggesting more cleavage than it showed and enough back to support the built-in engineering—no unsightly straps to slip. The dress fit as if it were custom made, which posed a problem because the fitting room mirror showed every seam and wrinkle in her everyday underwear. She reached under the floor length skirt and slipped her briefs off. Pantyhose weren't going to work either, but no one was going to see her legs.

She agonized briefly over using Rick's credit card to pay for it. The saleslady remembered her, of course, and didn't bother to call Mr. Rage for authorization. With a wrap and shoes, and a matching clutch, it all came to $1200. But after murder, credit card fraud was penny ante. She'd read *Crime and Punishment* and she'd seen *Crimes and Misdemeanors*. On the whole, she thought Woody Allen had a better measure of the age.

She changed after work, in the models' dressing room, where she left her civvies, and she borrowed some of the costume jewelry they kept for shoots—cubic zirconia and ruby glass, but they looked real and classic. She felt naked without her camera case.

Paul arrived in a cab, which waited while he came upstairs for her. His only comment on her looks was, "Very nice." No small thing—he could've just stepped off a shoot for a GQ tux layout.

The party was at the Cultural Center, one of the city's most stunning venues. It turned out to be one of those black tie things

Michael Sneed mentions in her columns. The attendees were the people you see on the society pages, businessmen, and politicians, and lots of lawyers—corporate attorneys, as well as prosecutors, a few expensive defenders and some judges.

She knew she should be terrified, surrounded by all the law enforcement personnel, but they were all clueless. She felt like a jaguar watching from the safety of a high perch as the hunters blundered by below.

She was surprised at the number of people who insisted that they be introduced to her, including the Assistant US attorney who'd forced her to testify.

"I'm Aaron Mercer—"

"The US Attorney. I know."

Mercer said, "I'm afraid you have the advantage, Miss—?"

"*Ms.* Lessing."

He blinked. She could tell the exact moment he figured out who she was and where they'd met before by the slight widening of his eyes. It was a measure, she decided, of how she'd changed since Dossi died that she enjoyed Mercer's confusion and discomfort. And she could recall their last meeting without blushing.

"You have friends in the State's Attorney's office?" he asked. The implication was why hadn't she used her influence to get the subpoena quashed?

"Actually, I'm still in FBI custody."

She glanced briefly at Paul, then watched Mercer process that information. Paul's reaction was impossible to read.

Joanne was spared further conversation by the arrival of Judge Tofler. She guessed from the way he came beaming up that he'd been pleased by her pictures and that he'd had too much to drink. Nevertheless, she smiled and took his arm and said, "Excuse me," as the judge led her away.

Mercer turned to Minorini. "What's going on?"

"Dossi's dead. Lessing's no longer a witness. Fair game."

"And you're sleeping with her."

"That's pretty crude, even for you."

"I don't like it!"

Minorini just shrugged and smiled.

There was something enigmatic about her. She'd climaxed for him—hadn't she? With women you could never tell for sure. But he suspected some part of her hadn't surrendered. He wondered why he felt compelled to know for sure whether she'd killed Dossi. Why he didn't just follow all the mob "leads" to their dead ends, file his reports, and forget it. But he knew he couldn't live with the uncertainty. He could live with Joanne, even knowing that she'd done it. He couldn't live with not being sure.

They caught a cab on Michigan Avenue afterward. As it turned onto Madison, Joanne looked up to find Paul watching her. *Cat and mouse.* He didn't seem the type to torture his prey. If he caught Dossi's killer, he'd just make an arrest. Wouldn't he?

She wasn't sure what perverse impulse made her ask, "Do you think you'll ever discover Dossi's killer?"

He'd been leaning toward her, now he sat back. "Discover, yes. Proving it is something else." He glanced at the cabbie, who seemed intent on the road. "People get away with murder all the time. If they're smart enough not to tell anyone."

What was he saying?

Something clicked, metaphorically, as distinctly as the zippery ratchet of handcuffs closing on a felon's wrists. She knew that she was caught. She should have been terrified, but she felt incredibly aroused.

She wondered if he had any idea how turned on she was. How could he? But what *was* going on inside his head? She said, "A penny for your thoughts."

"Now that's a cliché."

She just smiled.

"I'm hungry. Like to stop at my place for something?"

"Sure."

He licked his lips, slowly, and she felt her own lips parting.

214

She felt the pleasant squeezing sensation in her breasts that meant her nipples were coming to attention. She felt the strength abandoning her limbs. She offered no resistance when he pushed her gently back against the door and slipped a hand between her legs.

"Let's go somewhere private."

Paul's place was a tiny one-bedroom apartment on the twenty-fifth floor overlooking the Loop and Lake. Immediately to the right of the door was a galley kitchen with a pass-through counter to the living room. To the left was a closet, and a short hall to the open bathroom and presumably the bedroom.

He took her wrap and hung it with his own coat in the closet. Then he put his hands on her shoulders. The slight lift of his arms caused his suit jacket to pull open; she could see the dark shape of his gun. She shuddered.

He must've read her mind because he said, "Sorry. I forget it's there sometimes."

"But you need it. You may have to arrest a dangerous felon."

"Um-hmm." He leaned towards her and she retreated until she came in contact with the wall next to the kitchen door. She reached through the door way to put her clutch on the countertop. She slipped her hands beneath his jacket, but he caught her wrists and pinned them gently at her sides. He leaned forward to kiss her, thrusting his tongue in her mouth. She felt a sensation like slow lightning and a languor so profound she would have slid to the floor if he hadn't had her pinned. She felt light-headed. "Are you going to arrest me?" She was breathing faster.

"Are you a dangerous felon?" He was breathing fast himself.

"I plead the fifth."

"Then I'd better take you into custody."

The words gave her a start, though they weren't surprising given the context. She shivered with excitement.

Gently but very firmly he turned her around and lifted her hands over her head. He pressed against her, pushed her hands flat on the wall. He nuzzled the back of her neck, then said, "Spread your feet." He accompanied the order with a thrust of his knee, forcing her legs apart. He kept her hands pinned.

She let out a little sigh of pleasure. "I have rights . . ."

"You have the right to remain silent."

He seemed to lose track of what he was saying. She could feel his distraction as he pressed against her rear. He stepped backward until the only points of contact between them were his hands on her wrists. He let them go and ran his hands down her sides, all the way to her ankles. He removed her shoes.

She was leaning against the wall, now. Weak in the knees and everywhere else.

He reached around her, putting his hands together, on her throat, as if to strangle her from behind. Then he brought his hands down slowly, over her chest and breasts, pausing to slip his index fingers under the edges of her dress and to finger her nipples through the silk.

She let herself sigh.

He cupped her breasts, probed the creases beneath them with his fingertips, then slid his palms slowly over her abdomen, past her waist and down the fronts of her thighs. He squatted to feel down over her knees and shins and ankles. He stood up and ran his hands down her back and buttocks, over her thighs and calves. When he straightened, he rested his forehead against her shoulder.

A series of rhythmic shudders tensed her abdomen and innards. She was nearly hyperventilating.

She felt his fingers working her zipper. He lowered it slowly. He pulled the two sides of her dress apart and traced her backbone with his tongue—all the way down to her tailbone. He let the garment drop, and when she stepped out of it, he blew his breath out slowly. He kept one hand on the small of her back as he lifted the dress onto the back of nearby chair.

Then he finished his search, running a hand up the inside of one leg and down the other, gently, thoroughly probing the hidden space within her.

She spread her fingers wide and clawed the wall. She heard the brushing sound of fabric, then a soft metallic ratcheting. He reached for her right wrist and closed something cold and hard around it. He brought her arm down, behind her back.

She felt a little surge of terror, a huge wave of pleasure.

He held her cuffed wrist while he reached for her free one. There was a second ratcheting sound, and she was his. She should have been terrified, but she had never felt such intense arousal.

He turned her around and grasped her elbow. He led her to the couch, and seated her in the center. She sat with her arms pinned behind her and watched him remove his holster and his tie. . . .

Minorini awoke before sunrise, still dreaming that Joanne was next to him beneath the covers.

No dream. She lay half-facing him, arms overhead. She looked content. At some point last night he'd located his backup handcuffs and, after wrapping her wrists with protective strips torn from the sheet, he'd cuffed her to the headboard. Apart from an "Ahhh," or "Oh!" or "Paul!" she'd said nothing, no "stop" or "don't," but she'd let him act out every fantasy, clawing and biting when he told her to submit, knowing instinctively he'd meant the opposite. And—he realized with a start—letting him fuck her without protection.

What was really going on?

When they had finally climaxed—together—and she lay there with her arms overhead and her eyes drifting shut, she'd murmured, "I confess."

He'd stroked her satiny belly. He couldn't feel any tension in her muscles. "To what?"

"I killed J.R. And Hoffa. And Dossi."

That hit him like a sucker punch, but he managed to stay cool. "So?"

"And I stole the money for my dress." She seemed more asleep than not.

"From whom?"

"Rick."

217

"I'll pay him back. I love that dress."

"It was twelve hundred dollars . . ."

"Worth every penny."

He felt he was being worked over by the sandman. She'd said something about killing Dossi. Just kidding? He should follow through but . . .

He managed to pull the covers over them before he drifted under.

Sometime later the phone woke him. He glanced at the caller ID, then stretched to turn the ringer off. Haskel could wait.

Sunlight had crept through the window and lay across the bed like a bright comforter.

Beneath the covers, Joanne rolled onto her back and asked, without opening her eyes, "Who's calling?"

"No one."

She tried to lower her arms and opened her eyes when she got to the end of the slack in the chains. She turned her face toward him. She didn't seemed surprised or frightened, but beyond that, he couldn't read her look.

He said, "I want you."

She smiled ever so subtly and tugged at the tether. She spread her legs beneath the bed clothes and arched her body.

He could almost feel her will him to pull the covers back and look. Part of him pointed his response as he reached to stroke her beneath the sheet.

She raised her body to meet his open hand. "How much?"

By way of answer, he threw the covers off and rolled up, looming over her on hands and knees so she could see for herself.

The sun poured over them, and he paused to stare as if the light had changed her into someone else. It had. The sudden intensity brought out a tinge of yellow-brown, the color of an old bruise, between her right breast and shoulder, above the armpit, just where a rifle stock would rest if she had fired a long gun. He touched the spot and asked, "What's this?"

He felt her tense. She looked at the place. "A bruise, I guess."

"How'd it happen?"

"I don't recall. Does it matter?"

Did it?

She shivered and he noticed goose flesh forming on her arms and thighs.

"Cold?"

Her eyes widened and she nodded. "But you could warm me."

Performance art. The nice woman he'd been playing with had suddenly become a demon. But that was part of the turn-on. He smiled and nodded and fumbled for the handcuff key on the bedside table.

FIFTY-TWO

It was 9:00 A.M. when Minorini woke again. His caller ID told him Haskel had called again—twice. He rolled over and found Joanne gone. A pair of handcuffs lay like a Bizarroland glass slipper on her side of the bed. He felt hung over, though he hadn't had any alcohol the night before. She was like cocaine, and he was addicted.

He knew he should quit cold turkey—lay the situation out for Butler and walk away. Fuck his career. Fuck the Bureau. Most of all, fuck Haskel, who—Minorini was sure—was the leak.

Minorini tapped on Butler's door and when he heard, "Come in," he entered and closed the door behind him.

Butler said, "I heard you made an impression last night. Who was the woman, someone from *a service*?" Butler gestured to a chair.

Minorini took it. "If your sources are any good, they told you a Circuit Court judge was introducing her to everyone."

"You're skating on thin ice. Until this Dossi thing is closed, she's a material witness."

Minorini ran a hand over his face. "Let me run something past you."

"Go ahead."

"I think it's fair to say that Dossi knew we were watching him, especially after the bomb attempt. So he wasn't going to try to hit Lessing himself. But we can assume he must've wanted her gone." Butler nodded. "So he hires Terry Finn to blow her up. Finn screws up; Dossi fires him."

"Tell me something I *don't* know."

"Let's say next Dossi hired Armand Wilson to do the job. Meanwhile, the mob's getting antsy. As long as Dossi's in our scopes, there's a chance we'll nail him for something and he'll offer to cut a deal."

"I'm with you. As long as Lessing was alive we just might have nailed him. But who killed Dossi?"

"Wilson."

"How did you arrive at that?"

"Wilson was a *mob* enforcer. I found evidence that Dossi hired him, but maybe he was really working for someone else, someone who had a grudge against Dossi, or who thought Dossi was getting too high-profile planting bombs in yuppie suburbs. Or maybe someone thought he was getting careless in his old age, letting a housewife with a camera take his picture. So when Dossi hired Wilson to get Lessing, maybe Wilson's real orders were to shoot Dossi. Then Lessing's no longer a threat to anyone so no one has to shoot her." He sat back in his seat.

"Nice theory. Wilson kills Dossi; we kill Wilson. No witnesses left. No loose ends."

"Thanks."

"But Wilson was a pro. It doesn't make sense that he'd start a gun fight with Federal officers."

"Unless he thought one of them would make sure he didn't live to cut a deal."

"Come on!"

Minorini leaned forward. "As you said, it's all too neat. I did some checking. Carlos, Dossi's chauffeur, told me he was off the day Siano was hit *and* the day Doris Davis was run down. I followed up on his alibis for those days—He *was* off; it wasn't him.

"Carlos also said that the day after Lessing took those pictures at the Daley Center, Dossi had him drive to an isolated forest preserve and get out of the car. Another car drove up—a limo—and Dossi got out of his car, into the limo. It had dark-tinted windows, no license plate, and the driver had on a hat and dark glasses. Carlos couldn't ID him.

"Dossi stayed in the car about half an hour, then had Carlos drive him home. Carlos said he was real pissed off about something for days."

"So? We knew we had a leak."

Minorini nodded. "The housekeeper also remembers the chauffeur being off and Dossi driving himself somewhere when Siano and Davis were hit."

"She sure?"

"Yeah. She's been marking off the days on her calendar till she can go home for a visit. She keeps her to-do list on it—she showed me. Some of the things she had to do used to get on Dossi's nerves, so she'd wait to do them when he was out. She also recalls Dossi being out of sorts after his trip to the Forest Preserve."

"When, presumably, he got the word he'd been recognized."

"Yeah. Fast-forward to the day we get the Jane Doe subpoena for Lessing. Manuela remembers Dossi getting a call from his 'cousin Guido' from New York. Dossi took the phone and told the caller he didn't *have* a cousin Guido, but in a little while, he went out. Carlos said he drove him to the Harold Washington Library. Thinks he wanted to make a private phone call."

"Go on."

"I checked the records for all the pay phones at the library." Minorini handed Butler a sheaf of photocopies, one of which had a time and phone number highlighted in yellow. "Finn's phone."

Butler glanced at the page. "Nice work."

"Look at the number above it."

Butler looked. The call had been placed to a 312 area code number thirty seconds before the call to Finn. The timing was pretty good circumstantial evidence that the same person made both calls.

"It looks familiar but I don't . . ."

"Yeah."

"But why would Dossi wait until Lessing was called to testify? If he knew about her before . . . ?"

"Lessing wasn't much of a threat to Dossi until they issued the first supoena. At that point, he hired Finn. After we took her into custody, and until we set our little trap, no one—not even Haskel—knew where she was except you and me and the Marshals."

"So until we set our trap and leaked the location, Dossi couldn't find her."

"Just on a hunch, I pulled the records for all the calls made on that library phone up to the day Dossi got nailed, and guess what?"

"I can't wait."

Minorini handed him another sheaf of photocopies. "That phone wasn't used much, fortunately, and there's no way to *prove* who made the calls, but we're all creatures of habit. . . . Carlos is pretty sure Dossi was in the library on the days I've highlighted. I've written the subscriber's name next to the numbers."

Butler paged through he sheets. There were numbers marked for the day before Minorini left for Florida, the day they decided to set the trap. One was to the 312 number, another—labeled "Wilson"—was from out of state. There was also a call to an 847 area code number labeled "Judge Hollander."

"Wouldn't our hypothetical informant tell Dossi we were setting a trap and where Lessing really was? Why would he send Wilson into a trap?"

"As I said before, I think his informant had another agenda."

"I'm sure you're gonna tell me what."

"Wilson didn't know he was walking into a trap. Whoever sent him to Wisconsin, wanted him dead—so he couldn't talk if he were caught."

"How could they know we'd *kill* Wilson?"

"Think about it," Minorini said, though he didn't, himself, want to consider a fellow officer killing for the mob. Especially not Haskel.

"But after we decided to go with this trap plan, *everybody* knew the location of the dummy safe house."

"Not everyone knew I was taking the kid out of state."

"How is that relevant?"

"Maybe Wilson already knew where we had Lessing stashed. I'm sure—from what I learned about him—he wouldn't hesitate for a second to kill Carver or Reilly or me, but the thing with Wilson was he wouldn't hit a kid, wouldn't even hit someone in front of a kid."

Butler nodded again. "So even if he knows, earlier, where Lessing is, he won't kill her with her kid around. He's gotta find her, then find a way to separate her from her kid. But when his informant tells him about your little Florida trip, he sees his chance."

"And if, as you said, someone wanted Dossi dead and no loose ends why not pay Wilson to kill Dossi too?

"Reilly told me Wilson yelled 'fuckin' double-cross' just before he opened fire. If she were the leak, I'm sure she wouldn't have mentioned that."

"Unless she thought Haskel would, and wanted to set him up or cover her ass."

"But her shot wasn't fatal."

"What did Haskel have to say?"

"Nothing."

Butler saw what he was getting at. "It's circumstantial."

"Yeah it's circumstantial. But whose cell phone do you think this is?" Minorini pointed to the 312 number on the printouts.

"Haskel's?"

"Bingo!"

"But if *he* was the leak, why wouldn't he tell Wilson about the trap?"

"Maybe he did. Maybe Wilson suspected it was a double-cross and went there to kill him."

Or maybe he went there thinking that's where she really was after he didn't find Joanne in Kenilworth!

"Speculation," Butler said. "How're we supposed to find out for sure?"

"I can confront Haskel with what I've figured out. If he's guilty, he'll have to do something about me."

"Don't do anything without backup."

224

. . .

There were just a few things that didn't fit the theory he'd outlined for Butler—the first snow plow job; the fact that Wilson wasn't known to use a rifle; Dossi's picture under the seat of his aunt's car; and Joanne's lie about Carver being there all night.

She had no alibi and plenty of motive. And he bet if he dug into it—or into the Grayslake landfill—he could prove she'd had a gun. The problem was, he didn't want to.

He went back to his office to think about how to set up a trap.

FIFTY-THREE

Haskel had graduated the academy the year after Minorini and spent the intervening time working his way up the food chain. He had been in Chicago only two years, the last six months of which he'd worked with Minorini. On Butler's authorization, Minorini got his personnel files and did a credit check. There was nothing in his background or Minorini's recollection that would explain him selling out. Like Minorini, he was single—though Haskel had never married—and had an apartment downtown, on the near South Side in Haskel's case.

Minorini spent the day discreetly investigating him, asking questions of fellow agents, secretaries, attorneys, court clerks, and cops. He even located and interviewed a former girlfriend. She said he was a jerk, like most of the men she'd dated, but not exceptionally awful. Apart from expensive taste in clothes and cars, and reckless driving habits, there wasn't anything to raise any flags. Except the phone calls. Haskel had had the same phone number since coming to Chicago.

The next round of inquiry was done in a couple of sports bars and restaurants where Minorini'd developed confidential informants. None of them had ever heard of Haskel; no one recognized his picture.

It was about 9:30 P.M. when Minorini exhausted the last of his leads and remembered he'd only had coffee and a donut to eat all day. The holiday traffic was thinning for the night, but parking was still problematic. He spied a semi-legal spot on Wabash and realized he wasn't far from Miller's. The pub had decent food and Bass on tap. He parked and went in.

He ordered steak and a pint at the bar, sipping the latter while he waited for the former. The place was full. He watched the waiters and bartenders, observed skaters from Skate on State, businessmen, college students, and a pair of young men trying to disguise the electricity arcing between them across their table.

Another Christmas in Chicago. It felt like home even though he hadn't any family here. He thought of Joanne and Sean and wondered.

An odd couple at a small table near the back caught his eye—shoppers by their packages—in an uncomfortable tryst. Not quite Jack Sprat and his wife. A tall, cadaverous man with thinning brown hair and eyes hidden behind thick-lensed wire rims. His overcoat was draped on the back of a vacant chair beneath his companion's full-length mink. His suit was expensive and conservative. In contrast, the woman's moneyed, no-taste glitz reminded Minorini of Bette Midler in her prime. She was perched on the edge of her chair with her right arm resting on the mink in a clear "See? Mine!" gesture. The fingers of her left hand danced a drum roll on the table-top, causing the diamonds on her wrist and ring finger to flash like a suburban cop's mars lights.

Minorini knew the man, though it took a minute to recall from where. He smiled to himself. Chance favors the prepared. . . . He signaled the waiter and watched him two-step between tables of well-lubricated carolers.

"Yes, sir?"

Minorini pointed to the couple and said, "I'd like to buy my friend and his lady another round."

"Sure."

Minorini watched the waiter make his way to the bar and confer with the bartender, who poured a double shot of Red Label over rocks in one glass, then mixed a number of ingredients to make a burgundy colored concoction in another.

The waiter walked over and put the drinks in front of the couple. When he pointed out their benefactor, Minorini nodded and raised his glass to mime a toast. The puzzlement on the man's face changed to panic as he worked out where they'd met. He said something to the woman—the first definitive gesture Minorini'd noticed. She looked uneasy, but she didn't argue as he rose and walked to the bar.

Minorini remembered him from an investigation of sports betting. He was an accountant, basically an honest citizen whose expensive lifestyle made him vulnerable to undue influence, or rather whose wife's extravagant demands made him look for supplemental income. Stopping in front of Minorini, he brought Jimmy Stewart to mind, facing down Liberty Valance against impossible odds.

"Relax," Minorini told him, "The statute of limitations has expired."

"What do you want?"

"Information."

The accountant waited.

"The favor you owe me."

The man looked stricken but he seemed to screw up his resolve. "I'm clean."

"Good for you."

"What do you *want*?"

"I'd like to know where I can find the answer man."

"He'd kill me if I told you."

"He'll never know."

The accountant thought about it for a moment. "Then we're quits?"

Minorini made a cross over his chest.

The accountant looked around, as if to see if anyone was watching, then he said, "He used to put in a lot of receipts for Smith and Wollensky."

Minorini called Butler at his home to report. "FYI, I've got one more interview to do tonight, then I'm calling it quits."

"What did you find out?"

"Nothing yet, but I have a line on someone who'd know if Haskel was into any heavy betting or drug use."

"Well, keep me posted."

Smith and Wollensky was at 318 North State, tucked under one of the twin Marina Towers along the River. Minorini timed his arrival so that the answer man—so called because of his photographic memory and knowledge of the city's action—was just finishing his brandy.

He pointed at Minorini with the index finger of the hand holding his brandy snifter. "You did me a favor once." His other hand held a fat cigar.

"No," Minorini said. "You got off because your accountant refused to be intimidated."

That wasn't accurate either. Minorini had pulled his punches during the interrogation because he hadn't wanted to set the accountant up with a felony record. The accountant had kids to support.

"Extortion. Or that's what you'd call it if anyone but the Feds did it."

Minorini shrugged.

"What can I do for you?"

Minorini took out Haskel's picture and handed it across the table. "You know this man?"

"Should I?" He studied the photo. "No."

"You ever have the opportunity to pass along information about a Federal investigation in progress?"

"Wouldn't that be illegal?"

"Off the record?"

"Off the record, if you told me what you're fishing for I might be able to tell you where to drop your line."

"Any rumors of a Federal agent for sale or on the pad."

The answer man smiled. "You have a leak." He studied his glass, rolling it to coat the sides with brandy. "Not recently. About two years ago there was a rumor—just a rumor—that someone with the FBI had run up a sizeable tab with a sports bookie. Shortly afterward, the bookie alleged to be involved in this interesting series of events claimed he'd sold the debt to a long-term investment broker."

"Name?"

"Gianni Dossi."

FIFTY-FOUR

Late as it was when Minorini pulled into his parking garage, the parking spaces near the elevator were all filled. The garage was stark and silent, unheated, but well lit in deference to security. It reminded him of *Twilight Zone* episodes. He left his car at the far end. His footsteps echoed as he walked back.

There was a man sitting on the edge of the raised concrete dais that kept motorists from driving into the elevator doors. He stood up when Minorini approached.

Haskel.

His coat was open and he seemed unaware of the cold that was turning his breath to steam. His suit and shirt were rumpled, his eyes just sufficiently unfocused to convince Minorini he'd been drinking.

"Paul, old buddy." Haskel's speech was slightly slurred. "You been avoiding me."

Minorini hadn't been, but it was a reasonable assumption. He hadn't returned Haskel's calls. "I've been trying to wrap things up so I can leave for Christmas."

"You're working on the assumption someone wants this solved. You know what you do when you assume? And is your dialing finger broke?"

"What are you doing here, Wayne?"

What he was doing was blocking Minorini's path to the elevator.

"Doorman wouldn't let me in. I figured you gotta come home sometime. And here you are."

"The question is, why are *you* here?"

"We gotta talk."

"Not tonight." He started to step around, but Haskel side-stepped and blocked him.

"Butler said you're investigating *me*. Why?"

"You like to bet on sports, Wayne?"

"Just the football pool." Haskel seemed to be sobering up fast. Fear did that. "Someone accuse me of illegal betting? Who?"

"Not betting, Wayne. Paying off bets with information."

"What?" Haskel seemed relieved. "That's bullshit! Who told you that?"

Minorini heard a slight scuffing sound, a shoe scraping on the pavement as its wearer pivoted. He and Haskel turned in unison. Butler stepped into view like a B-movie character, complete with 9-mm pistol.

Minorini was momentarily at a loss. "Butler?"

Butler pointed the gun at Haskel. "Paul's put together a very nice case against you, Wayne. Your weapon, please."

Suddenly stone sober, Haskel looked at Minorini. "What did I do?"

"You gave Joanne Lessing to Dossi."

"You're full of shit!" His breath puffed out like a silent shout. "How— What kind of crap is that?"

Butler said, "Agent Haskel, give me your gun."

"Why did you kill Wilson?" Minorini asked.

Haskel reached for his weapon. "Video games."

Butler said, "Slowly!"

"The phone records, Wayne," Minorini said. "Dossi called you."

Haskel looked incredulous. Then Minorini could see him start to put it together. He glared at Butler. Instead of handing him the gun he pointed it. At Butler.

Butler fired.

The report was deafening. The range was so close Butler couldn't have missed.

232

Haskel looked startled. Blood began to seep from a hole below his collar bone.

Minorini took advantage of his distraction to step forward and take his gun. He held it out where Butler could see it. "Don't shoot, Butler."

Haskel coughed. His eyes widened—fear. But not of Minorini.

Minorini looked at Butler, still pointing his gun at Haskel. "I've *got* his gun."

The gun in Butler's hand wobbled slightly, as if he was trying to aim but found it too heavy for accuracy. "He was going to shoot you."

Minorini spun Haskel's gun in his hand, slipping his finger through the guard.

Butler fired. Haskel jerked as the bullet struck.

"At least we know we've got the leak plugged," Butler said.

Everything was suddenly clear. Butler, not Haskel, had gotten in over his head! "You—"

Butler's gun was pointing at Minorini now. Minorini had a sudden epiphany about Joanne's dilemma. He pointed the gun at Butler and fired. The noise slammed his eardrums and reverberated around the garage.

Butler looked surprised. He stared at the bright red fluid leaking from a hole in his chest. Then he dropped to the floor. The gun clattered to the pavement and skittered under a car. Butler didn't move.

Minorini felt Haskel's neck for a carotid pulse and failed to find one. Haskel's eyes were fixed and dilated. Minorini closed them and began to recite every obscenity he'd ever known.

When the enormity of what he'd done hit him, he groaned. He put the gun in Haskel's hand and aimed it at the car behind Butler's remains. He put Haskel's dead finger over the trigger and squeezed. Then he took the weapon, grasping it by the slide, and put it on the floor.

He was sitting on the floor, holding Haskel's head on his lap, when the first officers on the scene came to lead him away.

FIFTY-FIVE

Agent Minorini, there's a call for you."

"Take a message."

"The woman's called three times this afternoon. She sounds worried."

"Who is it?"

"Joanne Lessing."

He'd been watching a Chicago detective and two special agents sweat the sports bookmaker. It wasn't much of a job. Once he was sure Butler couldn't retaliate, the bookie had been happy to talk. He'd sold Butler's debt to a private party. It hadn't been a face-to-face meet, but he understood the ultimate recipient of Butler's marker was Gianni Dossi. And with recent events, he figured Butler'd got his marker back.

Minorini told the secretary, "Thanks. I'll take it in my office."

The Chicago cops had kept him all night. They *did* let him wash the blood off. And one of the detectives escorted him upstairs to change his clothes—so they could confiscate what he'd been wearing—before they took him to Area 1 Detective Headquarters. They also took his gun.

They kept asking the same questions. He kept repeating what he'd told the first officers on the scene: Butler had set Haskel up to look like the leak in a recent investigation and the fall guy in Minorini's own murder. Why? Because Minorini was about to discover Butler was in the bag for the mob. We'll check that out. Please do. What was Minorini's connection to Haskel? Partners for the last six months. So sorry for your loss.

Minorini had been through it before—from the other side.

When they finally let him go, he'd headed back to 219 South Dearborn, where the ninth and tenth floors resembled a torn-open fire ants' nest. The Special Agent in charge of the Chicago office demanded to see him first. After he laid the same case out for him that he had for Butler, substituting Butler for Haskel as the bad guy, he'd added what he learned from the answer man. He had to repeat the story for the US Attorney, three US Marshals, and half a dozen special agents. He would also have to talk to Internal Affairs in the next day or so. In the meantime, he was on paid leave—not suspended unless they found something incriminating. He wondered what they'd make of Joanne. He didn't care.

"Minorini."

"Paul, it's Joanne. I just heard the news. Are you all right?"

"I'll live."

"I'm sorry about Agent Haskel."

"Yeah."

"Is there anything I can do?"

"Spend the night with me."

She hesitated. "I have to pick Sean up at O'Hare."

"You got your car back?"

"No. I was going to take the Blue Line out there, and we can get the Air Transport bus home."

"Let me drive you. What time's his flight? And what time do you get off?"

"I'm off at four. His flight's at 8:30 if it's on time."

"I'll pick you up at four."

They went to Paul's place. They were scarcely in the door before he was on her, kissing her with a ferocity and hunger that were frightening. He said, "I need you," and demonstrated by tearing off their shoes and coats, shedding his jacket and tie, fumbling in his fervor to undo her snaps and zippers.

When he had her naked, he pushed her onto the rug and began to kiss and nip her with an intensity that was less than gentle. He was overwhelming, touching her, tasting her, pushing his tongue then his fingers in her mouth and between her legs. He spread her arms and legs and went down on her. Frantically. Then he thrust his fingers in and played her until she cried, "Oh, God, Paul!"

He thrust himself inside and started banging her until she had to bite her wrist to keep from screaming from pain and ecstasy. She wrapped him with her arms and legs and squeezed. . . .

Afterward, he lay on top of her for a long time, face averted, supporting his weight on his forearms. When he rolled off, she felt the pang of loss. He lay facing her with his head resting on his outstretched arm, looking somewhere distant. Tears leaked from his eyes.

She reached over to wipe them with a fingertip. "Was he a close friend?"

Paul looked at her. "No, but I got him killed."

"We've all got twenty-twenty hindsight."

"And I killed Butler."

"Give it time. The pain fades."

"You speaking from experience?"

She drew a quick breath, not quite a gasp, then paused, then said, "Yes."

He didn't press her to explain. He pulled her to her feet and sat her on the couch. She folded her arms tightly across her chest and drew her legs up in front of her. She felt weird, sitting there, naked, watching him tuck in his shirt and zip his fly. He kissed her on the forehead, and she realized—for the first time since she'd met him—he was unarmed.

"What happened to your gun?"

"Chicago Police have it."

"Did you have to—?"

He looked at her—naked and vulnerable. Maybe he *would* tell her. Some day.

He shook his head. "Standard procedure whenever there's a shooting."

His laptop was next to the coffee table. He said "Excuse me a minute," and lifted it up and turned it on.

She nodded. She got up and picked up her clothes and headed for the john.

He typed the commands to delete the hidden files he'd compiled on the Dossi case, files detailing his suspicions about Joanne. It wouldn't be enough. Sooner or later, I.A. would ask to see his laptop. They'd look for deleted files. He opened the folder titled FLU and scanned the filenames. I LOVE U was too obvious, most of the others too benign. He finally settled on an obscure virus that he knew would keep rewriting gibberish on his hard drive until he reformatted it. Two or three rewrites and it would be safe to wipe the drive and reload his original software. The geeks could spend the rest of his lifetime trying to reconstruct his files. Joanne would be safe.

They'd just passed the junction on the Kennedy when Paul said, "You're awfully quiet."

"I feel like a death row inmate who's been suddenly reprieved."

"Funny, you don't act like it. Lighten up." He tilted his head to look at her. "You sure that's all?"

She smiled. "Maybe a little of it's . . . I'll miss you."

He looked as if he were trying to decipher the thoughts behind her confession. "You don't have to," he said quietly.

"Is that a proposal?"

"Yes."

"What brought about your change of mind?"

"Only women can change their minds?" He held her gaze until she was afraid he'd crash the car.

She blushed and smiled wryly. "You don't know me."

"Who of us ever knows anyone? At least I know you don't snore. Or hang your unmentionables around the house."

He was laughing at her reservations. A week ago, she'd have given . . . But that was in another lifetime.

"Why don't you come with us to my mother's for Christmas—get to know the family? You might change your mind back."

Why had she said that? A death wish?

He glanced at her, then back at the highway. "Is that a yes?"

"A definite maybe."

"Sure, if it wouldn't put your mother out too much."

"She won't be happy until I'm married again. She'll be delighted."

She wondered why he'd changed his mind. Surely not just because she was no longer a witness. He must know! Before this whole thing, he'd said he thought she was an innocent. He couldn't still think so. It must be that he *knew* who killed Dossi and didn't care. Or maybe losing a friend had made him rethink his priorities.

The idea that Joanne was a murderer didn't disturb him as it should. He wanted her, wanted to make children with her. He didn't wonder what kind of mother she would make. He knew she was a great mother—Sean was proof, a mother who would kill to keep her kids safe. And she was a lover to die for. . . .

Sean's plane was delayed an hour, and when it finally pulled up at the gate, he was one of the first off. He almost knocked Joanne over in his hurry to hug her. Then he noticed Minorini and said, "I guess my ma's not a witness any more."

"You ever thought of a career as a detective?"

After Paul dropped them at the house, when they were settled in the living room with mugs of hot cocoa, Sean recounted his adventures in the keys. "What happened while I was gone?"

"I fell in love."

"Oh. OH!" He thought about it, looking confused, then said, "Congratulations. I think."

"Paul's coming to the farm with us for Christmas. What do you think of that?"

"I dunno. It's all right, I guess. You gonna marry him?"

"Do you mind?"

"Naw. I'll be going away to school in a couple years. I'm not gonna be around to take care of you forever."

FIFTY-SIX

When Minorini arrived at the Lessings's the morning they'd agreed to leave for the farm, there was no car in the carport. Joanne had told him she'd gotten it back, so he had to wonder.

Sean looked relieved to see him when he opened the door. "Mom went to the police station," he said. "They called and said they *really* needed to talk to her about that guy that got shot."

"Did they threaten to arrest her?"

"I don't think so, but she didn't think she had a choice about going."

That's how they did it. They didn't have to read you your rights if you weren't in custody.

"I'll go check it out."

The dispatcher buzzed Minorini into the back of the station and told him where to find Detective Gray. Gray was standing in the hall outside the interview room.

"I was just about to interrogate a suspect," he said. "Care to watch?"

Gray watched Minorini closely as he stepped aside to let him see the suspect. Joanne was sitting inside, behind the two-way mirror. He'd expected it. He tried to keep his expression neutral, interested but not personally involved. There wasn't anything he could do in any case. He'd warned her. He was sure she'd got the point. What she did next was up to her. He'd be seen as complicit if he protested. Maybe also if she gave it up, but certainly if he interfered.

And he wanted to see if she had the right stuff. She could do the crime, but could she live with it? Could she live with the accusation? If not, maybe she wasn't the one for him. It was a crapshoot, but he felt lucky. He felt like he'd picked the right lottery numbers. He smiled and told Gray, "Have at it."

Gray seemed almost disappointed, but he just nodded and went into the room. Joanne had seemed curiously calm, not a good sign since it was commonplace that only the guilty are comfortable in custody. Now she looked wary.

Gray said, "Sorry to keep you waiting so long, Ms. Lessing."

She shrugged. "What's this about?"

"I'd like to ask you where you were the night Gianni Dossi was shot. You remember the date."

"Are you asking me if I killed Mr. Dossi?"

"Did you?"

"Am I under arrest?"

"No."

"Why would you ask me such a thing?"

"We've got a list of people with a reason to want Dossi dead. We're trying to narrow it down by eliminating whoever we can."

"I see. And if I had killed him—somehow—you think I'd admit it to you?"

Gray didn't say anything.

Joanne stood up. "I'd like to go now."

On the other side of the mirror, Minorini was saying, "Yes!"

He knew that men of integrity would never condone what she had done, even to save their lives. But he'd been with the Bureau too long to have such scruples. What she'd done—though premeditated—was closer to the spirit of self-defense than Haskel's "justified" shooting of Wilson. And not even in the same ballpark as what Butler, or Minorini himself, had done. Furthermore, her ac-

241

tion would cost her far more dearly. She'd never go to jail, but she'd have it hanging over her the rest of her life.

As soon as she was out the door Gray said, "You and I both know she must've done it."

"Why? Because she benefited and we don't have a viable suspect?"

"We don't have *any* other suspect."

"Impossible!"

"Why? She's a hunter—you've seen her pictures. She's a crack shot. I talked to two or three people she went to high school with—they all said so. And she has the best motive there is."

"Yeah, but both of her brothers told me she never hunted with a gun—except once, when her old man dragged her along and she screwed up the hunt for everyone."

"What is it? You got a thing for her? Why? 'Cause she's the struggling single mom? Or 'cause you'd like to get in her pants?"

"She's just the last in a long line of innocents the Bureau's fucked over. And she's raised her kid to be a nice, decent human being in spite of his having a jag-off for an old man. I don't think she needs any more grief. Especially for something you haven't any evidence she had anything to do with."

"You took her to the morgue," Gray said. "Why?"

"To ID Siano's shooter. You've been tailing me. Why?"

"I'd give a month's pay to have seen her reaction. She pass out? Or laugh? Or ask if she should get a lawyer?"

"None of the above."

"And based on 'none of the above' you're prepared to vouch for her?"

Minorini didn't answer.

"You stayed pretty late after you took her home," Gray said.

"Am I a suspect too?"

"You got an alibi?"

"As a matter of fact, I do. And *she* was in the custody of a US Marshal."

"Carver, wasn't it? Funny. Half a dozen members of the delivery room staff told me he was with his wife delivering their baby when Dossi was blown away."

Damn, he was good! "Okay, but proving Lessing hasn't got an alibi's a long way from proving she did the hit. It would, however, put a poor SOB with a family to support out of work."

"That's the only reason you'd lie about Lessing's alibi?"

Minorini relaxed inwardly. "I've known Carver since I came to Chicago, and he's a straight shooter. As soon as he heard about Dossi, he told me what he'd done. I didn't even think about it. I told him, since Lessing wasn't hurt, no harm no foul. Just keep his mouth shut and forget it."

"You didn't tell him to lie if anyone asked?"

"Suborning perjury isn't part of my job description."

"Lucky for both of you."

"What does that mean?"

"I'm inclined to believe Carver, and his story supports what you've told me."

"So?"

"So I'm prepared to leave Carver out of it unless I get evidence I can use against Lessing."

Gray was watching him, humming. Minorini recognized the tune: "When a man loves a woman . . ."

"Seems like we got a real whodunit on our hands," Gray said. "What do you think?"

"I'd rather not speculate."

"FBI to the end, huhn? Well, no matter. No hurry. No statute of limitations on murder."

It was obvious *Gray* had connected all the dots.

FIFTY-SEVEN

The trip south was colder than it had been over Thanksgiving. Dry salt on the road—powdery. The sky seemed farther away; snow covered the corn stubble and all but the tips of the roadside grasses.

Paul and Sean talked about football—which neither seemed to follow passionately. There was a wariness between them that she hadn't noticed at the safe house. They seemed to be trying almost too hard to be pals—for her sake, she was sure. It was oddly uncomfortable. They were all relieved when they spotted the mailbox marked SCHROEDER.

The family greeted her pretty much as they had in November, perhaps a little more urgently because of her narrow escape. They were naturally curious about Paul, whom Allen and Ken had met before. She wondered why Paul hadn't mentioned that. But then, he seemed to want to fit in. He probably didn't want to make anyone uncomfortable by bringing it up.

At sunset, they all watched the red disk slip from a lemon-ice sky, below an icy gold horizon. Then the teenagers piled into a car to go see a movie; the adults settled in to watch one on the VCR.

After dinner, Paul parked in front of the TV with the guys while the women did the washing up. Their topic of conversation was Joanne's new beau, of course. Kate and Mary were almost too enthusiastic. When they'd dried the last plate, Elizabeth sent them to join their husbands and poured two cups of coffee. She pointed to a chair at the kitchen table and asked Joanne to sit.

"What's up, ma?"

"Joanne, how well do you know this man?"

"Well enough. I thought you'd like him."

"He's very nice, but are you sure you're not just feeling gratitude because he saved your life?"

He didn't save my life, she thought. I did. What she said was, "I'm sure. And I'm sure he loves me."

Elizabeth nodded. "That's that, then."

Joanne sent Sean to bed at eleven. The others turned in soon after, leaving her and Paul to watch the fire die. He was beautiful in firelight. She had to fight the urge to grab a camera.

He got up and put another log on, then took a little leather pouch from his pocket. He opened it in front of her with a flourish, and dumped the contents in her hand.

The diamond that landed on her palm must've been a full carat, sparkling like sunlit ice in the fire light. It held her attention like a magic spell. He was saying, "Let's make this official."

She let him take it from her palm and slip it on her finger as smoothly as he'd cuff one of the suspects he'd tracked down.

She was tired of going it alone. And he knew. He knew and wanted her anyway. Or maybe he wanted her *because* he knew. She didn't care. He wanted her.

He kissed her then, tentatively at first, then more passionately, until she felt light-headed. He undressed them both, and they made love on the rug. Afterwards, he lay looking thoughtfully at the fire while she put on his shirt and went to look out at the snow.

It was so cold. Cold as the trigger of her father's gun. She felt a déjà vu. Cold as guilt.

Out of the corner of her eye, she saw him take something from the wallet in his pants pocket and throw it in the fire. A small photograph.

It was browned almost beyond recognition by the time she crossed to the fireplace, but in the moment before flames burst from it she recognized Gianni Dossi—she was certain. One of her own pictures, taken at Dossi's house. Paul had had it all along.

245

"What was that?" she said.

"Nothing important."

The flame vanished as suddenly as it appeared, its gold fading to red ember. The ash was carried upward by the heat.

He laced his fingers through hers and pulled her down next to him. She was happy. In the red glow of the firelight, she could no longer see blood on their hands.

BOOKS BY A. J. CRONIN

DESMONDE

DESMONDE

BY A. J. CRONIN

Little, Brown and Company
Boston—Toronto

FIRST EDITION

T 08/75

LIBRARY OF CONGRESS CATALOGING IN PUBLICATION DATA

Cronin, Archibald Joseph, 1896–
   Desmonde.

   I. Title.
PZ3.C8772De4   [PR6005.R68]   823'.9'12   75-8649
ISBN 0-316-16163-2

Design by Barbara Bell Pitnof

ONE

1

On a windy March day early in the century, I was seated in the office of the prefect of studies, awaiting admission to the Jesuit Day School of Saint Ignatius and, after seven rough years in the free Council schools of the city of Winton, rather glad to be there. At my birth, my father, in the first flush of paternity, filled, too, with sanguine expectations of his own future, had entered me for Stonyhurst. When he died, six years later, after a painful and protracted illness, his laudable ambition remained unfulfilled: he left barely enough to pay the doctors and the undertaker.

Yet Saint Ignatius was not a bad substitute for the parent Lancashire institution. It was built, with its adjacent church, on an eminence not far from the city center, dedicated to the education of sons of the Catholic bourgeoisie and indeed, since the fees were moderate, of the working class. All the masters were Jesuit priests, for the most part men of birth and breeding, aloof, after the manner of the Order, and to me so intimidating that I sprang to my feet as the door opened behind me.

But it was another boy who strolled in, quite unperturbed, indeed, completely at ease. I sat down again and, with a half-smile, he seated himself beside me. Infinitely better dressed than I, he had on a dark flannel suit of distinguished cut, fine socks and shining shoes, a spotless soft white shirt set off by a striped green and black tie which I judged, correctly, to be his prep school colors. A linen handkerchief just peeped from his breast pocket, and as if this were not enough, a small cornflower was tucked, and worn with an air of scornful detachment, into his buttonhole. He was, moreover, so devastatingly good-looking, with his pale complexion, soft blond hair and flax-blue eyes, that I became more and more conscious, not only of my flaming crop of red hair, freckles, and long nose, but of my painfully poor attire: old flannel bags, blue jersey knitted by my mother, and a crack in the toecap of my wornout shoe which I had just acquired by a reckless punt at a ball that bounced from the schoolyard as I came up the hill. In fact, I hated him, and decided to pick a fight with him at the first opportunity.

Suddenly he stunned me by breaking the silence of that august book-lined chamber.

"Boring, isn't it. Punctuality is not the politeness of Jesuits." He began to sing.

" 'They left us in the lurch, waitin' at the church.' " Then, "I bet Beauchamp's in the pantry having his elevenses. Frightful guzzler, I believe. But terribly cultured. Old Etonian. Convert, of course."

He began again, rather more loudly: " 'They left me in the lurch, waiting at the church . . .' "

At that moment the door swung open and there swept in a fine, massive, imperious figure, well-banded by his soutane which, however, failed to conceal a pronounced and advancing corpulence. In his right hand he was carrying a plate on which reposed a large double cheese sandwich. This he placed on his desk, deftly covered with a napkin taken from his drawer. He then sat down rather heavily, with the words, half-excusatory, half an apostrophe:

"Edere oportet ut vivas."

"Non vivere ut edas," murmured the little snob beside me.

"Good," said the prelate who was, indeed, the redoubtable Father Beauchamp. "But, though you know your Cicero, uncalled for." He paused, looking from one to the other. "As I approached the sanctuary of my study I was greeted by most un-Lydian strains . . ."

[4]

"I am the culprit, reverend sir," my companion acknowledged very fairly. "I have the absurd habit, almost unconscious, when I am nervous or waiting on someone who is late, of erupting into song . . ."

"Indeed!" said Beauchamp grimly. "Then stand up and erupt now. But nothing vulgar, I beg of you."

I suppressed a gleeful chuckle. Now the little prig must really make an ass of himself. He got slowly to his feet. There was a pause. The pause lengthened. Then, fixing his gaze above Beauchamp's head, he began to sing.

It was the *Panis Angelicus,* that most lovely and difficult Latin hymn. And as the sweet and moving words filled the room, ascending, as it were, to Heaven, the stupid smile faded from my face. Never, never had I heard it sung so beautifully as now: clear, true, entrancing. Compelled, I gave myself to it. When it was over a profound, momentous silence followed.

I was stunned, dumbfounded. Although my knowledge of music was then extremely limited, I had enough good taste to recognize that the little dressed-up prodigy had a truly beautiful, an exceptional, a spectacular voice! Beauchamp too was obviously deeply impressed.

"Ha. Hum," he said, and again, "Ha. Hum. We must certainly speak of you to our choirmaster, the good Father Roberts." He paused. "You must be the Fitzgerald boy."

"I am Desmonde Fitzgerald. The Desmonde written with a final 'e.' "

"It shall be so inscribed," Father Beauchamp answered with unexpected mildness. "I have had in fact much correspondence with your father over the years. A most erudite and distinguished scholar. It was from him that I got my Trinity College Apocalypse, the Roxburgh Club's rare and much prized edition." He paused. "But when he wrote me some months before his death, he said you were to go to Downside."

"Maternal fondness has kept me at home, sir. And inflicted me upon you. Perhaps to the relief of the Benedictines."

"So you are now living in Winton?"

[5]

"My mother, who is Scottish, wished to return to her native land. She has taken a house in Overtown Crescent."

"A delightful situation, overlooking the park. I shall certainly call upon her . . . perhaps she will give me tea." A reflective look came over his face, and he moistened his lips. "As a Scot she will know of these delicious little iced French cakes, a speciality of the town. A survival, indeed, of the Old Alliance."

"I shall ensure, sir," Desmonde answered gravely, "that a generous supply is on hand for your visit."

"Good. Good. Ha. Hum." He turned, inspecting me from beneath his enormous eyebrows. "And now you?"

Thoroughly embittered by this glowing and intimate interchange, which had made me feel more than ever an outsider, I muttered from between clenched teeth.

"I am merely Cronin."

He seemed rather to like this. He beamed, almost benignantly.

"Ah, yes. You are coming to us on the Kelvin Scholarship." He leaned forward to inspect an open folder on his desk. "As, despite your length, you seem rather a 'modest crimson-tippit' youth, would it help your self-esteem to know that your papers were quite exceptional? Father Jaeger, who corrected for the examination, so regarded them. Does that please you?"

"It will please my mother when I tell her."

"What a good answer! Now you are no longer 'merely,' but most admirably, Cronin." He looked me up and down, kindly, not missing my burst shoe. "And at your convenience you may call on the bursar for the first instalment of your scholarship. The office is open from two till five."

The rich aroma of new-baked bread had now penetrated the napkin and was deliciously permeating the room. I was already drooling, and it became clear that the good prefect of studies was anxious to get on with his sandwich. Briefly, therefore, he informed us that we were both allocated to the upper fourth form, instructed us as to how we might reach the classroom, and dismissed us.

But as we passed his desk on the way out, he reached out a

huge hand and deftly picked the flower from Fitzgerald's buttonhole.

"During school hours, no floral decorations, if you please."

Desmonde flushed but said nothing, merely inclined his head.

But as we came out of the study into the corridor my companion smiled.

"That's Beauchamp for you. Wonderful brain. Insatiable stomach! I'll bet he makes a salad of my cornflower. And what an idiot I was to sing for him. Now I am stuck with another choir. After three years as the bleeding prima donna of my prep school."

"Perhaps your voice will break?" I suggested consolingly.

"It has done, very early. Now I am a beastly, confirmed Don Giovanni, a Mario, a Pinkerton, a blasted Papageno." Taking my arm, "I hope you'll like me, as we're to be together. I think I might like you. That 'merely' was very pretty. Do you play chess?"

"I play football," I said. "Do you?"

"Never kicked a ball in my life. But I'll come and watch you. I say, why don't we nip over for a quiet ginger beer before we start the toil of the day. There's a good-looking bun shop across the way."

"I'm stony," I said coldly.

"Haven't I asked you? Do come."

He guided me across the street to what was, in fact, a baker's shop which had come to be regarded as the tuck-shop of the school. Inside it was pleasantly cozy. We sat down.

"Two Schweppes stone gingers please, as cool as possible, and each with a slice of lemon, if you happen to have such a thing."

The woman behind the counter gave him an odd look, but a few moments later two full foaming glasses appeared, each with a slice of lemon swimming on top.

"Thank you, madam. May I pay you?"

He paid. It was a long time since I had enjoyed a ginger beer. The first long, cool draught was mellowing.

"Good, isn't it?" He smiled. "The citron does improve it. Now tell me about yourself. Apart from scoring goals, what do you want to do?"

I told him I hoped to try for a university scholarship and if lucky to go in for medicine. "What about you?"

He immediately became serious.

"I want very much to become a priest. And it would please my mother, too. She is a very dear, pious person." He smiled. "So when you are in Harley Street I shall be a Cardinal in Rome. Those red hats are terribly becoming!"

We both burst out laughing. Impossible to resist him. Half an hour ago I was itching to knock his block off. Now he had won me over. I liked him immensely. He drained his glass.

"Shall we have another foaming tankard?"

I felt my face getting very red. But I said very firmly:

"I'm sorry Fitzgerald, I can't stand you one back. And as I don't intend sponging upon you in future I must tell you that we, my mother and I, are frightfully hard up."

He made sympathetic mutterings. I saw he was dying to ask me more, but I had no wish to enlighten him further. And, indeed, he had the good taste not to press me. He said:

"All the best saints were poor, and loved poverty."

"They can have it," I said.

He smiled. "Anyway . . . for Heaven's sake don't let it interfere with our friendship."

Five minutes later when we left the shop, I made no objection when he took my arm and said:

"It's rather early, but would it bore you if we first-named each other? I do hate being called Fitzgerald. All we Fitzes are almost certainly descended from Charles the Second's bastards. He threw Fitzes at them with the *bâton sinistre*. It's a repulsive thought. I much prefer Desmonde, provided you never, never call me Des. What's yours?"

"I have a perfectly horrible name. I was called Archibald as a vain propitiation, quite useless, to my Montgomerie grandfather. And Joseph in honor of the saint. The combination is ludicrous. So I like to be known simply as A. J."

"But that's a delightful combination! A. J. Balfour, A. J. Cronin. I foresee fame for you."

We entered the classroom. He gave me a pleased look when we saw that our desks were together.

2

Desmonde's father had been a bookseller. But no modern novel, still less a paperback, had ever been seen to enter the precincts of the dusty little diamond-paned shop tucked away in a corner of the Dublin Quays, and known throughout Europe and beyond, as a storehouse of rare old volumes, special editions of the fine arts, historical pamphlets, the transactions of learned societies and suchlike treasures, sought after by intelligent collectors with an eye for something special at rather less than the outrageous prices demanded in London or New York.

Although he had not made a fortune—as he often told his clients when making a deal — Fitzgerald was comfortably situated and, twelve years older than his wife, he had prudently secured her future by a double life-endowment policy, which would afford her a substantial annual income on his death — an event which had in fact recently occurred.

His widow, Elizabeth, was Scottish, a Lanarkshire woman who had never been quite at home by the turgid waters of the Liffey. After a decent interval which had enabled her to sell the house and to secure a reasonable sum for the stock and goodwill of the business, she had come to Winton where, with the facility of a returned native, she had quickly found the small delightful terrace house to which Desmonde had referred when the good Father Beauchamp invited himself to tea. With a doting mother,

Desmonde had everything he might desire: fine clothes, pocket-money *ad libitum,* a new bicycle to spin down to school . . .

How different was my situation. My mother, daughter of a prosperous Ayrshire farmer, had been disowned by her family when she ran off with my Irish father and, the greater crime, became a Roman Catholic. After his death, persistence in this faith had killed all chance of reconciliation. But my brave little mother was not easily defeated. After a brief course of instruction she secured a post as a Health Visitor to the Winton Corporation. Her work took her to the notorious Anderson district of the city, slum areas riddled with poverty and destitution, where so many of the children were blighted and deformed by rickets. This splendid though exacting work suited my mother's cheerful and energetic temperament. The pay, scarcely commensurate with the effort and the results obtained, was precisely two pounds a week. After deduction of two shillings and sixpence for superannuation tax and a further seven and sixpence as weekly rental for our two-room "flat," precisely thirty shillings remained to feed, clothe, and maintain my mother and myself until the next twice-blessed payday came along. But let it not be imagined that we were miserable and starved in our sparsely furnished "room and kitchen" four flights up, interminable steps which I climbed at the trot, knowing that I was going home, and that always there would be something to eat there for a hungry boy. There was porridge in the morning, and if necessary in the evening, varied by that inimitable Scottish dish, pease brose and buttermilk, and Scots broth made from marrow bones and stiff with vegetables, home-baked scones or bannocks, and at the weekend a joint of beef, which after Sunday manifested itself on succeeding days as Hot Pot or Shepherd's Pie. Nor must I forget the sack of potatoes which arrived unfailingly every August, sent surreptitiously by an old worker on the parental farm. These were pilfered goods and how sweet they were, big floury King Edwards, baked in the oven and served with a pat of butter — I ate even the skin.

Nevertheless, my style and condition of life differed so

markedly from the ease and comfort of Desmonde's existence that our continued and growing friendship became all the more remarkable. We met always with such a sense of joy and renewal, never a trace of superiority on his side or envy upon mine, though he had spun down on his new Raleigh bicycle while I had walked the two miles to school because I had not a halfpenny for the tram.

Close friendships are usually frowned upon, if not discouraged, in most Jesuit institutions. But as Desmonde and I moved up through the various forms, increasingly devoted to each other, there was never a hint of anything suspect in our relationship. I was obviously not the type for a love match — I had gone almost immediately into the football team where, as center half, my genius for rough play had been observed and commended, while Desmonde, under his lighthearted charm, had revealed himself as a postulant, seriously intent upon his vocation. Every morning, before classes began, he was in church for Mass and Holy Communion. He persuaded me to join the Sodality, toward which I had only the slightest leanings. And as the school went down for various services at such times as Easter and Holy Week, kneeling beside him, I would see tears stream from his eyes, fixed upon the crucifix above the altar.

Desmonde was generally liked by the fathers, and with Father Roberts he was an especial favorite, regarded indeed as a gift from Heaven. With his fellow students he was too exceptional to be popular, being regarded by some as a snob and by others as something of a freak. I am obliged to confess that but for me he might have suffered many indignities from the tougher element in our little community.

But for all his sensitivity, he was not a coward. On one occasion, when cornered by a group of rowdies, scurrilously taunted, and invited to defend himself, he put his hands in his pockets and, with a smile, advanced his face invitingly.

"I can't fight you. But if you want to give me a bloody nose, just go ahead."

[12]

For a moment, a petrifying surprise held the group motionless, an open-mouthed still life. Then mutterings broke out in the horrendous Doric of Winton which could be construed as follows:

"He's no feart . . . don't hit him, Wullie . . . lee him alane . . ." remarks suddenly giving way to wild shouts of laughter, less derisory than flattering to Desmonde, who bowed politely, and, his hands still in his pockets, walked quietly away. But I feel sure that his heart was beating like mad as he seated himself on the low stone boundary wall with his back to the playground. This was his favorite seat during recreation. He never took part in our rough-and-tumble games, since he had never learned to kick or control a football. But on this perch, disdainfully he read the Office of the Day or something from Livy, his favorite author. His main preoccupation, however, was to watch the ebb and flow of life in the narrow little street, to drop a coin in the hand of any beggar, deemed legitimate, who importuned him, and above all, especially when the wind blew hard, as it frequently did on the steep hill, to keep an alert weather eye open for the straw-hatted, blue-uniformed girls who made their way, up and down, to the adjacent convent school.

These girls, all from good-class homes, were naturally regarded by the boys as chattering intruders to be ignored with lowered or averted eyes. Desmonde, however, had no such inhibitions. He studied them with curious, impartial detachment, as one might regard a strange, aboriginal race, and his comments, derisory, often amusing, were certainly devoid of amorous yearning.

"Here comes little tubby. I say, doesn't she waddle! And there's mother's darling, note the curly curls. Ribbons too, bless her. Oh, la la! Here's the tall blond effort. Rather a smasher, but for those enormous feet!"

This was merely schoolboy nonsense but, on days of real turbulence when sudden gusts swirled downhill, sending hats skimming and tempestuous petticoats ballooning to expose chaste blue serge knickers, I felt that he was carrying the game too far and that it evinced, perhaps, an unrealized attraction toward the other sex. Whether or not, it did become apparent, from bright-eyed side glances and suppressed giggles, that this frieze of young girls had become emotionally aware of the neat, nonchalant young Apollo perched upon the wall, who often produced from a side pocket the forbidden cornflower and tucked it in his buttonhole.

Only one person in the school seemed actively to dislike Desmonde: Father Jaeger, who took the fifth form and sponsored and trained the football team, a short, tough, ruddy, perennially active little man to whom I soon became devoted, and who in his turn seemed to have some interest in me. One day, as I came into his study he suddenly remarked:

"You're rather intimate with Fitzgerald."

"Yes, we are good friends."

"I don't like soft boys. Have you seen how he sits on the wall staring at the convent girls on their way up to school?"

I checked my reply. No one but an idiot argued with Jaeger. I merely said:

"That wall game is all fun. He's terribly good. Daily communicant . . ."

"That makes it all the more dangerous. A soft spot in that apple. I foresee great trouble ahead for your pretty, pious friend."

There the matter ended. Using the sleeve of his old soutane, he began to polish his little briar pipe — his one indulgence — and, clenching it between his teeth, unlit, since it was Lent, he launched into his favorite topic: the necessity for a man to keep himself clean, hard, and fit.

A passionate believer in physical fitness, he perennially greeted the dawn with an ice-cold bath followed by a series of Sandow exercises, and so influenced me that I adopted the habit and followed it faithfully until I became old, when I was tactfully admonished to drop it. In his youth, rumor had it, Jaeger had played for Preston North End. Certainly he was madly keen on the game, worked hard with the team, came to all our matches, and nourished the wild ambition that Saint Ignatius might one day win that most coveted trophy, the Scottish Schools Shield.

3

Yet Father Jaeger must surely have been mollified, surely Desmonde redeemed himself, when, quite out of character, he suddenly became a regular supporter of the school team. On Saturday mornings he would meet me at the corner of Radnor Street for the tram that bore us to Annesland in the outskirts of the city, where the playing field was situated. During the game he posted himself behind the goal of our opponents and when that citadel was pierced, particularly by a shot from my ruthless boot, he broke into an excited variation of the Irish jig.

When Jaeger made me captain of the team in my second term, he would have me to his little study upstairs in the presbytery to discuss tactics before and after each game. Long before it became standard practice in the professional leagues he insisted that the center half — myself — should not only act as a defender but go forward with the ball well into enemy territory and himself have a shot at the goal. And it was indeed this advice which enabled me, not only to delight my friend, but to win games that might otherwise have been lost.

After the game, whether triumphant or despondent, Desmonde took me back to his house for lunch, where quite often I would find my mother. Desmonde, with his tact and sensitive fine feeling, had brought our surviving parents together, not a difficult matter since both attended the Sunday High Mass at Saint Ignatius, and it was at once evident that the two women liked each other. I had reason to believe, too, without being presumptuous, that Mrs. Fitzgerald approved of my friendship with her son.

What pleasant occasions these were — always a delicious meal, nicely served in that delightful, beautifully furnished, sunny room overlooking the park. And what a treat, especially for my dear mother who had known such things in the past and lacked them for so many years. After coffee the two women went to the window seat to chat, or to take up some sewing which Mrs. Fitzgerald, who worked for the church, could always provide, while Desmonde and I took off on our weekly pilgrimage across the Park to the Municipal Art Gallery, a fine modern building of red sandstone not far from the Winton University. Already we knew it well and, as a concession to me, we went immediately to the room of the French Impressionists, sat down, and gave ourselves once again to the splendor of some twenty examples of this period. Best of all I loved the Gauguin: two native women seated on the beach against a gorgeous complex of tropic jungle.

"Painted during his first visit to Tahiti," Desmonde murmured.

But my gaze was now on the delicious little Sisley of the Seine at Passy, moving slowly to the equally delicious Vuillard, all lemon and deep purple, then to the wonderful Degas, *La Blanchisseuse,* the Utrillo, a simple street of a Paris faubourg, empty of people but full, oh, so full of Utrillo.

"His best period," whispered my mentor. "Early, when he mixed plaster with his paint."

But I wasn't listening, absorbing the atmosphere of canvases I now knew so well and coveted so avidly that I exclaimed:

"How I would love . . . to have just one . . . like these . . . in my room. So that I might see it, refresh myself with it, at any moment of the day or night."

Desmonde gave me an odd, serious look.

"You will have not one, A. J., but at least a dozen, in your home, within twenty years from now."

I laughed. This extravagant speculation was too absurd to demand an answer. Desmonde rebuked me with a faint smile.

He then stood up, deciding I'd had enough of the Impressionists, and moved into the corridor. I followed him to the end room given over to Italian paintings of the early and high Renaissance. These Florentine and Siennese religious compositions did not greatly interest me. I sat on the central settee while he made his way slowly around the circular room, stopping now at some particular favorite, peering close, breathing ecstatically, casting his eyes up to heaven.

"You're being dramatic, Desmonde," I said.

"No, A. J. These lovely old treasures, with their spiritual force, their simple grandeur of conception, induce in me a heavenly state of being. Look at this Piero della Francesca, and this heavenly Madonna, obviously the center of a three-part altarpiece, Florentine school about 1500, and this *Pietà* by Simone Martini. Pity they don't have a Fra Angelico, you'd like that, A. J. Ah, this is my most ecstatic: *The Annunciation*, by Bartolommeo de la Porta."

"Why de la Porta?"

"He lived near the Porta Romana. In 1475. A friend of Raphael. I love it so much I managed to get a little reproduction."

I waited with exemplary patience while he continued to rhapsodize, until I heard the strains of the orchestra tuning up in the concert hall below. I then stood up.

"Music, maestro."

He smiled, nodded, took my arm as we went down the wide stone staircase to the splendid theater which a benignant Corporation had provided for the citizens of Winton, and where on many Saturday afternoons the Scottish orchestra might be heard, free of charge, in programs of good music.

As we entered, Desmonde took one of the typewritten sheets at the door.

"Dash!" he exclaimed as we seated ourselves at the back of the poorly filled hall. "No Vivaldi. No Scarlatti. No Cherubini."

[18]

"But glorious Tchaikovsky, Prokofiev, and smashing, heavenly Moussorgsky."

"Your beastly Russians."

"They induce in me a state of heavenly being!"

He laughed, then was silent. The conductor had appeared, greeted by mild hand-clapping, and the first strains of the ballet, *Love of Three Oranges,* swept toward us.

This orchestra, then beginning to be known in Europe and the United States, was of remarkable quality for a provincial city. The Tchaikovsky was beautifully played, and after the interval, *Pictures at an Exhibition* was magnificent.

When the last crashing notes had died we sat for a moment, recovering, silent, until Desmonde said moodily:

"Nothing for us at the Kings this week, I'm afraid."

"What's on?"

"One of these idiotic musical comedies, *Maid of the Mountains,* I believe. What mountains? Everest, Kanchenjunga? or Pook's Hill? However," he added, "Mother had word from Dublin that the Carl Rosa company will be here quite soon."

"Good!" This was another of our passions, secret, and never to be divulged at school where undoubtedly we should be mocked. We both loved opera, and when it was in town would go on Saturday nights, to the sixpenny gallery seats in the Kings Theater. I insisted on this sixpenny outlay, all I could afford, but occasionally Desmonde, who detested the gallery, would produce two tickets for the stalls, which he tried to persuade me were complimentary, obtained by his mother.

"The Carl Rosa was jolly good last month," I said. "I did love the Donizetti."

"*Lucia di Lammermoor.*" Desmonde smiled. "Being a Scot, you would!"

"That girl was really superb. The Bridal Aria is jolly difficult."

"I'm glad you say Bridal, A. J. Crude to call it Mad Song. Yes, she's Geraldine Moore. Quite the toast of the town in Dublin."

"She's a darling, so young and beautiful."

"I shall certainly tell her that, A. J.," Desmonde said gravely, "when I meet her."

We both laughed. How could we foresee that this lovely and talented woman would play a major part in Desmonde's future, admittedly hectic, career.

Most of the audience had now filed out — we usually waited, since Desmonde hated to "crush out with the mob" — so I now glanced at him.

"Tea?"

He smiled: "Delighted, A. J."

My mother, from the beginning of our friendship with the Fitzgeralds, had said: "We must not sponge. We must return, as best we can, the hospitality we receive."

"But surely . . . we're not quite . . ."

"Yes, we are poor," she interrupted quite fiercely, "but we must never, never be ashamed of it."

Desmonde enjoyed his Saturday tea with me, but his first visit to my home had positively startled him. As we came out of the park and crossed into the mean district of Yorkhill, he viewed the cheap shops therein with ill-concealed distaste, his nostrils dilating as we passed the fish-and-chip establishment of Antonio Moseno who, already aproned and in his doorway, hailed me across the street.

"Howdya, Meester Cronin. Green pea ready. Chip-a-potata ready twenty meenutes."

"A friend?" remarked Desmonde, casually.

"And a jolly good one. He almost gives me double when I go in for a pennyworth of chips."

As we passed the little butcher's at the end of the row, the blue-striped, belted figure within gave me a wave of his arm in greeting.

"That's another friend," I remarked, forestalling my companion. "He's a Scot. And when my mother goes in just before he closes on Saturday night, she gets a first-rate bargain."

Desmonde was silent, and as we were now climbing the steep

hill on which the tenement stood, the reason became obvious. Indeed, when we reached our entrance and climbed the four flights of steps to the top flat, he steadied himself against me, groping for breath, speechless.

"I say, A. J.," he wheezed at last, "don't you find this rather too much for you?"

"Nonsense, Desmonde!" I rather laid it on. "When I've had my morning cold bath and run around the park three times — that's a mile — I absolutely spring up these stairs."

"You do?" he said flatly.

I took out my key, opened the door, and led the way into the kitchen where, before tactfully departing, my mother had spread a clean white cover on the little table and laid out the tea things, with a large plate of newly baked shortbread.

Desmonde collapsed into one of the two chairs, watching me in silence while I lit the gas ring, boiled the kettle, expertly brewed tea, and filled the two big cups.

He took a long, deep swallow and sighed.

"Terribly good, A. J. Most refreshing."

I refilled his cup and passed the shortbread. He took a piece, bit into it experimentally. Then his face lit up.

"I say, A. J., this is delicious."

"Homemade, Desmonde. Have another."

We set to work on the tea together. Indeed, with some slight assistance from me, Desmonde practically demolished the plateful.

"I'm worse than old Beauchamp." He apologized, hesitating before taking the ninth and final piece.

In reply I gave him his third cup of tea.

Thoroughly revived now, Desmonde looked around, his eye dwelling upon the curtained alcove behind me.

"Is that where you study, A. J.?"

I drew the curtain aside with my foot, revealing a narrow iron bedstead, neatly made up and spread with a gray counterpane.

"My mother's bedroom," I said. "You want to see mine?"

He nodded, silently. I took him across the miniature hall and threw open the door of the other room.

"This is my domain." I smiled. "Where I sleep, work, and take my exercise."

He followed me, in a state of total wonderment. The room was completely empty, except for a narrow truckle bed at one end and at the window a little dilapidated fold-down deal bureau, deemed not worth putting in the auction when our home was broken up.

As he remained still and completely silent, I took an India rubber from the mantelpiece, threw it against the wall, and as it came back at a sharp angle, caught it.

"My wall game. When I catch fifty, without a fault, I've won."

Still he did not speak, but came toward me, still with that strange, emotional expression, and to my acute embarrassment, took my hand and went down on one knee.

"A. J.," he exclaimed, raising his eyes to me, "you are noble, truly noble, as also is your dear mother. To live like this, spartan lives, nobly and cheerfully, is truly saintly. You shame me. Dear A. J." His voice broke. "Sign me with the Cross and give me your blessing."

Dreadfully uncomfortable, I was about to say: "For Heaven's sake, don't be an ass," but for some strange unknown reason I checked myself, murmured the names of the Trinity, and marked his upturned forehead with the Sign of the Cross.

Instantly he relaxed, got to his feet, and vigorously shook my hand.

"Now I feel I have the strength, the courage to emulate you. I must be hard on myself. And I shall begin now." He reflected. "It's a couple of miles from here to my house, uphill most of the way if I cross the park."

"Slightly more than two miles, all uphill."

"Good! I'm going to start now, walking fast, and I promise you I'll be home in twenty minutes."

"That would be a fine effort, Desmonde."

"I'm off, then." He took his cap from the peg in the hall and went to the door. "Thank you for a delicious tea . . . and for yourself."

I waited a moment while he went clattering down the stone steps, then went to the window of my room. True to his word, Desmonde was on his way, arms swinging, head thrust forward. So he continued, until gradually his pace slackened and he seemed suddenly to flag. He had, after all, eaten a considerable quantity of shortbread. And now indeed he paused, removed his immaculate handkerchief from his breast pocket, applied it to his brow, and resumed thereafter at a slower, a much slower pace. He was now at the end of the hill road, facing the main street. He paused, stood considering the flow of traffic and, as a cab ambled past, looking for a fare, his right arm shot up. The cab stopped, the door opened, and Desmonde flung himself into the back seat.

"Home, James," I murmured to myself. "And don't spare the horses." But he had tried.

The sun was now setting over the distant hills of Dumbarton, lighting the rooftops and furnishing my empty room with a magic splendor. As I gazed into the rosy glow of the sunset I wondered what the future held for Desmonde . . . and for me.

4

Desmonde, who never seemed to overtax himself with work, was naturally clever, and due to his father, he had the incomparable advantage of three languages. Completely fluent in French and Spanish, he could even converse, though more slowly, in Latin. Almost apologetically he explained to me how his father of an evening would take him for a stroll in Phoenix Park, stating firmly at the outset the language in which their converse must be conducted. To relapse into English was an offense, not punishable, but frowned upon by his accomplished parent, a scholar who was often called upon to arrange and catalogue the libraries of great houses in Europe.

As we came into our final school year it was a foregone conclusion that Desmonde would take all the language prizes while I, by intensive study, might succeed in mathematics, science and, with luck, English. It was already settled that Desmonde would go on to the seminary at Tarrijas, in Spain, while I would try for the Marshall Scholarship, sole passport to Winton University and a medical career.

My chances of scholarship were impaired by the fact that our football team was having an unprecedented run of success in the competition for the Scottish Schools Shield. This coveted trophy had never been won by Saint Ignatius and as we came through to the quarter finals, leaving a trail of vanquished schools behind, Father Jaeger, who had made me captain of the team the year before, was beside himself with ardor and excitement.

Every other evening long training sessions were held in the gymnasium and before every game I had a detailed briefing in Jaeger's study.

"I think we might just do it, A. J." Unable to be still, he pranced up and down the little study. "We are a young, a very young team, but keen, yes, keen. And we have you, A. J., taking the ball forward. Now remember . . ."

Desmonde came with me to all the matches, returning jubilant to our customary Saturday luncheon at Overton Crescent, where he delighted my mother by exaggerated reports of my prowess.

Now that his admission to the seminary was settled he was amusing himself, and the school, in his own fashion. He had first ascertained the date of Father Beauchamp's birthday by consulting *Who's Who,* and as the day drew near, he composed and typed a marvelous letter purporting to come from the Mother Superior of the adjacent convent school, a venerable old lady who rarely exposed herself to public view.

The letter, widely circulated among the school, ran as follows:

My dear, very dear Father Beauchamp,

If I had the courage I would address you by your delightful name of Harold, for I must now confess that I have long cherished a deep and passionate reverence for you. Yes, I watch you often, from my window, striding down the causeway, a noble, magnificent, corpulent figure, and with beating heart, I long to have known you when we were both younger. When you had just left Eton, laden with honors, and I was a simple maiden, student at the nearby Borstal Reformatory. What joys might have then been in store for us. Alas, Heaven willed otherwise. But now, cloistered though I am, I may, purely and without sin, declare my secret passion. And in celebration of your auspicious name day I venture to send you a birthday cake. Intuition, or perhaps rumor tells me that, despite the rigorous diet of your Order, you enjoy and are permitted to indulge yourself excessively in sweetmeats.

Heaven bless you, my darling.

I pray for you always — a solace to my love.

Yours adoringly,
CLARIBEL

Roars of laughter greeted this masterpiece as it was passed from hand to hand and thereafter endorsed with a huge chocolate cake in a beribboned box.

This box was then secretly conveyed to the jolly, stumpy schoolgirl whom Desmonde had inveigled into the plot. It was she who had actually provided the sheet of convent notepaper on which the letter was typed, and she who on the appointed day rang the school's doorbell and personally presented the gift to Beauchamp. Almost the entire school saw the box delivered and all awaited the outcome with ill-repressed anticipation.

All day long there was no reaction but, at five o'clock when the school had assembled for evening prayers, Beauchamp made his appearance to conduct the service. Before he began, almost absently, he said:

"Fitzgerald, would you oblige me by standing up."

Gracefully, Desmonde obeyed.

"You are Desmonde Fitzgerald."

"I have always been led to believe so, sir. If I am in error perhaps you will correct me."

"Enough! Fitzgerald, do you consider me 'corpulent'?"

"Corpulent, sir? That is a word, sir, which comprises a variety of meanings, from a gross obesity to a benign and graceful *embonpoint*, eminently becoming to a prelate of your dignity and stature."

"Ah! I assume you know, or at least know of, the venerable Mother Superior of our neighboring convent school?"

"Who does not, sir."

"Would you ever, for a moment, believe that she had passed her early life in a Borstal Reformatory?"

"Sir, you yourself must be aware that many of our greatest saints, eventually models of piety and devotion, were in their early years reprobates and malefactors, which did not prevent their ultimate canonization. Thus, should our Reverend Mother have been by chance to Borstal, would you wish deliberately to cast the first stone?"

A ripple ran through the school. We were all enjoying this immensely.

"Enough, Desmonde!" From the mildness of Beauchamp's tone it seemed almost as if he were himself enjoying the exchanges. "Enough, sir. Borstal or not, would you consider it possible that this venerable and saintly lady would conceive a secret passion for any man?"

"I would consider it eminently possible, sir!"

"What!"

"The word passion, sir, like your corpulence —" here the school did indeed laugh outright — "has many meanings. There is the passion, sir, that you might feel if, God forbid, I should ever annoy you. I would then return to my beloved mother in tears, exclaiming brokenly: 'Darling Mother, dear Father Beauchamp, our beloved prefect of studies, was in a raging passion with me.'" Desmonde had to pause until he could be heard. We were all in hysterics. "Then, sir, there is that very frequent use of the word when a charming woman might say casually to her friend, as she came from her garden proudly bearing a trug loaded with blooms: 'I have a passion for roses, darling.' Or again, a henpecked husband might say to his wife: 'You have a passion for clothes, confound you. Just look at this milliner's bill . . .' Then, again . . ."

"Enough, Desmonde." We were getting out of control. Beauchamp held up his hand. "Tell me, did you write that birthday letter that came with the birthday cake?"

"Sir, that is a leading question. Even in a court of law I would be given time to reflect and consider and if necessary to consult my legal advisers . , ." Desmonde broke off suddenly. He sensed that enough amusement had been extracted from the situation and that to go further would spoil the admirable effect he had created. So he bowed his head and said simply: "I did send the cake, sir. And I did compose the letter. It was all done in fun, sir. If it annoyed you, I am sorry and I will accept my punishment. And I am sure every one of us, who had a part in this silly joke, is equally contrite. I only hope that you enjoyed the cake."

There was a long silence. One might have heard a pin drop. Then Beauchamp spoke.

"Desmonde, I predict, without the slightest hesitation and with complete assurance, that if you do not fall by the wayside, you will end your days as a cardinal in the inner circle of the Vatican. You have the exact quality of diplomatic equivocation which is highly regarded in that august body. However, you are now a pupil under my authority who must be punished. So your punishment will be this —" he held us breathless for a long moment. "Next time, send me a cherry cake. I prefer it to chocolate."

It was a masterstroke. Beauchamp knew how to handle boys. We rose in a body and, led by Desmonde, cheered him to the echo.

With the long summer vacation drawing near, the school was now in high good humor. We had just won our semifinal match against Allan Glens, a famous Scottish school with a strong team we had greatly feared. And how well and with what pleasure do I remember the game, the grounds of the famous Celtic Club, the perfect weather, a sunny late afternoon, the cropped green turf, lawn smooth, so suited to our passing game, every member of the team in top form, the joy of victory, and the cheers that greeted us as we streamed into the pavilion, where Father Jaeger threw his arms around me in a triumphant hug.

Our greatest hurdle cleared, we were now in the finals where our opponents would be a little-known team from a small elementary school. With good reason, it was generally acknowledged that the Shield would at last be ours. I was in high favor. Even Father Beauchamp, not precisely a sporting man, would beam me a radiant smile as we passed in the corridor.

All our examinations were now over, the results already on the notice board. As anticipated, Desmonde had done superlatively well, taking half of the prizes, while I, a modest plodder, took the other half. However, also on the board was a communiqué from the university, briefly indicating, but with immense joy to myself and to my dear mother, that I had won the Marshall Bursary. Finally, on the board was the annual invitation to the boys of the upper sixth, inviting them to the convent dance given by the senior girls under the supervision of Mother Superior. This was an established custom between the two schools, doubtless to arrange a meeting between Catholic boys and girls of good education and high morals which might prove salutary, or even fruitful, now that they must face the liberty and temptations of unsheltered life. Naturally, we all regarded it as an immense joke.

The day of the momentous final was now upon us, the match fixed for five o'clock at Hamden Park, the famous international ground. For a schoolboys' event, the crowd was exceptionally large. Even now, more than sixty years later, it pains me to write of the event, of which the memory has so often recurred to sting me. We began in great style, swinging the ball about with precision and complete confidence, and for seven minutes we were obviously the masters, almost scoring twice. Then the incident occurred.

Our left back, a boy of no more than thirteen years, had the habit of running, even of walking, with his arms akimbo, and in this fashion he tackled one of the opposing forwards. His elbow barely touched the other boy who, alas, slipped and fell. Instantly the whistle of the referee sounded. A penalty!

The kick was taken, a goal was scored, and immediately our young team went to pieces. Then the rain began, drenching us in heavy sheets, driven into our faces by gusts of wind, a pitiless downfall that persisted through the second half into a premature early darkness, almost a blackout, with the pitch markings and the ball barely discernible. It was of course equally bad for our opponents, but they had their goal. The seconds were ticking away. In the last minutes of the game, the ball came to me on the touchline, outside the penalty area. I took one desperate blinding shot at the enemy goal. It was a good effort, sailing hard and true for the top corner of the net, when a fierce gust caught and diverted the ball, which struck the junction of the bar and the post, sailed high in the air, and went out.

Instantly the final whistle sounded. We were beaten, one to nothing. In the pavilion poor Father Jaeger, ash-gray from strain and suspense, immediately quelled our curses against the referee.

"You did your best, boys. We were handicapped by the storm, and," he added bitterly, "by the fact that you were wearing green jerseys. Now hurry and change, our bus is waiting."

I could not face the dinner that had been arranged for us. I hid myself in one of the washrooms, emerging only when the rumble of the bus had died. Then I took my bag and went out into the rain, faced with a long walk to the tram stop and a longer bumpy journey home.

Suddenly in the darkness a hand was on my shoulder.

"I've a taxi waiting, dear A. J. I managed to get it through the gates. Give me your bag. I won't say a word about the game and I'll get you safely home."

He led me to the cab, and into it. This was Desmonde, Desmonde at his best. Thankfully I lay back, utterly spent, and closed my eyes.

After we had cleared the gates and were on our way, Desmonde whispered:

"Are you asleep, A. J.?"

"Unfortunately, no."

"I'm not going to talk about the match, A. J., but I'd like you to know that I prayed like mad all the time, and when your shot just missed being a goal I nearly died."

"I'm glad you survived."

He was silent for some minutes, then:

"I'm leaving for Tarrijas, for the seminary, the day after tomorrow."

"So soon?"

"Yes. Mother is terribly upset. She'll come with me to Madrid. Then I may not see her till I'm ordained."

"That's very severe."

"Yes, I understand they're formidably strict."

Again silence, then leaning toward me he murmured:

"You know I love you, A. J."

"Like is the imperative word, Desmonde."

"Well, then, I like you immensely and I want you to promise to keep in touch with me. There's no ban on letters out there, so I mean to write you often. Do you mind?"

"Not at all, and I'll reply, when I'm not tied up with Quain's *Anatomy*."

"Thank you, thank you, dear A. J."

So the pact was made. And that is why I may continue this narrative with absolute accuracy despite the fact that we were often apart for many years.

The taxi drew up. We were now outside my home.

"Thank you sincerely, Desmonde, for being so decent. It would have taken me more than an hour."

I gave him my hand. I have a vague idea that he tried to kiss me on the cheek as I got out of the cab, but it was not successful.

"Good night, Desmonde, and thank you again."

"Good night, my dear A. J."

5

I slept late next morning, from sheer exhaustion, and had to forgo my usual run in the park. Although the school prize-giving was not until late afternoon, my mother had taken the whole day off from work. She brought me my breakfast in bed, a special treat, and on the tray, in addition to my porridge, there was hot buttered toast and a plate of bacon and egg. Not a word did she speak of the game, although I read in her face maternal compassion tempered by a determined brightness.

She sat with me while I cleared the tray, then:

"I have a surprise for you, dear." And from the hall she brought a flat cardboard box, took off the lid, and exposed a new, extremely good-looking dark blue suit.

I gazed, enraptured, amazed.

"How did you get it?"

"Never mind, dear. You know that you must have a decent suit for the university. Hurry and try it on."

"How did you get it?" I repeated, seriously.

"Well . . . you know that silly old silver brooch . . ."

"The one with the ring of pearls."

"I didn't want it, I was tired of it, a useless old thing . . . I sold it . . . to a decent little man who knows me in my district."

"You loved that brooch. You said it was your mother's."

She looked at me in silence. Then:

"Please don't make a fuss, dear. You had to have a suit for the prize-giving, and especially for the dance afterward."

"I don't want to go to the dance. I'll hate it."

"You must, you must . . . you never have any amusement or social life." She added: "I had a letter about you this morning, delivered by one of the college servants. From Father Jaeger."

"Do let me see it."

"Certainly not. It's my letter and I shall prize it. Besides, I don't want you to get a swelled head."

She paused, while we confronted each other on the verge of laughter.

"He did mention that he hoped you weren't laid up, as you didn't turn up for the dinner. And if you've time he'd like you to come up and see him, before he goes off on Monday."

"He's going away?"

"So it appears."

I pondered, puzzled. At least I would have the answer tonight.

"Do try the suit, dear."

I got up, horribly stiff, and with some difficulty took my bath. A clean white shirt and a new light-blue tie had been set out beside the suit. I dressed with care, enjoying every moment, brushed my hair carefully, and presented myself for inspection, fully aware that I had not been as well turned out for at least five years.

My dear little mother looked me up and down, walked slowly around me, then looked again. No burst of admiration, no superlatives, no lovey-dovey "Oh, my darling," but it was pleasant to read her eyes as she embraced me and said, quietly:

"It is a perfect fit. Now you look *yourself*."

All that day I lazed around, easing my bruises, and getting in the way of my mother, but at five o'clock we were both seated in the school hall where most of the boys were already present with their parents and friends. Desmonde was much in evidence but, as he explained, his mother, busy with arrangements for their departure, was enforcedly absent. However, it was he who started the proceedings by leading us into the school song, the new version composed by Father Roberts. The effect was rather spoiled by the noise of latecomers looking for seats and dragging chairs, and almost at once Father Beauchamp appeared on the platform. After a short prayer, when everyone stood, he read an account of the school's progress during the past year, then began to distribute the prizes. Parents of sons so rewarded beamed; others less fortunate did not conceal their chagrin. A woman behind us was heard to remark rancorously to her neighbor:

"Oor Wullie was fifth in Religious Knowledge. Whet wey did he no' get a prize."

Finally, speaking more slowly, Beauchamp came to the upper group and presently Desmonde was called to the platform to accept his books, receiving some applause as he gracefully bowed and retreated. Then it was my turn. And how relieved and pleased I was, for my mother's sake, at the roar that greeted my appearance and continued until Beauchamp raised his hand. He began to speak, presumably about me, since there were more cheers, but although I caught the phrase "our admirable Cronin" my attention, and indeed my eyes, were fixed on an envelope which lay on top of my pile of books.

At last the ordeal was over. Beauchamp awkwardly shook hands with me and I hobbled back to my seat, where my mother, crimson with pride, pressed my hand and gave me a look I shall never forget, a look that sustained me during the hard years that followed.

Another prayer, and we were all dismissed and crowding toward the doors. I saw my mother down College Hill to the tramway stop, and before I put her on the tram I handed her the envelope.

"This is five guineas in cash, my prize for the English essay competition. Will you kindly go to your little jeweler friend and get back your brooch."

Before she could answer she was in the tram and moving off, while I, feeling horrendously sentimental and dramatic, turned up the hill again.

At the school, the tower clock showed twenty minutes after six. I went immediately to Father Jaeger's study. He was there, seated in his usual chair, not busy in any way and looking, I thought, rather more than usually pensive.

"I hoped you would come, A. J. Your mother got my letter?"

"Yes, she did, sir, and sternly refused to disclose its contents."

"Good!" he said, and smiled. "I did want to see you, A. J., not to talk about the game — that's all dead history — but because I may be . . . going away, fairly soon." He glanced at his wrist-watch. "But aren't you supposed to be at the dance?"

"The more of that I miss, sir, the better. And I did want to thank you for giving me the essay prize. You knew I needed the money."

"What nonsense is this. Your essay was miles ahead of the others. You have a bit of a gift in that direction."

"Well, sir," I laughed, "I shall employ it in writing prescriptions. But please tell me, are you going on holiday?"

"Not exactly, but I shall be away."

A silence fell. I saw that he was not smoking. I said:

"Shall I fill you a pipeful, sir?"

This I often did for him, when we were talking football. However, he shook his head.

"I'm rather off my pipe, A. J." He paused. "I seem to have a ridiculous spot on my tongue which is interesting your future colleagues, somewhat."

"Does it hurt?"

"Moderately." He smiled. "But I shall know more on Monday, when I go back for their report."

I was silent. I did not like the sound of this at all.

"So they might keep you to have it out?"

"We shall know next week. Possibly I might go later on to our base at Stonyhurst. At any rate, I wanted to say goodbye and wish you well in your university career. I have no doubts about you, because you have got it here —" he touched his brow — "and here." He closed his fist and thumped himself hard on the chest. "I can't say," he went on, "that I have the same confidence in the future of your friend. Fitzgerald is like the curate's egg, good, very good, in parts, but the rest of it . . ." he shrugged and shook his head. "But, really, A. J., you must get to the dance or they'll think you're funking it. I'll see you downstairs. I am going to the church for a while."

He came to the door of the school, stood, and put out his hand, which clasped mine firmly while he looked straight into my eyes.

"Goodbye, A. J."

"Goodbye, sir."

He turned and moved toward the church, while slowly, very slowly and sadly, I made my way across the street and uphill to the convent. I had read tragedy in Jaeger's brave eyes. And with reason.

He had a cancer of the tongue, already with secondaries in the larynx and elsewhere. Six months later, after three operations and untold agony, he was dead. His one little indulgence, in a life of stark austerity, had killed him.

Some premonition of this must have been in my mind as I was admitted to the convent. The dance was already in progress, couples moving sedately around under the watchful eyes of a group of senior nuns seated on the platform, Desmonde doing his best with a few capers to enliven the party.

Dancing had not been in my curriculum, but I took up one of the wallflowers, who were gathered in a distressful group, and made the circuit with her several times while she breathed heavily into my right ear as we trod on each other's feet. I then turned her over to an unsuspecting boy and sat down beside a nice, quiet, gray-eyed girl.

"Thank goodness, you're not dancing."

"No," she said. "I'm entering my novitiate tomorrow."

"For the convent here?"

She inclined her head. Then: "Is that boy, carrying on there, Fitzgerald, the one who's going to be a priest?"

"Yes, he goes off to the seminary on Monday."

"You're not serious. In two days' time?"

"Why not?"

"I couldn't believe anyone could go on clowning like that, practically on the eve of giving himself to Our Lord."

I said nothing, having no wish to be drawn into a discussion on prenovitiate behavior.

"You must be the A. J. Cronin boy. The good footballer who just won the Bursary."

"How on earth do you know?"

She smiled. "We talk about you boys over here."

"Yet you're going to be a nun?"

"Yes, I am, I can't help it."

This delightful answer made me smile, and we began to talk very agreeably to one another, until suddenly she checked herself. "I think I must go now."

"So soon, just as we are beginning to like each other?"

She blushed, most attractively. "That's why I must go . . . I'm beginning to like you too much."

She stood up and held out her hand.

"Good night, A. J."

"Good night, dear little Sister."

I watched her to the door across the room. I hoped she would look around. She did, for a long, long moment, then lowered her eyes and was gone.

I decided to go too, but at that moment all the nuns on the platform stood up as a very old and venerable nun appeared, escorted by a young sister and walking slowly with a stick. Instantly a chair was produced, placed in the center of the stage. She sat down.

The dancers had immediately become still, for this was the convent's Mother Superior. After gazing down benevolently she said quite distinctly:

"Would the Fitzgerald boy come forward."

Immediately, nimbly, Desmonde mounted the platform, bowed and stood before her to attention, then gracefully sank to one knee.

"You are the Irish boy who sings?"

"Yes, Reverend Mother."

"The Father Beauchamp has spoken to me of you. Firstly, dear Desmonde, for your peace of mind, I would wish to assure you that I did not receive my education at the Borstal Reformatory, which you seem to know of, in the vicinity of Eton."

Desmonde blushed as the surrounding nuns dissolved in giggles. The famous letter had apparently become a convent joke.

"Do forgive me, Reverend Mother. It was stupid fun."

"You are already forgiven, Desmonde, but you must do penance." She paused. "I am an old Irishwoman, who still pines for her homeland to which now she will never return. Would you oblige me, therefore, by singing one, just one, Irish song, or ballad, that might ease my longing."

"I will indeed, Reverend Mother. With the greatest pleasure in the world."

"Do you know 'Tara'? Or 'The Minstrel Boy'?"

"I know both."

"Then sing." She closed her eyes and turned an expectant ear as Desmonde took a long breath and began to sing, first one, then the other, of these old ballads. And never did I hear him sing better.

> *The harp that once through Tara's halls,*
> *The soul of music shed,*
> *No more to chiefs and ladies bright,*
> *That harp of Tara swells . . .*

> *The minstrel boy to the war is gone,*
> *In the ranks of death you'll find him;*
> *His father's sword he has girded on,*
> *And his wild harp slung behind him.*

> *"Land of song!" said the warrior-bard,*
> *"Though all the world betrays Thee,*
> *One sword, at least, thy rights shall guard,*
> *One faithful harp shall praise Thee!"*

The minstrel fell! — but the foeman's chain
Could not bring his proud soul under;
The harp he loved ne'er spoke again,
For he tore its chords asunder,

And said, "No chains shall sully thee,
Thou soul of love and bravery!
Thy songs were made for the pure and free,
They ne'er shall sound in slavery!

And what a tableau! Against a frieze of nuns, the old, the very old Mother Superior, eyes closed, half reclining in her chair, and at her side, this angelic, fair-haired, blue-eyed youth, pouring his heart out in song.

When it was over, no one moved, until Reverend Mother spoke, through streaming tears.

"Thank you, dear Minstrel Boy. May Our Lord bless and keep you for giving an old woman a taste of Heaven, before she may get there."

She rose, helped to her feet, and smiled to us below.

"Now let the dance resume."

When she had left the stage, the fun did indeed begin, led by Desmonde, elated by his triumph and ready for action. He had induced the ugly stubby little number, now identified as captain of the hockey team, to join him in a combined version of the Irish Jig and the Highland Fling.

I would have wished to go over to him for just one last good-bye. But we had really said this after the game, and to the lively strains of "The Campbells Are Coming," thumped out on the piano, I went out into the cool night air.

My mother was waiting for me when I got home. As I kicked off my shoes in the hall she called out:

"I hope you're hungry, dear. I have a lovely Welsh rarebit for you."

I was hungry. I stepped into the kitchen. She was there, arms outstretched, the brooch gleaming on her bosom.

TWO

1

Desmonde entered the Seminary of Saint Simeon in the village
of Tarrijas, some ten kilometers from Toledo. His letters to me
thereafter were frequent but irregular. Following the initial letter, which gave an interesting account of the seminary and its
whereabouts, they became rather dull and repetitious, since they
had little to offer beyond the minutiae and monotony of monastic life. However, toward the end of Desmonde's preparation for
the priesthood, a letter reached me which had a definite interest
and, indeed, a direct bearing on Desmonde's subsequent career.
I shall therefore reproduce the first and the last letters in detail.

As for myself, since I shall eventually come into Desmonde's
life again, it may be briefly noted that my career at the university was proceeding rigorously in circumstances little different from those that had attended my schooldays. The same half-
empty little flat, the same plain food and porridge, the same loving devotion of my mother. Ambition alone sustained us. We did
not complain, since we were not alone. Other poor students were
there, vying with each other, desperate for success. In that era,
now remote, large sustenance grants were not lavishly and indis-
criminately bestowed. Clever, ambitious boys would come from
poor farms in the North carrying a sack of meal to sustain them
till the next Meal Monday, a free day by university statute to
enable them to return to the parental farm for fresh supplies.

Yet however harassed by hard work and recurrent examinations, I often thought of Desmonde and, refreshed by his letters,

I had an odd conviction that when he was ordained I should again see and be near to him.

My dear A. J.,

Behold your beloved friend, your *fidus Achates,* in Spain, almost within sight of the noble walled city of Toledo, embraced by the benign sun of the Midi, but miserable, forlorn, desolated at the parting from my mother, and in dread of the long joyless future stretching endlessly before me.

But first I must serve the sweets before offering you the bitters.

Two days after our last meeting, I set out for Rome with my dear mother who, although far from well, insisted on accompanying me. Our journey was pleasant and uneventful and on arrival we proceeded to our hotel, the Excelsior in the Via Veneto, where we were shown to our rooms, large, cool, and away from traffic noise.

The purpose of our stop in the Eternal City was not only to rest, although this was almost a necessity for my mother, but to renew certain contacts made by my father during his frequent visits, when he had come to purchase old manuscripts of books and to review and catalogue the libraries of great houses. It was pleasing to find that he was not forgotten. And soon, indeed, our telephone began to ring, and cards were left for us at the concierge's office. Old Monseigneur Broglio called, a frightful old bore with a large appetite, who did however get us the entrée to the Vatican. There were others. Most delightful and hospitable of all, the Marchesa di Varese had us several times to her absurdly large and beautiful old house on the Via della Croce. My father had spent many weeks as her guest arranging and cataloguing her enormous, and enormously valuable, library. I feel sure she was half in love with my dear dad, for she was particularly nice to me, promising to help me in any way if I had need of her.

She it was who supplemented the old Monseigneur in arranging our audience with His Holiness. And how memorable, how touching was that meeting, not a private audience, of course — this accorded only to royalty or to the famous — but a meeting in the great hall, fifteen minutes in advance of the general audience.

We were there in time, I assure you, I in my black suit, my mother also in the required black, the fine dress and lace mantilla provided by the Marchesa. We waited in a little anteroom, then were conducted to the near end of the audience chamber, a part sealed off by a velvet rope. There again, we waited for perhaps two minutes. When the Pope entered, accompanied by the papal secretary, I experienced a tremor almost ecstatic. Such dignity, serenity, such an abiding sense of goodness that it radiated toward us as, briefed by the secretary, he greeted us by our names and spoke of my father — whom he had known when a cardinal — and "all that he had done for the Church." He talked first to my mother, then to me, extolling the great good that active young priests could accomplish in the world of today and, with a look in his eye that may have previsaged Toledo, enjoined me on the virtues of self-sacrifice and penance. This might well have continued beyond the specified fifteen minutes, for I could see His Holiness was not bored with us, but suddenly behind us at the far end of the hall, the great doors swung open and a great horde swept in of . . . guess what, A. J. ? . . . American Navy sailors, who came forward en masse with unsuppressed excited cries: "There he is, fellers! There's His Holiness. Quiet now, don't shout!"

When silence was restored and they were all grouped in their own section, the secretary indicated that we should kneel.

I did so, but His Holiness made a restraining touch upon my mother's shoulder and whispered; "Do not kneel, dear lady."

He then blessed us, before these silent, attentive witnesses.

Do you remember, A. J., that moment in your room when I asked you to bless me? This was the same unreal, unworldly, inexplicably presanctified feeling, magnified of course, but in essence identical. In future, therefore, I shall with difficulty refrain from addressing you as your Holiness.

We were conducted out by the private staircase, and that evening dined in state with the Marchesa. Next day we were in the *rápido* for Madrid.

Since my mother had looked forward to this Spanish visit and had saved a substantial amount from her annual income to pay for it, I decided not to go direct to the seminary but to spend two more days in the Spanish capital. On our arrival I took a taxi direct to the Ritz Hotel where, with dispatch and supreme courtesy, we were installed in a suite overlooking the gardens.

What a superb hotel, A. J., I unhesitatingly award it two extra stars beyond the four it already possesses. My mother had a real rest, relaxing under the orange trees, while I took a good look at the Prado — disappointing rather, too many huge portraits of Spanish kings, but with, of course, that wonderful, unsurpassable Velázquez, *Las Meninas*. Mother did worry a little over the lateness of dinner, but when we sat down all was forgiven. A mouth-watering cuisine.

On the morning of our third day I made all arrangements for a courier to see my mother safely, that evening, into the compartment I had booked for her on the Madrid–Paris–Calais express. We set off in a large Hispano-Suiza limousine for Toledo and the seminary.

At the forbidding gates of that institution, as my dear mother embraced me in a last goodbye, I had a sudden frightful premonition that this was indeed a final parting, that I should never see her again. I waited, watching the car until it was out of sight and also, let me admit, until I had wiped my eyes after a good weep. Then I passed through the huge gates of the seminary and asked the gateman, in Spanish, to take me to the Father Superior's office. He seemed surprised that I spoke his language, and very willingly picked up my suitcase and escorted me across a wide courtyard toward the central part of the college, a delightful old Andalusian abbey on which, however, two horrible tall modern concrete wings have been added. Inside, we went up a fine old black olivewood staircase. Then, outside a forbidding door of the same dark wood, he put down my bag. I gave him a couple of *pesetas*. Again, he seemed surprised and pleased.

"It is useful the *señor* has Spanish. All the servants are Spanish."

"All men?"

"But assuredly, *señor*. Father Superior Hackett would have no others."

I knocked at the door, received no answer, but went in, unutterably startled and surprised to see a tall, dark priest kneeling in prayer on a prie-dieu before a crucifix fixed on the wall. Beneath the crucifix in an enclosed glass receptacle lay, believe it or not, A. J., a severed human hand. Before I could recover, the kneeling figure spoke.

"Go outside and wait."

I removed myself, still carrying the bag, and stood outside for at least ten minutes before the voice again materialized.

"You may enter."

I entered, put down the bag, and as a chair seemed to be in place for me in front of the desk, sat down.

"Get to your feet."

I obeyed, surveying my future Superior with considerable misgiving as he sat there, studying a folder that, with deeper misgiving, I knew to be my dossier. Have you ever seen the Phiz drawing of David Copperfield's stepfather? This was it — the same stature and general repulsive appearance, the same dark, brooding, sadistic eyes. I did not at all like him. In fact, he made me feel exactly like little David before they sent him to the factory to wash bottles.

"You know, dear Desmonde, with the final 'e', that you are a full three days late in coming to me." The sarcasm in his voice was bitter, not amused.

"I am sorry, Father. My mother accompanied me, and as she seemed tired, we spent two days in Rome before coming on to the Ritz in Madrid where, again, I felt it prudent to stay overnight."

"A truly filial devotion. And what did you in Rome, my child?"

"We had a private audience with His Holiness, the Pope."

I thought that would sink him. It did not. He continued to smile, and I assure you, A. J., I did not like that smile.

"And what did His Holiness say to you?"

Misguidedly, I spoke the truth. "He extolled the virtues of penance and self-sacrifice."

Immediately, he raised his big fist and suddenly thumped the desk so hard it made everything on the desk jump. Alas, I jumped too.

"These are the very words I should have spoken to you. And I speak them to you now, for they are the motto of this college and they are particularly applicable to you, an effete, completely spoiled mother's boy! If I did not already see it written on your face, it is here, written in your record." He glanced at the folder on his desk. "Tell me, do you know *anything* of mortification?"

Again, misguidedly, since, though still fearful, I was becoming rattled. I said, "Yes, I do. My greatest friend takes an ice-cold bath every morning and runs two miles before he even has his porridge."

His eyes glistened hungrily. "That's my man. Could we ever get him here?"

"He's already on his way to becoming a doctor."

"Pity! What a missionary I would have made of him. We specialize in missionaries here, Desmonde with an 'e.' I have in the past twelve years already sent out seven, of which three have shed their blood in darkest Africa."

This bloodthirsty fellow was now alarming me, A. J. He was worse than Jack the Ripper.

"To come to the point. I am obliged to punish you for your flagrant disobedience of my order. You are gated for two weeks. And the room I shall give you will possibly not remind you of the Ritz."

He banged the bell on his desk. Immediately a servant appeared. The Ripper instructed him. The man looked surprised, but picked up my valise, and we departed, moving out of the lovely abbey and across to a remote part of the concrete building. Here, he led the way down the basement steps to a small, dark, cellarlike cubicle with a minute window that afforded a horrid vista of some outdoor lavatories. The cell itself was foully dirty and in frightful disorder.

I gazed at the dirty bed, turned upside down on the floor, then turned to the fellow who was still holding my bag.

"Who occupied this room?"

"A student expelled only yesterday."

"What for?"

"I believe for smoking the cigarette, *señor*." Then he added in a low confidential voice, "This is the punishment cell, *señor*."

I brooded for a moment. I would not, simply would not have it.

"Do not go! Wait here with my baggage. I will return."

He seemed almost to expect this. He smiled and put down the bag.

I went up the beastly steps, straight back to the Ripper's office, and went in.

He looked up from his desk. I was convinced he expected me.

"Yes?"

"I will not accept that stinking dungeon. I am at least entitled to cleanliness and decency."

"And if I don't obey your demands?"

"I shall walk straight out of here to Toledo, charter a taxi to Madrid, take train to Rome, and report the matter to the Holy Father."

"Very well," he said mildly. "Goodbye, Desmonde with an 'e.' "

I stood there, blazing, while he resumed his work at the desk. Then I turned, went out, and slowly made my way back to the cell. Now I no longer felt like little David, but like one of the bottles he had half washed out. I could not, of course I could not do it, and the Ripper knew it. How should I look, returning to my mother at the Ritz . . . No, never, never, I must make the best of it. There was still some spirit left in me. The servant was still standing by me. He knew I'd be back.

"The little room would look better, much better, *señor*, if it were cleaned."

I met and read his eyes, and thanked God for my fluent Spanish, a fact unknown to that sadistic bastard in his study.

"What's your name?"

"Martes, *señor*."

I took out from my pocketbook a beautiful, new, crisp fifty-

peseta note and held it toward him. I knew it was a fortune to him; he knew it, too.

"Martes! Bring a friend, with soap and water, everything for cleaning. Get fresh bed linen, fresh curtains, find a carpet from another room. Make everything lovely and fresh, and the money is yours."

He put down the valise and was off like a flash. I waited just long enough to see him return with another of the college servants, whom he introduced as José. Between them they were loaded with a variety of brushes, cloths, and buckets of water. As I went up the steps I heard them getting madly down to the job.

For about an hour or more I wandered around the grounds, inspecting some dilapidated tennis courts into which cows from the neighboring fields had obviously strayed to leave cards, a yard with several high *pelota* walls, an old football field. I looked into the church, Old Spanish and, I admitted to myself, most devotional, unspoiled, quite lovely. Classes were apparently in session, for I met no one.

Finally, I returned to my quarters. Both servants were awaiting me outside and, indeed, followed me inside. In a word, I was staggered by what they had accomplished. The little room had been scrubbed and polished until it shone. A new linen curtain adorned the clean little window and a natty little Spanish rug lay on the tiled floor. Another gift from some empty room upstairs was a padded wicker armchair. The chest of drawers, still exuding a healthy aroma of beeswax, was now revealed as a veritable Andalusian antique. And finally, the wreck of a bed had been put together and serviced with well-bleached fresh white linen.

I looked gratefully at my two benefactors, both smiling and expectant.

"Nice room now, *señor*. Quiet. Lovely cool in summer."

I took out my pocketbook and extracted another brand-new fifty, fresh from the cashier at the Ritz. When I handed one fifty to each, their joy was a pleasure to behold.

"We come often, when everything is quiet, to keep it nice, nice, *señor*."

"Do that, Martes and José, for now you are my friends."

When they had gone, looking back with more smiles, I unpacked, and put my things away in the newly papered drawers. Then I stood my two little pictures on the chest, pushed the empty suitcase under the bed, and with a last look around, went out.

And there in the ward, coming toward me, was my enemy.

"Been busy, Fitzgerald?"

"Not more than usual, Father."

"Let's have a look."

He went down the steps. I did not follow. Presently, when he had obviously examined everything, opened my drawers and fingered my underwear, he emerged, smiling. And how I distrusted that smile.

"Congratulations, Fitzgerald. You've done a wonderful job. I didn't know you had it in you." And he put a genial hand upon my shoulder.

Retreating from this false embrace, I looked him in the eye.

"You know I did not do it. So don't try to make me out a liar. Whatever you think of me I have never been that, and you'll never trick me into being one."

He was silent. Then in his normal voice, he said, "Not bad, Fitzgerald. I may make a missionary of you yet. Now it's time for our delicious *mercenda*. Come, and I'll show you the refectory."

This was a large hall in the far new building with a platform at one end, and below, perhaps twenty long tables at which my future comrades were getting ready to stuff themselves. Hackett showed me to the end of one of the tables and then took the center chair at the platform table where, on either side, he was flanked by two priests. Grace was then said and, as a youth began to read at a lectern from what apparently was the *Book of Martyrs,* the lunch was served by Martes, which suggested I might receive some tasty bits.

Alas, the dish was a tasteless *olla podrida* of rice and peas, semi-liquid and floating with snippets of tough beef, which must have been severed with a hatchet. I nerved myself to eat my portion, knowing that if I did not learn to get down this fodder, I would undoubtedly starve to death. Some sour goat cheese, followed with a hunk of bread, which actually was not bad, this followed by a bowl of black liquid masquerading as coffee. I managed this bitter brew in gulps. At least it was hot.

Meanwhile, I had been surveying the other inmates whom, for the most part, I detested on sight, in particular, a big ugly brute of a youth who sat at the head of the middle table and was addressed as Duff.

In regard to the clergy, one, and only one, seemed aware of my existence, a little waif of a man, red-cheeked and gray-haired, who kept moping and mowing in my direction. When I inquired of my

neighbor as to his identity, he muttered, since silence was imposed:
"Father Petitt, music master."

Dear God, I thought, this is the last straw, and when we got up and gave thanks, and he seemed to be making signs to me, I hurriedly rose, mingled with the crowd, and made tracks for my little cell. This was the free hour, in which I began to compose and write this letter, now completed late, by candlelight, on the following day.

As I cannot risk subjecting it to the censoring of bloody Hackett, I shall entrust it to my little Spanish friend, who will mail it in the village. Do forgive this long, labored screed, dear A. J. I wanted you to know exactly how I am situated and what, if I survive, is in store for me over the next four years.

Do remember me to your dear mother.

Most affectionately yours,
DESMONDE

P.S. The neat little severed hand is now revealed as the relic of one of the boys, a young priest, killed and mutilated in the Congo, his body recovered by Belgian troops who preserved and sent the hand. This gives Hackett one good mark in my book, that he should preserve and reverence it.

2

What was one to make of that long and rambling, so typical letter? I allowed my mother to read it, since she was fond of Desmonde and interested in his priestly progress. She shook her head. "Poor boy. He will never do it."

But a long succession of letters, arriving periodically, seemed to contradict this foreboding. Moody, complaining, lit by occasional humor or bursts of fury against Hackett, they were so repetitious and, indeed, so unworthy of Desmonde, that I have suppressed them. Weighed against the events that were to follow, this was a dull period in Desmonde's life. Its virtue was his persistence, as in succession he became subdeacon, then deacon. In the early stages of his novitiate, his only friend among a rough lot was a boy as sensitive and intelligent as himself, nicknamed "Looney," with whom he foregathered at recreation hour to play dreary games of tennis with antique rackets and wornout balls on a court well marked by sun-baked bovine excrement. At other times they would pace the cloister of the old abbey in silence, absorbing the beauty and peace of this much neglected part of the college. On wet days they foregathered in the library to read, although not from the volumes of the martyrs, with which the shelves were loaded, but other and less saintly books. They also got together to compose rude clerihews and limericks, mostly dedicated to Hackett. These, written in disguised hand, were discreetly dropped in the lavatories and other more public places.

With the one exception of Father Petitt, Desmonde received little comfort from his priestly instructors, whom he often offended by revealing that he knew more than they were attempting to teach. But Petitt, the elderly, pink-cheeked, rather timid little priest, already described as "moping and mowing in an introductory manner," was from the first extremely well-disposed toward Desmonde, whose school report had been of paramount interest to a choirmaster lost in a musical wilderness. Petitt could not really lay claim to this attribution. He played the church organ, taught the piano or violin on demand, and mustered enough voices to decently control the hymns, litanies and plainsong, which would otherwise have been bawled beyond recognition. How he had come to the seminary was a matter for conjecture, since Petitt was not only reticent but so painfully shy that a direct question would make him flush. He had undoubtedly been musical from an early age, and while still in his teens had played with one of the Midland orchestras, his instrument, appropriately enough, the flute. How, or why, he had suddenly decided to study for the priesthood he would never reveal. So, also, was he silent on the many changes, the shuttling from one parish to another, to which he had been subjected after his ordination. He was not made to be a success, even in the service of the Lord, but his knowledge of music remained, and he felt it a blessing to find himself finally at Saint Simeon's. Here he was beloved by all, and particularly by Father Superior, who favored "the little fellow" in many ways.

Soon after Desmonde's first meeting with Father Petitt, he was gently lured to the music room, a long, low raftered chamber, high up above the cloisters of the old abbey, remote from concrete and from all other distracting sights and sounds.

"Sit, Desmonde, and permit me to talk to you."

As they sat together on a frayed old sofa near the upright piano, Desmonde saw that the little fellow was nervous, and breathing quickly, as he began:

"My dear Desmonde, your report from Saint Ignatius made special mention, among your other attributes, of your exceptional voice. When I read of it, I trembled with ill-suppressed anticipation. Now, do not be alarmed." He laid a hand on Desmonde's arm. "I would not for worlds throw you to the wolves by requesting you to sing with that howling mob in church, who yell their way through the hymns and the easy pieces of Bach and Haydn I have drummed into them. No, my dear Desmonde, I have a long-treasured hope." His voice trembled. "A possibility, a dream, a project that I have nursed through many fruitless years." He paused. "Before I go on, would you oblige me by singing to me."

Desmonde had now been captivated by "the little fellow."

"What would you like me to sing, Father?"

"Do you know Schubert's 'Ave Maria'?"

"Of course, Father."

"It is difficult." He indicate the piano. "Shall I accompany you?"

"It's not necessary, thank you, Father."

Desmonde loved this beautiful hymn, and he sang it now with real enjoyment.

When it ended he looked down at Father Petitt. The little man was sitting with his eyes closed, his lips moving in silent prayer. At last he opened rather watery eyes and, inviting Desmonde again to sit beside him, he said:

"My dear Desmonde, I was thanking Our Blessed Lord for answering a prayer I have made to Him for more than three years. Will you listen while I explain. And by the way, may I continue to call you Desmonde?"

"I wish you would, Father."

It was the first time Desmonde had been so addressed since he entered the seminary. And he listened intently while, for almost ten minutes, Father Petitt poured out his heart to him. A long silence followed this emotional outburst. Then:

"Will you try, Desmonde?"

"If you think I should."

"I believe it a God-given opportunity you should not throw away."

"Then I will."

They shook hands. The little man smiled.

"My idea is that you come up here during your free period in the afternoon, twice a week, say Tuesdays and Fridays, from three till five. We'll chat together and work, yes, work hard. For your relaxation I'll play you Beethoven, or whatever you prefer. And at the end I'll arrange for some refreshment to be brought up. I didn't do so today since I was not sure you would accept."

Desmonde went down to the stark austerity of seminary life with a new interest, the prospect of a relaxation he had always enjoyed, and an objective impossible almost to achieve, but which stirred his blood when, occasionally, he permitted himself to visualize a possible victory, murmuring, savoring the words, "The Golden Chalice."

The Tuesday and Friday sessions began and were regularly continued. In all his singing Desmonde had never had a tutor — he sang naturally, and had acquired many technical faults. Little Father Petitt set him many difficult pieces and did not fail to criticize.

"Desmonde, don't dwell on that last note as if you loved it and were afraid to let it go. That's a vulgar, sentimental trick. Try that passage again, you had just a trace of vibrato there. Avoid vibrato like sin. It's the damnation of many a good tenor. Don't blow up your high notes for effect, dying away like an expiring frog." Father Petitt resumed. "And now, Desmonde, what will be your 'choice' song at the contest? This is important, for much of the judging is based upon it."

Desmonde reflected for only a moment.

"I would wish to sing the Prize Song from *Die Meistersinger*." He added: "Wagner is not a favorite of mine, but this song is magnificent. Not only inspiring, but aspiring, reaching out for success, which makes it suitable for us."

Petitt nodded.

"Yes, a superb song. But long, very long, and difficult. Well, soon we will see what you can do with it."

On certain days Desmonde was not permitted to sing. He

rested on the sofa while "the little father" sat, with a cushion, at the piano and played, played selections from Brahms, Liszt, Schubert and Mozart, many of them Desmonde's favorites.

Regularly, at quarter to five, Martes would come up with something from the kitchen, normally reserved for the priests' table. Often he would come earlier and stand outside the door, listening. From some remote cupboard Father Petitt produced a kettle and spirit lamp on which he brewed tea.

This undreamed-of relaxation from the rigorous seminary routine, so in accord with Desmonde's tastes and natural disposition, undoubtedly saved him from abandoning his vocation, or perhaps from a breakdown. He referred to it continually in his letters, relating how gradually, subtly, he came to take possession of the attic room until he could come to it whenever he was free from the routine of the day. He wrote all his letters in this blessed seclusion and, stretched on the old couch, rested for half an hour, fighting down the inedible lunch, before starting work for the afternoon. He had uncovered a great pile of German music from the cabinet in the piano bench. He played through this and sang from it, too, until his sight-reading became perfect. Some of the lighter pieces he learned by heart. Two of Schubert's songs, "Der Lindenbaum" and "Frühlingstraum," he particularly liked, and that sweet lovesong of Schumann, "Wenn ich in Deine Augen seh." Serious songs there were, also: Brahms' "Tod das ist die kühle Nacht," and surprisingly, in English, some excerpts from Handel's *Messiah,* best of all, the touching, "I know that my Redeemer liveth."

One afternoon, when he was singing his heart out on a favorite piece from Handel, "The people that walked in darkness," he did not hear the door open behind him. And when he turned, there was the great, the ominous figure of Hackett. He had been listening in the doorway.

Desmonde almost fell off the bench. He trembled, thinking, this is the end, as Hackett slowly came toward him. But what was this? A huge, approving hand laid on his shoulder, and the words, not hurled at him, but mildly spoken:

"That was truly beautiful, Fitzgerald. I'm no professor, but I know the best when I hear it. Keep on, keep at it, and win, for the honor, and for the college, the Chalice."

He paused. "By the way, would you like to change your bedroom to one of the bigger rooms upstairs?"

"Thank you, Father, but, no. I like my little cell."

"Good for you, Fitzgerald. I'll make a martyr out o' ye yet."

He smiled, actually smiled, turned, and was gone.

Desmonde went down the old abbey staircase as noisily as possible, singing a hosannah at the top pitch of his lungs. No need to creep now. He was sanctioned, even sanctified; the little attic study was his own.

Desmonde's dislike of Father Hackett had been modified by the unexpected kindness his superior had shown him. Yet he could not quite accept the persistent and insistent missionary complex that seemed the dominant factor in the teaching of the Seminary and the substance, more often than not, of Father Hackett's short but powerful sermons.

One Sunday the morning discourse made a particular impression upon Desmonde. Father Hackett began quietly extolling the virtue and necessity of missionary endeavors, in obedience to the command of Christ: " 'Go therefore and make disciples of all nations' — Matthew XXVIII, 19. And Saint Paul has voiced the same command: 'Woe to me if I do not preach the Gospel' — Corinthians IX, 16. Christ has repeatedly stressed the Church's evangelical mission, the need to preach the Gospel and to educate its members to the greater knowledge and consciousness of God.

"The core of the Catholic Church is missionary in nature," Hackett insisted. "An obedience to the command of Christ to exert a moral influence for social justice, to build schools, hospitals, dispensaries for the poor, the ignorant, the oppressed."

He then moved on to the great names in the missionary history of the Church, a subject dear to his heart, beginning with Saint Paul, who had carried Christianity to the Gentiles, the Apostle James the Greater in Spain, and the Apostle Thomas in his conversion of the Malabar Indians. And, thereafter, Saint Martin of Tours in France, Saint Patrick and Saint Columban in Ireland, Saint Augustine, the first Bishop of Canterbury in the year 596.

Father Hackett then went on to speak of the great Jesuit missionaries, citing the case of the Jesuit Matteo Ricci, who early in the sixteenth century made the great breakthrough in China by an intensive study of the Chinese language and culture. His gifts of a clock and a spinet won the favor of the Emperor Wan-li and subsequent freedom to preach and teach. And in India, the Jesuit Roberto de Nobile, adopting the dress and manner of life of the Brahmans, outdid them in austerity and made thousands of converts among the upper classes.

"Do not imagine for one moment," Hackett went on, "that all this sublime work was accomplished without sacrifice, the supreme sacrifice. In one year in the Congo alone, one hundred and six priests, twenty-four brothers and thirty-seven sisters were cruelly murdered in the performance of their holy work."

Father Hackett paused and, with a break in his voice, declared:

"Here, from this Seminary, one of the many young missionaries we have sent forth over the years to all parts of the world, that noble and distinguished youth Father Stephen Ridgeway, was brutally murdered and his body hacked to pieces while bearing the word of God into the wild and unexplored jungles of the Upper Congo.

"You are aware of the sacred relic recovered by Belgian soldiers and sent to us by the Belgian fathers at Kadiri, the hand of this brave and noble youth, severed from his arm by a slash of the savage pangas and miraculously, I repeat, miraculously preserved, fresh and undefiled, as though it still were a living part of Stephen's living body.

"You have viewed this relic, exposed to you for veneration at the Mass we celebrate on the anniversary of Stephen's glorious martyrdom. It is my most precious possession, and will be shown in all its miraculous freshness when I apply for the canonization of this saintly youth, the pride of this seminary and a model, an inspiration and incentive to all of you here.

"What joy in Heaven, and to me, humble advocate of the missionary life, if, beyond these brave good souls who have already chosen this *via dolorosa* others among you would come and say to me: 'I, too, accept the message, nay, the command of Christ to 'Go forth and preach the Gospel.' "

Again a pause, then: "Stand up, and let us all sing that splendid hymn, the battle cry of all who lead the fight for Jesus, 'Onward, Christian Soldiers.' "

Clearly, Father Hackett was now better disposed to the novice he had formerly so harshly treated. Yet Desmonde could not altogether respond to the advances made by his superior. An unpleasant thought kept nagging him, and on the afternoon following the Father Superior's impassioned sermon, this found expression in the music room when he suddenly exclaimed to his tutor:

"Doesn't Father Hackett's missionary complex strike you as being rather cheap? If he feels so strongly on that subject, instead of urging us out to martyrdom, why won't he take a turn out there himself?"

Little Petitt dropped the sheet of music he was holding and looked at Desmonde sternly.

"That is a most uncharitable and uncalled-for remark."

"But isn't it true?"

Again he studied Desmonde with a kind of angry surprise.

"Don't you know that Father Superior spent twelve years of his life as a missionary? Immediately after ordination he went to India to work among the Untouchables — the lowest and most despised of all humans. With his own hands he built a little dispensary, then started a little school, began to clothe and teach those ragged, starved children whose days and nights were spent in the gutters of Madras. He literally pestered his friends at home for money to clothe and feed these little unwanted children, taught them the catechism, led them into Christianity, while all the time living in the humblest, poorest quarter of the city where cholera is almost endemic.

"Of course, through his unsparing tending of the sick, he went down with cholera, recovered, and was invalided home.

"In his absence a young American priest had carried on his good work and joined up with Father Hackett when Hackett returned. Together they achieved miracles, until an epidemic of yellow fever struck the up-country province of Lingunda. Leaving his fellow priest in charge of the Madras mission, Hackett left for the plague center. Six weeks later, after heroic devotion to the sick and the dying, he was himself stricken, nearly died, and was invalided home so wrecked, so devastated by that frightful disease that he was refused permission to return. Since it was now imperative for him to live in a warm climate, he was given this relatively easy appointment in Spain."

A long silence followed this brief exposition by Father Petitt, during which Desmonde remained perfectly still, a strange expression on his face. Suddenly he sprang to his feet.

"Please excuse me, Father. I must leave you." And he rushed from the room.

Perhaps little Petitt had an inkling of the meaning of Desmonde's sudden departure, a premonition that he would soon return. He went to the piano and began softly to play his favorite "Ave Maria."

He was still playing, and continued to play when Desmonde did come back, at the same time turning to inspect his pupil and to murmur slyly:

"You look happy. Good confession?"

"And forgiveness from a saintly priest," Desmonde said humbly.

3

Desmonde was now settled down at the seminary almost comfortably, rescued from earlier miseries by his God-given voice. His fastidious palate had even come to tolerate the unsavory messes of the regime, since these were now mercifully ameliorated by fruit, notably peaches, from the surrounding orchards. He was even on surprisingly good terms with the Father Superior, who had begun to suspect hitherto unforeseen possibilities in this strange novice.

Desmonde's letters were now infrequent, altogether less anguished, indeed, full of hope and tinged with a sense of dedication, an ardor that seemed to grow as time went on. One might say enthusiasm but for the fact that the discipline of the college had tempered Desmonde's natural ebullience.

During this phase, benign and prolonged, Desmonde passed through the various stages of his novitiate. And how pleasing this was to his mother, who longed to see her son a priest.

At least once every two or three weeks we went on Sunday to lunch with Mrs. Fitzgerald. The conversation always was centered on Desmonde. Now almost an invalid, she was living for the great event, yet I doubted if she would survive to see her son ordained. I was now within sight of my final examinations, and her symptoms of cardiac involvement, pallor, shortness of breath, and marked edema of the ankles, were only too apparent to me, a diagnosis confirmed when she showed me the medicine prescribed for her: little pillules of Nativelle's digitalin. I was now "houseman" to Sir William Macewen, living in, with full board and lodging, at the Western Infirmary, and so ameliorating the burden my mother had heroically borne for so many years. Soon I hoped to be able to recompense her fully by sending her resignation to the Winton Corporation, terminating the work that had kept us both alive for so many hard years.

This satisfactory, almost benign state of being, for Desmonde and myself, continued for some further months until suddenly, out of the blue, a letter arrived, stamped with the familiar Spanish postmark. A letter so bulky and hurriedly written that I suspected disaster even as I unfolded it.

My dear A. J.,

I have been in despair, cast down, humiliated, abused, ground into the dust, almost expelled, my priestly vocation in jeopardy, and all, I repeat, in my honest and unprejudiced opinion, through no fault of my own. Only now am I able to raise my bowed and bloody head, to give you the full circumstances of the case and to invoke your sympathy.

I believe I already mentioned, in a previous letter, that one of the few ameliorations in our strict regime is the weekly walk we are permitted to take to the town every Thursday afternoon. We go in a group, unchaperoned, with permission to buy fruit or other legitimate refreshment from the various vendors who are always about, in anticipation of our visit. Our absence from the Seminary is never permitted to exceed one hour.

I need not tell you how eagerly we anticipate, not only this brief escape from our hard routine, not alone our momentary contact with the normal outside world, but also the many delicious fruits which we may purchase for a few *pesetas*. What else is there in this typical little Spanish village to excite us: the single dusty, winding, street, lined with little houses, all blinding white in the perennial sun, with groups of old black-clad women seated in front, stitching and gossiping. Dark little passages lead into the dark little shops which, solely because of the nearness of the seminary, sell extraneous articles: soaps, toothpaste and brushes, simple medicines, postcards and even sweets. In season, too, mainly to seduce the students, they are piled with grapes, Malaga oranges, and peaches.

I am especially fond of peaches, as indeed are many of the other novices, and we are always met at the entrance to the town by a young woman, a girl, to be exact, who takes advantage of the other vendors by coming toward us with a big, flat pannier slung from her shoulder and heaped with ripe, delicious fruit. In the interest of her business, she has established a friendly relationship with us and it has become more or less customary for us to stand and chat with her for a few moments, practicing our Spanish, before we continue into the town.

On this particular Thursday of ill-omen, I had been held up by Father Petitt, my admirable music master, who was rather excited by receiving long-looked-for news from Rome of the proposed song festival. I was, in consequence, late in passing through the gates and when, by hurrying, I made up on my companions, I saw to my chagrin that all the peaches had been cleared.

"Oh dear, Caterina, you have kept nothing for me."

She shook her head, smiled, showing her nice white teeth.

"You are too late. You must never be late for a meeting with a lady."

All this was in Spanish, but as you have always accused me, A. J., of swanking my languages, I will continue in English.

"Yes, you are too late, nice little priest, and you must never be late for a rendezvous with a lady."

My colleagues, in particular Duff, the raw-boned Aberdonian, who detests me, had begun to enjoy my predicament as I said:

"I am sad. I thought I was your favorite customer."

"So you are sad, truly sad."

"Yes. Truly sad."

"Then smile now, your beautiful smile." And to my surprise and delight, she produced from behind her back two of the biggest and most luscious peaches I had ever seen.

The chuckles and guffaws around me had subsided as, slinging the pannier to one side, she came up to me holding a peach in each hand.

"Did you think for one second that I would forget you? Take them."

I felt in my pocket to pay her and, to my dismay, discovered that I had no money. In my haste I had forgotten my purse. My distress must have been obvious, not only to the onlookers but to her, as I stammered.

"I am so sorry. I cannot pay you."

She came quite close to me, still smiling. "So you have no money? I am pleased. For then you must pay me with a kiss."

She placed a peach in each of my hands and, as I stood there helpless, threw her arms around me and pressed her lips against mine in an embrace that was unquestionably passionate, at the same time murmuring in my ear, "Come any evening after six, my darling little priestling, to 17 Calle de las Piñas. *For you it is free.*"

When finally she disengaged herself, looking up at me with her dark sparkling eyes and that same entrancing smile, the ominous silence was broken by a shout from the Aberdonian.

"Enough fellows. On to the town."

I followed in a state of dazed euphoria. That close and luscious embrace, tinged with the fragrance of peaches, had quite unmanned me. More or less isolated at the tail of the procession, I did, eventually, and to some degree, revive myself by consuming both of the delectable fruits.

Even on our return journey to the Seminary, no one spoke to me. Temporarily, at least, and through no fault of mine, I had become a pariah.

Next morning it did seem as though a thaw had set in, but at eleven o'clock I received a summons to appear before Father Superior in his study. Somewhat rechilled, I complied, my anxiety deepening when, on entering the room, I observed the tall, cadaverous figure of Duff standing by the window.

"Fitzgerald, a most serious charge has been laid against you." Father Superior, seated at his desk, made the accusation immediately. As I remained silent he continued. "That of embracing the girl Caterina and, furthermore, of having immoral relations with her."

I was stupefied and, suddenly, enraged. I looked at the Avenging Angel by the window. He avoided my gaze.

"Who makes these charges? Plum Duff?"

"The name is Duff, Fitzgerald. He was present when you embraced the girl Caterina. Do you deny this?"

"Absolutely and completely. It was she who embraced me."

"You did not resist her?"

"It was impossible. I had a large ripe peach in each hand."

"She had given you these peaches. Without payment. Does not that suggest intimacy?"

"She is a jolly, friendly girl. We were all her customers and, in a sense, intimate with her. We all laughed and joked with her."

"No' me." A sepulchral voice came from the window. "Ah saw frae the furst she was a hoor."

"Silence Pl . . . Duff. Of all the others you were her special

[64]

intimate, her choice, in fact. So that she arranged an assignation for that evening, to which you replied O.K."

I was now livid with rage.

"I have never in my life uttered such a corrupt and vulgar term. Who accuses me of using it?"

"Duff has keen ears."

"They are big enough."

Father Superior ignored this and resumed the attack.

"I have made inquiry. This Caterina Menotti, if not precisely a prostitute, is regarded officially as a *fille de joie*."

"Didna' ah tell ye, yer Reverence. She even gien him her address."

"Quiet, you Scottish oaf." Father Superior's evident annoyance with Plum slightly cheered me. But he went on: "Do you deny that you have ever visited her at this address?"

"If I had visited her, why should she give me her address? I would certainly have known it."

Father Superior looked inquiringly at Duff, who blurted out:

"She must of telt him to remind him in case he had forgot it."

A chilly silence followed this assumption, then Father Superior made a gesture toward the door.

"You may depart, Duff."

"I'm sure your Reverence kens I only brought this to your notice from the highest possible personal motives of virtue and the good name o' the college and forbye because there's nae doubt in my mind but what Fitzgerald . . ."

"Depart, Duff, instantly, or I shall be compelled to punish you with marked severity."

When Duff had departed, shaking his head, the Rector was silent, studying me reflectively. Finally he spoke.

"I don't believe for a moment, Fitzgerald, that you visited that house, or that you had carnal knowledge of that girl. If I did, you would leave the college this very afternoon. But you behaved in a manner that laid you open to a suspicion of grave misconduct, and one which disgraced and dishonored the college. I shall have to consult with my colleagues as to what your sentence must be. Meanwhile, whether you must go, or whether you stay, I give you this advice.

"You are obviously inordinately attractive to the other sex. Be on your guard, therefore, against advances that may be made to you. Remain always in control of yourself and your emotions. Be discreet, calm, ready to withdraw at the slightest sign of danger. Do this, and you will spare yourself much pain, grief, and subsequent disaster. Now you may leave. You will know your fate by tomorrow afternooon. Go to the church and pray that I may not be compelled to send you away."

I bowed and went out, straight to the church where, I assure you, I made my entreaties wtih fervor. I knew how severe Hackett could be — only a few months before, he had dismissed one of the younger novices for smoking a little end of cigar. Warned once before, this fellow had disobeyed the order. It was enough.

On the following day I continued to suffer until five o'clock, when our good choirmaster Father Petitt came toward me, and put his arm on my shoulders.

"I am deputed to tell you, Desmonde, that you are to remain. You are gated until the end of the term but, thank God, you are saved, not only for your vocation but," he smiled, "for our foray in Rome next month."

I had begun to thank him when he added: "Yes, you may be grateful to me. I think I swung the decision in your favor. I don't have a voice like yours, not once in a hundred years."

So there, dear A. J., is a verbatim report on the latest and most serious trial and tribulation of your most affectionate friend. I long for news of you. Do write to me immediately you have the results of your final examinations. You don't know how often I picture you, studying hard, in your bare little room. In return I will brief you on the proposed visit to Rome, with all the details, everything I have hitherto withheld.

Ever yours most devotedly,

DESMONDE

4

————

I had now passed my final examinations for the M.B.Ch.B. and had taken a temporary assistantship with Dr. Kinloch, an old and widely respected general practitioner in Winton. This was not my ultimate objective, nor the simple M.B.Ch.B. the last degree I meant to achieve, but it would keep me near my mother for at least six months, and with an annual salary of £400 would enable me, at last, to remove her from her work in the slums and to relieve the hardships she had bravely borne for so many years.

When I called to see Mrs. Fitzgerald it was now in a professional capacity. I was seriously worried by her deteriorating condition and, when she permitted me to examine her, the diagnosis was never in doubt: acute mitral stenosis with partial occlusion of the coronary artery. I persuaded her to allow me to bring Dr. Kinloch in consultation. He confirmed the diagnosis and, while cheering the patient and prescribing for her, gave an even more grave prognosis: she must rest in bed pending an improvement in her general edema. Indeed, as we drove back in his little cabriolet, he said:

"With that heart she might go at any minute."

The dream of her life had been to see her beloved son ordained a priest of God. Now it was necessary to tell her that, in her present condition, she would never reach Rome. I could not bring myself to deliver this crushing blow and my mother, now free to visit her friend every other day, and wiser than I, begged me to refrain for at least one more month.

So it befell that Desmonde's mother, falling asleep one night in a bright vision of her son's future, did not awaken to reality, disappointment and despair. She died peacefully and without pain.

Desmonde, summoned immediately by telegram, arrived the day before the funeral, his manner sad yet restrained, without the abject manifestations of grief that might have been expected of him. I saw at once that he had changed, that his five years in the seminary had left their mark upon him, leaving him more restrained, rather more in control of himself. My mother epitomized it: "Desmonde has grown up."

Even at the graveside, he bore up well although tears, and bitter ones were shed. Immediately after the funeral, since he had been granted only three days' leave, he talked with the lawyer. His mother's annuity died with her, but she had saved for him an amount exceeding three thousand pounds. He would also receive monies accrued from the sale of the lease of the house. Many of her nice clothes, including her fur coat and a brand new costume, no doubt intended for the ordination, she left to my mother, together with some of her best furniture, eminently acceptable gifts that moved the recipient to tears. For myself, who expected nothing, there was a gift outright of one hundred pounds.

Desmonde's train did not leave till midnight and that night, after my evening surgery, I sat late with him in his silent house and drew close to him again, as if we had never been apart.

Inevitably he spoke of his mother, concluding with a truism:

"Isn't it amazing, the good a good woman can do to a man."

"And the bad, a bad one can do. There's plenty of them around."

"Always the realist, A. J." He smiled. "What are your plans, now you have your degree?"

I told him this was merely the first step, that I meant to take my M.D., and then to try for the M.R.C.P., adding:

"That's a hard nut to crack. Terribly difficult."

"You'll do it, A. J."

"How do you see your future?"

"Less clearly than yours. I shall be ordained in a matter of weeks, and as I haven't always pleased the powers that be, I've a sad foreboding that, after a training period at the seminary, I shall be sent to do penance in some rough parish, probably Irish, since I am an Irish citizen."

"You won't like that."

"No, A. J., but it may be good for me. My views have changed rather, under the tender solicitude of the good Father Hackett."

I looked at him inquiringly as he went on.

"This Hackett is a strange fellow, A. J. I began by hating his guts. And he gave every manifestation of loathing me. I thought him a bully and a sadist. He's not really, simply a zealot. He's imbued, saturated with missionary zeal. He would like all his students to go forth into the wilderness to preach the word of God. I thought him a maniac. I don't now. He's a throwback to one of the Apostles, probably Paul. I have come to like and respect him — in fact he has rather got me."

"Do you see yourself as a second Saint Patrick?"

He flushed. "Don't laugh, A. J. How do we know what's ahead of us? You might suddenly chuck medicine and become a popular author. I might one day lay my bones in some tropical jungle."

Impossible not to laugh, loud and long. And in a moment he joined me.

"Anyway, I understand and respect Hackett now, and I'd like to repay him. There's a competition in Rome. Promoted by the Società Musicale di Roma with lots of backing from the Vatican, open to young priests newly ordained or to novices on the eve of ordination. The basic idea is to encourage the use of the voice, in the sung Mass, the litanies, and so forth. Quite a noble idea, and nobly named the Golden Chalice. Father Hackett would like me to try for it." He paused. "We're a small college at Tarrijas, with an inferiority complex, far less well-known than our counterpart at Valladolid. What a lift it would give us, and what publicity, if we could put the trophy — it's a golden chalice — in our front window."

"When is the happy event?"

"Next June. So you can picture me following scores of others — Italy is bristling with young tenors — onto a platform deco-rated with a blasted panel of experts, lay and clerical, and sing-ing my heart out before an audience, normally in the hundreds."

"You'll win, hands down, Desmonde. Want to bet?"

He smiled. "With my ordination so near, A. J., I am barred from donating coins of the realm to a very dead, canny Scot." He looked at his watch. "I'm afraid we'll have to go now. Let's walk down to the Central."

When he had taken a last look around the house he took his bag and, pausing sadly on the threshold, shut and locked the front door. "It's a Chubb lock. The agent has the key."

As we set out for the station, he took my arm with his free hand.

"Too bad keeping you up so late, A. J."

"I'm often up late, or in the middle of the night. Let me take your bag."

He shook his head. "I carry my own these days. Listen, A. J. May I ask you a medical question?"

"Of course." I wondered what was coming, but never ex-pected what followed.

"It's rather an odd question, but do answer me seriously. If a human hand was severed at the wrist, would it eventually decay?"

"Absolutely! After a week it would stink to high heaven, putrefy, then liquify and finally rot, leaving only the bones, which would in time separate into the carpal and metacarpals — little knobs of disintegrating calcium."

"Thank you, A. J. Thank you very much."

No more was said, and soon we were in the Central Station. I saw him to his third-class compartment.

"Don't wait, dear A. J. These prolonged farewells are hell. Besides, I know, absolutely know, that one day our lives will be together again."

We shook hands. Then I turned away and walked quickly from the station. I hoped he was right, that we should one day meet again. I also hoped the last tram for Western Road had not gone.

Six weeks later Desmonde was ordained and, fulfilling his forebodings, officially notified to proceed to the Church of Saint Teresa in the parish of Kilbarrack in Southern Ireland. But much was to happen before then, as Desmonde will now relate.

5
___

On the morning of our departure, Father Superior came himself to my little cell to awaken me one hour earlier than usual. When I had dressed, he stood while I threw some things in my suitcase. Then we went together to the church where little Petitt was awaiting us. Both he and Father Hackett had already said their Mass but both remained in the front seat while I said mine, and I assure you I did not omit a petition for heavenly aid in the endeavor now before me.

When I had finished, Father Hackett took me by the arm and conducted me to his study, where Martes was standing by with good hot coffee, not the habitual refectory sludge, and fresh hot rolls. My Superior watched me in silence while I made a good meal, but refused, quite nicely, when I asked if he would take a cup.

When Martes had cleared away he said:

"I have arranged for you to have a car to Madrid."

"Oh, thank you, Father. That local is a beastly train."

"It is not a beastly train. It is a most useful train for our peasants and farmers taking their produce to the Madrid markets. It is, however, rather slow and uncertain in its arrival. Hence the car, not a Hispano-Suiza, nevertheless a car."

"You are right, Father," I said at once. "I am always putting my foot in it with you."

"Not so much as usual, Father Desmonde. Not nearly so much. In fact, while you are far from perfect, you are a much improved young man. I have taken great pains with you, and in return," he paused, fixing me with a steady eye, "I want you to bring the Golden Chalice to the college. It is, in itself, a bauble, a sorry trophy, but it would bring great prestige, not only to you, which is unimportant, but to the college."

He stood up, as did I, and moved to the prie-dieu. I followed.

"I am going to accord you a great favor. Kneel, take this blessed relic, and say a prayer for your success and mine."

I knelt and, I assure you, with great reverence took the little hand, so smooth, the skin so pliable it had the feeling of a living hand. Gently I pressed it and it seemed as though the fingers responded, enfolding mine with a touch both intimate and tender, as though unwilling to release, unwilling to relinquish this contact with a life once experienced and remembered now in tranquillity and joy. In this manner I made a truly fervent petition, not only for immediate success, but for a good life and a happy death.

"Well?" said Father Hackett, when I stood up.

"It is miraculous. There is the touch of Heaven in these fingers."

"You must tell that to your doctor friend who demands putrid flesh and rotting bones. Now come, it is time for you to go."

The car, a solid little Berlier, was already in the yard and beside it, with my suitcase and his own carpetbag, Father Petitt. When we were in the car, the luggage safely in the boot, I saw Father Hackett, as we set off, make a big Sign of the Cross, blessing us. In the beginning I had hated this dedicated priest. Now, though he deliberately repelled all affection, I truly revered him.

In about an hour we were in Madrid and in the *rápido* for Rome, Father Petitt exercising an almost maternal solicitude upon me, imposing silence, forbidding the window to be widely opened, suspecting drafts from all points of the compass, as though I were a chicken just out of the egg. At Rome Station, however, his confidence evaporated, and he was glad to have me

[73]

summon a porter to transfer our bags to a taxi which I duly directed to the Hotel Religioso, where rooms had been reserved for us by our Superior.

Alas, the Religioso was a sad blow. Piety might be practiced here, but all temporal virtues were totally in abeyance. As I surveyed the bare, linoleumed, liftless hall, the precipitous, uncarpeted stairs, and finally our two monastic little rooms overlooking the railway shunting yards from which, amid a grinding, snorting, puffing consortium of engines and their appendages, clouds of steam and smoke billowed toward us, my heart sank. With four full days remaining before the songfest, what a preparation for our ordeal! And I had hoped for such leisured, pleasant ease in this reunion with my favorite city.

I glanced at little Petitt. He did not mind, not a bit, but I was bitterly cast-down and at the midday meal, a *polenta* mélange served on a wax-clothed table with flies embracing the sauce stains, my melancholy deepened and continued until the shades of night began to fall.

And then, A. J., Heaven responded to my unspoken prayers. As we sat staring at each other in what I might call the commercial room, a frightened youth in an outside porter's uniform approached us at the double.

"A lady at the door, sir, in car, asking for you."

I made for the door, also at the double, and there, yes, yes, A. J., there in a big, new Hispano-Suiza, was my friend the Marchesa. She had read of our arrival in the evening paper, *Paese Sera di Roma,* and had instantly gone into action.

"Come, come at once, Desmonde. You must not remain here an instant longer. I am afraid even to enter. Come to me."

"I have a little friend, a priest, Madame. He wouldn't take up much room."

"Bring him, bring the little priest at once. Come, both of you."

Needless to say, we did not refuse, and in no time at all we were in the big car with our belongings — I in the back seat with Madame, Father Petitt, still dazed, in front with the chauffeur, gliding toward distinguished affluence, leaving the youthful porter gaping in our wake, stunned by the tip I had recklessly thrust upon him.

It was after ten o'clock when we reached the Villa Penserosa, past the hour of dinner, and although refreshments were pressed upon us, I declined.

"Dear Madame, we have been stuffed with so much *polenta* since we became inmates of the Religioso that all we now long for is a good restful sleep."

"You shall have it." She spoke aside to the maid who stood waiting for instructions. "And as you are obviously tired, I shall say *buona notte* until tomorrow."

Our adjoining rooms, with a luxurious bathroom between, were, to the last detail, perfection. A suit of silk pajamas had even been laid out on my bed. Father Petitt had not the habit of a nightly bath, so I luxuriated for half an hour in deep, hot, soapy water, rubbed myself down with a turkish towel, donned the gift pajamas, in which I felt more unreal than ever, and fell into bed. Instantly, sleep overwhelmed me.

Next morning, agreeably late, we were awakened by break-fast: a large pot of steaming, freshly roasted coffee, with a little napkin-covered basket holding a tier of warmed Roman rolls, that special and richer variety of the French croissant. When I had dressed I went downstairs to find my hostess awaiting me in her little boudoir sewing-room, where all her charitable stitching was accomplished.

"Good morning, my dear Reverend Desmonde. I see from your fresh and shining air that you have slept well. Your little friend is now safely ensconced in the library with a book. So now you belong entirely to me."

She stood there smiling, facing the hard morning light without a qualm. Inevitably, she looked older, her hair now a silvery white, but her fine eyes were as lively and her mind as wittily alert as ever. How unutterably irresistible she must have been as a young woman. Even now she was a darling.

"However," she added, "all fresh and dewy you may be, but where, oh, where did you get those trousers?"

"Madame, these trousers, now only three years old, are the finest work of the finest sartorial artist in the village of Tarrijas."

"They are certainly unique. And the jacket?"

"This jacket, Madame, although venerable, is virtually a religious object, cut down, and suitably adjusted by the aforementioned tailor, from a discarded jacket previously in the possession of the Very Reverend Father Hackett."

"It is undoubtedly a relic. Come, Desmonde, and view yourself."

She pulled open the door of a cupboard on which a large pier mirror had been inset.

I had never seen so much of myself for a long, long time, and while the face remained passable, the rest of me might have been found on the trunk and legs of an aged and decrepit tramp.

"Yes," I reflected aloud, thoughtfully. "A little sponging and pressing would make me as good as new, Madame."

She laughed outright. "Desmonde, you are incorrigible. Listen, you must be quiet and rest until Saturday, but this morning you are coming with me, to visit my friend Caraccini."

"A priest?"

"No, merely the best tailor in all Italy. Don't worry about your friend. He is very happy in the library."

We set out in the beautiful big landaulet, not the Hispano as I had imagined, but a brand-new Isotta Fraschini, drove down the Via Veneto to the Excelsior, turned left, and drew up at a window displaying no goods, adorned simply with the word Caraccini.

We entered, Madame greeted with immense deference by a dapper little man in an immaculate dark gray suit. My needs, my situation, were fully discussed; bales of cloth were inspected, felt and selected. I was shown into a commodious cubicle where an underling in shirt-sleeves taped and measured all over me.

"You understand, Caraccini, everything must be finished and delivered by the evening of Friday."

"Madame la Marchesa, it is impossible. But for you," Caraccini bowed, "it will be accomplished."

All was not over, since Madame still wanted more fun, for thus she regarded and named her charity to me, and I was led into a nearby haberdasher's, one of obvious and unimpeachable distinction. Here my dear friend went a little wild, and in the end a variety of elegant and expensive garments had been chosen and set aside for immediate delivery. Finally, we dropped into the custom shoemaker's in the same street. Here my feet were sedulously measured and two leathers selected, one light and the other somewhat heavier, both pairs commandeered for the following Friday. How, one might ask, could such skilled work be accomplished in so short a time? The answer is in the fact that Rome is a city of craftsmen, and of women too, tucked away in little rooms and alleys throughout the city, receiving the work for speedy delivery and laboring, often through the night, to complete it. One would hope that such expertise would be amply rewarded. Alas, this is not so.

"Just a light little lunch," Madame said, when we emerged from the shoemaker's. "Then home, to rest, rest, rest until Saturday."

She led the way into the Excelsior bar where, seated at the bar, she proposed a sherry and a Parma sandwich. The car was parked outside the hotel. Soon we were on our way back to the Villa Penserosa. When I tried to thank her she would not hear a word of it.

"Quiet, dear Desmonde. You know I loved your mother and was so sorry when you wrote me of her death." She added, "You know also that I love you too, my dear boy."

As we approached the house she murmured, "I wonder what your little friend has been doing in your absence."

Immediately we were inside she took my arm and led the way to the library.

There, indeed, was the Reverend Father Petitt, seated in the same chair, with the same book upon his knees, open at the same page, a beatific smile upon his face and a gentle rhythmic sibilation coming from between his lips.

"He has not moved one millimeter," Madame gasped.

"Oh, yes, Madame," said the maid who had admitted us. "He ate a very good large lunch with a bottle of the good Frascati."

"He looks sweet when he is sleeping," Madame said. "Like a child."

"He has taught me a great deal," I said. "And if we should have any luck at all on Saturday I shall owe it all to him."

"What a nice thing to say, dear Reverend Desmonde. And now you must go to your room and rest. From now until Saturday it is rest, rest, rest, with little talking. Do you know that Enrico does not speak a word between his performances?"

"I am not Caruso, Madame."

"We shall see on Saturday." She smiled. "And now I must rest also, for I am tired. You see, I am an old woman now."

"Please don't say such evil words, Madame. You are as gracious, as charming, as darling as ever. And you have been an angel to me today."

She shook her head, still smiling, as she preceded me upstairs, then turned and went into her room while I entered mine.

6

Saturday dawned fine, and Desmonde, who had slept restlessly, rose early and drew up the venetian blinds to let the sun into his room. He then lay on his bed for ten minutes, considering the prospects of the day. Admittedly he was nervous. He wanted to win the Chalice, not entirely for personal success, but to please, and indeed repay, Father Hackett, the Marchesa, and especially little Petitt. And, as he told me afterward, his thoughts kept going back to the final of the Schools Shield which I had longed to win and which, alas, had been lost.

A knock on his door cut short his foreboding. The little fellow, dressed, and having already said his Mass, came into the room.

"Good night?"

"Quite good. And you?"

"Perfect!" This with an emphasis that gave perfection the lie.

"Beautiful day for us."

"Perfect."

"I left everything for you down below, when you're ready."

"Down below" was the little Sanctuary in the basement where, every day since their arrival, they had both said Mass.

"I'll be down straight away."

"Good!"

Desmonde did not shave but quickly got into his old suit and went downstairs to rejoin Father Petitt in the Sanctuary, a little rough stone grotto equipped with a simple altar, a crucifix, a statue of the Virgin, and two prie-dieux, a retreat for prayer and emergency services often found in large Italian houses. Father Petitt, with customary foresight, had brought everything necessary from the seminary.

Desmonde said his Mass, with Father Petitt acting as server, and it may be assumed that their prayers, those of the young priest and the old, were leavened by the same intention. Afterward, when Desmonde had made his thanksgiving, they went upstairs to a substantial breakfast, English style, of bacon and eggs, marmalade and toast.

As they were served, the elderly tablemaid whispered to Desmonde.

"Madame la Marchesa begs you to make a large breakfast, for it must be a very small lunch."

"We will obey," Desmonde said, smiling. "Madame la Marchesa will not herself be down?"

"Rarely she comes before ten o'clock."

The reply gave Desmonde a sudden understanding that his patroness, so lively and so charming, so active on his behalf, was, in years at least, an aging woman. Now he knew that he must do his utmost to succeed, if only to thank her.

After they had breakfasted, Desmonde with a good appetite, Father Petitt less so, they went together to the library.

"This is the beastly bit," Desmonde said. "Hanging on. By a thin rope over a cliff. I suppose I can't go out."

"Absolutely not. And you should talk little."

"God bless Caruso. If only I could sing like him."

"You will, if you remember all I told you. Be quiet, don't move around. Half of those young Italians will be flinging themselves about the stage with hands on their hearts. Now, listen. While you were shopping with *la Marchesa* I made inquiries. For your own choice song, which follows the set pieces, you will sing what?"

"As we decided. The Prize Song from *Meistersinger*, in the Italian translation."

[80]

"No, no. Listen to me. The cardinal from the Curia who is on the committee of judges — a very, a most important man — is a German cardinal. So you must, must, sing your Wagner piece in the original German."

"I prefer it that way. Is the hall large?"

"Very large, with a wide, high balcony. And it will be filled, every seat. The acoustics are excellent. On the stage will sit the judges, all important and informed people, teachers and professors of music, members of the Curia, including the cardinal, and members of the Society. I asked if our marchesa might sit with them but the answer was 'no.' It would be deemed favoritism and would prejudice the judges against you."

"I can believe that. Where will the Marchesa sit?"

"All competitors — the number has been screened down to twenty — will sit in the front row. And in the row behind, railed off from the auditorium, will sit special guests, including our good hostess."

"Good! Steps up to the stage, I suppose?"

"Exactly. Each candidate goes up in turn, sings two set pieces, is judged and given his marks. After all have been marked, and the marks are counted, ten are eliminated."

"And can go home, poor fellows."

"Certainly, they are dismissed. Again, for those who remain, one very difficult set piece. Again the candidate is marked and the marks counted. The low six are eliminated. And again, for the remaining four, the other very difficult set piece, after which two are eliminated and two remain. These two must choose each one song, sacred or not, on which they are judged, one sent down and the survivor awarded the prize."

"A fairly cold-blooded procedure."

"It is eminently fair, dear Desmonde. And for one to succeed, all others must fail. Besides, it gives a whole afternoon of excitement and good singing to the *aficionados*. And there are many, many of these, I assure you, ready to cheer."

"Or to howl you down." Desmonde looked at his watch. "Only ten o'clock. Another two hours of waiting misery."

He got up and began to wander around the room, looking over the shelves so nobly stocked. Suddenly, on a bottom shelf, given over to smaller and more personal books, his eye was caught by a little green book entitled *Heraldry of Ireland*. Oddly, it seemed familiar. He took it up from the shelf and opened it to the flyleaf. There, beneath his father's familiar bookmark, he read the words, written in ink, now faded:

For my very dearest Margarita with my deep affection and profound regard

DERMOT FITZGERALD

Desmonde remained motionless, holding the book, while a wave of emotion, of revelation and understanding, swept over him. He knew now the reason for the kindness so warmly bestowed upon him in this house. He saw, too, that the book had been held and fondled many times. Quietly he replaced it, leaving it perhaps a fraction of an inch out of line with the other books. Then he moved away.

"Going up to change now?" Petitt asked.

"Yes, it's about time."

He went slowly upstairs. As he was about to go into his room, he saw the marchesa coming toward him, looking fresh and rested, beautifully turned out in a suit of dark Italian silk.

"Good day, Desmonde dear."

He did not answer, but took her hand and, looking deep into her eyes, he kissed her fingers one by one. Always Desmonde was full of these silly little tricks and always the recipients seemed to like them. She smiled.

"I would blush, Desmonde, if I did not have my rouge on. What have you been doing with yourself all morning?"

"I have been reading, Madame. A most interesting book on heraldry. I was pleased to find that we Fitzgeralds were mentioned therein."

Did she understand? Later that morning he saw the book

had been lifted and replaced. But now, too quickly perhaps, though still smiling, she said:

"Now go and get ready for the fray."

Desmonde retreated to his room, washed and shaved more carefully than usual, brushed his hair, then put on his new clothes. How white and fine was the shirt, how light and well-fitting the suit. The shoes too, of pliable soft leather, had nothing of the rigid feeling of new shoes, but clung to his feet like gloves. The best is always the best, thought Desmonde, and what a pity it is always so expensive.

He could not view himself completely in the little bedroom mirror, but went downstairs smartly, hoping that all was well. The marchesa was in the hall with Father Petitt, walking up and down, obviously awaiting him. Both stopped dead when he appeared, as indeed, did he.

"I can't believe it's you, Desmonde," Father Petitt gasped.

Madame had not spoken but was circling him critically.

"Do clothes make such a difference?"

She smiled. "Dear Father Desmonde, how should I look in a washerwoman's old skirt and shawl? Never mind, I am pleased, very, very pleased with you. I knew Caraccini would not fail us. Perfection, there is no other word. Now come to lunch, such as it is."

"You both had a good breakfast?" Madame asked, as they sat down at the sparsely plenished dining room table.

"Wonderful," little Petitt chuckled.

"The finest since I was a boy back on the farm!"

"You were never on a farm, Desmonde!"

"Of course not, Madame, but I must, at all costs, dramatize the breakfast."

"Well now, for every reason, you will get little. And all is for the voice."

A cup of strong boullion was served with a raw egg floating rather repulsively upon the top, and afterwards, thin slices of fresh pineapple floating in the juice of the fruit.

"This clears the throat," Madame asserted, looking at the

clock. "And now we have time only for coffee. It is a bore, but they are so fussy and official at the Philharmonic, we must be early."

Coffee, strong black coffee, was swallowed. Then they were in the closed car, driving through sunny streets to the big auditorium off the Via di Pietra, where already crowds were moving toward the long row of clicking turnstiles.

"We go to the offices. Everything is very stuffy and old-fashioned here," Madame said briskly, leading the way to a narrow door beyond.

Here also a crowd was milling around, but the Marchesa, armed with Desmonde's letter, immediately commanded attention. They were shown into an inner office, thence to the auditorium proper, where Desmonde and Petitt found places in the front row, specially reserved for competitors. Madame la Marchesa was seated in a special reserved enclosure not far behind.

Already the auditorium was more than half-filled, and crowds were flowing in. On the stage, too, where the trophy, the Golden Chalice, was enthroned on a velvet podium, activities were increasing. From time to time, young priests of various sizes and conditions materialized, and nervously seated themselves on the candidates' bench.

Little Petitt moved restlessly. "Such waiting. These preparations are very trying for you, are they not?"

"Yes," said Desmonde. "I'm going to close my eyes. Nudge me when they're ready."

For perhaps twenty minutes Desmonde kept his eyes resolutely closed, ignoring the noise and the sense of movement around him, until his vision was restored by a tap on the shoulder. He then saw that the other candidates were lined up beside him, but that the committee of judges had assembled on tiered seats to the left of the stage, while at the rear a Philharmonia quartet was about to open the proceedings with the *Veni Creator Spiritus*. Everyone joined in this beautiful hymn, candidates, audience and committee alike, so that a great volume of sweet sound swelled and filled the hall.

The secretary of the society now stepped forward and in a brief speech outlined the object of the contest: to sustain and increase public interest throughout all Europe in the sung Mass, to maintain and keep alive that most historic, most beautiful offering to God, which now, alas, was threatened by the rush and hurry of this modern age, sacrificed to the demand for shorter, and still shorter, services. He then thanked the members of the Curia, and in particular His Eminence the German Cardinal, for attending on the committee so that the judging and allocation of marks would be absolutely just and impartial. He then looked meaningfully toward the crowded balcony and begged the many partisans who had come to support their candidates to realize that justice would be done and to refrain from demonstrations of all kinds. He then announced that the contest should begin.

Immediately ten candidates on the far side of Desmonde got up and mounted the steps to the stage, where they were seated on a long bench in one of the wings. The first test piece was announced, and after the quartet had played it through, the candidates, announced aloud one by one, came forward to sing it.

Desmonde, as may be imagined, listened intently. All were good choir voices, somewhat lost in the big hall, but two of the younger candidates were so manifestly nervous that they obviously did not give their best, while a third almost provoked laughter by a variety of enticing gestures, hand on the heart, first one then both arms outflung, all implying dramatic and emotional fervor.

Now came the turn of the second ten. Of these Desmonde was the last to come forward, somewhat disturbed, not only by the fact that the candidate immediately before him, a novice from Abruzzi, had sung superbly, ending to a great ovation from a crowd of supporters in the gallery, but also by the fact that his own appearance, so quietly distinguished, had evoked catcalls and laughter from the same gallery.

Desmonde, however, remained quite still before the great sea of faces stretching beneath him, waiting in apparent calm until he achieved complete silence. Only then did he launch into the lovely Brahms. Now there was no jeering from the gallery, but a great burst of applause swelling up the main body of the auditorium.

Presently the marks were announced, and the ten losing candidates removed from the stage. The process of elimination was resumed.

The next set piece for the remaining ten was a particular favorite of Desmonde's. His appearance, no longer greeted by derision from the gallery, was warmly applauded from all the other parts of the hall. He was at ease now and sang even better than before. As he went back to his place to prolonged applause, he caught the eye of the cardinal fixed benignly upon him.

Again the marks were read aloud, to the usual mixed reception, and the disconsolate six removed from the stage. Now, no more than four candidates were alive to face the final set piece, and of these it had now become apparent that Desmonde and the novice from Abruzzi would survive to meet in the grand finale.

An intermission now occurred, during which the quartet played the first part of Vivaldi's *Four Seasons*.

Meanwhile, Desmonde and the Abruzzian were called before the committee and given the respective totals of their marks, which indicated that Desmonde was leading by nine points. They were then asked to name their "choice" piece. The selection of the little novice was "O Sole Mio," a great favorite, in fact a crowd-pleaser to an Italian audience, though less so to these informed committee critics, who now looked expectantly at Desmonde. Obviously, since he was already ahead, he must choose a simple piece to avoid all possibility of technical error. However, to the astonishment of the committee, he said: "I choose the Prize Song from *Die Meistersinger*."

A silence. Then: "You will sing in Italian?"

"Not at all." Desmonde permitted his glance to rest for an instant on the cardinal. "I will sing in the original German."

Another silence. Then the president said, "That will be a

great treat for all of us . . . but of course you know the difficulties . . . the risk . . ."

At this point the cardinal intervened.

"If this brilliant young priest wishes to sing this superb song, then you must let him sing it. He is not afraid, nor am I."

Thus, when the Vivaldi came to an end amid some polite applause, the president of the society stepped forward and announced the choices of the two finalists. The novice from Abruzzi must sing first.

And some moments later the lovely melody of "O Sole Mio" fell upon enraptured Italian ears, long familiar with a song popularized, sung by countless mediocre tenors, throughout the country. The gallery went wild, even joining in the song. Alas, worse was to come, for the little Abruzzian, scenting triumph in this mass success, actually raised his right arm and conducted the yelling choir. More, more applause when he had finished. He returned to his seat flushed and smiling.

Now Desmonde must sing, to a restless, excited, seething gallery. He advanced, waited patiently at the front of the stage, calmly observing the Marchesa and Father Petitt watching him with straining intensity. Then at last there was total silence. He began to sing.

As the superb opening bars of that magnificent song swelled upward, the test song of the Mastersingers, purposely difficult, a strange trancelike stillness seemed to embrace, to elevate and ennoble the listeners. Desmonde himself seemed to lose himself in the Wagnerian meaning and intention of this noble song, the straining aspiration it bestowed upon the singer. He became Walther seeking the recognition of his splendid voice and admittance to membership of the elite, the immortals. All, all he gave, knowing, and rejoicing in the supreme effort.

When it was over and he stood, his eyes uplifted, exhausted and unknowing of his surroundings, a dead silence fell upon his listeners. Then came a roar that lifted the roof, sweeping upward from all parts of the great auditorium from the standing, cheering crowd.

A standing ovation, unsurpassed in the history of the society, went on and on until the cardinal came forward and, his face wreathed in smiles, took both of Desmonde's hands and shook them repeatedly.

"My dear Father Desmonde, words fail me. Believe me, we shall know more of you in Rome, and soon, since I personally will see to it. You are too precious to be lost in the wilds of Ireland." Then he raised a hand to still the audience.

"Members of the society, ladies and gentlemen. Your overwhelming response has confirmed our careful markings that Father Desmonde Fitzgerald is the winner of the Golden Chalice. And as honorary president of the society I have great pleasure in presenting the chalice to him now, together with a little replica that he may retain as a constant reminder of his triumph here today."

Amid further cheers, he held up the chalice, to which was attached a small jeweler's box, and presented it to Desmonde.

People were now leaving the hall. Indeed, the Abruzzi party, with other disappointed groups, had already sadly departed. The Marchesa and Father Petitt had come forward to the foot of the platform steps.

"Your Excellency, may I present my hostess and my tutor."

"Present! Good Heavens! Come here at once Margarita, you naughty girl." He kissed her hand. "I see you are at your old games, entertaining distinguished Irishmen, always handsome ones, too."

"Father Desmonde has just lost his dear mother. So I have adopted him."

"Then we must get him back to Rome, soon, for you."

"And you, little Father . . ." He had turned to Father Petitt. "It is you who have taught your pupil some useful tricks."

"Oh, your Excellency!" Between past tension and present excited delight, Petitt scarcely knew what he was saying. "Desmonde is himself bursting with all sorts of tricks."

The cardinal smiled. "Let them give you the case for that lovely thing. Otherwise it may be coveted and stolen. You have your car, Margarita? Good! Then I shall bid you all a very happy *auf wiedersehen.*"

When he had gone, the marchesa took Desmonde's arm and pressed it to her side.

"You see, darling Desmonde, my heart is still beating like mad. Oh, I am so excited, so deliriously happy. I can't tell you how wonderful you were, standing before all that crowd, like a young god, and singing, singing like an angel. But we must get home. Father Petitt has his case, and I have got you. Now come."

They left by the stage door. The car stood outside, and they were off, exhausted but triumphant, to the Via della Croce.

Together in the rear seat, while little Petitt sat in front clutching his trophy to his breast, the Marchesa drew Desmonde's head upon her shoulder.

"Tonight we shall rest and tomorrow also, for you must be worn out with strain, and I, an old woman, am quite exhausted, supporting you with all my strength when you were singing. But on Monday and all of next week we shall have fun, with lots of parties, and the opera too, here in Rome, and also a quick trip to La Scala, where I have an *abonnement.*"

"But, dear Madame, I should be in Ireland soon."

"The Irish won't mind. They are an easygoing people. And also, you have earned and deserve a holiday. Finally, as my adopted son, you must obey me. I want you to be happy."

"Father Petitt will stay, also?"

"We could not detain him if we wished. Once he has the chalice engraved with your name and college, he will be off like a rocket to give Father Hackett the joyful news."

When they reached the peace and comfort of the Villa Penserosa, Desmonde went immediately to his room and wrote a few words on one of his cards. He then took the card and his little gold replica, summoned the maid, and asked her to place both on madame's dressing table. He then took a hot, relaxing bath and, wrapped in a big towel, lay down on his bed. How pleasant to think of his success and of the coming festivities.

Kilbarrack seemed a long way off, a different world, in which he would return to the crudities of peasant life, to a dilapidated church filled with artistic horrors, Stations of the Cross so lurid as to hurt the eye, little faceless, factory-made statues of the Virgin in blue and white, a pervading smell of candle grease, stale incense, and odors normally associated with the stable. Well, he must endure it. In the meantime, let there be joy, music, refinement and all the pleasures he had so richly earned.

THREE

1

The arrival of Desmonde at Kilbarrack was not auspicious, nor did it raise the dampened spirits of the new curate. The day had been wet from morning, and the railway journey from Dublin to Wexford a painful reminder of the native indolence of Irish trains. One hour late at the junction, he had to wait another hour for the local that dawdled to his destination. Here, disgorged with his suitcase to the rain-swept single platform, he looked in vain for a cab. Ten minutes went by before a wagon appeared, drawn by a nag that in all probability had never won the Irish Derby.

"Hey! Hey! Can you give me a lift."

From beneath a mantle made of sodden potato sacks came the answer.

"Sure and I can. Step up, your reverence."

Desmonde stepped up, hoisting his valise to the rear of the car and taking his seat beside the driver.

"So you expected me?"

"I did." The driver laid the whip gently on the horse's dripping rump. "I met the noon train for ye on the Canon's instructions. I'm Michael."

"Sorry you had the double journey, Michael."

"Ah, 'tis no trouble, your reverence, no trouble at all. I do all kinds of a job for the Canon, besides bein' sidesman at the church. I'll take you by the cattle market and up the High Street, 'twill give ye a look at the town."

Kilbarrack, no different from a hundred other unflourishing country towns, was no surprise to Desmonde. He had known them as a boy. But as they jogged past the litter-strewn yard, the corner pubs, the licensed grocer, the butcher, baker, the ironmonger's spread of farm implements across the pavement, and again more pubs, all viewed through a curtain of mist and rain, he felt himself a long, long way from the Via Veneto and the delightful mansion of the marchesa in Via della Croce.

Did the jarvey read his thoughts?

"Bit of a change for you, your reverence. And for us an' all. The whole town is buzzin' with the luck we have getting our new young father fresh and straight from none other than the Holy City."

"I hope I'll do well for you, Michael. I'll try."

"You will an' all. When I saw ye standin there on the platform sae young and handsome, for a' the rain, I fair took to ye." As they had turned uphill away from the main street, he bent down to Desmonde, lowering his voice. "You'll forgive me, your reverence, if I give ye a bit of a word to the wise. The Canon's a fine man, a grand man, he's done wonders for us here, but 'tis not a bad notion to go sweet and gentle with him for a start. Once ye know him and he knows you . . . he'd fight the devil himself for ye, if you grasp my meaning. Well, there's the church for ye, with the school to the side, across the yard, and the presbytery behind."

The church, built of a good gray stone, twin-spired and surprisingly large, impressed Desmonde with its size and quality. It dominated the town and, with the adjacent school and presbytery, all of the same fine-cut stone, was offset by a grove of trees that merged up into the woods beyond.

"It's wonderfully fine stonework, Michael, both the church and the school."

"It is, sir, an' all. And 'twould have to be, to please Madame Donovan."

But now they had drawn up before the neat porticoed stone

house and the driver was lifting out the valise. Desmonde jumped down.

"What do I owe you, Michael?"

"Nothing whatsoever, your reverence. It's all a little matter between the Canon and myself."

"Take this, Michael, from me."

"May I live to be a hundred," Michael touched his hat and whipped up, "before I let your reverence pay me."

Desmonde watched him go with a sense of warmth behind his damp, chilled ribs. Then he turned, took up his bag, and pressed the bell.

Almost at once the door was opened by a short, neat, full-fleshed little woman in a well-laundered, well-ironed white overall, who greeted him with a smile that revealed her own even teeth, creditably white for her age, which could have been fifty.

"So it's yourself at last, Father. Come right in. We were afraid you had missed the noon train. You must be drenched. Let me take your case."

"No, no, thank you."

"Then let me have your coat, it's fair soaked." He removed the coat and gave it to her. "Now, I'll show you to your room. The Canon is out to a meeting of the school board, but he'll be home by six."

As they went into the tiled hall, which afforded Desmonde a fleeting impression of a massive hat-and-umbrella stand, a statue in a niche, and a huge brass gong, she continued, after neatly arranging his coat on a hanger, "I am Mrs. O'Brien, the housekeeper, and have so been, by the grace of God, for the past twenty-odd years."

"I'm very happy to know you, Mrs. O'Brien." Desmonde held out his free hand. She took it with a pleasant smile that made her dark eyes sparkle. Almost black they were, against her smooth pale skin.

"But how cold and damp you are," she half turned as she

[95]

led the way up the waxed oak staircase, "and half starved, no doubt. Did you miss your dinner?"

"I had breakfast on the boat."

"So here you are all the way from Rome to Kilbarrack with nothing but rolls and coffee in your stomach." She turned toward him in the upstairs corridor and pushed open a door. "This is your room, Father, and I trust you'll find it in order. The bathroom is the end of the passage. I'll be with you again in no time at all."

The room was small and simple. A white enameled single bedstead well made up with spotless linen, a crucifix above; a plain deal chest of drawers against one wall; a little fold-down mahogany bureau against the other; behind the door a prie-dieu of the same polished wood; a square yard of carpet beside the bed on the glistening linoleum floor; and over all, the polished sheen of cleanliness and care. A room such as Desmonde had hoped for—not quite a monastic cell, of course, but suggestive of the ascetic life without loss of essential comfort. He put his suitcase on the chest, opened it, and began to unpack his things, slipping them into the drawers below. The photograph of his mother he placed on top of the bureau, and beside it his little framed replica of the Bartolommeo *Annunciation*.

He then became aware that his feet were uncomfortably wet and, kicking off his shoes, he had begun to peel off his sodden socks when there came a knock on the half-open door. Mrs. O'Brien stood there with a tray.

"I'm relieved, Father," she smiled, "you've had the good sense to change your feet — they were fair squelching. Now just leave your wet things and I'll take them down for a proper drying." With one hand she lowered the flap of the bureau and put down the tray. "Now here's your tea, with something to keep you going till supper at seven o'clock."

"Thank you immensely, Mrs. O'Brien. You are terribly kind."

"Have you plenty dry socks?"

"I believe I have another pair."

"One other! That will never do, young Father — not in

Kilbarrack with our roads, not to mention our weather. We'll have to start the needles clicking." She had been glancing at his pictures. "I see you have your treasures set out."

"One is of my mother, who died last year. The other Lady, I believe, needs no introduction to you."

"Indeed not, and how nicely you put it. And what would befit you more, Father Desmonde, than to come to us in such company? Now take up your tea while it's good and hot."

She gave him a smile of real warmth, picked up his wet socks and shoes, and went out, quietly closing the door.

The tea, indeed, was hot, strong, immensely elevating. Equally delectable were two hot buttered home-baked soda scones and a thick slice of Madeira cake that still bore the fragrance of the oven.

Desmonde's view of Kilbarrack, preformed with deep foreboding, but softened already by his reception, now mellowed further — melted, one might say, under the succulent impact of that heavenly cake. Restored, fortified, he thought: I will take a look at the church. He found the dry socks, pulled on his slippers, and went downstairs.

On his first approach, with the inimitable Michael, he had noticed a glass-covered passage leading across the courtyard. Conspicuously, it opened off the far end of the hall. A moment later he was on his way to the church.

On his last day in Rome Desmonde had made a final sentimental pilgrimage to Saint Peter's. The image of that noble creation was fresh in his mind as he entered the parish church of that dirty, impoverished Irish country town. He expected, and braced himself for, a shock, a chapel of conventional design with a lurid altar and daubed horrors of the Stations of the Cross deforming the walls.

He did, indeed, receive a shock, which caused him abruptly to sit down. He could not believe his eyes. The church was exquisitely and supremely beautiful, pure Gothic, the stonework of the finest quality and workmanship. The nave was lofty, with aisles on either side. The Gothic pillars, supporting arches of delicate tracery, led the eye upward to the lofty roof. The Stations of the Cross were also cut from stone, simple in design but executed with grace and delicacy. The main altar, richly gilt and with a magnificent fretted reredos, lit up the Sanctuary and compelled the eye.

Instinctively Desmonde dropped to his knees, to give thanks for this heavenly, unexpected blessing, a noble church in which he felt he could strengthen and expand his sacred calling, increase his love and devotion to his Savior. He was still in prayer when suddenly, an organ pealed, and a choir of boys' voices began to sing the hymn "Crown Him with Many Crowns."

Immediately Desmonde rose and hurried to the rear of the church, then up a winding staircase to the organ loft. A choir of boys, conducted by a young man, was practicing the hymn, and at Desmonde's sudden materialization they broke off.

"Oh, please don't stop. I'm sorry to interrupt you." He went forward to the young man and held out his hand. "I am Father Desmonde Fitzgerald."

"I'm the schoolmaster, John Lavin, Father. We're having our usual practice."

"Forgive me," Desmonde said. "I'm literally stunned to hear such fine singing . . . and that unusual lovely hymn too, down here in the wilds of Wexford."

"It's all due to Madame Donovan, Father. She loves the boys' voices in really fine part singing, so of course she has to have them."

"You've trained them splendidly. And you know your timing well."

"Thank you, Father." He paused. "If you're on your rounds, and free, one day perhaps you'll call in on my wife and me, and our new baby." He smiled shyly. "We're very proud of him."

"I will, I will." Desmonde lapsed into the Irish idiom, then shook hands, smiled to the boys, and went out of the church, still barely recovered from what he had seen and heard therein.

At the presbytery Mrs. O'Brien met him in the hall.

"The Canon is back, Father Desmonde. And he'll see you at

supper. Which I'm serving right away. Would you care to go into the dining room, the door's open and there's a nice fire for ye."

Desmonde washed his hands and went into the big dining room, where a glowing peat fire lit up the fine old mahogany furniture: table, chairs, sideboard, all of that solid, serviceable wood. At the double windows he had a striking prospect of the distant sea, some fine fields and woodland, and, the roof visible among the trees, a large country house.

"Do you like our view, Father Desmonde?"

Canon Daly had asked the question. A short, thickset man with the chest and arms of a coalheaver, a round cannonball of a head dusted with gray, topped by a red biretta and without benefit of neck, sunk deep into the massive shoulders. His face was brick-red, with deep-set honest blue eyes; his expression candid, open, but with the capacity to be formidable.

"I do like your view, Canon. And I love, am completely bowled over by your magnificent, most tasteful and artistic church."

"Aye, 'tis one of Pugin's best. None better. I was pleased your first thought was to go down to it."

Mrs. O'Brien had now brought in supper. A noble joint of beef, side dishes of potatoes and vegetable.

"Sit in," said the Canon. He took his place at the head of the table and picked up the carvers, which he proceeded to use with such vigor and dexterity that Desmonde quickly had before him a plateful of well-sliced beef, floury potatoes and fresh spring cabbage.

"We are not fancy here, but we get enough to eat."

"It's delicious, Canon," Desmonde responded after the first few mouthfuls. He had eaten little during the journey, and now joined the Canon in attacking the good food with enthusiasm.

Watching him covertly, the Canon seemed pleased.

"I'm glad you're no' one o' they fancy finnickers as I feared ye might be. In fact ye're a hale lot better than the Roman dude I was led to expect."

"I'm no Italian, Canon, just an Irishman who has lived a long time in Scotland."

"Do ye say so? Well, well, ye're like myself. I was near eighteen years in Winton with my parents before they came back to their homeland. And you can tell it frae the way I talk."

"Your accent makes me feel at home, Canon, and it suits your rugged strength."

When full justice had been done to the main course, Mrs. O'Brien cleared, and brought in a deep-dish apple tart, then quietly went out.

"You've got the right side o' Mrs. O'B. already, lad. She was a' excited when I came in, singin' your praises." He handed out a generous section of apple pie with lots of juice, and helped himself in similar fashion. "And I think the world o' her opinion. She's been with me over twenty years and never has she failed me."

"The church, Canon. Your superb church. How under high Heaven did you get it? I know Ireland and the Irish. You never got it from the pennies of Kilbarrack."

"You are dead right, lad. A' the pennies in a' the collection boxes in a' the country, for ten years, would never have built it." He had finished his dessert and rising, he went to the sideboard, took up the bottle that stood openly thereon, and measured into his tumbler exactly two fingers of amber liquid.

"I got it from this, lad, and from the most lovely, pious, charitable, munificent lady in all Ireland."

Burning with curiosity, Desmonde watched the Canon sit down and hold the glass up for his inspection.

"I don't allow liquor in the house, lad. But I'm an old man, and this is different. It is the one drink I have in the day, two fingers, and not a drop more, of Mountain Dew."

Desmonde was now wildly interested, but he dare not press the Canon, who took a little sip of Mountain Dew, inhaled slowly, then set it down tenderly, saying:

"The finest, purest, maist exquisite and devilish expensive malt whiskey in a' the world. Made with the finest peat water and bottled in a special Donegal distillery, matured at least six years in bond, then sold by the Dublin office all over the world, to them that likes the best. And owned, lock, stock and barrel by the lovely lady who planned, built, decorated and paid for our darlin' church."

After this peroration the Canon took another little sip, and gazed benignly at Desmonde, who murmured:

"What a wonderful thing to do. She must be a most charitable old lady."

At this the Canon burst suddenly into a wild fit of laughter, in which he was joined by Mrs. O'Brien, who had come in to remove the dessert.

"Aye, she is charitable," the Canon resumed, when quiet was restored. "I'd be feared to tell ye what it a' cost. There was just one thing left out, worse luck, by sheer oversight. Did ye notice the altar rails?"

"Actually, I did, Canon. Very old, and wooden. Rather out of place."

"Ye see, ye noticed it right away. But never mind, lad, I'll have them changed one of these days for a set worthy of the church. It's the main object of my life now. I'm hintin' at it to Madame Donovan a' the time."

"Madame Donovan!" Desmonde echoed.

"You know the name?"

"Never heard it in my life until I came here."

"Well, ye'll hear it plenty now. That's her house ye were lookin' at through the window. And forbye she has another beautiful residence in Switzerland."

"Why on earth Switzerland?"

The Canon's left eye, viewed over the glass, took a slow, significant droop and he murmured a single word:

"Taxes."

Allowing this to penetrate, he added: "Madame is not only

a lovely, accomplished, talented woman, but as clever and tough a businesswoman as you'd meet in the City of London. If you knew her history you'd know I am speakin' the truth."

A silence followed while the Canon enjoyed and finished his Mountain Dew. Then, in a different manner:

"I was prepared for a hard case before ye came, lad. And to deal with you hard. However, from what I see of you, the trouble simply is, ye've had far too much social life, gaddin' about Rome and gaein' to parties wi' rich —" here he looked at Mrs. O'Brien — "old ladies. In fact, ye've been a bit o' a playboy. So my order is this, and if ye look at my ugly auld face ye'll see I'm a man to be obeyed: no invitations to be accepted here without my permission."

"Yes, Canon."

"Ye understand."

"The schoolmaster, Canon, whom I met in the church, asked me to look at his firstborn baby."

"Babies is different. Ye may go, but don't stay. Just look, say somethin' nice, then out."

"Yes, Canon."

"Good! Now, we're early bedders here, and as I'm sure ye're tired after the journey ye may turn in now if ye wish. I'll take the ten o'clock and you'll do the eight. Michael's always in the vestry, he'll show ye a'. Mrs. O'Brien will wake ye in the mornin'. Now, a good night to ye, lad. And it may please ye that what I have seen o' ye is highly satisfactory."

In Desmonde's room, all his damp things had been dried, ironed and neatly laid out. The bed was turned down, and a hot-water bottle had been placed between the immaculate sheets. When he had knelt to say his usual prayer, and glanced at the two familiar photographs on the bureau, he got into bed and, with a profound feeling of gratitude, closed his eyes.

His first day at Kilbarrack had been a most surprising success.

2

At half past seven Desmonde, refreshed by a sound sleep, was in the church where Michael, in the vestry, had laid out the vestments for the day.

"Usually we have only a scattering at the early Mass, your reverence. But there's quite a crowd this morning."

"Piety, Michael? Or curiosity?"

"Maybe a touch of both, your reverence."

Now Desmonde, in fact, was himself in a state of high curiosity in regard to the donor of the superb church.

"Does Madame Donovan, by any chance, frequent the eight o'clock Mass?"

"She does indeed, sir, every weekday, and the ten o'clock on Sundays. That's her own private little pew at the end of the front seat."

"Indeed, Michael."

"But she's not here this mornin', being in Dublin on business at her office. They do say, however, that she'll be back Saturday."

Desmonde knew always when he had said a good Mass, rather than one impaired by personal worries and distractions. He was satisfied with himself when he had left the altar, made his thanksgiving, and returned to the presbytery.

After an excellent breakfast he set out for his initial tour of Kilbarrack. How pleasant to be saluted and greeted as he made his way down to the Cross Square. Not all, however, were so friendly. Outside Mulvaney's tavern on Front Street the crowd of youths and men idling on the corner were silent, barely allowing him passage room, and when he had gone, following him with laughter and rude remarks. Desmonde was not perturbed. The Canon had warned him that this was the pest spot of the town.

Recollecting the invitation of the schoolmaster, he inquired the way to Curran Street where, closely regarded by the neighbors, he knocked several times on the door of Number 29. He had decided to avoid an afternoon call, lest he be pressed to stay for tea and so contravene the Canon's injunction.

Now, however, there was no response except for sounds of an infant's wailing coming from inside the little house, so, as the door stood ajar, Desmonde pushed it open and went in. And there, in the corner of a neat living room, a sweet little baby was howling its little head off in its cot. Embarrassing, no doubt, but not for Desmonde.

He immediately went forward, picked up the child, burped it, and cradling it warmly against his breast, began to pace up and down the room, singing Schubert's "Frühlingslied," which he conceived to be the nearest thing to a lullaby. The result was magical. The little thing snuggled against him and immediately went to sleep.

Elated by his success, Desmonde dared not spoil it by putting the baby down, and so continued singing and walking up and down the room. The front door, meanwhile, had blown open and in no time at all a gathering of the neighboring women, mostly in their morning dishabille, had clustered around on the pavement like bees around a honeypot, and were even pressing into the house.

"Oh, God, Janie, take a peek at his reverence."

"Did ye ever in your life. 'Tis the new swate young father from Rome."

"He may be young, begor', but he can handle the wean."

"Oh, God, 'tis a lovely sight, and the lilt o' the voice of him, the doat."

Then one, bolder than the rest, exclaimed, "Excuse me, Father. Mrs. Lavin has just slipped out a minute to the baker's up the street."

The room was slowly filling up, causing Desmonde some anxiety, not for himself but for the child. He decided to go outside to meet the mother.

"Gangway, please! Gangway for his majesty the baby."

Once he was outside in the cool air he felt more comfortable. But he had reckoned not of his audience. As he padded slowly up the street, still crooning to keep the child asleep, his followers, swollen by more and more spectators dashing out from their homes, had become a legion.

Worse was to follow. Janie Magonigle at the outset had shouted to her own little nipper.

"Tommy, dear, sprint down to the *Shamrock* office and beg Mick Riley to slip up quick with his camera."

Scenting a sensation, Mick had obliged, and before Desmonde reached the baker's, he responded to a call from behind, turned, and was startled by two sharp clicks.

"Thanks, your reverence. We'll have ye in the *Shamrock* Saturday."

At this precise moment, fortified by a long chat with the baker's wife, Mrs. Lavin came out of the shop, a loaf under each arm.

"Oh, dear Lord, what in all the world . . . !"

Even as she ran forward, Desmonde soothed her, then briefly explained all.

"Will you take him now."

"I can't with the bread, Father. He's sleeping so good and peaceful with you, please, please take him back with me to the house."

It was a procession to arrest and delight the eye — the young priest with the baby, the young wife with the loaves, followed by a horde of ecstatic admirers. Mick Riley had finished his film by the time they reached Number 29 Curran Street.

"Come in, do come in, Father," the mother breathed, in a visible tremor, as she flung the loaves onto the hall table.

"Another time," Desmonde answered hurriedly. "I'm due back at the presbytery. But let me tell you this. You've got the best and sweetest baby I've ever held in my arms."

The infant was handed over, still angelically fast asleep, and Desmonde set off hard for the upper town. But not before three hearty cheers were called for him, and with these still ringing in his ears he dashed into the presbytery, hoping that subsequent days in Kilbarrack would be less memorable than his first.

At supper that evening the Canon remarked casually:

"Old lady Donovan will be back from Dublin on Saturday, Desmonde. No doubt you'll see her on Sunday."

"Did she telephone you, Canon?"

"No, indeed. And it may interest you to know how news travels in Kilbarrack. This morning Madame telephoned Patrick, her butler. Patrick naturally gave the news to Bridget, his wife. Bridget told the girl in the kitchen, who told the milkman when he called. The milkman then told Mrs. O'Brien and Mrs. O'Brien told me."

Desmonde smiled. "You know the event before it happens!"

"Yes, lad." The Canon leaned forward and patted Desmonde's hand reassuringly. "And that's why I know you'll be front page news, with photographs, next Saturday morning. Now don't upset yourself. I understand it was all done with the best intentions, and 'twill do ye a power of good in the parish."

Sunday dawned warm and fine, hopeful harbinger of a good summer, a season of the year that Desmonde loved, particularly since he had known the benign, perennial sunshine of Spain. The Canon had announced that his curate would take the ten o'clock Mass, while he, though preaching at the ten, would take the eight o'clock. This unusual arrangement puzzled Desmonde, until his superior, sitting across at breakfast remarked, with a side glance at Mrs. O'Brien who had just come in with a rack of fresh toast:

"I want to display you in style to the old woman. It would suit my purpose fine if she sort of took to ye." The Canon added: "What the purpose might be ye'll learn in the Lord's good time."

This prearrangement annoyed Desmonde. He had no wish to be made a puppet in the Canon's schemes, and made up his mind to ignore the private pew, whether occupied or empty, at the end of the front seat.

When the ten o'clock bells had ceased and he was fully robed and approved by Michael, he followed the four little altar boys dressed as friars to the altar with his eyes determinedly lowered. Yet as the Mass proceeded, he was absurdly and annoyingly conscious of a scrutiny, penetrating and prolonged, fixed on himself and all his actions.

After the Gospel, the Canon ascended the pulpit to preach.

Desmonde, two little boys on each side, was seated on the right side of the altar. Only then did he direct a cold and impassive glance toward the private pew. He started, started so visibly and with such surprise that his little acolytes looked at him in wonder.

A young woman was in the pew, stylishly, elegantly dressed in a gray tussore silk suit, a flat-brimmed straw hat tilted rakishly on her nut-brown hair. With a calm, self-possessed expression, she was deliberately studying him. As her cold gray eyes met his and did not fall or falter, he immediately averted his gaze. This was not Madame Donovan. Perhaps it was her daughter, or some rich relative, and her open, rude curiosity in regard to himself he found both objectionable and offensive.

The Canon had now concluded his sermon, notably shorter than usual, and during the succeeding hymn the collection baskets were being passed. Out of the corner of one eye Desmonde noted that this modish interloper, in her expensive clothes, contributed nothing, not even a silver sixpence.

The hymn over, Desmonde returned to the altar and proceeded with the service. At the Communion he did not expect the woman to receive the Sacrament. He was wrong. She knelt, last of all, at the altar rail, and as he placed the Eucharist upon her tongue he saw with relief that her eyes were closed.

Soon the Mass was over. A final hymn, and Desmonde returned to the vestry. His thanksgiving completed, he hurried to the presbytery, eager for his breakfast-lunch, and for enlightenment on the mystery of the woman.

The Sunday midday meal of roast beef was not yet *au point,* but Mrs. O'Brien had coffee and a toasted scone on the dining room table for Desmonde to break his fast.

"Canon," exclaimed Desmonde, when he had swallowed his coffee, "who is that excessively rude young woman in Madame's pew?"

The Canon exchanged a look with Mrs. O'Brien, who had come in with fresh coffee.

"You mean that good lookin' one in the good claes and the swanky wee hat?"

"Exactly! Was it Madame's daughter?"

"Could it be the granddaughter?"

"Possibly! She looked young enough!"

"Desmonde!" The Canon glanced at Mrs. O'Brien repressively. "We're not makin' fun o' ye. And our bit of a joke has gone far enough. You fancied Madame an old woman, and we had a little fun over it. That was Madame Donovan herself in the pew this morning!"

Desmonde sat up. "You can't mean it. She was no more than twenty-four or twenty-five."

"Add another ten to that, lad, and ye'll just about hit Madame's age. She is a fine woman in body and spirit. And young in heart. Forbye, she takes care of herself, she *does* look young."

"So, she is actually the head, the owner of . . . everything . . ."

"When you know Madame's story, if ever she tells it tae ye — and I cannot, for I'm her confessor — you'll fully understand the way she's capable to run her business, control it and a' her other affairs, with a will of iron."

"I can believe that! The way she stared at me."

"Now, dont' be hasty, lad. I've an idea she has taken tae ye. When we chatted after Mass she invited you to tea, Tuesday, at Mount Vernon."

"It shows her manners when she invites me secondhand."

"Again, don't be hasty, lad. I'll warrant you a written invite comes by Patrick — that's her butler — when he's up for Benediction. Now wait and see if I'm right or wrong."

The Canon's prediction was fully justified. At half past six that evening, Desmonde opened a sealed envelope, unfolded a sheet of finest quality handmade notepaper, embossed in block letters with the address:

Dear Father Fitzgerald,
   If your clerical duties permit, would you come to me for tea at four o'clock next Tuesday.

Sincerely,
GERALDINE DONOVAN

"What cheek," Desmonde muttered. "What bloody awful cheek. *Would you come.* I'll show her I'm not her lackey!"

4

The fine weather continued and Tuesday was sunny with a refreshing breeze that sent fleecy clouds chasing each other across the sun. Desmonde had been fully occupied during the morning and after lunch he decided to take a siesta. He lay down on his bed in his underwear with an eye on the clock, not to ensure punctuality but because of his determination to be late for his commandeered appointment at Mount Vernon.

He had a nap, rested for a further half hour, then got up, shaved, washed, and brushed his hair. He then put on his fine, light Caraccini suit, with a clean shirt and collar. The result was satisfactory, indeed pleasing, and as the clock now showed four o'clock, he set out in leisurely fashion for his destination.

When he passed through the wide gateway of Mount Vernon and advanced up the broad drive it was in fact almost half past four. He did not hurry. The house was now in view, a fine Georgian house with a pillared portico such as may be seen in many an Irish estate. But this house differed, in that its immaculate appearance indicated a care and maintenance rarely, if ever, seen in the run-down, dilapidated, quasi-historic mansions of the Emerald Isle. The long double row of windows gleamed; the frames were freshly painted, as was the door on which the heavy brasses shone. The sloping roof was immaculate, and in front a cut-stone terrace with balustrade, obviously an addition, completed a picture worthy of the front cover of *Country Life*.

Desmonde mounted the steps and rang the bell. The door was opened by an elderly manservant, not in tails, but in a livery waistcoat, who showed the visitor into a large hall, the marble squares superbly covered by a Kirman Lavar flower carpet which Desmonde, as his feet sank into it, correctly deemed to be of the seventeenth century. A fine Lavery portrait of an elderly man hung on the near wall above a silver-laden Chippendale side table, while on the opposite wall there was a portrait of a woman in fancy dress by the same hand. At the rear of the hall a lovely broad staircase swept gracefully up, with a statue, probably Greek, on the landing, while below, two wide passages led away from the hall to the right and to the left.

Following his mentor to the right, Desmonde did not fail to observe through an open door the comfortable library, appropriately lined with volumes.

At the end of the corridor he was shown into a large domed apartment which had once been the great conservatory of the mansion but which, with skill and taste, had now been converted to a kind of drawing room known in Ireland as a saloon. Again, Persian, or perhaps Chinese, rugs, faded with antiquity, littered the parquet floor. A grand piano, open, at one end, silk-covered settees and armchairs on both sides, flowers everywhere in careless abundance — suffused, too, by the warmth and radiance of the April sun — it was a rococo setting sufficiently overpowering to the uninitiated visitor.

At the far end of this room a slender, elegant woman was seated at a small buhl table, reading. Her complexion was pale, carefully tended, her features fine and regular, her expression, even while she read, firm and composed, her beautiful chestnut hair in a bobbed shingle which intensified her youthful appearance. She was perhaps rather more than thirty, and simply yet beautifully gowned in dark gray silk, entirely without ornament but quite strikingly adorned by an oriental scarf of gray-and-scarlet silk.

Desmonde, by no means overpowered, had given his hat to the servant who admitted him and was now standing quite erect, hands by his side. Indeed, for some moments he stood thus, silent and still, delightfully aware that, as he had intended, his lateness had annoyed her.

At last, having failed to force him into some rustic gaffe, she looked up, but did not rise. After studying him for a further moment, with critical unfriendly eyes, not neglecting to note, however, the smart Roman cut of his clerical suit in which, she was obliged to admit to herself, he looked stunningly handsome, she said coldly:

"So you are our new curate."

"I believe so, Madame." He did not move.

"I hear that, for a playboy, you are good with babies."

"If you hear nothing worse of me, Madame, I shall be grateful."

She half smiled, yet suppressed it.

"Since you are apparently known in the town, affectionately, as Father Desmonde, shall I so address you?"

"I could not so presume at our first meeting, Madame, but later I might be worthy of your affection."

Feeling that she was getting the worse of these exchanges, she said, "Sit down."

He did so, quietly, easily, without affectation. She continued to study him, with her clear steel-gray eyes.

"At least you are a change from our late curate. I had him to tea. Only once. It was enough. He sat on one corner of his chair, lips clamped together, his cup clanking in his hand, speechless with fright."

"At least he was not a playboy, Madame."

"No, he was not. A good, hard-working priest, dull as ditch-water. I rejoice that he has been given his own little parish. Would you like tea?"

Desmonde smiled his beautiful smile.

"I came here in the expectation of your justly famous tea. I am glad you won't disappoint me."

She pulled the wall cord beside her chair and put down her book, a superbly bound copy of the *Imitation*, saying:

"My *à Kempis* came from your father. I knew him and liked him greatly."

"I thank you, Madame. For my father, and from myself."

Almost at once tea was brought in by the manservant. He carefully put down the heavy silver tray with its service of antique Spode and a three-tiered cake stand.

"Thank you, Patrick."

He bowed and went out, shutting the doors silently behind him. Beginning to pour the tea, she remarked:

"Irish servants are the best in the world, Father, if you train them. If you don't, if you spoil them, they are the worst. Remember that, in your dealings with the presbytery staff."

"Our good Mrs. O'Brien is more likely to spoil us than to be spoiled."

She seemed to regard this as a mild rebuke, but said, "I have no wish to be spoiled. Or to be surrounded by flunkeys. The good Patrick is my butler and chauffeur, his wife, Bridget, my excellent cook, aided in the kitchen by Maureen, a local girl. For my simple garden, the son of one of my farmers comes to attend to it three times a week."

He received this information in complete silence, as though he considered it redundant or even in rather bad taste.

She was obliged, therefore, to turn her attention to the tray.

"Cream? Sugar?"

He made a quiet gesture of negation.

The cup she handed to him, pure and undefiled, was hot, fragrant, delicious. She watched him sip it like a connoisseur as she sipped her own, then raised her eyebrows questioningly.

"Tea made in Ireland is always good, Madame. But this, like manna, must come from Heaven."

"No, from a special plantation in Ceylon, shipped direct to us here. What would you like to eat?"

He took two of the wafer-thin watercress sandwiches. They were delicious. Then he put down his plate.

"What! No cake? Bridget won't sleep tonight if you don't take a slice. I thought all curates liked cake."

Obediently, he took a slice of the rich homemade cake, saying:

"Not only curates. The clergy in general." He went on to relate, quite amusingly, the old schoolboy episode of Father Beauchamp and the cake. But, reminding herself that she had meant to be severe with this young priestling, she barely smiled.

"I don't care to hear a good priest ridiculed. I once heard your Father Beauchamp preach a sermon that was truly memorable."

"In Winton, Madame?"

"Yes. I was briefly in that city."

Desmonde was silent, swept by the strange and indeed incomprehensible conviction that once before, briefly, he had seen this remarkable woman who was now offering him his second cup of tea.

"I am still waiting for your horrendous impression of Kilbarrack. It must be a shock to you after Rome."

"It is not a shock, Madame, for I am as Irish as your dear good self. What *is* a shock, a great, undreamed-of joy, is the truly beautiful, the superb, church in which I am permitted to serve Our Blessed Lord. Nor, can I forbear to add, the unexpected pleasure of this invitation, to take tea at her house, with the blessed donor of the church."

"What a lot of words, Father Desmonde!"

"Yes, I'm a fool when I'm deeply moved. I spoil it all with a tirade. Simply, I love and adore the church and bless the giver of it."

"I love my church too, Father Desmonde. That is what keeps me in this remote part of Ireland, that and my house, which I also love. For since my husband's death I have become a woman of many affairs, with fully staffed headquarters in Dublin. I must go there often. Yet, with a direct private wire, I make many of my decisions here, and go as seldom as possible." She paused. "But why am I speaking of myself?"

"Because I am listening with the greatest interest and attention. Madame, you may have heard weird and untrue stories of me from Rome. I was merely polite in that city. And bored.

But now, to be in my own country, in the society of an Irish lady, so charming and fastidious, so noble and . . . oh, heavens, dear Madame Donovan, you must stop me . . . I came determined to be as rude to you as you were to me in church this morning. I have so loved being with you this afternoon, that I have run away with myself again." He stood up. "And it's time now for me to leave . . . I have Benediction tonight, and the good Canon insists on punctuality."

"Then you must come earlier next time." She smiled, warmly, and stood up. "I'll walk with you to the door."

She stood with him for a moment on the paved portico. The first distant stars were already showing through the still warm air.

"Is it not heavenly?" she breathed. "A heavenly evening. If you are late Patrick will drive you."

"Thank you, no, Madame. I shall enjoy the walk."

"We have a shortcut through the upper wood to the church. One day I will show you. Good night, Desmonde." She gave him her soft, warm hand.

"Good night, dear Madame."

She watched him go smartly down the drive, hoping suddenly, strangely, that he would turn to look back.

He turned and looked back.

When he had vanished between the high pillars of the gate, she went to her room and looked at herself, all warm and glowing, in the mirror. It was a pleasing sight. She half smiled. Then, moving away sharply, she said out loud:

"Don't be a fool, Gerry. Please don't!"

5

Desmonde, not a notable walker, was a full six minutes late for Benediction. But after the service, when he appeared at the presbytery, the worthy Canon, usually a stickler in the matter of punctuality, chose to ignore the peccadillo. And later, as they sat down to dinner, he unfurled his napkin with a flourish, tucked it securely around his neck, and smiled.

"You had a nice time with her ladyship, lad?"

"Delightful, Canon. I'm afraid I overstayed my leave."

"Ah, what of it! Did she . . . sort of, as ye might say, take to ye?"

"After her preliminary attempt to take me down a few pegs, she was most kind. In fact we got on famously."

"I kenned ye would, I kenned ye would." The Canon chuckled, as he took up the carvers and slashed through the crackling of a promising leg of lamb. "All in a good cause, Desmonde, lad."

During the next few days there was no word from Mount Vernon. On Sunday the main ten o'clock Mass was normally reserved by the Canon for himself, since the later hour gave him time to prepare his thunderbolts and a much larger congregation on which to discharge them. The earlier, sparsely attended, eight o'clock service was therefore taken by Desmonde.

On the following Sunday as he came to the altar, he could not fail to observe that the sacrosanct reserved pew at the end of the front row was occupied by Madame Donovan, who normally came at ten o'clock. She was wearing a short black cashmere coat cut in a military style with a wide collar and flap pockets, a pleated skirt, silk stockings and stitched shoes, and on her head a chic black cloche hat, worn low on the forehead. She looked a full ten years younger than her age, and to say that she was smart would be a vulgar understatement. In any of the fashionable Paris churches she would have drawn admiring glances.

During the Mass Desmonde did not once look toward her, but at Holy Communion when she came forward and knelt at the little wooden altar rail, looking up as he placed the sacred wafer between her parted lips, her eyes remained open and met his in a spiritual exchange that was touching and sweet.

In the vestry, as he disrobed, he saw that the Mount Vernon closed landaulet stood outside, and when he emerged she was waiting on him, brisk and slightly impatient.

"I am driving to Dublin today. Important business that I must see to. Will you let the Canon know. I shall be at the Shelbourne, as usual, for ten days or thereabouts." Suddenly she smiled, showing her small, white, even teeth. "By the way, my spies inform me that you got a thorough drenching on your rounds the other morning. Haven't you a raincoat?"

"It's not a garment much worn in Rome." Desmonde laughed, and his teeth were quite as attractive. "I have the parochial umbrella, a tremendous canopy which blows inside out with delightful facility."

"You must have a raincoat," she said, laughing. "If not in Rome, it's a garment much worn in Kilbarrack. Now, *au revoir.*" She held out her hand.

After the Sacrament, he could not do more than gently press her fingers. But when she had gone he knelt and, before beginning his Office, said a prayer that she might journey safely on the crowded Sunday roads. And return soon.

Life moved on normally for the next few days, during which Desmonde became more and more conscious of the absence of his new friend. But on the Thursday, evidence that she had not forgotten him came by express delivery in the form of a superb new raincoat. A Burberry, quietly gray in color and, when he tried it on before the expectant Canon, a perfect fit.

"It's the very thing for ye, lad. Downright handsome, and that clerical gray is just right." He smoothed the fine-proofed gabardine, well pleased by this sign of interest from Madame Donovan. "She's taken to you, Desmonde, and later on, if you watch your step, she might listen if ye bring up the matter of the altar rails."

Desmonde was silent. He had already made up his mind to treat this oppressive and delicate matter with great reserve.

Six days later, evidence of Madame Donovan's return reached the presbytery: a telephone call asking both Desmonde and the Canon to lunch on the following Sunday.

The Canon was pleased but sent his regrets, accepting only for his curate.

"It's yourself Madame wants to see, Desmonde. And you know how I enjoy my nap after the Sunday dinner."

So Desmonde set off alone for Mount Vernon, bareheaded and wearing, as a gesture of gratitude, his fine new raincoat. As he came up the wide drive Madame was strolling on the terrace, very informal in a pink blouse and gray linen skirt, a straw garden hat strapped under her chin. She held out both hands with a smile.

"Good heavens! Is it raining?"

"Madame, the weather is irrelevant. I am modeling your delightful gift so that you may admire it."

"I do admire it. And you! You look most unclerical, like a young faun disguised as an advertisement for Burberrys. Now, take it off at once."

He did so, thanking her simply. She took the coat, folded it over one arm, and offered him the other. "Now we must saunter for at least ten minutes or Bridget will be serving everything half-raw."

They began to walk up and down on the terrace.

"You were absent longer than I had hoped," Desmonde said.

"There was an annoyance that I had to squash." As he looked

at her inquiringly she went on: "Some enterprising Japanese in Tokyo, who were already making bogus Scotch whiskey and selling it under faked Scottish names like 'Highland Fling' and 'The Sporran,' have now turned their attention to Irish whiskey. In bottles similar to ours, practically the same labels, they have titled their rotgut stuff: 'Mountain Cream.'" She paused. "Of course it does not bear comparison with our superb matured malt whiskey, but the confusion is damaging."

"You sued them?"

"In Tokyo! Good heavens, no. And I've had enough of law-suits. No, I simply sent out an S.O.S. to all our agents, dealers, and wholesalers that if they stocked and sold the Japanese imitation they would cease to act for us." She paused. "Before I left Dublin we had been flooded with obedient, consenting cables, telegrams, and express letters." Abruptly she dismissed the subject. "Are you hungry, after your walk?"

"Ravenous!"

"Of course, I must warn you that you will not get anything half as satisfying as Mrs. O'Brien's Sunday dinner. What is it to be today?"

"Boiled pork, I believe, with whole onion sauce."

"How the good Canon will snore after that! I admire and esteem the Canon, Desmonde, but sometimes he is too pos-sessive. My beautiful church was not given to him, but —" she lowered her voice — "to Almighty God, for His most blessed help and support during a period of suffering and trial."

Desmonde was silent for a moment. Then he said quietly, "I would wish you to understand, my dear, most dear Madame Donovan, that I would never, but never, accept your most kind and welcome invitations in order to use and debase them by seeking some advantage, spiritual, or temporal, from you."

She pressed his arm, turned, and looked at him.

"I knew that, Desmonde, from the moment I saw you."

The melodious notes of a gong broke into the silence of this touching intimacy.

"My punctual Patrick is calling." They went into the house.

"There is the washroom. And at the end of the passage, the dining room. I'll be with you in a moment."

The dining room was all Chippendale, polished and gleaming, the long formal table unset but, by the window where the sun came in, a small oval side table laid very elegantly for two.

"Isn't this cozier?" she said, coming in. "I always eat here by choice."

They sat down. She was still wearing her fetching little straw hat.

"Madame," Desmonde was compelled to say, "I must still use the word with discretion, in a personal sense, but may I tell you that I love your darling little hat. It's a Boulter's Lock Sunday hat. I want to take you on the river."

"Could you punt? In your Burberry?"

"No, but I could look at you, lying languidly on cushions in the stern, an unopened parasol by your side, one lovely hand trailing in the cool, limpid water, as we glide under drooping willows."

She smiled, looking happily into his eyes. Then she collected herself and looked away.

"I warn you, Desmonde, you will get nothing but fish here today. And it was all in the sea not later than six o'clock this morning."

Patrick was now serving the soup, in two-handled thin Dresden bowls, and whispering in Desmonde's ear. "Good day to your reverence. 'Tis the *bisk homard*."

The thick lobster soup was delicious, floating with little ends of claw, topped with a blob of cream, and served with cheese straws.

"Again?" asked Madame Donovan. "If you will, I will. There's not much to follow."

"Oh, please. It's delicious."

After the second serving of soup there was a pause while the butler carefully uncorked a mildewed bottle.

"Don't decant it, Patrick."

"Will Madame try it?"

She made a gesture of negation.

"It ought to be all right. It's been waiting long enough."

The clear, amber wine was poured. Desmonde sipped, and looked at his hostess across the little table, with silent reverence. It was a venerable Chablis, mellowed to a honeyed fragrance.

"Yes," she smiled. "It's awfully good. And so rare, we must finish the bottle."

Now the next course was being served. Grilled fillets of sole, garnished with anchovies, and ringed on the platter by honest Irish mashed potatoes.

"Eat lots," Madame said. "There's only fruit salad to follow."

The delicious fish, grilled to a turn and impeccably fresh, was irresistible. Desmonde did not reject the platter when it came around again. Nor, indeed, did Madame.

And afterward, how cooling and refreshing was the compote of fresh fruits, well chilled and served in antique silver communion cups.

"Coffee in the sun-room."

They seated themselves on the big settee facing the window to drink the strong, black mocha. Desmonde, suffused by a euphoria almost beatific, felt his eyes drawn compulsively toward her.

"Well . . . what next?" she asked, smiling. "Do you wish to emulate the worthy Canon?"

"That is an insult, Madame . . . as if I could leave you!"

"We could rest on separate ends of the sofa. It is a joint attitude, perfectly pure, and known, I understand, as toe-to-toe."

"Are you sleepy, Madame?"

"Decidedly not."

"Then I must speak to you, Madame, if you permit, of a matter which has been on my mind, insistently, from the moment I saw you."

"Yes?" She murmured, doubtfully. Surely, helped by the Chablis, he was not about to make some premature declaration that would spoil everything. No, he was not. Taking her hand, he said, very seriously:

"Dear Madame, ever since our first meeting at Mount Vernon, I have had the conviction that I had seen and heard you before. And now, after two delightful hours spent intimately in your presence, I must tell you how insistently you remind me of Geraldine Moore, who in Winton some years ago brought me to my feet, cheering like mad, by her sublime performance as Lucia in Donizetti's *Lucia di Lammermoor*." He paused. "And then your lovely portrait in the hall . . . as Lucia."

She seemed slightly put out. Then she smiled.

"Ah, Donizetti, how he could wind himself round your heart-strings. But, my dear Desmonde, I thought all of Ireland, including your dear self, knew that I was Geraldine Moore before my marriage, and that for four years I had sung with D'Oyly Carte and the Carl Rosa. And I recollect that I did sing Lucia during that visit to Winton. And also, I believe, *Tosca*."

"We heard you, Madame, in *Tosca,* my friend and I. We left the theater in tears."

She half smiled: "You can blame Puccini for that, not me."

"Then, why, dear Madame . . . ?"

She stood up. "One day, Desmonde, when we know each other better, I will bore you with the story of my life. Now, what we both need is a good brisk walk. Give me a moment to change my shoes and I will show you the shortcut from Mount Vernon to the church."

They set off uphill through the grounds, crossing trim lawns that surrounded the rose garden and the little pillared pseudo-Greek summerhouse, which stood beside a well-tended *en tout cas* tennis court.

"I keep this in good order, since some of my office staff like to play when they come down. My schoolgirl niece likes to play, too."

Now they were in the big orchard.

"All apples, and a few plums," she said. "We can't grow much else here."

And finally they reached the pine wood. Desmonde saw that a path had been cleared through the trees.

"It's all good walking," she said. "I have it trimmed regularly. And look, over the tops of the trees you can just see the roof of the church."

"It is lovely," he said. "What a view!"

"Yes . . . I come up here every day to look." She held out both her hands. "Now, go and wake the Canon. And come again soon . . . soon."

She turned and was gone.

6

The blight of Lent had now fallen upon Saint Teresa's, and the worthy Canon, who loved his joint of prime beef, his leg and saddle of lamb, his fat boiled pork, and perhaps best of all, his daily dram of Mountain Dew, yes, the worthy Canon who disciplined others, was even more severe upon himself. He abstained and fasted rigidly. In a word, he suffered. It was in this season and in this mood that he composed and discharged his famous thunderbolts.

During the month, as a further penance, the Canon took the eight o'clock Mass, Desmonde the ten o'clock, and after the Gospel of this Mass, while Desmonde and his servers sat beside the altar, the Canon mounted the pulpit to preach.

Today, the second Sunday in Lent, the church was packed to the doors, a tense and quivering congregation, aware from experience of what to expect, as the Canon, a long lace surplice over his soutane, the biretta firmly anchored on his skull, slowly mounted the rostrum and, with a brooding brow, turned, faced his audience and paused. The pause lengthened until, in a rising crescendo, with a voice of Stentor, there came forth, thrice repeated, to a final shout:

"Hell! Hell! *Hell!*"

When the shock wave beneath him had passed, the Canon began.

"Do I utter that dreadful word as an oath, as a foul and ribald curse to be tossed about by, and between, the ungodly on the street corners or in the pubs? Go to hell! The bloody hell with you! A hell of a good time! Damn it to hell! I'll see you in hell before I stand you another.

"No! I speak of Hell as the bottomless fiery pit into which, to their everlasting doom, Satan and his rebel angels were hurled from Heaven. Hell, the tortured, hopeless home of the damned throughout the ages. Hell, the inevitable ending of the wicked, the fearful bourne to which go all who spit in the face of God, those, even in this congregation now before me, who persistently refuse Grace and die, God help them, in mortal sin, and are plunged into Gehenna to join the infernal legions of the damned, writhing, entangled in their agony. Did you never pause to contemplate the fearful unending agony of the damned? Did you ever burn your finger, holding the match short, when you lit your pipe? Would you ever want to try and hold a finger for one minute only in the flame of a simple tallow candle? Never! No one but an idiot would so harm himself. Reflect, then, on such a pain, multiplied a million times, and suffered all over your body. Not for one minute, not for a million years, but for all eternity.

"Immersed in a boiling lava, flames ablaze around and upon ye, suffocated by the smoke, steam and all the foul stinks and spume of the inferno, pronged and tortured by a' the little devils with red-hot forks and pincers, the groans, the shrieks and the curses of a' the other lost souls about ye, a seething, writhing, intermingled mass of hellish agony, and through it all, the wan continuous torturing, eternal thought that ye have only yerselves to blame, that ye had yer chance and threw it back, with a curse, in the face of the Almighty, that if only ye had listened to yer poor auld Canon on a certain Sunday, ye wad be above, in Heaven, in the company and companionship of the Elect where, clearly seen, mind ye, where reigns light, sweetness and eternal joy in the Divine Presence of the risen Lord."

Silence, complete, deathly, followed this peroration. And the Canon was quick to seize the advantage.

"I speak to all here in this beautiful church, this veritable cathedral, gift of the munificent, saintly lady, our Madame Donovan. Many of you, thank God, are good true practicing Catholics. But there are others —" the Canon's voice rose. "You at the back there, jammed in the back seat, slinkin' in to stand by the door, you that never take your coat off for an honest day's work, but only for a fight. You that gets corns on your behinds, wearin' out the arses of your trousers, sittin' on the pavement with your backs to the wall of the corner pub. And you bedizened Jezebels, hidin' yourselves with pretended modesty behind the pillars, you what gets yoursels aal done up pretty with the powder and paint, puts on a fancy shawl, and strolls out of an evening by the front, seeking whom you may devour . . . and God pity the poor fool when he wakes up of a mornin'. To you I say, and to all in this church, steeped in the filth of mortal sin, I say again, the eye of the Avenging Angel is upon you. And if you deny that, and toss it off with a curse, then I tell ye: *Mine Is!*"

Seated on the narrow bench, weighed down by his heavy vestments and deafened by the Canon's thunder, Desmonde felt himself begin to wilt. His meager breakfast, scrupulously apportioned, did nothing to sustain him — he was not built to live on Lenten fare, and to ask a dispensation would be sheer futility. Wistfully he thought of his dear friend, absent so many days now from Mount Vernon, wondering what could delay her return, pervaded by a sense of longing to be with her again.

He had been out, on his daily rounds when she telephoned ten days before, and the Canon had taken the message that she must leave immediately for Switzerland. Could this be for fiscal reasons? Impossible! Her three consecutive months in summer, spent at her residence near Vevey, must surely maintain her necessary Swiss domicile, already well established by law.

Puzzled and confused, he had a sudden longing that Madame Donovan might return soon. But at that moment a long sigh of repletion, followed by the scraping of chairs and boots, warned him that the sermon was over. He stood up while the Canon stalked by, genuflecting in passing the tabernacle.

Immediately Desmonde returned to the altar and, with increasing fatigue, succeeded in completing the Mass. Within twenty minutes he was upstairs in the presbytery.

He went immediately to his room and lay down on his bed, already made and spread with a clean coverlet by Mrs. O'Brien. After a few moments of complete inertia his thoughts returned to Madame Donovan and, once again, he wondered if she had returned. The nature of her absence remained an enigma. And why, why must his thoughts turn so insistently to this woman, herself, in a sense, an enigma? Was he in love with her? He stirred restlessly. Pure love was permitted between man and woman, and she was, admittedly, ten years older than himself. But how sweet she was, how lovely, fragrant and charming. Witty too, and with a keen and lively intelligence . . .

The faint sound of the gong, always tactfully muted by Mrs. O'Brien in the Lenten season, forced him to his feet. In the dining room the Canon was already seated, mournfully regarding the small plate of macaroni cheese which, with its counterpart at Desmonde's place, constituted the sole decoration of the table.

As Desmonde sat down he felt the Canon raise his eyes, a glance that was considerate, almost tender.

"You're pale, lad. 'Twas a long Mass. I'm going to break the rules and give you a glass of sherry."

"Only if you take one also, Canon."

The Canon, who had half risen, sank back, reached out across the table, and took Desmonde's hand. He pressed it warmly.

"That is a sign of true affection and regard. I shall treasure it. And so we'll suffer together."

"At any rate, you gave us a smashing sermon."

"Smashing, maybe." The Canon carefully conveyed a string of macaroni to his jaws. "But I'll tell you straight. The maist o' the bloody lot o' them will have forgotten it a' before they're halfway down the hill to Murphy's shebeen. Do you think there's enough cheese in this sludge? It's tarnation tasteless. And why don't they grow the macaroni thicker?"

No answer was expected. The Canon resumed.

"Mind ye, lad, I don't go a' the way wi' the med-evil conception o' devils wi' toasting forks. I only use it to try and frighten them. But there is a Hell and the punishment is the worst of a', sadness and desolation, the loss forever of the sight and presence of our Divine Lord. And I tell ye, lad, I'm downright depressed, not alone by the state of the parish, but by the immoral condition of the whole bloody world at large."

Another string gone, sucked off the fork.

"There's na difference now, at all, at all, between what's right and what's wrong. Everything goes. Cheating in business, infidelity in marriage, the beastly irregularities of sex at all ages. Go down by the pier of an evening. What do ye see, washed out by the tide, a shoal of filthy condoms, like diseased fish, floatin' out to God's ocean as evidence of man's immorality."

The Canon skillfully forked and engulfed the last of the macaroni.

"I tell you straight, Desmonde lad, in no uncertain terms — the world of today is fucking its way to hell!"

Having delivered this powerful aphorism the Canon picked up his plate and, with a circular motion of his large tongue, licked it clean of sauce.

"There, now — clean as a whistle. No need to wash it at all, at all."

He rose and patted Desmonde on the shoulder.

"Now out you go for a breath of air. 'Twill dae ye good. Stroll down to the Mount and see if Madame is back yet."

7

Desmonde left the presbytery by the side door, cheered by the kindness of the Canon, a man of iron rarely given to expressions of approval or affection. The lane leading to the wood was steep. Desmonde took it slowly, pausing when he reached the great belt of trees above. Then, resisting the temptation to rest on the grassy dell that marked the end of the lane, he entered the private cutting that reached down to Mount Vernon.

The resinous scent of the firs was reviving, full of promise of the estate beneath. Desmonde felt his spirits liven and his heart quicken. How fond he had become of the lovely old house which, within and without, fitted so exactly his sense of beauty and good taste. Perhaps, too, though he doubted this, the lady of the manor would have returned — Madame Donovan, his friend, his dear friend whom he loved, in the best and purest expression of that noble feeling.

Alas, when he broke from the wood and Mount Vernon lay exposed beneath, the house was shuttered, the garden deserted. Nevertheless he went down, pausing to study the little Greek atrium which served as a tennis pavilion, then on to the terrace of the great house. Here he began to walk up and down, enjoying an amusing, vicarious sense of ownership.

Suddenly the front door swung open and there, in her best Sunday clothes, was Bridget.

"Oh, your reverence, do please come in. To see you walkin' outside, like a born stranger!"

"But you are all closed up, Bridget."

"Not at all, sir. I'll have the blinds of the sun saloon up in a second. Madame would never forgive me if I left you out there, all by your lone. And an' all, there's a letter for ye."

The prospect of the letter was decisive. Desmonde followed Bridget into the house and, true to her word, she quickly rattled up the venetian blinds of the sun-room. Then, before he could stay her, she put a match to the kindling beneath the logs arranged in the fireplace at the far end of the room.

"Now, sir, may I give you a good cup of tea and a nice bit of cake? Patrick is off for the day and the gurl is down to her mother's, but 'twill be a pleasure to serve you."

"If you're sure it's no trouble, Bridget. I would love a cup of tea . . . but no cake."

"Ah, 'tis that blessed Lenten starvation on ye. I'll have a real good cup to you once the kettle boils. And your letter."

When she had gone Desmonde sat down by the fire. The good, well-seasoned logs had already begun to blaze and crackle. How good it was to be here again. He let the warmth of the fire and the ambience of the room sink into him, longing to read his letter, yet protracting the pleasure of anticipation until he had had his tea.

This came quickly, a large steaming cup. Never had he tasted anything so good, so fortifying, so delicious in flavor. Indeed, when Bridget came again to the door to ask if he would have a second cup he exclaimed:

"That's the best cup of tea ever, Bridget. Was it something special?"

"To tell the truth, your reverence," Bridget smiled, "seeing you so tired like, I put a good drop of the 'Dew' in it."

"No seconds, then," Desmonde laughed. "But I'll tell Madame how wonderfully you revived me. Bridget, may I sit by the fire and rest for half an hour, since you've had the kindness to light it?"

"It's not you may, sir, but you must. Madame told me the freedom o' the entire house was yours should ye come down."

When she had gone, silently closing the door, Desmonde took a deep breath and opened the letter.

My dear, my most dear Desmonde,

I hope you will have honored me by visiting Mount Vernon in my absence and that you will then receive and read this letter.

When I telephoned the presbytery to speak to you, the Canon answered, since you were out on a sick call. I therefore said no more than that I was leaving urgently for Switzerland. You will now learn the reason of my sudden departure.

Claire, my niece, daughter of my poor sister who died tragically some four years ago, after a horribly disastrous marriage, has been in my care ever since. Undoubtedly she had an unhappy childhood, which may account for a certain irresponsibility, one might even say wildness, in her character. For the past two years I have had her at one of the finest finishing schools in Switzerland. The school, beautifully situated high above La Tour de Peilz, is most conveniently near my house at Burier, where she spends her holidays with me during the summer.

All has seemed to be reasonably well with Claire, although her reports have indeed referred to some indiscipline and breaches of rules, mainly attributed to high spirits. However, last evening I received a telegram from the headmaster, Major Coulter: Claire had been expelled and I must come to remove her.

Naturally I telephoned at once. It appears that Claire, and another of the girls, after going to the dormitory as usual at 9.30 P.M., climbed out by one of the windows after dark, jumped to the ground, removed their cycles from the bicycle shed and freewheeled down to Montreux. Here, wearing their school uniforms, they went to a dance hall where they readily found partners in a jamboree that went on till after midnight. Fortunately their uniforms had given them away and the doorman of the hall telephoned the headmaster, who tore down in his car, arriving in the nick of time, just as the two girls were preparing to take off with a very doubtful-looking young man in his sports car.

I need not to tell you, Desmonde, how upset I am or how I begged Major Coulter not to do anything decisive until I arrive. I hope to be able to persuade him to keep Claire for another year, after which she would surely be less irresponsible and more adaptable to our quiet way of life. At present I fear she would be rather unmanageable here, if Major Coulter insists on an immediate expulsion.

I shall leave immediately for Dublin by car, and hope to get there in time for the afternoon boat.

While I am away, do walk down to the Mount occasionally and go into the house — you will be expected, and Bridget will give you the freedom of the larder. Sit in the sun-room and think a little of me. I assure you my thoughts will be of you.

Most affectionately yours,

GERALDINE

Desmonde read the letter twice, and not because he failed to understand it. His heart lifted at the intimacy, even the tenderness, of the hurried phrases. And while he regretted the necessity of her sudden trip to Switzerland, this absence had given proof of the feelings that bound them — respect, devotion, love in the purest sense of that misused word. Convinced that she would quickly induce the headmaster to keep her troublesome niece, he could now look forward to her almost immediate return.

Desmonde folded the letter, thrust it into his inside pocket, and jumped to his feet. Elation, induced by Madame, and perhaps by Madame's Mountain Dew, demanded action, an immediate response. His eyes fell upon the piano. Impulsively he sat down, opened the keyboard, and ran his fingers over the keys. A soft-toned Bluthner, exactly to his taste. For some months now he had not sung, but now, irresistibly compelled, he filled his lungs and broke into that loveliest of all hymns: *O Salutaris Hostia*.

How well his voice sounded in the big room. Rest, perhaps, was the reason. He knew that he was singing better than ever before. In the same mood his next choice was Pergolesi's *Salve Regina*. Then, lightheartedly, for a complete change, he sang Purcell's "Passing By."

He now began to play and sing snatches of his favorite operas, improving as he went along and thoroughly enjoying himself. Finally he let himself go over Paca's last aria in an opera he loved: *La Vita Breve.*

Suddenly he glanced at the clock above the mantelpiece. Good Heavens, it was ten minutes past four. His First Communion children would already be gathering for him at the side altar. He had less than fifteen minutes to be there.

Bridget was in the hall, seated, as he came out of the sunroom. She rose at once.

"Father Desmonde, I've been listening to the wireless, fair entranced. Never did I hear Dublin so loud and clear. It's them records they play, John McCormack, Caruso, all them great ones."

"I'm glad you enjoyed it, anyway, Bridget. And thank you for all your kindness and hospitality. Especially the lovely tea."

"Come again, Father." She opened the door. "And soon. Madame would want it."

Desmonde took the hill at a good pace, recovered his breath going down the lane, and was in the church at exactly half past four.

The little children, a round dozen, all five or six years old and all from poor families, stood up as he drew near. Desmonde's mood was radiant. Rather than address them from the altar, he sat down and gathered them around him in a little group.

This was only the second lesson, and he picked up the thread of the first by describing how Jesus, entering Jerusalem with his disciples, knew that He was going to His death. As He was soon to die, He wanted to leave something by which He would be remembered. And what better if that symbol of remembrance were Himself. So Desmonde resumed, simplifying the Mystery in words which the children might understand and, as he went on, feeling that he had captured the attention even of the little ones.

At the end he invited questions, careful to encourage rather than belittle, and, when possible, to praise. He then fixed the hour and the day of the next session, handing to each of his pupils a sweet from the supply he kept in a cupboard, and dismissed the class.

As he walked toward the vestry a little girl, one of the smallest, followed and took his hand.

"When Jesus comes to me, will I love Him as much as I love you, Father?"

Desmonde felt the tears spring to his eyes.

"Better, my darling. You'll love Him much, much better."

And lifting her up he kissed her on the cheek, put an extra sweet in the pocket of her pinafore, and carried her back to the others.

8

Desmonde's popularity was not confined to the children of the town, who would run to him and take his hand whenever he appeared on the streets. The adults of the community, at first regarding him with curiosity and suspicious awe, were now almost entirely his friends, won over by his ready smile, constant good nature, and the interest he displayed in listening to those who chose to inflict their woes upon him. After all, he was an Irishman just like themselves, although fancied up a trifle by the Pope in Rome.

He was generous, too. Scarcely a week would pass without Mrs. O'Brien coming to him with an apologetic smile, after the shades of evening had cast a friendly obscurity upon the back door of the presbytery.

"You're wanted again, Father Desmonde."

"Who is it this time? Old Mrs. Ryan, or Maggie Cronin?"

"No, it's Mickey Turley . . . just out the nick."

"Tell him I'll be down in a couple of minutes."

"You're too good to all these deadbeats, father." Half smiling, Mrs. O'Brien shook her head. "They take advantage of ye."

Desmonde put his hand on her shoulder and gently, affectionately, shook her.

"What's a shilling or two in the sacred cause of charity. Here am I, warmly housed and wonderfully fed by the best housekeeper in Ireland, who washes and irons my linen to perfection, brushes my suits, keeps my room spotless and, no matter how hard she's been working, greets me always with a charming smile — who am I to turn away some poor soul with nothing but the few rags that cover him."

"The maist o' them will drink it."

"At least a good Guinness will warm them and send them on their way. Now lend me half a crown from that purse you always carry on ye and I'll pay ye back tomorrow."

Still laughing, but still shaking her head, Mrs. O'Brien handed over the coin. She was still there, waiting for him, when he came up from the back door.

"I'm not trying to buy popularity, Mrs. O'B. There's a tough crowd in this town that will never, never, have anything to do with me."

But not long after he had made this remark, the Thursday before Easter to be exact, an event occurred that caused him to modify his views.

It was the monthly market day, an event of some importance in the little country town, when the farmers of the neighborhood came in to sell and buy their livestock. The streets were crowded with carts, wagons, trucks, and a constant slow-moving procession of farm animals being driven in and out of the town. All was bustle, excitement and confusion.

Desmonde enjoyed these market days, and on this Easter Thursday he walked briskly down from the presbytery to enjoy the spectacle. He was halfway down the hill when, at the main crossroads below, an old farm truck, descending too fast, collided violently with a heavy wagon cutting across from the side street. No one seemed hurt, but the shock of the impact broke the tailboard of the truck and instantly a stream of little pink piglets gushed out, leaping and frisking, their silky ears flapping, their tails curled with delight, their little trotters scampering toward freedom. Instantly a crowd formed, yells and curses rent the air, blows were struck, and everywhere hands reached and grabbed after the elusive little porkers.

Out of the melee two little piglets sneaked away unseen and took off up the main street at full speed, still unobserved, making direct for Desmonde. He saw he must stop them, lest they come to an untimely end, and raised both his arms arrestingly. But the two truants, instead of halting, turned left and bolted into an unsalubrious narrow alley known as the Vennel. This was worse than before since here, unquestionably, they would be stolen for the stewpot. So Desmonde gave chase, running hard, following all their jinks and capers, and finally running them to earth in a blind passage with no exit.

Quite as exhausted as he, they gazed at him fearfully, but seemed reassured when he picked them up, one at a time, and held them in his arms under his raincoat where, indeed, they snuggled warmly against him. Desmonde then waited until he had recovered his breath, and set off for the scene of the disaster.

Here, indeed, the crowd had multiplied. All hell had broken loose and a police officer, Sergeant Duggan, whom Desmonde recognized as one of his parishioners, was trying, but failing, to control it.

"Sergeant!" shouted Desmonde. "Make way for the Church."

This unusual demand did actually cause a passage to open, and Desmonde found himself in the center of the ring facing the two combatants.

"Michael Daly! You know me and I know you. Your farm's along the road from Madame Donovan's estate." A dead silence had now fallen upon the mob as Desmonde went on:

"You have lost two of your pigs."

" 'Deed an' I have, two of the best, sows they were, for rearin' and breedin.' "

"Farmer Daly, if you could have them back, would you shake hands with this fellow here that ran into you?"

" 'Deed an' I would."

The silence was now petrifying as Desmonde slipped open his coat, and with a gesture that would have done credit to Masqueline and Devant, produced and held up on high, one in each hand, the two little porkers.

For a full minute that dead silence continued, broken only by

a feeble female voice, recognizable as that of old Maggie Cronin:
"Oh, God! 'Tis a bloody miracle."

Then pandemonium broke loose: yells of surprise, laughter, stark bewilderment. The deity and the devil were equally invoked. Then, as Desmonde handed over his trophies to their owner and brought the two men together to shake hands, there was a roar of applause.

"You got me out of a nasty situation, Father." The sergeant spoke into Desmonde's ear. "I'm going to see you get what you deserve." He held up his hand. "Listen, all of ye. The trouble has been settled to perfection. Instead of fighting and a bloody riot, blessed peace has been restored. And all through the efforts of the cleverness of wan man — his reverence here, known affectionately as Father Desmonde. Come on now, all of ye, three hearty cheers for his reverence."

The cheers could, indeed, be heard at the presbytery, to which Desmonde returned, between laughter and, absurdly enough, a warm satisfaction and sense of accomplishment.

As he passed by the side door of the church he noticed that a small girl, who stood there alone, had raised her right hand, making a timid signal in his direction. He immediately moved toward her, recognizing her as one of the brightest of his Communion class. He saw also that she had been crying. He put his arm around her thin little shoulders.

"Why, Peggy, what's the matter?"

She burst into tears again. "I can't come for my Communion, Father. I don't have a proper frock."

He remembered saying that it would please our Lord if the girls could come dressed in white.

"It's not really important, Peggy. You can come as you are now."

"Like this, Father? The other girls would laugh at me."

He saw now how poorly she was dressed.

"Did you ask your mother?"

"Yes. She was angry." The tears flowed again. "She said if I wanted a new dress I could go to Jesus for it."

Desmonde was silent. He had made a mistake. In the fact of such poverty one should not command. But this child must not be hurt. He smiled at her and pressed her thin shoulder blades.

"Tonight, Peggy, before you go to bed, I want you to kneel down and, just as your mother said, ask Jesus for your new dress." She looked up at him in wonder. "Don't tell anyone, just say your prayer. You promise?"

"Yes, Father." The answer came in a tearful whisper.

"Now, off you go, and we'll both see what happens."

Briskly Desmonde entered the presbytery and immediately was met by Mrs. O'Brien.

"Oh, 'tis glad I am to see you safe back, Father. There's been such a fearfu' commotion down the street. What in all the world was the matter?"

"Just a little bit of trouble for your friend Sergeant Duggan. He'll tell you about it, no doubt. Now, never mind. Here's that half crown I borrowed off you. And in return . . ."

"In return? Isn't it my own half crown?"

"In return," he smiled winningly, "I want you to do something for me . . ."

He spoke to her earnestly for just four minutes. Then before she could protest, he was off, bounding upstairs to the study.

That evening, as they sat down to supper, the Canon leaned forward, with narrowed eyes and a quivering of the lips that betokened some fearful joke.

"They tell me y'are a great success in the lost property business."

Easter Sunday dawned fine, in splendid colors of gold and pink. Desmonde's prayer for a good day had been answered, or perhaps the Irish weatherman was for once in a good mood. So too was the Canon, rejoicing in the feast of the Risen Christ and the blessed ending of his Lenten martyrdom. He greeted his curate with the traditional cheek-to-cheek embrace.

"You will celebrate High Mass, Desmonde. And I shall assist you."

Desmonde flushed at this unexpected honor.

"Ye deserve it lad, the way ye have bothered wi' the children. And besides, I've gotten sorta' fond of ye."

A vast quantity of spring flowers had been sent up from Mount Vernon. The high altar, superbly decorated with narcissi and Easter lilies, was a sight of splendor and fragrant beauty. Michael, the sidesman, himself with a flowery buttonhole, reported to the vestry that the church was overflowing, packed to the door.

"Never saw the like, they're standin' in the aisles."

"Ye're not nervous?" the Canon whispered. Desmonde shook his head. "I tell ye because Madame's home, and will be watchin' all." He added: "I hope she notices our poor ould altar rails!"

The organ pealed, the voices of the choir rose in the opening anthem, and the procession moved into the church, Desmonde superbly robed in festive vestments of gold and white satin, preceded by eight little altar boys dressed as friars, and followed by the Canon in stately humility.

Desmonde's first glance was toward his communicants, seated in the front seat: all as he had wished, the boys with white and gold armlets, the girls all in white, some merely in white starched pinafores, others in white summer frocks and one, in particular, neatly, beautifully dressed, in a white voile tunic, that could be serviceable thereafter. Desmonde looked no further, but mounted the altar steps, genuflected, and began the Mass.

Slowly, with perfection of movement and color, the ceremony continued. A tapestry woven in gold and scarlet slowly unrolled. Only when the Canon turned to read the Epistle did Desmonde look toward that end front pew, realizing with a start that Madame's eyes were steadily fixed upon him. She looked happy, a good augury for the news she would give him from Switzerland, and, in her neat suit of fine blue Donegal tweed, as fascinating as ever.

The service resumed, the bell rang for the Consecration and again, presently, for the moment of Holy Communion. The children stood, came in perfect order, knelt at the altar rails, and Desmonde, alone, came slowly to place the Eucharist, for the first time, upon the childish tongues. Then came the parents of the children, followed by great numbers of the congregation, the Canon descending now to assist Desmonde. And finally, the last of all, came Madame, kneeling, looking upward to receive, and meeting, in that same glance of spiritual love, the eyes of Father Desmonde.

Soon, now, the Mass was over. The organ played, the choir sang the final hymn, "Christ the Lord Is Risen Today." Back in the vestry, as they disrobed, the Canon whispered:

"Perfection, lad. You never put a foot wrong."

Back in the school hall the children were seated at a long table for their Communion breakfast, a substantial meal of cereal, bacon and eggs, toast, tea, and fruitcake, served under the supervision of the schoolmaster. Madame was already there with a little prayerbook, *The Key of Heaven,* for each child, and soon Desmonde and the Canon came in.

"Don't rise!" called the Canon, stifling an incipient movement. "Go on with your breakfasts. And God bless you all."

He turned to Madame Donovan and bowed. "Happy to see you home again, Madame. Didn't you think, thanks to you, that the church looked beautiful?"

"The Mass was beautiful." She turned to Desmonde. "It was perfection. I was deeply touched. And these sweet children, so well prepared . . ."

"Ah, yes, Madame," cut in the Canon. " 'Twas a lovely sight. If only the rails at which the poor little things knelt had been more in keeping . . ."

"Be quiet, Canon," Madame laughed. "You may get your rails sooner than you expect. In the meantime, how do you stand with your Dew?"

"I have not lipped it during Lent, Madame. And even out of Lent I sip, once a day, no more than two fingers-full, as Desmonde will testify; yet, an' all, I have a feeling I may be getting low."

"You'll have a fresh case from Dublin immediately."

The Canon bowed low. "I thank a most generous lady."

"And what of you, Desmonde? Would an invitation to drink tea be acceptable?"

"Eminently, Madame."

"Good heavens," Madame smiled at him. "We're behaving like characters in one of Cavalli's horrible operas — *L'Ormindo* for choice. You may come at four."

When she had gone Desmonde walked around the long table, before following the Canon to the door. As he passed the girl in the voile dress, he met her radiant glance and whispered: "That was a good prayer, Peggy dear."

Upstairs in the presbytery, Mrs. O'Brien, looking flurried for once, was in the dining room.

"I'm sorry, Canon, and Father Desmonde, I've been so busy with the children's breakfasts, as ye see, I have only a ham sandwich for you. But I've a lovely saddle of lamb for this evening."

"Don't worry, Mrs. O'Brien. You never fail us. And I'll take my daily drop of the Dew with the sandwich."

"Wasn't it a tremendous congregation," said Mrs. O'Brien, putting the bottle on the table. "Never, never in my life did I see the church so full . . . and with some of the tough characters from Donegan's Corner."

"Are you acquainted, Mrs. O'Brien," said the Canon, measuring an exact two inches into the glass, "with that old song that begins: 'As I came out one morning from Tipperary town . . .'?"

"No, Canon."

"Well it ends like this, or nearly so." And the Canon boomed forth: " ' 'Twas the little pigs that done it, och, the dear little pigs.' "

"Desmonde," resumed the Canon, when Mrs. O'Brien had departed, shaking her head, "I see a case of the Dew on the horizon and also, God willing, a set of altar rails in pure Carrara marble. Go down for your tea to dear Madame and be very, very, sweet to her."

In the early afternoon Desmonde set out to walk to Mount Vernon. He was happy, supremely happy: that admixture of spiritual joy and physical well-being that matched the brightness of this lovely day. How well everything had gone this morning: his splendid Mass, the sweetness of the children's First Communion. He prayed every day to the Holy Spirit for success in his vocation. That prayer had indeed been answered.

As usual he was early at the Mount: Madame had gone out on a round of visits to her tenants but Bridget, emerging from the servants hall, where she appeared to be entertaining friends, assured him that he was expected for four o'clock tea. And indeed, Desmonde had barely begun to walk up and down the terrace when the big landaulet swished up the drive and Madame stepped out, briskly, before Patrick could get to the door.

"Take all these things to Bridget." She spoke sharply. "The scones, soda bread and vegetables."

"May we have some of the scones, Madame?" Patrick spoke with unusual humility. "You did say, Madame, with your kind permission, that we might have a few friends in to have a bit of an Easter party."

"Take them all!" She turned on her heel, came up the steps, and to Desmonde, who had bent forward to kiss her hand, "Not now, please."

Only when Patrick had removed the car did she smile, faintly, a rather forced smile, barely showing her beautiful teeth, pressed firmly together.

"You must forgive me. I'm in a teasing mood. The more you give, the more people demand from you. New water pipes, more tiles on the barns, a new floor in the kitchen and, if you please, two new bathrooms with hot and cold showers."

Desmonde smiled. "What a pity, Madame, that today's Irish peasant won't walk in his bare feet to the yard pump to wash himself."

"No wit, please. And last evening a worrying, most ungrateful letter from Claire. But enough. Go into the sun-room and I'll be there presently."

Madame was indeed in a bad mood, and not alone for the reasons she had stated. Always she had been regarded as the luminary, the leading figure, the cynosure of all eyes at her own beautiful church, Saint Teresa's. But now, this handsome little curate, emerging from nowhere, or at least from Italy, had stolen her thunder. This morning she had felt herself slighted, almost ignored and, though she repressed the feeling, had even wished that he might make some slip, a human *faux pas,* in the perfection of his performance.

She had decided, while making the upsetting round of her tenants, that Desmonde must be taken down. He was altogether too complete. There must be a flaw in his perfection and it had become her duty to expose it.

She was smiling when she entered the sun-room, took both his hands, and made him sit beside her on the sofa.

"Desmonde, dear, Bridget has given me the weird story of your magic radio that afternoon when I was out. Come, now, you really were regaling yourself with a few student ditties."

Desmonde smiled. "The piano was so inviting. I trust I was not taking a liberty, Madame."

"Good Heavens! Of course not. And as it's still some little time until we are served tea — they're having quite a party in back — I would love you to sing to me now."

He glanced at her oddly.

"I have hitherto refrained, Madame . . . since you don't sing yourself."

"Tut, tut! You'll hear about that one day, and perhaps soon . . . I adore to hear good singing and now I wish to be entertained."

He paused. "What shall I sing to you? A hymn, an old Irish song, something operatic?" She was looking at him inquiringly. "When I was in Italy I had the advantage of hearing many of the best operas . . . in Rome, but mainly at La Scala in Milano."

She forced a laugh. "Did you make the pilgrimage to Milan on foot?"

"No, Madame. I had the extreme good fortune to be taken by Madame la Marchesa di Varese, in her imported Rolls-Royce. As you may know, she is an elderly lady, with her own box at La Scala, passionately devoted to music."

"And to you?" As he ignored the question, which was almost a sneer, she continued: "So what is your taste now, in operas?"

"I tired of the little tearjerkers." He smiled as he used the phrase. "Of dear Donizetti, and Bizet, and Puccini. *La Bohème,* for example, is such nonsense. My taste turned to the grand operas, Verdi and Mozart. *Don Giovanni* is a great opera. I also love the Spaniard, Falla."

"Surely you forget Wagner."

"I am always carried away by Wagner's thunder, against my will. But he has written some extremely fine pieces."

She looked up at him endearingly. "Do you know the Prize Song in *Die Meistersinger?*"

"That is probably one of the most beautiful songs ever written . . . Yes, Madame, I know it . . . moderately well."

"Could you, would you sing it for me? It is frightfully difficult . . . ?"

"For you, Madame, I will try . . ."

She seemed almost to relent. "Don't worry if you break down, dear Desmonde. We'll choose something simpler."

"Thank you, Madame," Desmonde said simply. He was now

perfectly aware that she had chosen this song, deliberately, to embarrass him, a feeling that became a conviction as she explained:

"You won't mind if I call the servants and their friends into the passage. They are all dying to listen to you."

Desmonde suppressed a smile. She could not know that this was his winning Prize Song or that he had sung it in private performance in the salon of the Marchesa's villa, to an audience of over a hundred of the best of Roman society.

"It will make me more nervous, Madame, but if you wish, please do call them."

He waited until she had called and settled them in chairs outside, leaving the door half open, until she had seated herself, almost purring like a dear little cat about to sip cream.

"You forgive me in advance, if I disappoint you, Madame?"

"Of course, dearest Desmonde. Now do begin, we are all waiting."

He did wait, another moment. Then quickly he played the introduction and, lifting back his head, began to sing in the original German.

Firmly determined to sing well, he knew after the opening that he was at his best and would never sing better.

Indeed, he sang it to listeners enchanted, and when at last he finished, the silence persisted for a full minute before a perfect crescendo of applause broke forth in the passage.

Desmonde did not leave the piano, but when quiet came, called out: "As this is Easter Sunday, when we praise with joy the Risen Christ, I can't leave you without one hymn in His honor." He began without delay to sing his favorite hymn, the lovely *Panis Angelicus*.

No applause when he finished, but a reverential silence, immeasurably more impressive. He glanced toward the sofa Madame Donovan was in tears. Blindly, she made a sign that he should close the door. He did so. Then again she signed, that he should join her on the sofa. Here, half reclining, she took hi head in both hands and pressed it toward her, so that he felt the warmth of her tear-stained cheek.

"Desmonde," she whispered. "You have overwhelmed me. Your beauty, your charm, your perfect manners, your inviolable purity, and now . . . that lovely, lovely voice. What must I do? I wish you were my confessor — but that would hurt the good and worthy Canon. I wish you were my son . . ."

"Madame," Desmonde interposed reasonably, "that is a physical impossibility . . . you are no more than nine or ten years older than I."

"I wish, then, that you could offer some solution in my extremity. I am Héloise, and you are Abelarde."

"No, dear Madame, I am not Abelarde, who was a rather dirty, unpleasant fellow. I am a priest truly in love with a charming, distinguished woman who, I believe, has a equal fondness for me. There is no solution other than to love purely, in the sight of God, and to be content with that love."

She sighed, disengaged herself, and sat up.

"Desmonde, we must first have our tea, if only in the cause of propriety. Then I will try to explain why I feel so bewildered and so lost. Do ring for Patrick while I try to repair my face."

Desmonde pulled the bell cord, then wisely stood looking out of the window, with his back to the room. He foresaw eulogies from Patrick, who was indeed on the point of erupting, and stilled only when Desmonde half turned and raised one finger to his lips.

Presently Madame returned, looking fresh and apparently composed. She poured the tea and they drank it in silence. Some fine slices of buttered soda bread were on the tray. He took several, remarking that it had been some time since he had tasted this home-baked Irish bread.

She said: "I imagine Mrs. O'Brien is too busy to bake it."

This was the limit of their conversation, until Patrick had re-entered to remove the tray.

Only then did Madame turn to Desmonde, and in a firm voice, she began:

"I had been singing two years with the Carl Rosa when, during the Dublin season, it became evident that an elderly gentleman had become interested in me. Always the same box, and only when I was singing. He was Dermot Donovan, owner of the Donovan Distillery Company — a rich and prominent Dublin personality. I was flattered, and when, one evening, a note came around asking if I would take supper with him, I accepted. We went to Jamme's where, treated almost with reverence by Jamme himself, he commanded a delicious supper. It was delightful to be entertained by such a man, tall, solidly well-built, and with trimmed gray hair and gray mustache. He drank only a thimbleful of his own Mountain Dew. I had a half bottle of Perrier Jovet.

"When we had eaten, in the seclusion of our private room, he took my hand and said, very seriously, "Gerry! I am in love with you and wish to marry you. I am seventy years of age, comfortably rich, and able, I believe, to give you a full and happy life. I don't ask you to decide at once. Come down to Mount Vernon, my place in Wexford, and see for yourself."

She paused. "In a few words, I came here. I married Dermot Donovan. There were, of course, the usual screams in the newspapers: 'Spring Weds December.' 'Little Songbird in a Golden Cage.' But I never, no, never, regretted my marriage." She paused. "Strange though it may be.

"Dermot was a man of high principle. He was one of those Irishmen, and they are not uncommon in Ireland, taught in the Jesuit schools and colleges that sex is a dirty and offensive thing, to be avoided at all costs. He had lived his life as a lay priest, and now at seventy he had no desire to possess me sexually. All this was explained to me beforehand. He had his own bedroom, I had mine, an arrangement acceptable and agreeable to me, since my love for him had nothing of sex in it. I was his dear companion. He loved me to sing to him of an evening, and as time went on I learned shorthand and typing and became his personal secretary. We traveled, usually to the spas of Europe. In winter we took a cruise, to the West Indies, to Jamaica, to Tahiti.

[150]

"We spent five happy years together. Then, quite suddenly, in Vichy, after complaining for only a few days of a pain in his chest, he died. He was buried in France.

"Back in Dublin, his will was read. The dear, dear man had left everything to me — his personal estate and the business. Naturally, I was grateful, and happy too. But before the will was probated an objection was raised by two men in the Dublin office: the manager and the cashier. They demanded a post mortem, on the grounds that the sudden death of my husband was suspicious."

Madame paused, moistened and compressed her lips and went on.

"So the body of my poor man was dug up, and brought to the Dublin mortuary for examination. The certain cause of death: rupture of an aortic aneurism.

"Was that enough for those two devils in the office? It was not. They brought a plea that the marriage was invalid since it had never been consummated.

"I was forced by law to be medically examined." Again Madame paused, and her eyes were hard as steel. "You may understand the misery and humiliation this caused me. The finding: I was *virgo intacta*.

"The case came before old Judge Murphy, a wise and, thank God, an honest man. He tore these two scoundrels apart. 'Because this good woman was faithful to her old husband, because she did not allow herself to be seduced by some younger man, you would deny her the rights and rewards of her fidelity. Case dismissed without possibility of appeal.' "

Madame took a long sighing breath, but her eyes were steely.

"You may imagine that I was now a nervous wreck, but I was not quite out of it. For it was my turn now. I put the best London firm of chartered accountants into the office. They went through the books with a fine-toothed comb. As I had already suspected, the two would-be beneficiaries had been quietly helping themselves to the till for months. And they had stolen even more: the foreign receipts were short by nearly one hundred thousand pounds. They are still in Mountjoy Prison."

"Madame, how brave you were!"

"That's about all, dearest Desmonde." She took his hand. "Except to say that I had a breakdown to end all breakdowns. I was dead out for two months, and when I came to, my voice was gone. They told me I would never sing again. But what of it?" She smiled. "I'm a fighter, Desmonde. I've taken charge of the business, built it up to triple what it was before, established Swiss residence, cutting taxation in half, and here I am, as good as new."

When Desmonde returned to the presbytery, he found the Canon upstairs in the study, drinking coffee before a fine, glowing peat fire. No one could manage this intractable fuel better than the Reverend Daniel Daly.

"They drove you back, lad. I heard the car." He added, inquiringly: "A good ten minutes ago."

"I went into the church. To thank the good Lord for a wonderful Easter Sunday. To say a prayer for my little communicants, not forgetting your kindness, and Madame's also."

"Well done! Will you join me in a coffee? Ye observe I keep my vow — I had my Dew middleday." He handed Desmonde his cup. "Go in the kitchen, fill me up again and take a cup to yourself. Mrs. O'B. is out, but the pot's on the stove."

When Desmonde returned, a cup in each hand, the Canon had drawn forward a chair for him at the other side of the fire.

"Thank ye, Desmonde. Not bad stuff this, though it gets one up, the middle o' the night. Did you have a good dinner down by?"

"Quite simple, Canon. The kitchen was rather on holiday."

"We had a grand saddle o' lamb here. The best I ever put my teeth into. Mrs. O'Brien was real upset you missed it. She kept a bit for you for tomorrow. And mind you, cold saddle of lamb with a baked potato is even better than the hot." He paused, to sip coffee. "By the way, I heard ye had a bit of a sing-song down by."

Desmonde smiled. "Canon, you get the news in Kilbarrack even before it happens."

"Not at all, lad. 'Twas Patrick when he rang up to say you'd not be here for dinner. He near burst the wire. You know, lad, the more I hear of your accomplishments the more I get depressed. For it means that I shall lose you soon. The archbishop has been speakin' of you, your talents, your manner, your personality. He wants you in Dublin for his own entourage, or for the cardinal. And what shall we do then? Myself, and Madame. You know she loves you, Desmonde. And so do I." He paused. "By the way, how did Madame seem to be, today?"

"Much as usual. But she did seem upset early on."

"And well she might be." The Canon finished his coffee and put his cup down beside the fender. "She rang me late last night, told me not to say a word to you, not to spoil your Easter Sunday." He shook his head. "On Saturday evening she had an express letter from that headmaster in Switzerland. After all the trouble she took to smooth things over, the niece has been expelled." The Canon drew a long distasteful breath. "There appears to be an Italian gentleman, if I may use the word, from Milan. He seems to have a substantial business of an unknown nature, and is rich, aged, say twenty-eight, with one of the choicest and most expensive Italian cars. He was staying, presumably for tax purposes, at the most exclusive hotel on the Lake and, like a gentleman of the type I've implied, has three times persuaded the niece, Claire, to break bounds at night, for purposes unknown, returning to her dormitory just before dawn." After this sardonic peroration the Canon paused then, in his natural voice, added: "Third time out, the little bitch was bloody well caught, and deservedly."

"I'm terribly sorry for Madame," Desmonde said. "Is she all bad, the girl?"

"It seems she's like her mother. Willful, attractive and fond of the men. Anyway, at eighteen it's high time she was finished with school and under stricter supervision. And that is just what Madame has asked me to give her."

"Shouldn't Madame take charge of her, now that she's going to her Swiss house?"

"And let this Italian bastard keep after her? No. No, Desmonde, she must be removed from his illicit attentions. I promise you I'll knock some sense into her, and you must help me. I'm meeting her in Dublin the day after tomorrow. Patrick will drive me up."

"It's a long journey for a young girl to take alone."

"Tuts! 'Twill all be arranged, lad. She'll be put in the train at Geneva. At Paris a representative of the school will meet her and put her on the Calais express. At Calais it's a step to the boat, and in London a man from Madame's London office will put her on the train for Fishguard. And I'm on the quay waiting for her in Dun Laoghaire."

"Anyway, she must have made the trip several times before." Desmonde added, "Does Madame leave soon?"

The Canon nodded. "To add to her present woes, the boys of the Inland Revenue are asking if she intends to give up her Swiss residence. She must get there presto, once she has settled the girl down at the Mount."

"Such changes!" Desmonde said. "I don't like them. Canon, if you're not thinking of bed yet I'd like to ask you about a letter I had this morning."

"I saw the envelope, with the heading on it, in your mail. Don't have anything to do with them, Desmonde. Or their movement."

"You know about it, Canon?"

"Small though it is, I do. They're puttin' out circulars to all the young members o' the clergy: protest against the continuance of priestly celibacy! Pah! They're just a bunch o' bastards wantin' weemen."

"You're all for celibacy, Canon?"

"My views on celibacy can be expressed in five words: 'Lump it and like it.' We priests are men, Desmonde, which makes it hard at times. But we are followers, disciples of our Lord Jesus, also a man, who was celibate. And from the practical point of view, what use would a wife be in a presbytery? Before long she'd be wearing the vestments and hearing confessions. Don't you know, too, from your experience in the confessional, how many marriages are failures, bringing misery in their train — the nagging, the quarrels, the fighting, the infidelities, the 'get the hell out of here, you bloody bitch.' Less than a tenth of the marriages of today are happy and successful. And the children? Do you want half a dozen o' them yelling, squabbling, playing hide-and-seek in and out o' the confessionals?"

"The High Anglican Church, very near to us, seems to sanction marriage with some success."

"They're situated differently from us, lad. We priests live beside, or on top of our churches. The Anglican vicarage is often a mile or more away, private and secluded. Married life to them is a thing apart. No, Desmonde, the rosy dream of matrimony of any young priest is not based on reality. 'Tis just a projection of his own two balls."

A silence fell, broken by the sound of the side door being shut and bolted, followed by the footsteps of Mrs. O'Brien moving to her room below, then quietly closing her door.

"There's the answer to your question, Desmonde. Who could look after us better than that good, pure — I repeat, pure — woman?"

He stood up and stretched. "I'm weary. I'll take the bathroom first tonight, if that's all right with you."

Desmonde laughed. "Then I can soak a bit longer. Shall I put the light out here?"

The Canon nodded. "Good night, my dear, very dear lad."

"Good night, Canon, with my deep affection and dutiful respect."

Thus ended Easter Sunday in Kilbarrack. The happiest, and the last, that Desmonde Fitzgerald would ever spend there.

All arrangements had been made, as previewed by the Canon, and at eight thirty on Thursday, after he had said the eight o'clock Mass to a mere handful of the faithful, and breakfasted substantially thereafter, that worthy dignitary departed for Dublin in the landaulet, driven by Patrick. Wearing his best Sunday suit and wrapped tightly in a thick black ulster which would undoubtedly protect him from the elements should he be obliged to wait, exposed, on the Dublin quays, his expression was firm and composed although, indeed, for a cleric who rarely quitted his own diocese, the expedition was both an excitement and an ordeal.

"All being well," he remarked to Desmonde, who saw him off, "we'll be back around four o'clock. Though, mind ye, I can't guarantee the mail boat."

"Don't omit your lunch, Canon," said Desmonde, with solicitude.

"If I have the time, I'll drop in at the Hibernian — they know me there," added the Canon, with the air of a man of the world. "But if I'm pushed —" he made an inconsequential gesture to the left — "Mrs. O'Brien has put up a bit of a sandwich for me."

Glancing left, Desmonde was relieved by an outsize package on the seat, carefully wrapped in oiled paper, and bulging with assorted food. Assuredly the Canon would not starve.

"Take care of yourself while I'm away, lad," cried the Canon, as the big car began to move.

What a good, simple, honest man was this old parish priest, yet strong, too, formidable in the cause of virtue. So thought Desmonde as he went toward the church. When he had said Mass he made his way over to the school. He had not visited there for some time, and after a chat with the master he went around the classes, saying a few words to the children in each, pleased by the morning freshness of the children and the greeting they all gave him.

Desmonde was still smiling as he went to the presbytery. Here Mrs. O'Brien was waiting for him.

"There's a message for you, Father, from the Mount. 'Twas Madame Donovan herself, she's expecting you to lunch today. You're to come when you're free. A light luncheon, she said." Mrs. O'Brien shook her head. "And what a pity. Here am I with two of the nicest sweetbreads ye ever saw, ready to cook for you special."

"I *am* sorry. But keep them, Mrs. O'Brien. The Canon and I could share them for dinner."

"I will, I will. But sure, one of them is but a couple of swallows for the Canon. I'll have to put in some chops as well. And now, there's a sick call for you, as well. Old Mrs. Conroy at the Point. She's bedridden, you know, and would like you to take the Sacrament. I'll give you something else for her too. She's a poor old soul, though a terrible talker."

The Point was on the far side of the town, so Desmonde decided to take the car. After he had washed, he went back to the church, removed a Host from the tabernacle and placed it in the little purse reserved for that purpose. He then drove off in the old Ford. Mrs. O'Brien had already placed a parcel on the back seat.

Mrs. Conroy, one of those old ladies who like to make the most of a visit from the clergy, was sitting up in bed, wrapped in her best shawl, with a lace cap upon her head. Neat and tidy, adorning the poverty of the little cottage, she welcomed Desmonde with effusion.

After he had administered the Sacrament she pointed to the chair which, at her direction, the neighbor who looked after her had placed beside the bed.

"Now, Father dear, 'tis a great honor. I'm sure ye understand, the fella that was here afore ye, I disremember his name, never had it, nor deserved it, but then he was a dull sort of a clod, and never came but three or four times to see me aal the time he was here. Ye are the chip of a different tree, it's clear to see, even with my poor ould eyes, lookin' at your dear handsome smilin' face, and they tell me it's wondrous things ye have accomplished, the two pigs that was killed stone dead by a truck in the market, and ye put your fair blessed hands upon them and lifted them back to life, I tell ye, the neebors tell me the cheerin' could be heared down here. What's that you're callin', Lizzie, a parcel from Mrs. O'Brien? God bless her, there's a kind wumman for ye. And what would be in it? Scones, butter, the half of a boiled fowl and a hale can o' tay! Ah, now, the saints be praised, and Mrs. O'Brien too, just when we're near outa the tay, 'tis mate and drink to me. Let Lizzie give ye a cup, Father."

Rather than disappoint the old chatterbox, Desmonde accepted and drank the tea, which he duly praised. Thereafter he sat and listened until he felt he might leave without giving offense.

After his escape, Desmonde drove the long way around to the Mount with both car windows down, deeming it wise to aerate himself from the odors of Mrs. Conroy's bedroom, before presenting himself to Madame. Thus, it was precisely noon when he arrived.

"You are barely in time," Madame said chillingly. "Bridget has just sent word that the soufflé is *au point*. Once it falls in, it is of course uneatable."

"I have been on an errand of mercy." Desmonde excused himself, as he followed his hostess into the house. "To Mrs. Conroy."

"That old gossip! Not half so ill as she pretends. Is she still complaining?"

"Yes, Madame, that you don't send her enough of your delicious hothouse tomatoes."

"You'll soon see if they are delicious. With Patrick away, I warned you it would be a light lunch. Salad and cheese soufflé, followed by —" she smiled — "coffee."

They seated themselves and almost at once Bridget's girl brought in the soufflé, golden brown, beautifully risen, puffy as an old man's breath.

"Tell Bridget it is a success," Madame said, already slicing into the glorious bubble.

Each place had already been set with oval plates heaped with a fresh vegetable salad.

"It is unbelievably delicious, Madame." Desmonde sighed after a few forkfuls. "Like an angel's kiss."

"Do they kiss up there? Don't the wings get in the way?"

A silence followed while they devoted themselves to the food. A single glass of the same Chablis had already been poured, ice-cold.

"We were enlivened this morning," Madame said, looking up, "by the strains of martial music. A fife and drum band, to be exact."

"I believe the Hibernians were on the warpath."

"A route march."

"Possibly."

Madame shook her head, smiling. "Desmonde, my dear Desmonde, Bridget's girl, who was at the ten o'clock, brought back a very different story. You are now numbered among the elect, surpassing even the Canon." She paused to spear a reluctant slice of cucumber. "Did he get off safely this morning?"

"He did, Madame, exactly to the second, fully accoutred and stocked with rations, against all hazards and contingencies."

"What a dear old man he is — simple, faithful, strong and true. A saint, in fact. I love him." She added, "Even when he annoys me."

"Have you a grain of affection left over? For his curate?"

"Don't tease, today, dearest Desmonde. You know you have become half of my life. And I shall miss you dreadfully for three whole months. How I wish you could come to my place in Burier. It is quite lovely, and large, a real country house. I hate to be confined. Lots of parkland and a heavenly view of Leman. A convent near, at La Tour de Peilz, very convenient in Protestant Switzerland, where I hear Mass in the little chapel. Beauty, peace, complete isolation. But no Desmonde. And, besides, I shall worry all the time about Claire." She paused. "I dread meeting her today. We are always at odds. She is exactly like my poor sister, intractable, irresponsible, unpredictable. I have begged the Canon to try and put some sense in her. And you must try, too, Desmonde. Can you stay with me till they arrive?"

"I am free all afternoon, Madame."

"Splendid! Then we'll have coffee in the sun-room, and afterward you must sing for me."

"Won't you . . . try to sing with me?"

She smiled, sadly. "I am not Trilby, and you, Desmonde, are not Svengali, if such people ever existed. No, my phrenic nerve is irreparably gone. Yet my speech, thank God, is not impaired."

She rose, gracefully, as usual. "I'm afraid that's all. No good offering you cheese after the soufflé."

The afternoon had passed, ecstatically as planned, and now, some three hours later, having taken tea, they were seated on the long settee in the sun-room.

"Desmonde," she murmured. "This, I believe, has been the sweetest afternoon of my life."

"You speak for me, too, Madame."

"Tinged, intensified, by the agony of separation, Desmonde." She paused. "I must leave within the next few days, first for Dublin, where I shall spend a week at the office, reviewing everything, then for Geneva. So this may be the only time I shall be with you alone." She took both of his hands. "I therefore wish you to know, that once I have persuaded my friends at the Inland Revenue that I am back in Switzerland, I shall take the express that goes direct through the Simplon to Milan, and there I shall proceed to the firm of Moreno and Calvi, expert in all arts and skills appertaining to ecclesiastical marble. Desmonde, because of you, I intend, at last, to embellish my church with altar rails of the finest Carrara marble. There I will kneel when I receive the Eucharist from you."

"I am overwhelmed, Madame. And the Canon will be in seventh heaven."

"You may have the pleasure of bringing him the good news. So that is settled." She stood up, still holding his hands. "Desmonde, just this once — it may be a sin, I do not care. I embrace you as a woman who loves a man."

Opening her arms, she took him to her, offering all her body, withholding nothing. Their lips met in a long, exquisite, prolonged kiss.

Where this might have ended must remain in doubt, since the crunch of the big car on the gravel caused reason to intervene. They drew apart, and almost at once the Canon burst in, buttoned to the throat and followed by a tall, thin girl with a white, dirty face, the front of her dress stained with vomit, her big, dark, weary eyes drawn fearfully toward Madame.

"So you are back, Canon," Madame managed to remark, pale and breathing rapidly.

"As ye see, Madame, safe and sound. And with your young lady, who's a bit the worse o' the wear. 'Tis a deadly crossin' from Newhaven when the wind's high. Waitin' there on the quay I was glad of my ulster."

"You did famously, Canon, and I am grateful."

" 'Tis a pleasure to serve you, Madame, and as I happened to be in Dublin I took the liberty of calling at the warehouse for the case ye so kindly promised me."

"That was wisely done." Madame inclined her head. "Claire, you may go to your usual room. I am quite sure you need nothing to eat. Take a bath first."

"Thank you, Auntie. And thank you, Canon." Claire turned and went out.

A brief silence followed.

"I took the further liberty, Madame, of asking Patrick to wait. I thought you might kindly permit him to finish the day by drivin' us home."

"Naturally, he will do so. I am sure you are weary yourself, so I will not detain you."

She escorted them to the front door. Here, the Canon bowed and went down the steps. Madame gave Desmonde one swift, burning glance.

"Three months is not forever. Remember that I love you."

Back at the presbytery, welcomed by Mrs. O'Brien, the case of Dew safely in the hall, the Canon was himself again, and in an answer to his housekeeper on the question of supper, thoughtfully replied: "I had a chop or two at the Hib, sampled some of your sandwiches on the quay, and finished the remainder off with Patrick on the way home. However . . . ?"

"Something light, maybe, Canon. A sweetbread?"

"The very thing, with a bit of cheese and a biscuit to follow."

Mrs. O'B. smiled at Desmonde. "I believe you would like that, yourself, Father."

During supper the Canon, in the manner of Marco Polo, reverted to the rigors and hazards of the expedition. As regards the niece, he merely said:

"She seemed a poor bit of a thing, half dead wi' that awfu' journey. And starved as weel. Onything she had to eat went over the rail into the Irish Sea."

"She seemed terrified of her aunt."

"And with good reason. Onybody that does wrong to Madame knows what to expect." He paused to sip his Dew, perhaps a slightly larger portion than usual, because of the fresh stock on hand. "How did you get on yerself today, with Madame?"

"Wonderfully." It was the appropriate moment. Desmonde rose from the table. "Canon, I am deputed by Madame Donovan to inform you that before the end of the year you will have altar rails of the finest Carrara marble."

As though electrified, the Canon sat, motionless. Then he sprang to his feet.

"Oh, thank God! And thank you, Desmonde. I kenned ye would do it, that Madame would do onything for ye." He put his arms on Desmonde's shoulders and embraced him. "Oh, glory be to God, and to Madame. We'll have the finest church, all complete, in the whole of Ireland. Wait till I tell Canon Mooney in Cork. He's aye been sneerin' at our auld rails, the Carrara will kill him. Oh, I must get on the phone instantly to Madame, to thank her . . ."

"No, Canon, wait. She's not in the mood now with the niece just back on her. Compose one of your beautiful letters overnight and send Michael down with it in the morning."

"Oh, you're right, lad, right as usual. I'm in no fit state. But I'll phone Mooney, 'twill give him a bad night. And I'll give Mrs. O'B. the great news straight away. Och, lad, I'll never forget you for this, never, never. Sit down by the fire, I'll be back in two ticks, then we'll talk it all over from beginning to end."

And the Canon, his Dew forgotten, dashed through the door, and downstairs to the kitchen.

Madame had gone and the days seemed less bright. No longer did her charming, attractive figure adorn the church. Instead, the little end pew held only a solemn-faced Patrick and a sub-dued, sulky Claire. Sadly missed, too, was the generous hos-pitality of the Mount.

"It's no' quite the same without her," the Canon commented more than once, adding: "I hope she hasn't forgotten her promise."

Madame had not forgotten. Toward the end of the second week two architects arrived and, without delay, began their operations in the church, measuring, calculating, discussing, and with a silence more cutting than speech, ignoring the Canon's suggestions and proposals, which would undoubtedly have ruined the entire project. They conversed only with Desmonde, in rapid Italian that had the warmth of expatriates discovering their own language, spoken perfectly, in a foreign town. And from these exchanges Desmonde was able to assure his superior that all would be perfect, both in quality and design.

Indeed, after three days, before the two strangers departed, they presented the Canon with a skillfully tinted design — a picture, in fact, of the finished work. The Canon gazed, and was immediately in ecstasy.

" 'Tis beautiful, 'tis superb, oh, dear Lord, it is heavenly!' "

Looking over his shoulder, Desmonde was equally enchanted. A superb curve of veined white marble, supported, in groups of three, by delicate yellow pilasters, saved from over-elaboration by a median gate of beaten bronze.

"You were right, Desmonde, lad, to leave them to it — they're experts, artists. Ah! what a joy 'twill be when it's here. Did they mention when the work would start?"

"Almost at once, Canon. They asked me where their men could stay — the Station Hotel, I thought . . ."

"Ay, they'll get dacent rooms there. I'll see to it. I'll speak to Dolan myself."

Hugging the drawing, the worthy old man went immediately to the church porch and hung it there for all to admire.

Every week now, on Tuesdays and Fridays, the Canon, accompanied by his curate, made the pilgrimage to the deserted Mount to see that Madame's instructions were being strictly observed.

On the Tuesday following the departure of the Italians, the Canon and his curate took their leisurely walk to the Mount, the Canon remarking as they approached the house: " 'Tis like a body without a soul."

Patrick, as usual, anticipating their visit, met them at the front entrance.

"Well, how is your charge today, Patrick?"

"As usual, I'm afraid, your reverence. Miserable all the time, nothing to do, naebody to talk to, barring ourselves. She wanders around like a knotless thread."

"No letters written or received."

"None whatsoever, your reverence. Not a scrape of a pen. I check the post carefully myself."

"Does she not take up a book?"

"She's not a reader, Canon." Patrick hesitated. "Don't you think, your reverence, that Madame is just a bit over-severe with her? With all respect, that's the opinion of ourselves in the kitchen. She's a slip of a thing who's been a bit wayward, maybe, but there's many o' us makes mistakes when we're young. Why, Madame has even forbidden the glass of light wine to her lunch that she's used to at her school. She's no appetite without it.

Don't you think t'would be a kindness to let her have just one glass o' the Barsac we have on occasions ourselves — mild stuff, from Findlater's in Dublin."

The Canon pondered, glanced at Desmonde.

"I say no." The response came firmly. "Madame must be obeyed."

"Weel," said the Canon slowly, "I say yes. Justice must be tempered with mercy."

"Thank you, Canon," Patrick said. "She'll maybe eat a bit now. She's up by the tennis court if ye wish to see her."

He led the way through the house and out across the rose garden to the pavilion. On the court, dressed in her ordinary blouse and skirt, Claire was making the best of her solitary state, serving six balls from the far end of the court, walking slowly to the near side, collecting the balls, then carelessly, absently, banging them back again.

"That's no sort of a game!" growled the Canon, and after a further listless volley, he touched Desmonde on the shoulder. "For Pete's sake, lad, take your coat off, get a bat, and knock the balls back to her."

"I have no racket."

"There's plenty in the pavilion." Patrick disappeared, and was back in a moment with a brand new racket. " 'Tis a good one, a Spalding."

Desmonde stripped off his jacket and stepped onto the court, where he was greeted by a surprised, welcoming smile.

"I'm not much good," he said. "But I'll try and give you a game."

They started off with a knock-up. She began by moderating the speed of her serves, which he returned with an underhand stroke. Desmonde had a good eye and soon they had some creditable rallies that provoked applause from the spectators. Finally they played a set, Desmonde still serving underhand, which, though only by six games to four, he lost.

The change in Claire was remarkable. She looked a different girl as she followed her opponent from the court. Flushed and smiling, she thanked, in turn, the Canon, Desmonde, and finally Patrick.

"It's just what I've been longing for," she added.

"Father Desmonde looks the better o' it, too," commented Patrick. "Maybe you'll let him play again, Canon, when he comes down."

"I sanction it." The Canon nodded amiably. "But look at the way he's sweatin'. He'll need tennis claes."

"There's plenty o' them. Madame has white shirts and shoes and pants in the lockers — for the office fellas when they visit us. I'll have Bridget wash and iron a set o' them."

Claire's eyes had brightened. She's nothin' like as bad as Madame makes out, thought the Canon. Madame can be gey hard, ay, hard as steel, when she's crossed. And, aloud:

"I perceive it's been dull and miserable for ye, missie. We'll ease up a bit on ye now. If Father Desmonde is free, he'll give you a game Thursday. Away now, and get yourself shifted, you're all sweatin'!"

They watched her run down to the back door of the house, where she turned to wave to them.

"I'm in the same condition." Desmonde laughed. "Wringing wet. Perhaps Patrick would drive us home."

" 'Twould suit me," said the Canon, who was not looking forward to the uphill walk back to the presbytery.

"I'll see that the water is turned on in the pavilion," Patrick murmured to Desmonde, as he led the way to the garage. "You'll get a decent shower after your game Thursday."

The two visitors were driven off, suffused by a comfortable feeling of a kindly act, well done. Watching from the window of her little bedroom, Claire felt happy for the first time in many weeks.

14

The following Thursday was wet and the official visit to Mount Vernon was postponed. In the forenoon Desmonde worked with the Canon over the quarterly accounts, writing off the expenses of the presbytery against the income from the church collections. The balance was small indeed, so small that the Canon shook his head.

"We'd never manage to keep things going, Desmonde, if 'twasn't for Madame. Think of all that she gives us, or pays for. The fine wax candles, lovely vestments, and flowers, the heating and lighting, even the incense. And now, them wonderful rails." He paused. "I wonder how she is now, over there?"

As if in answer to the Canon's query, the noon mail delivery brought a letter from Switzerland, addressed to Desmonde, who immediately read it aloud to his superior.

My dear Desmonde,

I have been frantically busy since my arrival here, but now I seize a moment to unburden my troubled lonely heart and also to inform you that all arrangements for the new altar rails have been completed. You must tell the good Canon that I have sanctioned the proposed design — it is quite lovely. I have also chosen the various marbles, also superbly beautiful, and now Signor Moreno, head of the Moreno Company, has just telephoned to say that all these precious goods have been crated, and will be shipped by freighter direct to Cork one week from today. Accompanying them will be four of his best workmen, who will see to the delivery of the crates, and unpack and install the marbles. This should take a week or ten days, so perhaps the good Canon will accordingly reserve rooms for the men. I suggest the Station Hotel. Tell Dolan to give them rice and macaroni dishes — that's their usual diet.

Among all my longings, I cannot wait to see my lovely gift actually in being, in my lovely church, and to kneel there, to receive the Sacrament from your dear hands, dearest Desmonde. What joy, spiritual and, yes, temporal — but of the purest ray serene.

Desmonde flushed and paused, looking across at the Canon, who nodded understandingly, saying: "I know, lad, I know. If it hadna' been for you I might have waited long enough . . ."

Desmonde resumed.

Nor must we forget our worthy Canon, who will soon be in a position to exult over his friendly enemy in Cork.

The Canon chuckled. "She kens aal . . . What a woman!"

On other matters of less importance, I have had a most unpleasant time, interviewing Major Coulter, Claire's late headmaster, who, in addition to lecturing me, as if I were to blame, on the adverse publicity suffered by his school through Claire's escapades, presented me with a sheaf of bills sent to the school after her departure, debts unofficially incurred by my darling niece, for showy dresses, a bead necklace, and white gloves, all quite unnecessary. To put it as charitably as possible, she seems to have no sense whatsoever, not only of the standards of common decency, but of the value of money, particularly when it is not her own. I do trust that, with the Canon, you are supervising her behavior and ensuring that she doesn't communicate with her former confederates, or get into mischief there.

Again the Canon intervened. "Isn't that just what we're doin', and seein' to, forbye, that she stays in good health."

And now dear friend, with all good wishes, I must say *au revoir*.
Let me know at once when the shipment arrives.

Most sincerely yours,
GERALDINE DONOVAN

Desmonde hesitated, then folded the letter and returned it to
its envelope. A postscript had caught his eye which he thought
wiser not to disclose.

Desmonde, I cannot sleep. I, who always slept peacefully, soundly
as a child, lie awake at night, often for hours, *une nuit blanche*,
thinking, thinking . . . of whom? Write to me soon, my darling.

GERRY

Leaving the Canon to his final additions, Desmonde rose and
went to the church to kneel before the tabernacle, always his
solace and comforter, his refuge in every difficulty. He prayed
that Madame's insomnia might yield to refreshing sleep, but beyond all, he prayed that their mutual love might be restrained,
to remain within the bounds prescribed by Holy Church. For
himself he had no fear, but as for his dear, dear friend, his
patroness, the postscript of her letter troubled him. He promised
himself, and Heaven too, that his reply to the letter, while no
less affectionate than before, would be tempered by a cautionary
prudence.

The children were now beginning to assemble for his catechism class, among them the little ones he had brought on for
Holy Communion. The bishop's visit was not due until late
September, a week or ten days after Madame's return, but Desmonde, who wanted his pupils to shine before his lordship, had
started early. Assuring himself that the glass jar, in the cupboard in the sacristy, was still amply stocked, Desmonde began
his instruction, which went on until noon.

The sun continued to shine and at lunch the Canon remarked:
"You better do Vernon this afternoon, lad. 'Twill take us

[171]

over the weekend." Then as Desmonde looked at him inquiringly: "I have a four o'clock C.C. meeting on my hands. And to tell the truth, I don't care for that stiff uphill walk on the way back, instead of my usual nap. So you might as well run down yourself in future, see that all goes well, and have your bit of a game forbye."

Desmonde, accordingly, made his way alone to the Mount, arriving soon after two o'clock.

Claire, already on the court in short white ballet skirt and singlet, greeted him joyously.

"I'm so glad you've come, Father Desmonde. I was desolate yesterday. Patrick has put your togs all ready in the pavilion, and he's most decently given us new balls. So do hurry and change."

Desmonde went into the pavilion. As promised, everything was there, beautifully washed and pressed: white flannels and singlet, white sweater and tennis shoes — an inviting sight. In four minutes flat, Desmonde emerged, transformed.

"I say, you do look spiffing!" Claire's dark eyes had widened. "Absolute Wimbledon."

"All but my game, Claire."

"We'll see to that! Now come on, the first thing is to teach you the overhand serve. No more popping the ball over, underhand, as Auntie might do if she tried it."

The lesson began. Desmonde was an apt pupil — he felt so free and easy in his light clothing — and soon Claire decided that the set might begin. Her serves came crashing in, unsparingly, until at last Desmonde learned to time and return them. His own serve began to take shape, affording him the delicious sensation of a brand-new ball, hit hard and true with the center of a first-class racket.

Claire took the first set six games to one, and the second six to two. Halfway through the third, Patrick appeared with a jug of iced lemonade and glasses on a tray, which he placed on a table in the veranda of the pavilion.

"You *are* kind, Patrick," Desmonde said, coming to the net.

"Please thank Bridget for doing my things so nicely. And thank you for the new balls."

"It's a pleasure to see your reverence lookin' so well. Ye know, you were quite pale and peaky for a while, just before Madame left. As for the niece, the good exercise has made her a different cratur."

He waited, watching the game resumed, then joined Bridget, who had a vantage point by the pantry window.

"They're a beautiful pair out there," Bridget commented. "But . . . Do you think it's quite in order, quite safe, so to speak, to let them be tegither . . . alone?"

"Ah, they're just playin' like a couple of children."

"Madame wouldn't like it, Pat."

"What Madame doesn't see won't grieve her. It's my opinion she's been far too hard on the girl. Ever since we've been kind to her she's blossomed like the rose."

"Cut the poetry, Shakespeare! Ye never ca'ed me a rose. Ah, well . . . ah, well. Just look at that Father Desmonde, there. Anybody but a blind man would see she has fallen for him. He would turn the head and the heart of any wumman, young or old." Moving off, she added a parting shot. "As Madame could well tell ye."

When the third set was over, the players retired to a bench on the veranda and poured the lemonade.

"I did enjoy that," Desmonde said. "And I've always rather stupidly despised ball games."

"There's one or two of them warrant investigation." Claire put both feet on the railing, leaning slightly back to allow the breeze to exert its full cooling effect — an effect which was, indeed, assisted by a slight billowing of her short skirt. Hurriedly, Desmonde averted his eyes from the delectable vision thus revealed.

"Shall we play again?"

"I don't want you to overdo it, Desmonde. You'll feel stiff tomorrow from that overhead serve. But do come again on Monday. I'll be seeing you, Sunday, in church. Take your

[173]

shower now, before you cool off. I'll bring my dressing gown over tomorrow, so I can take one too. It's more companionable by far."

She got to her feet and, before skipping down the steps, planted a light kiss on his cheek.

On her way to the house she turned twice to wave her racket and to blow another kiss.

Great excitement now animated Kilbarrack as the cry went around: "The Eyetalians are here!" Accompanied by numerous crates, large and small, four quiet, debonair little men had been welcomed by the Canon and shown in state to their hotel. Almost immediately the work on the altar rails began. And how skillfully, how expertly did it proceed. And so silently, since the Canon, after some misguided attempts to interfere, was obliged to watch, which he did almost continuously, without words. And with what envy did he regard Desmonde, chatting away to them, making them smile and chatter back.

"What was that a' about?" snarled the good Canon.

"They are happy to be here, and with the accommodation so kindly provided. But as they are all highly skilled and experienced technicians, they wish not to be disturbed. Also they have brought with them all their own delicious food and wine, and wish no food from the hotel."

"Ma Goad!" groaned the Canon. "What will Dolan do with a' them lashins o' macaroni I made him buy."

Not alone was the Canon in his silent vigil. Piety suddenly became the rage in Kilbarrack, crowds flocking to the church to cross themselves, kneel, stare, and wonder.

"Have ye been up the day, yet, Mick?"

"I have indade, but I'll go up with ye again. 'Tis as good as the theayater. The way them little fellers slide around in their sandals, knowin' where everything goes and slidin' it in like clockwork. And a lovely job 'twill be when it's done, an all."

Parochial duties were necessarily reduced to a minimum, and Desmonde, with time on his hands, was drawn even more frequently to Vernon, to the tennis court. He had become fond of the game, and with his keen eye and swift reactions, had surprised Claire on his latest visit by winning in three straight sets. Far from annoying Claire, this had delighted her. Always gay, full of fun, and in her own phrase, "ready for anything," she had proved herself an amusing, uninhibited, and carefree companion. Now they shared the pavilion together as a living room in which towels, clothes, slippers, bathrobes and the rest, were scattered and littered around.

"Isn't this fun," Claire would exclaim, coming out of the shower, loosely robed. "I'm glad I got kicked out of that school. First of all because I hated the bloody place, and secondly because now I've got you."

And she began to sing: "Falling in love . . ."

"Enough, little birdie, you're off-key. This is how it goes."

And he sang it through for her.

This was the good summer which occasionally, though rarely, steeps the southwest of Ireland in benign and constant sunshine. Desmonde was now deeply tanned and he had put on muscle, so that the Canon, scanning him approvingly, had exclaimed:

"You're lookin' great, Desmonde, and more of a man."

This afternoon, striding down toward the pavilion, to change before Claire should appear, Desmonde did indeed feel unusually fit, carefree and cheerful, a euphoria that owed much to the prospects of this lovely afternoon, and the pleasure of being with his carefree opponent who was, in fact, on the spot when he leaped up the steps of the veranda.

"Out, birdie, out!" he cried. "I'm going to strip."

"And what difference does that make? I'm putting a new lace in my shoe. And aren't we the best of intimate pals?"

"Turn your back, then."

"What for? Are ye like Nora Macarty on her weddin' night?"
And without moving she began to sing.

Little Nora Macarty the knot was goin' to tie,
She washed all her trousseau and hung it up to dry,
Then up came a goat and he saw the bits of white,
He chewed up all her fal-de-rals, and on her weddin' night,
Oh turn out the light quick, poor Nora cried to Pat,
For though I am your bride, sure, I'm not worth lookin' at,
I had two of everything I told you when I wrote,
But now I've one o' nothing, all through Paddy McGinty's
    goat.

Claire burst out laughing: "That's a great song, Des, you should hear the two Bobs at it. So let's see you with one of nothing."

Desmonde shook his head and began, with as much discretion as possible, to change.

"And don't call me Des, Claire. The name is Desmonde, with the final 'e.' "

"Ah, what's the odds, I'll soon be calling ye darlin'. Here I go again, just once more." And she sang: "Let me call you sweetheart, darlin', I'm in love with you . . ."

Out on the court, Desmonde said: "I'm going to knock the stuffing out of you, for that."

They played without rest, two hard sets, and after a short adjournment to the pavilion, a final two, leaving the honors even. As they came off the court shortly after four o'clock, Patrick was waiting for them.

"Bridget thought you must be tired of that auld lemonade and wonders if ye wouldn't like to come in the house for your tea."

Desmonde glanced at Claire, who exclaimed, "I think we'd love it, don't you, Desmonde?"

They went into the pavilion to change, Claire, according to

custom, taking the shower first while Desmonde went into the men's changing room. He had barely stripped off his singlet when a wild shriek from Claire brought him out again.

"Oh, Des, quick, quick, look at my eye."

Standing stark naked, bedewed by the shower, like Aphrodite risen from the foam, she now ran toward him, put her hands on his shoulders, and upturned her face.

"Something in my right eye, a fly perhaps, hurting, hurting. Please look."

Desmonde inspected the eye, pressing back the lid, but could see no insect of any kind. He did however see Claire, her slim beautiful body, tight little pink-tipped breasts, and the delicate little tuft guarding the ultimate mystery from which, perhaps, came the strange fragrance that made his head swim. He felt his own body react, violently, hotly, as he stammered: "I see nothing . . . perhaps the spray . . ."

"Oh, it was so sharp, and sudden . . ." She let her face rest against his. "I was frightened. Don't move, dear, this is helping me." Now she was almost in his arms. "This is what I was longing for, hoping that you would hold me close, wanting you, wanting you. You know I'm crazy about you, darling. Hold me this way, often, often . . ."

When at last Desmonde disengaged himself, his heart was beating fast. He took one last look at her, standing there with arms outstretched, then stumbled into his changing cabinet.

Fifteen minutes later, they were both in the sun-room, oddly silent, relieved, almost, when Patrick, who had just brought in a well-stocked tray, seemed to hesitate before leaving the room.

"Might I take no more nor a minute, sir, to ask you a favor?"

"Certainly, Patrick."

"Well, 'tis like this, your reverence. The A.O.H. will be givin' their annual concert next month, for charity ye understand, and bein' one of the officials they've asked me to ask you a great favor . . . If you would consent to appear on the programme, just to sing no more nor a couple of songs, not classical, ye understand, just two o' the good old Irish ballads."

"Go on, Des, say yes," Claire urged, as Desmonde hesitated. "I've promised to do a turn myself."

"She has indeed, sir."

"Well, I will, then," Desmonde said.

"Oh, thank ye, sir, thank ye, indeed, the boys will be delighted. Ye've made yerself so well liked, so popular, goin' amongst the people, bein' one of us, despite your position and education, 'twill fill the house to hear you."

When Patrick had bowed himself out, Desmonde turned to Claire.

"Give me my tea, you hidden persuader, and some of that cake before you finish it."

When the tea and cake had been given and absorbed, Desmonde said seriously:

"Claire, dear, we must be careful in future. No more of these sudden sorties from the shower. They are dangerous."

She did not answer, but smiled, her tight-lipped enigmatic smile, which barely uncovered her little white teeth. When they had finished tea, and thanked Bridget in the kitchen, she said:

"I'll walk up the hill with you."

She took his arm and in silence they set off. At the summit of the woodland cutting, in the little grassy glade, he held up his hand.

"No trespassers, please. This is private property, where I come to meditate."

"Will you think of me?"

"Unfortunately, yes."

"What a nasty thing to say. You must atone by kissing me."

He kissed her.

She watched him as, without looking back, he walked down the hill.

16

Desmonde was now in better physical condition than ever before, or indeed, than ever he would be again. Unhappily there was a fly in the ointment, possibly of the species that flew out of Claire's eye. No matter how hard he worked in the parish, winning commendation from the Canon for completing tasks that had long awaited attention, he seemed unable to tire himself out, and often at night he would lie for hours inviting the sleep that did not come.

Mentioning his trouble at supper one evening, the Canon nodded understandingly.

"I had the same thing myself, when I was a young priest. It's in the nature of man — repression taking its revenge. You don't play so much tennis these days?"

"I was overdoing it, Canon. A priest has no place on the tennis court, every day of the week."

"Maybe . . . maybe," the Canon said thoughtfully. "Why don't you take a good hard walk at night before ye turn in? Or a little drop o' the Dew might send you over."

"Thank you, Canon." Desmonde smiled constrainedly. "I think I'll try the walk."

He wondered if his worthy Superior had an intuition of the struggle going on in his mind, of the fight he was waging to keep away from Vernon and from Claire. He did, nevertheless, set out about an hour after supper, striding up the hill and half running down. This, followed by a hot bath, gave him some relief, and exhausted sleep of two or three hours' duration, before the restless tossing set in again.

Often he thought of the casual manner in which he had treated Madame's mention of her insomnia. Were they suffering, she as a woman, he as a man, from the same malady? He did, however, continue with the palliative of the hard nightly walk, setting off with his torch when the darkness was oppressive, meeting the Canon's anxiously approving glance when he returned. That wise old man knew precisely the cause of Desmonde's disorder. As a young celibate he had suffered it himself.

One night of unusual humidity, the air warm and still, Desmonde breasted the hill and flung himself down on the grass to rest. He had closed his eyes, instinctively wondering if sleep might come to him. He did not hear the sound of quiet approaching footsteps rustling the fallen leaves. Only when his whispered name, and the sound of hurried breathing, caused him to turn on his side, did he sense that Claire lay beside him. Was it reality or was it a dream? Her arms enfolding him, her voice, breathless from hurry, whispering again: "Darling, darling, why didn't you come to me? I've waited, waited, hungry for you. And when I saw your torch tonight I couldn't wait another sleepless night. Come, darling, come to me, love me."

He was in her arms now, lost in the blessed relief, the joy of her embrace, their lips together, hands touching, fondling, seeking and finding, finding, with her skillful guidance, the entrance to appeasement and the delirium of undreamed delight.

A long sigh broke from her. She was still, remaining locked in his embrace. Then she whispered:

"Darling, wonderful darling, that was the best ever —" She checked herself. "I felt that it was love, true love. I came to you, did you not feel it, how I quivered. I had been longing for you so long." Then, after a silence: "I must go now, dearest, or they will miss me at the house."

Another kiss and she had risen, was gone.

Desmonde lay for a moment as though dazed, his eyes still closed, his being pervaded by a calm satisfaction, as though every nerve in his body were at peace. At last he got to his feet and began to walk downhill.

Alas, the nearer he came to the presbytery, the more a realization of his predicament dawned upon him. His glow faded, supplanted by a slow fear and chilling remorse that drove him directly to the church. He entered by the side door and, without turning on the switches, flung himself down upon his knees before the altar.

The side door banged open and, flashing his torch, the Canon came barging into the church. He did not at first discern Desmonde, but finally a beam of light caught up and illumined the still, kneeling figure of his curate.

"So this is where ye've been hidin' yerself. And me lookin' for ye all over. There was a sick call for ye. The old Duggan man, way down at Ardberg. I had to do it fer ye. And ye know how I hate drivin' at night."

Desmonde remained silent.

"What's the matter with ye?" The Canon angrily drew near. "Are ye deaf or dumb?"

Still no answer. The torch flashed into Desmonde's face. A brief silence. Then:

"Good God! What's the matter? Are ye ill? This bloody night walkin' has exhausted ye."

A tremor passed over the kneeling figure. A hand was raised, shielding the death-pale face against the light. The Canon's voice altered.

"Here, lad, enough of these midnight vigils. Let me give you my arm. And come away up to my room." He helped Desmonde to his feet. "Mrs. O'Brien is long asleep. But I'll make ye a good strong cup o' coffee. I'm needin' one for my own self onyway."

So presently Desmonde was in the Canon's warm room, seated in the Canon's deep armchair, eyes down, gulping his coffee with a shaking hand.

"Father, I must confess to you."

"Ah?" The Canon raised a restraining arm as Desmonde attempted to kneel. "Sit where ye are, lad. I'm listening."

"Father . . . I am in love . . ."

"Ah! A wumman?"

"Yes."

"Well, there's naething so wrong with that, so long as ye've come out with it to me. Wha is't? That little bitch, Claire?"

"Yes, Father."

"I'd sworn it. There's nae good in that little bitch. She would make love to a lamppost."

"No, Father. No . . . no . . . no. She is a sweet, innocent little thing."

"Indeed, now. Well, lad, you'll put that same sweet and innocent little thing right out of your sweet innocent stupid head."

A silence. In a voice that trembled:

"I cannot, Father. We . . . we have already consummated our love."

"Consummated . . . your love. What in the name of God do you mean?"

"Tonight, as you are aware, I went walking . . . in Kiloan Wood . . . couldn't sleep . . . deeply troubled . . . by chance we met . . ."

"You met."

"We tried to resist, father. It was impossible. We . . . we loved each other."

A shocked look came over the Canon's ruddy face. Slowly he said:

"You mean you had her?" Then, peering into Desmonde's lowered eyes, ear cupped for the faint answer.

"We loved."

"A physical union? Oh, God Almighty. Holy Mary and all the Saints. What a bloody to-do! You went fucking in the dark in Kiloan Woods, come back half dead and call it love." The Canon's voice rose to a shout. "I see it all now. And ye come back to be petted and gi'en coffee. Go to your room, you dirty little brute, but first take a bath. Ye'll get no absolution from me yet. But what's to do in the parish . . ." He threw up his hands. "If this gets abroad 'twill mak' all the devils in hell dance the fandango!"

17

Physically and emotionally exhausted, Desmonde slept as one dead until the persistent whir of his alarm clock, set for seven o'clock, awakened him to the realization of his position. For some moments he lay motionless, then raised himself on one elbow. He had the eight o'clock morning weekday Mass. He must get up. But before he could stir, there came a knock at his door, which opened to reveal the Canon, fully dressed.

"Good morning, lad. How do you feel?"

The sympathy, the humanity in the Canon's voice, startled Desmonde, who stammered an answer.

"Well, well, now, that's good news. Though you do still look a bit white about the gills. So there's no need to hurry. I'll take the eight o'clock for ye. I've asked Mrs. O'Brien to give ye a right good breakfast, since you missed your dinner last night. Over that sick call." The emphasis on these last two words was stony. "And if you'll step down to the church, I'll be in the sacristy."

A nod, what might have passed as a smile, and the door closed quietly.

Desmonde got out of bed, knelt, according to his custom, to pray, then shaved, washed and dressed. His appearance in the small square mirror above his washstand was disheartening, but he went fairly steadily to the dining room where, beyond the hatch that opened to the kitchen, Mrs. O'Brien greeted him.

"Good morning to you, Father. You must be starved. And out

so late too, at poor old Mr. Duggan's. I'll have your breakfast through to you in a minute."

Indeed, with her customary efficiency, she was as good as her word, this cheerful, bustling, dark-eyed little woman of fifty who must, in her youth, have been pretty, and who now, with no more help than one village girl in the kitchen, managed the presbytery in all its ramifications.

The breakfast was exceptional, even in a house noted for its table. Fried soles that had come fresh from Wexford before dawn. New-baked rolls and dairy butter. Honey and cream cheese. Strong steaming coffee with clotted cream.

Desmonde, faint from lack of food, did justice to this noble spread and, though he divined it some part of the Canon's design, when he rose from the table much of his anguish and apathy had gone.

He knocked on the hatch and lifted it to thank Mrs. O'Brien, whom he knew to be favorable toward him — this surely was a moment when he needed all possible goodwill.

"Did you enjoy it, Father Desmonde?"

"Immensely."

Her dark eyes sparkled and she smiled, showing her nice white teeth. She loved to be praised, especially from this nice young priest, such a handsome boy.

When Desmonde entered the church, Mass was over and the Canon, having finished his thanksgiving, was in the vestry.

He smiled, a conciliatory smile, as Desmonde appeared, and surprisingly, held out his hand.

"Did ye have a good breakfast, lad? I told Mrs. O'Brien to make it special."

"A wonderful breakfast, thank you, Canon."

"Good, good. And I'll warrant you slept well."

Desmonde reddened, murmured almost inaudibly, "Yes."

"Then come and sit by me, lad. We'll have a bit of a chat, and forgetting all the hard words of last night, try and straighten things out for you and all of us.

"Now don't be thinkin' that the sky has fallen in on you because you've made a bit of a false step. You're not the only one, by a long chop, that's done so. It's hard for human nature to be celibate. It would surprise ye to know how many a dacent priest has made a slip, once in a while, and has had to pick himself up quick and tell the Lord he was sorry."

The Canon paused reflectively, and looking at him, Desmonde became suddenly the victim of a strange optical illusion. He saw, not the Canon's ruddy honest features but, just for one second, the sweet, docile, dark-eyed face of Mrs. O'Brien.

"Well now," the Canon sighed. "One thing is certain, you cannot have anything more to do with the girl. To do so would be fatal. Do you see that yourself?"

"Yes, Canon. It's hard . . ."

"Of course it's hard, and if it were harder 'twould still have to be obeyed. You want to continue as a priest, where already you have made a great success and where the future is so bright and shinin'. You want to continue to serve the Lord God Almighty as his blessed and anointed servant."

"I do, I must."

"Well, then, leave everything to me. I will see to it that Claire does not come near you again. I have the power and the influence in that quarter, and believe me, I will use it. Just you put her out of your mind. If you don't, 'twould be stark ravin' madness, the disaster that all hell is awaitin.' " He stood up. "Now, take the car, and away down to see how poor old Duggan is this morning. I think it's maybe pneumonia, and if it is he'll have to be lifted to the Infirmary."

As he was bid, Desmonde drove out to make the sick call. He found the old man better, which he thought a good omen, and attended by the District Nurse, who assured him it was only a chill.

On the way home he saw that they were putting up posters for the Hibernian Concert, and was able to distract his mind by thinking of the songs he would sing — all truly Irish, he decided, tender, sentimental, patriotic. He parked his car at the Cross, scene of his adventure with the piglets, and went on foot to visit another of his invalids, greeted all the way by touched caps and cheerful, friendly, respectful salutations. How good to be on such pleasant terms with his parishioners, to be revered, yes, even loved, in this old country town. He began gradually to realize how foolish, how dangerous, had been his conduct.

It was lunchtime when he got back to the presbytery and, after that light meal, the Canon had more work for him, which kept him busy well into the evening. And how comforting, at dinner, to find the Canon as well disposed to him as ever.

The days that followed were filled, by the Canon's design, with a plenitude of parochial duties, comings and goings that kept Desmonde busy and on the move. There was no sign of Claire — not a word was heard from her — and Desmonde, true to his given word, tried to banish her from his mind.

The day of the concert finally came around and Desmonde, his spirits restored, decided to give of his best, the more so since the Canon had honored him by promising to attend.

The night was dry and fine, crowds began early to flock to the Town Hall and when the Canon and Desmonde arrived and took their places, reserved in the front row, the hall was filled to capacity, overflowing even, into the street.

Desmonde had been given the final place of honor on the program. He had feared, greatly feared, that as she had promised, Claire might appear. But as the evening wore on, mildly entertaining, there was no sign of her. And now it was his turn. He mounted the stage by the wooden side steps and, amid applause, sat down at the piano, immediately behind the footlights.

Dead silence as his fingers moved over the keys. Then he began to sing.

The minstrel boy to the war has gone,
In the ranks of death you'll find him;
His father's sword he has girded on,
And his wild harp slung behind him . . .

He could not have chosen a better opening. Cheers echoed to the roof, stilled only when he raised his hand. He had decided to give of his best, to honor Ireland and his Irish birth.

He sang next "Killarney," then, in turn, "The Star of County Down," "Terence's Farewell to Kathleen," that lovely song composed by Lady Dufferin, "The Meeting of the Waters." Then for a touch of comedy he suddenly launched into: "I Met Her in the Garden Where the Praties Grow." His heart swelled as he filled the hall with the dear old Irish melodies. Finally he sang:

"Off to Philadelphia in the Morning!"

It was sensational, a triumph beyond triumphs, deafened by the thunder of the applause. Among the great mass of cheering faces, he could see the Canon clapping like mad and behind him, Mrs. O'Brien, waving her tear-damp handkerchief wildly. They would not let him go. He had to sing more. It was of course his favorite end piece, his favorite hymn.

Dead silence when he began. Dead silence when he finished. Then the riot broke loose. They were up on the stage, crowding around, shaking his hand, patting him on the back — he had to be rescued and rushed backstage through the wings and down to the dressing rooms below.

He was sitting here, exhausted, when the Canon came in, accompanied by Sergeant Duggan.

Coming directly to Desmonde, the Canon took both his hands.

"Never, never in my long life, did I have such a heavenly treat. And Mrs. O'Brien too. You could see it in her face, she was just in the seventh heaven."

"Count me in too, Father Desmonde," said the Sergeant. "I'm not a Roman. Before I come here I was an Orange Lodge member up North. But I tell you straight, when ye sung that last hymn, I could have dropped on my knees. And now to be practical, I can't let you out the front doors. It's too dangerous — there's hundreds outside waitin' for ye." He looked at the Canon. "But I'm sure you know the back way up, sir, by the Vennel. I could let you out the side door . . ."

"That would be fine, Sergeant. Father Desmonde looks tired. I'd like to get him home."

Out in the cool night air, the Canon took Desmonde's arm, leading him through a network of narrow passages.

"You have Kilbarrack in the hollow of your hand, lad. The people love ye. Wait till ye see the church on Sunday, packed to the doors. Your little slip is over and forgotten. You're on top of the world."

As they drew near the presbytery, the Canon continued. "I know ye, lad. Ye'll want to go in by for your little prayer of thanksgiving. I'll go in the house and see what's doin' in the way o' supper."

Desmonde entered the church by the side door. Although tired, he was in a state of suppressed elation, of thankfulness and joy.

Except for the sanctuary lamp, the church was, as usual, in darkness. No, perhaps not completely dark, since in the farther aisle a single amber light had been switched on, above his own confessional. He drew near and there, in that faint glow, standing, waiting, was a woman, a girl, Claire.

The shock was severe, but Desmonde stumbled across the darkened church, came close to her. He was the first to speak.

"Claire. Dear Claire, we have been forbidden to meet. You should not be here."

"You think, darling, that because your bloody Canon lashed and lambasted me with his tongue, you think I could keep away from you?" Her voice was perfectly calm and contained as she continued: "You know that I love you, and I know that you love me. We could never be separated."

"No, Claire dear, but . . ."

"There are no buts, Desmonde." The voice was hard now. "We are tied together unalterably."

"Yet, darling Claire . . ."

"Unalterably Desmonde, for you will be the father of our child. I am pregnant, Father Desmonde, by you, and in a few short months there'll be a little one really calling you father."

"But Claire, dear," Desmonde stammered. "How can you be . . . I mean, only three weeks since we were together."

"I thought you'd say that, and that your bloody Canon would throw it at me too. Now listen to the God's truth, and like it.

"When I came to you that night in the wood my period was just due, that's why I came, I was burnin' hot. You served me and I was caught. No period — instead, sick in the mornin', and the feeling a woman gets all over and especially down there. I knew I was pregnant."

"Darling, how could you be sure?"

"Ah, it's out, as I expected, not from you, but from the Canon. After three weeks with no period, I took the train to Cork, to Dr. Dudley Martin, the best-known woman's doctor in Ireland. He examined me, outside and in, and gave me this signed certificate."

Dazedly, Desmonde took the paper, a prescription form written over in black ink.

"I can't read it here, darling, I'll have to take it upstairs. Do you want to wait or will you come back tomorrow?"

"I'll be at the presbytery. Eleven o'clock sharp, and see that you're all there ready for me, as I'll be ready for you."

Her voice altered, softened to entreaty.

"Now hold me darling, only a minute, and kiss me just the once. You know I love you with all my body, heart and soul, just as you love me. And I'll never let you go."

She threw herself into Desmonde's arms, passionately gave him her lips, then spun around and a moment later was gone. Desmonde turned slowly and stumbled out of the dim church. Alas, the Canon must be told immediately, and joy turned into sorrow.

18

Implacably, the next day dawned. The Canon, who normally slept like a felled ox, had passed a restless night. Desmonde had not slept at all. Even the good Mrs. O'Brien admitted that she had not closed an eye till three in the morning. Gloom lay heavy on the presbytery as breakfast was eaten, the Canon insisting that strength must be maintained for the coming ordeal. The two Masses had been said, a telephone call to Dr. Martin in Cork had, alas, proved the authenticity of Claire's certificate, and now, as the eleventh hour drew near, Mrs. O'Brien had polished the dining room table while the Canon, after arranging four chairs squarely in position, placed an enormous Bible in the center of this formidable set piece.

"We have to frighten her," he muttered. "Then I'll lay into her. And let us be all ready, seated, like a court of law, before she comes in."

Accordingly they seated themselves, the Canon at the head of the table, Desmonde opposite, Mrs. O'Brien on his left.

"Ye're not really wantin' me, Canon," Mrs. O'Brien quavered, uncertainly.

" 'Tis more dacent to have a woman, a good woman on the board. Besides, 'twill confuse her. So sit where ye are, Mrs. O'B."

The silence of expectancy fell upon the group, broken by the little clock on the mantel, which chimed eleven cheerful strokes.

" 'Tis fast," murmured the Canon.

"No, Canon dear, 'tis four minutes slow. I forgot to put it on this mornin'."

Again silence. The slow little clock now showed six minutes past the hour.

"She's feared," exclaimed the Canon with a note of triumph. "All may be well, Desmonde."

At that precise moment the doorbell rang, firm, rapid steps were heard, and Claire, beautifully turned out, swept into the room. Wearing the smart light navy Swiss dress that had caused Madame such anguish, Madame's cloche hat and short black cashmere coat, both appropriated, sheer silk stockings and patent leather shoes, she looked stunning, as though she had stepped out of the Place Vendôme into the Ritz Bar.

"I'm so sorry to be late," she apologized, sitting down and tossing her gloves onto the Bible. "I simply had to have my hair done." She then leaned over and kissed Desmonde lightly on the cheek. "How are you, my darling darling? I've brought you a little present. A lovely soft shirt with soft collar attached. You'll need it when you drop the dog collar." And she placed a neatly wrapped flat parcel before him.

For a full two minutes, stunned silence held the court speechless. Then the Canon cleared his throat.

"You know, young wumman, what a serious, a deadly serious situation you have placed us in."

"I, Canon? Was there no partner in the crime?"

"Yes, our Father Desmonde here was inveigled into it. A brilliant young priest with a great, a grand future in the Church, made that single slip. Do you want him to lose everything, to suffer all his life for it?"

"Leave out the suffering, Canon. So far Desmonde and I have had a lot of pleasure together and we want it to continue, don't we, Des?"

Desmonde flushed. Claire's smart, charming appearance, her style and composure, had restirred his vital organs. He did not reject the hand she held out to him.

The Canon leaned forward and his voice rose.

"Let's cut the fancy talk. What will ye take to let Desmonde off the hook?"

"Do you mean take a pill, Canon, maybe from your lady here, to have an abortion and kill my baby?"

"You'll excuse me, Canon," Mrs. O'Brien faltered. "I have to go."

She got up, slowly. No one made the effort to detain her as she left the room.

"I am talkin' of money, that's what I mean!" the Canon shouted. "How much will ye take down, and to go with the money in your hand to a nice quiet maternity home where all will be done for you?"

"And come home with me bastard in the mornin'," Claire sang. Then, in a hard voice: "How much down?"

"Two . . . three . . ." Watching her face, the Canon went on slowly, "Four . . ." Then explosively, "Five hundred golden sovereigns."

Claire laughed, a low, amused, bitter laugh.

"Admittedly, Canon, 'tis more than the thirty pieces of silver that sold Our Lord, but it won't buy me, Canon. I'm no little dirty farm servant, knocked up by the plowboy, that can be paid off in cash. I love Desmonde. I know, Canon, know that he loves me. We'll give our beautiful little baby our name, together."

Silence. Then the Canon, now thoroughly enraged, played his last, his trump card.

"Then there's only one thing for it. We'll disown you, totally and absolutely. Desmonde will continue here with his priestly duties, and you'll be left with your misbegotten bastard."

Claire laughed outright, throwing back her head and showing all her little white teeth. Then her teeth came together and her lips firmed in a hard narrow line.

" 'Tis just what I expected of you, Canon. So go ahead. And I will go ahead!" Her voice hardened, and her eyes narrowed. "I'll take the first train to Dublin, to the office of the *Irish Citizen*, a popular paper, ye may know, with Protestant tendencies and noted for its anticlerical attitude. I'll give them the whole story. It will be a front page feature, with photographs an' all. They'll be down after you with cameras and reporters. You'll be the talk of Ireland, laughed at, cursed, spat on, prayed for, despised."

A long silence, then in a low voice.

"You would not do such a thing, Claire."

Claire leaned forward, staring straight into the Canon's eyes.

"Don't you know me yet, your bloody, stupid reverence?"

Again, a long, long silence. Then the Canon sighed, stood up, and threw out his hands.

"I've done my best. But 'tis no use, Desmonde. I couldn't stand the shame, the dishonor on my beautiful church, the new altar rails and all, and Madame returnin' the end of the month and the bishop due for Confirmation. You'll have to clear out with her. And the sooner the better."

But suddenly, as though inspired, he raised his eyes and his arms to Heaven and, in a grief-stricken voice, while Mrs. O'Brien, standing by the door with tears in her eyes, gazed in awe, he cried out:

"Oh Lord God Almighty in Heaven, there's something wrang wi' your Holy Roman Catholic Church, when a sweet young priest, the flower o' the flock, just because he makes a single mistake, then corrects it by honestly marryin' the girl and givin' his baby a name, must be kicked out o' the Church like a mangy hound dog.

"It's a' the fault o' these auld bastards at the Vatican, wrapped in cobwebs and sae bluidy holy they think it's a sin tae haud their article when they go and make their watter. 'Tis no' only unjust, 'tis bloody unreasonable and agin nature. 'Twill have to be changed, oh, 'twill have to be changed, dear Lord, that is my humble prayer before Yer heavenly throne."

The Canon then confronted Desmonde sternly.

"One thing I must do, and will do, even though I may break the rule of the Church, though God knows not the spirit. I'm not having you go out of here and live and sleep in sin with that girl.

And I'm not having your child born in sin, a bastard. Regard this as a marriage *in extremis,* but a marriage it will be. So fetch up the girl here within the hour. I'll be at the side altar with Mrs. O'Brien as witness. Don't fail me Desmonde, or ye'll never have a moment's peace thereafter."

And so, within the hour, Desmonde stood with a now very very frightened Claire while, in the presence of Mrs. O'Brien, the Canon solemnly read the service and made them man and wife. He then blessed them and abruptly turned away. Only Mrs. O'Brien remained, and with tears in her eyes kissed first Claire, then Desmonde.

"Kneel down, both of the two of you, and pray for God to bless you in your marriage, as I will pray for you myself."

The poor old Canon, indeed, was at the end of his tether. He offered no resistance when the following day, Saturday, was hurriedly fixed for Desmonde's departure. Claire made her preparations, and got the tickets, while Mrs. O'Brien packed Desmonde's things, weeping at the memory of the happy day of his arrival. Desmonde forced himself to make a final visit to Mount Vernon, to say goodbye to Patrick and Bridget.

Everything was accomplished quietly and well, since Desmonde wished, above all, to make his exit in peace. Alas, on the morrow, when the farewells were over and he was in the horse-drawn cab with Claire, driving to the station, the sound of the fife and drum band burst suddenly upon his ears. The cab was surrounded by marching men, the horse loosed from the traces, and replaced by men on both sides of the shafts. Then, as the band struck up "Wearing o' the Green" with redoubled vigor, the cab slowly rolled off.

"Oh, God, Des!" Claire cried in high glee. "They're pulling us to the station, giving us the royal send-off. What an honor. What fun! And look at the banners!"

Now that the horse was gone, the processional Hibernian banners held aloft were clearly visible, each covered with a white sheet on which, in black paint, slogans had been splashed.

GOOD LUCK TO OUR DES

WE LOVE YOU DES. HAPPY WEDDING

FAREWELL DEAR MINSTREL BOY

CHANGE THE LAW

LET OUR PRIESTS WED

Claire was beside herself with pride and delight. When, finally, they were out of the cab and in the train, she lowered the window of the compartment, waved and blew kisses to the sea of faces below. Then, taking Desmonde's hand, she drew him to the window beside her.

How the cheers rang out! Three for Desmonde. Three for Claire. Then a voice shouted: "Three for the baby."

This set the crowd into a turbulence of laughter and cheers. Then, as the train started slowly to move, all else was stilled and the band struck up fortissimo: "Will Ye No' Come Back Again." In this manner did Father Desmonde Fitzgerald take leave of his parish in Kilbarrack.

FOUR

1

Before leaving Kilbarrack Desmonde had wisely written to his father's old housekeeper, Mrs. Mullen, now indeed a very aged though still active woman, asking her to find him a decent three room and kitchen apartment well-situated on the Quays. Desmonde knew the Quays from boyhood and felt that he might find there a simple and quiet retreat until he knew more clearly what lay ahead for his wife and himself. By the same post he had also written to the headmaster of his preparatory school, Saint Brendan's.

When the happy couple arrived at the station Desmonde took a taxi direct to the Quays, Claire viewing the busy streets en route with delighted anticipation.

"Dear old Dublin! Here we come!"

At Mrs. Mullen's the bridal pair were welcomed with less enthusiasm. The old woman's face expressed concern and bewilderment, but she had found a furnished apartment almost next door, which she thought might suit, and toward which, after she had draped a shawl about her, she conducted them.

Desmonde, who had expected the worst, was relieved and pleased as he viewed the three rooms, not ill-furnished, and the bathroom with hot and cold taps. As the rent was reasonable, he immediately took it for a preliminary six months and had the luggage brought in from the waiting cab. Mrs. Mullen, dismissed with the present of a pound, promised to tell the landlord to send the lease.

"Well, darling," Desmonde exclaimed cheerfully, "how do you like our new home?"

"It's not what I'm used to, Des. It's *low*."

"I think we're lucky to get it, so soon."

"You're used to this low-class district, Des. You were born here. But I was brought up in more ladylike surroundings."

Ignoring this, Desmonde said:

"Well, how about stocking up with some grub? As I remember, there's not a bad little grocer's on the next corner."

"Then you go, Des. I want to unpack and rest. Do remember my condition, dear."

Desmonde went out to Kelly's little corner shop, where, fortunately, he was not recognized, and bought tea, coffee extract, milk and sugar, bread, tomatoes, plain biscuits, a pot of Robertson's marmalade, cheese, butter, some slices of cold ham, bacon and a dozen eggs. Pleased with this substantial cash order, the aproned proprietor, no longer John Kelly, agreed to send the boy around with them at once.

If Desmonde expected congratulations for this neat show of efficiency he was disappointed.

"Look, Des, look, will ye." Exposing a dress somewhat creased, Claire continued, "That bitch of a Bridget that I told to pack my things has made a rag of my lovely new muslin."

"Won't the creases iron out, dear?"

"Where's the iron? Will ye oblige me by telling me. No, 'twill have to go to the cleaner's."

At this point came a knock at the door. It was the grocer's boy.

"Well, let's have some grub, darling. We'll both feel better after that. Would you like to knock up something while I unpack?"

Claire stared with hostility at the packages on the table.

"I must tell you at the beginning, Des, I'm not the cook and washerwoman type. I've been well brought up and I'm not used to it. Why don't we just nip up to the Hibernian for supper."

"And come back to find the bed not made up, all the sheets

and blankets still in the hall out there, and my clothes still unpacked!"

"Ah, Des, you're lovely when you get a bit red and excited." She stretched out her arms. "Come and kiss me, love. Wasn't it darling in the train, all the little bumps helping us up and down and in and out. And ye're right, we must get the bed sorted. I'll do it, if you make the supper."

Desmonde had set two eggs to boil on the little scullery gas stove and was beginning to lay the table when loud lamentations drew him, running, to the front room.

"It's the bed, darling. It's been taken down — the bits are all over, and so heavy I can't shift them."

It was one of those old Irish beds, solid oak and large enough to hold a family.

Desmonde approached the backboard.

"Let's try this first, and get it against the wall."

Together, straining hard, they lifted the bed, which seemed to weigh a ton, until Claire, with a gasp, let go her end. With a thunderous crash the backboard resumed its situation, flat on the floor.

"We'll need help, Des. It's too much for us."

"We must do it, Claire. It's a challenge. We can't sleep on the floor."

As Desmonde bent over the backboard once again, the doorbell rang.

"Who the hell can that be?"

Without answering this pertinent question Desmonde went to the front door and opened it.

A young man stood there, bareheaded and smiling.

"I'm Joe Mullen, Father, sir, old Mrs. Mullen's grandson. She thought you might need a bit of a hand, getting in. With the bed, especial."

Desmonde held out his hand.

"Come in Joe. I'm very glad to see you. It's the bed, of course."

He led the way to the front room, where Joe looked at the bed and nodded.

"It's one of the old brigade, sir. I think I know its tricks."

He took off his jacket, revealing splendid arms, and took the backboard in both hands. One straining heave and it was up, tilted against the wall.

"If you'd just put your hand on that, sir, so it doesn't slip, I'll have the end piece up in no time at all."

As good as his word, Joe soon had the end piece up and arranged in position. Then, holding it up with one hand, he took the side beams and slotted them into position back and front. The center piece followed. And there the framework of the bed stood, awaiting the mattress, a huge affair that Joe expertly slung into position.

"There you are, sir. I think I'll leave the blankets and sheets to madam."

"Thank you, Joe, a million times. Now you must tell me what I owe you."

"Not a brass farthing, sir. The name of Fitzgerald is still honored on the Quays. Besides, I'm not so ill-off myself."

"What do you do, Joe?" asked Claire.

"I'm a professional footballer, madam. Center forward for the Dublin Harps. I get good money for that. Then, since I'm free afternoon and evening, except on Saturday, Mr. Maley has made me a waiter in the lounge of the Hibernian."

"Mr. Maley?"

"He's the gentleman that bought the old Hib, and with his good Irish wife has made a wonderful place out of it — you wouldn't know it from the old Hib. Come in and see me there, both of you. There'll always be a glass of sherry for you on the house."

"Thank you, Joe," said Claire. "We will."

"Well, now, I'll be off, wishing you both a good night's rest in that fine old Irish bed."

When Desmonde came back from showing Joe out, he looked at the bed, then at Claire.

"What a fine young man that is, so strong, so well-built, and so polite."

"He certainly is, dear. And mighty handsome, too."

In the kitchen, the eggs were hard-boiled but, sliced with tomatoes and eaten with toast and coffee, they made a satisfactory meal.

"And now for bed, darling. I'm dead beat. We'll leave the dishes till tomorrow."

As they undressed and rolled into the cozy big bed, Claire breathed:

"Isn't this lovely, darling, the big bed, after dark woods and fusty railway coaches, so warm and cozy. Come to me darling, please, please."

He came to her, knowing that twice in one day was a bad, sad practice, but unable to resist, and afterward, hand-in-hand, they fell deeply into sleep.

Never, over many, many years, had this old Irish bed, that had witnessed so many lyings-in and so many layings out, never had it harbored such a strange and ill-assorted couple as this young man and woman who now lay upon its broad expanse fast asleep, still holding hands.

2

It was eight o'clock when Desmonde awoke from a good night's sleep. After a moment he got up and rolled up the blinds, letting a flood of sunlight into the room. Claire, one eye open, lying there like an indolent cat, murmured sleepily: "Come back, Des. It's so lovely, with all that sun."

"I would, Claire, but I have my appointment with Dr. O'Hare this morning."

"Ah, yes. Well, get yourself a cup of coffee, love, and some toast." As he pulled on his dressing gown and prepared to go, she added, "While you're at it, dear, you might make it a double order — 'tis just as simple as one."

Five minutes later, he was back with a small tray on which two cups of coffee steamed invitingly beside two slices of hot buttered toast. Removing his own share of the breakfast to the little dressing table, he handed the tray to Claire, now propped up on both pillows.

"Des, what a darling you are. I picked the right one when I picked you. We really ought to make this a regular feature every morning."

Sipping luxuriously in bed, she was silent. Then after a substantial bite at the toast she shook her head sadly. "Des, darling, I have a confession to make to you and I better get it over with now, and have your absolution, rather than go on worrying myself to death. Des, dear, I am no use whatsoever in the kitchen. I can't cook, never have done, and as I have been brought up as a lady . . ." He looked up quickly to see if she was joking, but she was not — and she went on with a kind of proud sadness. "I have never put a finger in dishwater or scrubbed a dirty pot in my entire life." Allowing this to sink in, she continued. "So maybe your old Mrs. Mullen would give us a hand or find us a scullery girl."

"We'll see what can be done, dear, when we're settled in."

"If we want to eat, there's lots of good, cheap, little restaurants just around the corner in O'Connell Street, that's to say if the Hibernian is too expensive for you, dear Des."

"We'll see about that, too, dear. In the meantime I must be off."

"I do hope you get the job, Des. It's awful to have you hanging around here just doing nothing."

"And what do you propose to do this morning?"

"Oh, I'll just take a stroll up Grafton Street to look at the shops. By the way, love, have you just a little something for pocket money to see me around and so forth?"

"Certainly, darling. I'll just see to the dishes and get dressed first."

Desmonde took the breakfast dishes back to the kitchen and washed them with the leftover supper dishes. Mercifully there was hot water. The good Joe must have switched on the heater before before he left. When he had dried the clean dishes Desmonde put them back in their places on the dresser shelf. He then shaved quickly before the miniature mirror hung over the sink and went back to the bedroom, where he dressed. Then, unlocking his suitcase in the cupboard, he took ten pounds from his store of ready cash, not failing to look at his passbook, which showed a disquieting balance of eight hundred and sixty-two pounds. He now realized how much he had spent or given to charity of the three thousand inherited from his mother.

"I'm off then, Claire dear. Will this serve you for the time being?"

She came out from the cover of the sheet, where she had been watching his every movement.

"What? Oh, Des, 'tis you. Oh, yes, dear." Taking the money, "This will see me around for a bit. Now good luck to you, darling. I'll say a little prayer for you."

When he had gone she counted the notes and then snuggled down for another nap.

Desmonde walked to the end of the Quays, turned right, and made his way up to Grafton Street, pleased to find himself again in the famous street, justifiably the pride of Dublin. He continued until he reached the corner affording a view of College Green. He had intended walking to Ballsbridge, but now a sudden exacerbation of the tiredness he had felt all morning made him decide to take a tram. He knew very well the reason of his fatigue and decided that he must take the matter up, nicely and reasonably, with Claire.

A tram soon came around the bend and stopped at his signal. Once seated inside, Desmonde was again swept by nostalgia, hurtful memories of his early boyhood, as the tram clanged its way along this very route he had so often followed on his way to school. His feelings intensified as he descended from the tram at the Ballsbridge terminus and walked through the Public Gardens to Saint Brendan's School.

Some late scholars, in the familiar green and black blazers, were hurrying across the playground as he slowly followed them to the entrance doorway. No need to ask for directions. He well knew his way past the classrooms and along a private corridor leading to an end door on which he knocked discreetly. Voices within indicated that Dr. O'Hare was engaged, so Desmonde seated himself on the bench outside. As a suppliant he was well prepared to wait. In perhaps a quarter of an hour the door was opened and a well-dressed, officious-looking woman was shown out by the headmaster and escorted courteously to the end of the corridor. Returning, Dr. O'Hare saw Desmonde and silently beckoned him inside. Ensconced at his desk he indicated a chair, and when Desmonde was seated studied his visitor for a long, long time. Desmonde, too, respectfully returned that look, shocked, almost, by the signs of age on the headmaster's lined and sagging face.

"Well, Desmonde, I had your letter and perused it with deep surprise and sadness. What, I wonder, would your dear father, so honored, so distinguished, have thought of it. In his old age it would probably have killed him. Were you unhappy as a young priest?"

"Far from it. I loved my work at Kilbarrack, but it was a choice between behaving like an honorable man or leaving a young woman of good family to suffer shame and dishonor alone."

"So the girl was pregnant."

Desmonde inclined his head in silence.

"Well, now I see you in a better light, Desmonde. So now you are married, a castoff from the Church, in straightened circumstances and badly in need of work."

"As always sir, you put the case with your usual lucidity and sense of justice."

"Don't flatter me, Desmonde, or I shall have nothing to do with you. Now listen, what can you offer me as a teacher?"

"I could teach Latin, French, Italian and even Spanish. I am fluent in these languages. And I believe I am reasonably good with the younger boys. I was quite successful with my First Communion and catechism classes at Kilbarrack."

"Just so," Dr. O'Hare reflected. "Well, Desmonde, I could take you on to teach Latin and French to the two lower forms. For the rest, you could help me in the office, correcting papers, helping me with my correspondence, filing, and so forth. The normal salary would be twenty pounds a month, but because of our past pleasant association and because you are obviously in need, I would make it twenty-five pounds a month."

"Oh, sir, I am so . . ." The headmaster held up his hand.

"All this, Desmonde, is on one condition. That I am now, and will so remain, completely ignorant of the circumstances of your life. You are simply an old, esteemed pupil who had come to me seeking employment."

"I . . . I think I understand, sir, and of course I agree."

"Yes, Desmonde, if it came to the ears of any of the parents that I had knowingly engaged a man with your reputation to teach their young children I should be in a very difficult position — unless I could instantly disown you."

"I understand, sir. And I agree. There hasn't been a word here in Dublin, about . . . about Kilbarrack."

"Then you are engaged, Desmonde. As from tomorrow at nine o'clock. I repeat the terms. The normal salary would be twenty pounds a month. Because I am truly grieved for you, I shall make it twenty-five pounds."

"Oh, thank you, sir. From my heart. You will see how I will serve you."

"Good, Desmonde. Now leave me. I have the sixth form in five minutes."

Desmonde left the school walking on air. He was saved. A regular position, one he would love, and a salary that would keep Claire and himself beyond all want.

He no longer felt tired, and stepped it out all the way to Dublin. Here he felt he must celebrate, and stopped off at Bewley's for a large cup of coffee and two wheaten scones, each with a pat of fresh butter. He knew Bewley's coffee of old, quite unbeatable, so fragrant and strong, with a little pot of thick fresh cream to enrich it. It was heaven, although he did rather fancy one of the good-looking pork pies his neighbor was biting into — but that was an expense, and must come later. Afterward, he strolled to Saint Stephen's Green and sat there on a bench in the sun among the students who usually passed the midday hour in that pleasant square of greenery in Dublin's busy heart.

He got back to the little house on the Quays, now known as "home," at three o'clock. Claire had not yet returned, but almost at once the doorbell rang. A smart van stood outside and on the doorstep was the driver, in a natty green uniform.

"Does Mrs. Donovan Fitzgerald reside here?"

Quite taken aback, Desmonde nevertheless answered in the affirmative.

"From Switzer's," said the man, placing two large beautiful beribboned boxes in Desmonde's arms. He then leaped into the van and was off.

Desmonde re-entered the house slowly, placed the two luxurious looking boxes on the living room table, and studied them with mixed emotions, murmuring to himself with a questioning wonder: "Mrs. *Donovan* Fitzgerald."

He was not long in doubt. At four o'clock Claire dashed in, beautifully smart in her best clothes, and bursting with exhilaration and excitement as she flung her arms around him and exclaimed:

"Oh, darling, I've had such a wonderful time. Let's sit down and I'll tell you. Well, I went, naturally, to Switzer's in Grafton Street and spent a marvelous hour there. You've no idea what wonderful things they have there, regular Paris style, and better. Well, besides looking, I did a bit of shopping . . ."

"Is this it here?" he interrupted.

"Yes, darling, some of it. Two heavenly dresses, latest models. I just couldn't resist them. Of course I can't wear them for long, darling, I shall be starting to show. But after, you'll love me in them."

"But, Claire, these must have cost the earth. How did you manage to . . ."

"Very simple, darling. I told them I was Madame Donovan's niece and wanted to open an account. You've no idea — Madame's name is a password in Dublin. You should have seen them all around me, bowing and scraping."

"But these things will have to be paid for."

"Ah, they don't send their bills for six months at Switzer's. Especially to anyone with the name Donovan."

"I see you have adopted it."

She laughed. "Ah, what's the odds, darling. I'm entitled to it."

"Did that conclude your adventures?" he asked, after a pause.

"Not at all, not at all, by no means." She giggled. "Remembering Joe's invitation to the Hib, I dropped over to the lounge and had the promised glass of sherry. Joe is a darling. He must have mentioned me to Mr. Maley, the manager, the nicest fellow you could hope to meet. He said:

" 'Joe tells me you are niece to one of our most distinguished clients.'

" 'Yes,' I said. 'I am Mrs. Donovan Fitzgerald.'

"We shook hands.

" 'Are you lunching with us?'

" 'I had intended to,' says I, bold as brass. 'Unfortunately I find I have rushed out without my purse.'

" 'Oh, madam, don't let that trouble you. I'll reserve your table now. And you may lunch à la carte as a guest of the hotel.'

"Well, Des, to cut a long story short, I had the best lunch ever, the lunch of a lifetime, *pâté de foie gras*, grilled salmon, strawberry mousse, and Irish coffee. Then, bowed out with smiles. So here I am, darling, back home and dying for a pee-wee, I must rush. Will you get us a cup of tea, Des, while I'm occupied in the bathroom."

When she had gone to execute this laudable performance, Desmonde went slowly into the kitchen to make the tea. She had not once asked him if he had succeeded in his interview with Dr. O'Hare. Now, for the first time, he realized the folly of his marriage and was struck, as by a blow, with the premonition of disaster.

Apart from the monthly salary, itself a life-saving asset, Desmonde was happy in his new position, and as the weeks and months passed he became accepted and, always good with young children, liked at the school. He did not see much of his colleagues, since when he was out of the classroom Dr. O'Hare kept him busy in the office, often after school hours and, observing the new master's efforts to please, had come to take an interest in Desmonde, suggesting that later on he might study for his Ph.D.

Claire, too, in her own fashion, welcomed and approved Desmonde's breadwinning effort.

"It'll be a blessing, Des, not to have you hanging around the house, like a sick dog, when I'm out and about in the town."

Claire, however, was less out and about the town than before, since she was now most perceptibly pregnant and approaching the date of her delivery. Desmonde's wish that her confinement should take place in the Mater Misericordia Hospital had been brusquely negatived.

"I want none of that Convent Miserarium."

"But the Mater has a worldwide reputation, Claire. My friend A. J. took his obstetric training there."

"It may be all right for the students, Des. But for the patients — stand outside and hear the screams. I want no nuns hanging around, flinging holy water at me. I've had a good long talk with old Mrs. Mullen. She's brought many a child into the world and she'll bring ours."

Desmonde, naturally, was constrained to acquiesce, doubtfully, yet impressed by Claire's hardihood. He had a talk later on with his father's old housekeeper which did partly reassure him. And indeed, when the event did take place, everything passed off with the greatest ease and facility. Desmonde, who had spent no more than an hour pacing anxiously outside, was called in by Mrs. Mullen, truly official in a large starched white overall, to be presented with a lovely baby daughter, all warm and cozy from the soapsuds, her dark eyes, as she lay in his arms, bent upon him in tender wonderment. Claire, surveying this touching scene from her position of leisured indolence in bed, exclaimed:

"Did I do well for you, Des?"

"Wonderfully, thank you, dear, dear Claire. A lovely child, with your lovely dark eyes."

"Thank you, Des, dear. I'll remember these kind words when we have our next set-to."

"I hope it was not too hard for you, dear."

Here the old lady professionally intervened.

"I tell ye, sir, in all truth and honesty, I never had such a patient in all my life. She bore down hard without a scream, and when the baby came out, that's the worst bit, sir, she no more than uttered a little whimper. And I tell ye this, for I'm sure it's of interest to ye, there's not a cut, not so much as a scratch on her dear little you-know-what. 'Tis as fresh and good as ever 'twas."

The old woman was in her best form, and when she had done everything to her satisfaction, she smiled at Desmonde.

"That's the lot, sir. Mother tidied up and comfortable, baby washed and asleep, the little crib set up there by your bed, all ready for her, the mother comfortable in bed and half asleep, so I'll be off, till first thing tomorrow morning."

"Good night, and thank you, Mrs. Mullen," said Claire. "You're a darling."

Desmonde followed the old woman into the passage, put his arms around her, and kissed her withered cheek.

"Dear, dear Mrs. Mullen, you're an angel, and have made us all so happy with your goodness and skill. Money can never repay you, but please tell me your fee."

"A couple of pounds is the usual, sir. But from you I'll take one."

Desmonde felt the ready tears spring to his eye. He took from his pocket the two five pounds he had removed from his store in the cupboard, and silently handed them to her.

"Oh, I couldn't, sir, indeed I couldn't . . ."

"You must, I insist, after all you've done, borrowing the crib for us, and everything."

"Well, sir . . . I'll take one, and thank ye kindly, but no more." And she tucked one of the notes into Desmonde's breast pocket. "And now, good night. I'll be around first thing in the morning." On the doorstep she turned. " 'Twould have been a happy moment for your dear honored father if he could see his lovely granddaughter, just her alone, and no more."

Desmonde went into the bathroom and got ready for bed. As he climbed in beside Claire he whispered:

"Are you asleep, darling? If not, I want to tell you how happy you have made me. I feel that baby will draw us closer together, close the little gap that seems to have sprung up between us."

"And who made that little gap? And what would any wife think of a husband that walks in one night and tells her straight he doesn't want her six nights in the week?"

"It was stupid and tactless of me, Claire. I love to love you. But I'm like a bit of chewed string if I get too much of it."

"There's some men can't get enough of it. But there's still a lot of priest in you, Des. Well, now that I'm in milk and *safe*, I'll maybe see more of you." She kissed him, adding: "If baby wakes in the night, get up and bring her to me."

Almost immediately she was asleep, and soon Desmonde followed her, clinging to her soft, warm body.

4

And now, on Saturdays and Sundays, when the weather was fine, the little family might be seen taking the air, along the Quays, across the bridge, even as far as Phoenix Park, Claire beautifully turned out in one of the new Switzer dresses, the baby in the handsome pram her father had bought for her, and of course, Desmonde, enjoying the admiring glances directed toward his equipage. Claire had taken advantage of this happy interim to present Desmonde with the bill for the dresses, some sixty-odd pounds, sent again with a threatening letter. He could not protest, particularly when she, alone, had attended to the difficult matter of the child's christening.

"You wouldn't want to do it, Des?"

He hesitated. "But it must be done."

"Give me the marriage lines the Canon gave you and I'll see to it Sunday at the Carmelite. There's always a crowd lined up there after the eleven o'clock. You're still agreed on the name Geraldine?"

Claire had insisted on this, as a propitiation to her aunt, whom she still hoped to win round with the help of the lovely child.

So Claire had set off while Desmonde waited in agony of pained suspense, dispelled when Claire reappeared, smiling broadly.

"All over, lad. The little one's a Christian now, God bless her."

It was then she presented him with the Switzer bill. Yes, Desmonde was happy, at least as happy as one might be in his invidious position. His teaching at Saint Brendan's had saved him from at least the worst of his remorse, and when this did at times torment him, when he was alone, he would cry to Heaven: "You threw me out like a rotten apple. Why should I come back to You?"

His better relations with Claire were enhanced by the help he gave her with baby Geraldine. Every evening when he returned from school he would bathe, dry and powder the little one and make her comfortable with a fresh diaper for the night. On Saturdays and Sundays he was exclusively the baby's nurse, rewarded now with a smile of loving recognition that warmed his heart.

One day when he was so occupied, while Claire sat reading the morning paper, she remarked idly:

"What's a note-of-hand, Des?"

"A bit of paper, some sort of agreement that you sign with your own hand."

"Is that all there is to it?" She laughed, and laid aside the paper to watch him powder and rediaper the babe. "You've a real way with her, Des, you handle her a treat. And she loves you now, you can see it in her eyes."

Desmonde smiled. "Are you about ready for our promenade now?"

"I'll just go and change my dress. It's a pity we can't all go out for lunch somewhere, we would be the admiration of the Hib!"

"She's a bit young for that yet, darling."

"Ah, yes, of course. But speaking of lunch at the Hib, Des, didn't you promise to take me for a slap-up celebration when I had stopped being a milk bar?"

"I did indeed, Claire dear, and I'll not fail to keep my word. How about next Saturday? We'll get Mrs. Mullen to look after Gerry."

"It's a date, Des. And I'll want it with all the trimmings. Saturday's the best day at the Hib. All the gang's there."

For the next few days, the prospect of the coming luncheon was never far from Claire's mind. Never failing to remind Desmonde of his promise, and preparing herself, in her own ways, for the celebration, she departed on unknown missions several times during the week, returning with sundry parcels that caused Desmonde to wonder how much money had been expanded on these apparent luxuries, and what might be the source of such unsuspected wealth. However, he refrained from pressing the matter, anxious to preserve the benign harmony that now lay like a sweet melody upon the house.

Desmonde had been induced, more or less by royal command, to perform his marital duties more frequently than before.

"You really are a great lover," Claire complimented him after one strenuous performance. "I don't want to swell your head, darling, but you leave a woman satisfied and fulfilled. There's some, God knows, that leave you up in the air, waiting for what you haven't got. But you're the goods. I knew that the first time I had you in Kilbarrack Wood."

"That was a short and," he added quickly, "sweet event."

"I've no time for them that drags it out, darlin', like layin' down a cigar and goin' back to it. Besides, 'tis a sinful perversion in the eyes of the Church. No, no, I'll take your way, lad, you've got *poontang*. But I'd like a bit of variety. So next time why don't you just go in from behind. There's them that tell me it's even better."

Accordingly, two nights later, suitably exhorted, Desmonde, although trying to postpone the event, did as he was bid, but all the time haunted by a horrid recollection of two mongrels he had once disgustedly observed performing in identical fashion in the main street of Kilbarrack.

At last Saturday dawned, faintly gray, yet full of the promise of sunshine. While Desmonde made coffee and attended to Gerry's needs, Claire rested in bed, rising at eleven to prepare herself for the pleasures of the day. Meanwhile, Desmonde had dressed himself and visited Mrs. Mullen, who promised to look after the baby that afternoon.

At twenty minutes after noon, Claire strolled into the living room and struck an attitude, inviting Desmonde's admiration. She was wearing a smart green dress he had not seen before, new green gloves, and a large, flashy green hat, also new.

"How, Des?"

"Stunning," he murmured sadly. "You look like a very expensive French tart out for the kill."

She laughed. "I like that, Des. I just came into a little money unexpectedly and thought I'd go the limit. Today, especial, I want to attract attention. There's some of the fellows up there at the Hib think I don't have a husband. Did you order a cab?"

"It's such a lovely day I thought we'd just walk up."

"All right, penny-pincher. At least we'll give the neighbors a treat."

They set off, arm in arm, when Mrs. Mullen appeared, followed by the old lady's shocked and sorrowful gaze. At one o'clock precisely they strolled into the hotel and through the lounge to the dining room. Here, the headwaiter obsequiously bore down upon Claire.

"Have you a nice table for us?"

"The best, madam. Your usual, by the window." And he conducted them thereto and seated them, whispering, "May I tell madam how ravishing she is looking today."

"None of your blarney. What have you got to eat for us? And we'll want a bottle of Perrier Jouet. This is a delayed wedding celebration. Meet my husband, Desmonde."

"Oh, I am pleased to know you, sir. Will you choose." He produced two large, elaborately ornate menu cards, offering one to Claire, the other to Desmonde. "Now, if you'll excuse me, I'll go and instruct the wine waiter as to your champagne."

Eventually a choice meal was ordered, the champagne opened, sampled, and served. Meanwhile Claire surveyed the long room, commenting upon the various personalities she recognized. Her own attire and affected mannerisms were certainly attracting attention, looks, whispers, suppressed laughter, that seemed equally inspired by Desmonde. A quietly dressed man in a dark business suit, lunching alone at the adjoining table, had several times encountered Claire's smiling glances and now, inclining toward her politely, he said:

"Forgive me, dear lady, but from the proximity of our tables I have gathered, without seeking to do so, that I am in the presence of a happy wedding celebration."

"It is indeed, sir," replied Claire, delighted at last to have someone to talk to. "And long delayed, through the remarkable circumstances of our love and marriage. Would you take a drop of champagne to celebrate with us?"

"I must not drink at luncheon, since Saturday is a very busy day, but, dear madam, if you would allow me one little sip from your own glass . . ."

Willingly, Claire proffered her glass, to which the stranger barely applied his lips.

"You were speaking, dear madam, of difficult circumstances."

"I was indeed, sir. Would you believe it, looking at him now, so gay and happy, that my darling husband was once . . ."

Desmonde pressed her arm and tried to turn her toward him, but she shook him off.

". . . once a young and much beloved priest at Kilbarrack."

"Don't tell me, dear madam, that he is the famous Kilbarrack curate everybody has been looking for over the best part of two years, and that you, dear lady, must therefore be the niece of our own Madame Donovan."

"For God's sake shut up, Claire," Desmonde groaned.

But Claire was now fully wound up.

"You hit the nail on the head both times, sir. But that's not all the story by a long chop. Desmonde, darling, keep your feet out of the way, you're hitting me with them all over. I could tell you, sir, of the difficulties of our courtship, both of us madly in love. I thought I would never get him, until one lovely starry night I made after him in the lovely woods of Kilbarrack."

"Waiter, the bill!" Desmonde called wildly. But the waiter, with arms folded, his back turned, and listening hard, would not have missed this for a five-pound note.

"Yes, sir, the lovely woods of Kilbarrack, where he used to stroll of an evening. And there indeed we consummated our love with such unrestrained passion that, while I caught Desmonde, I was caught too."

"Oh, God! Shut up, you drunken fool," Desmonde hissed into her ear.

"Pregnant, dear lady?" This from the benign stranger.

"You have it in a word, sir. And at the first go, showing the depth and strength of our love."

"Oh dear, oh dear," sighed the kindly gentleman. "And that's where your troubles began."

"You've said it, sir. But I had picked the right one. This handsome, brilliant young priest, fresh and famous from Rome, walked out of the Church and made me his dear wife."

"True nobility, dear lady. And how did your aunt, dear Madame Donovan, take the news?"

"Like one of the furies of hell, sir. For just to whisper in your ear, she was madly in love with Des herself. Des, for God's sake stop kickin' me. And what's Joe doin' there, making faces at us like a madman?"

"Just one little point more, dear lady. How did you adjust yourself to the nonsacerdotal life?"

"Just to perfection, sir. We have the loveliest little baby in all the world, called Geraldine after my aunt, a comfortable house on the Quays near where Desmonde's very famous dad used to live, while my brave bold husband has got himself a splendid position . . ."

"Be quiet, Claire, you damned idiot," Desmonde hissed in her ear. "Stop it at once."

". . . splendid position," Claire continued blandly, "teaching languages at Saint Brendan's School."

"Madame, I am overcome with admiration."

Desmonde leaned across his wife and interposed furiously.

"Sir, I'm afraid my wife and I are somewhat exalted. Perhaps on another occasion."

"In point of fact, sir," he looked at his watch, "the pleasure of listening to you has kept me late, very late, for my office. But you must permit me. A little belated wedding gift and a small honarium in acknowledgment of the wonderful information you have freely given."

He signaled to the waiter and asked for both bills, his own and that of the adjoining table. Both were brought and quickly signed by the generous gentleman. He then stood up.

"Again, thank you, madam, for a truly remarkable and most fortunate experience. No need to wish you well. I foresee for you a sensational career. As for you, sir," he offered Desmonde his hand, "you have my sincere and profound sympathy." Turning away, he added, "I have added the tip to the bill."

He swung around and made his way quickly to the door. Immediately, Joe approached their table. He was in his waiter's uniform and had obviously just come on duty.

"Hello, hello, Joe," Claire chuckled. "Come and drink our healths in champagne."

"I never touch the stuff, madam, and if I may say so in the presence of your husband, you've had a damn sight too much of it today." He turned to Desmonde. "Didn't you see me give you the warning sign to shut her up?"

"He must have, Joe dear. He near kicked the shoes off me."

"Well, I'll put you straight now, madam. That gentleman that was pumping you is the head editor of the *Sunday Chronicle*. And every word you told him, multiplied by ten, will be in the paper tomorrow."

"Good God, Joe!"

"You may well say it, sir. You'll find yourself bang on the front page tomorrow."

Claire gave way to fits of delighted laughter.

"I've made you famous at last, Des darling. Am I not a darling wife?"

In the effort to refill her glass she upset the bottle, flooding the table with the last of the champagne.

"Don't you think, sir, if I gave you a hand with her and got her into a cab? She'll begin to sing in a minute."

With Joe's help Desmonde got his darling wife on her feet, and taking one arm firmly, while Joe took the other, made an erratic progress toward the door, during which Claire bestowed her proudly smiling glances all around. But all was not yet over.

As they came to the entrance steps two photographers were waiting upon them, with flashbulbs and clicking cameras. But at last they got her into a taxi. On the way home she did indeed begin to sing, maudlin rubbish, clasping him toward her the while in voluptuous embrace. And he had a horrid feeling that another taxi was following them.

At last they were in the seclusion of their little house, where the good Mrs. Mullen sat awaiting them.

"For God's sake get her to bed," Desmonde cried, releasing her so that she fell, in all her absurd finery, spreadeagled on the sofa. "I've had enough! And I'll stand no more of it from her, the drunken bitch."

He turned and walked out of the house, turning inevitably to his usual retreat, to the quiet and solitude of Phoenix Park. He knew that he must free himself from her. And that without delay.

5

Desmonde did not leave the park until evening, almost closing time. As he walked slowly back to his house it seemed that more than the usual number of promenaders were on the Quays. And Mrs. Mullen, in her best shawl, was pacing up and down on the pavement as though awaiting him.

"I'm glad you're back, sir. There's been a regular commotion around here. Have ye seen the papers? An early special edition of the *Chronicle*."

"No, I haven't."

"Well, ye may do so now. A fellow from the *Chronicle* office just opened your door and flung in a copy."

"Bad news?"

"The worst, sir. Oh, God, I'm heartsick and sorry for ye. Me that lived to serve your honored father. And held you in my arms as a child."

"Oh, well! I'll go in and look. Have you seen to baby?"

"I have indeed, sir. She's had her bottle and is all bathed, tidied up, and asleep in her cot." She paused. "Madam's in bed too, snoring her head off."

"Thank you, Mrs. Mullen, from my heart. What in all the world would I do without you."

He went into the house, locked the door and picked up the paper lying on the rug. In the living room he switched on the light and opened the paper, shocked instantly, appalled and horrified by the banner headlines screaming from the front page.

RUNAWAY PRIEST FINALLY HUNTED DOWN

The handsome young ex-cleric all Ireland has been seeking, found at last luxuriating with his would be fashionable, over-dressed lady wife, lunching in state . . . Salmon and champagne . . . postponed wedding celebration . . . As the champagne flowed in madam's direction, we had the story in full from her sweet painted lips . . . "I wanted him from the first moment I set eyes on him," she burbled. ". . . a sweet schoolgirl from my exclusive Swiss finishing school . . . My dear aunt, famous Madame Donovan, had for some time been after him also . . . Indeed, on my unexpected return from school I caught her with arms around him in a passionate embrace."

Desmonde closed his eyes in agony. But he forced himself to read on, shrinking from the headlines of every paragraph.

Tennis a deux . . . walks in the lovely woods . . . already he was mine . . . saw it in his eyes. The first kiss . . . But alas his sacred office . . . Adored by all the parish . . . Certain advancement promised by the archbishop. Would he be promoted away from the parish? I shivered at the thought. It was now or never . . . knew he went walking at night . . . fighting down his passionate love . . . Caught him in those same lovely woods! And there on the greensward under the stars, I made him mine!

Desmonde could not continue. He felt physically sick, but even as he put the rag away from him his anguished eye caught two more headlines:

Pregnancy shyly confessed to him in the confessional . . . He stood by me. Love conquered all.

And the photographs, emphasizing her drunken stagger as they left the hotel. And worse was to follow:

[225]

Now living at Number 20 the Quays, masquerading as language master at the select Saint Brendan's School, this son of a famous Irish father, striving desperately to regain his self-respect, has succeeded in passing himself off as a clean young bachelor . . .

It was the final blow. Desmonde lay back on the couch, overcome by shame, disgust and blind rage.

His marriage had, from the first, been a tragic mistake into which his own folly had forced him. He had used every effort in adjustment and propitiation to make a success of it. And he had failed. He could not continue — indeed, it was now only too apparent that Claire was tired of him, that while he had certainly not been the first man to possess her, he would be, sooner or later, superseded by another, richer, or more attractive than himself.

These were his thoughts as the sounds of slow movements in the bedroom, followed by dragging footsteps and the opening of the inner door, caused him to look around. Claire stood there, a loose dressing gown flung over her nightdress, slippers on her bare feet. She scuffed to the sofa and sat down.

"Get me a cup of tea."

He had resolved, above all else, to keep his temper. He handed her the paper.

"Wouldn't you like to read this first."

She glanced at the newssheet with befogged vision until the headlines caught her eye. Then she began to read, mouthing the words to herself.

Meanwhile he went into the kitchen and made her a cup of tea. Continuing to read, she slobbered this down, still half-asleep, still not quite free of the alcohol in her blood.

"Well," she said at last. "I've put you on the front page, Des."

"By making a drunken exhibition of yourself, and of me. I shall most certainly be kicked out of the school on Monday, and I'll never, never get another decent job in Dublin. I'll be out on the streets without a penny to support you and our child." He

[226]

paused, continuing in a controlled voice. "Don't you think, Claire, that it's time we called a halt in our marriage. Take Gerry to your aunt and stay there for a while until we see how things are with us."

"So you're sick of me. Well, Des, I'm just as sick of you. You're a dull fellow to live with and, to speak the truth, you're no longer much good in bed. There's others could lick you at that job. You never take me to the movies, but keep nagging me to go walking in Phoenix Park. And I'm sick to death of the kind of life you've brought me down to, this little slum flat, me that's used to living like a lady with servants and all. Not to speak of an empty purse when I go shopping, so I have to get everything on tick. For weeks now I've had the idea to go back to my aunt with Gerry. We'll be welcome there."

Desmonde took her hand.

"I'm truly sorry to have been such a failure, Claire. Yet I'm relieved in a way. It makes my suggestion that we separate for a while more reasonable."

"Oh, shut up your talking, Des. You're full of words. I'm just as ready for a change as you, and I'm glad we can do it without a fight. Now go into the kitchen and cook me a bit of supper. Lunch is long gone and I'm half-starved. Can you do me some rashers and a couple of eggs?"

"I believe that's about all that's left," he said, getting up.

He hesitated. An hour ago he would have refused to serve her but now, with the prospect of an amicable parting in sight, he thought it better to obey.

"Fry some bread with them. I'll stretch for a bit, I'm still a bit woozy."

The larder was indeed bare. Only the bacon, a couple of eggs, and a stale loaf remained, but he fulfilled the order, reserving two strips of bacon to make a sandwich for himself. He had eaten nothing.

"I've made a good cook of you, Des," she commented, using a crust to polish the plate. "Before I had to do with you, you could scarce boil an egg. Ah, I feel better now. But would you

[227]

mind giving baby her bottle tonight. Everything's there in the cupboard. I'll have so much to do tomorrow I'll just toddle back to bed."

When she had gone Desmonde set about preparing the child's feed, an operation to which he was now accustomed. Later, with the little one on his knees, gurgling at her bottle, yet watching him always with her dark, wide-open, loving eyes, he felt an immense sadness sweep over him. He loved the child and would miss her dreadfully. Yet it was better she should go to Madame Donovan who, whatever her feelings toward him, would ensure that the child was properly cared for. Yet this must be no more than a temporary expedient. When he had picked himself up and restored his position in life, he would claim her again.

The feed over, he changed her diaper and tucked her in her cot. Mamma was already giving tongue in measured snores that indicated she was again asleep.

Desmonde returned to the living room, arranged a makeshift bed for himself on the couch and, having removed his suit, lay down in his underclothes. The prospect of Monday bore heavily upon him, but at last he fell asleep.

6

On Monday morning Desmonde awoke early, feeling rested and refreshed, but excessively hungry. He had eaten almost nothing on the day before. He got up, made tea, and breakfasted on a jagged slice of the remaining loaf, supported by two strong cups of tea. He then went through to the bathroom, washed and shaved with extreme care and returned quietly to the living room, where he brushed his suit and dressed. Nothing was stirring in the bedroom as he let himself out of the house and set out on the long walk to the school.

He walked slowly, since he was early, trying to avert his thoughts from the interview with Dr. O'Hare that must surely lie ahead. And once again he was swept by an overwhelming impulse to pray, to implore help from Heaven, for some divine act of intervention that might save him. Once again he resisted it.

And now he was at the school, some little boys from his class, lifting their caps, waving and smiling to him as they walked on ahead to the classroom. Some moments later he was about to follow them, when at the doorway one of the head boys of the school, a sixth-former, held up his hand.

"You are not to go in, sir. Dr. O'Hare's orders. He wishes to see you in his study immediately."

Desmonde's heart sank. He stood there, looking at the boy, who averted his eyes. Then, without a word, he turned abjectly away and walked slowly to the headmaster's room. He knocked and was immediately bidden to enter. He obeyed.

Dr. O'Hare was seated at his desk facing two women, both overdressed in their Sunday clothes, both armed with rolled umbrellas and an expression of outraged propriety.

"Mr. Fitzgerald," Dr. O'Hare began, without delay. "These two ladies, each mother of a boy in your class, have startled and shocked me with a horrifying story that apparently appeared yesterday in the Sunday *Chronicle,* a paper that I myself never read. Fitzgerald, answer me truthfully, were you at one time a priest in the parish of Kilbarrack? Did you seduce a young girl in your congregation, and when she was with child, marry her and leave the Church?"

"I did, sir."

"Then why in the name of heaven did you not reveal this when I engaged you?"

A pause, whispers between the women: "I was sure the good doctor didn't know nothing."

"Well, sir," Desmonde said, slowly, painfully, "I was afraid that if I told you, you might not take me on."

"We was sure, doctor, that you never had the least suspicion," said one of the women. "But now?"

"Yes, now, madam. Fitzgerald, I am obliged to tell you that your position in this school is now terminated. You will leave instantly without returning to your classroom. Here is your salary paid until the end of the month."

Desmonde took the envelope held out toward him, stood for a moment in silent anguish, then said, in a muted voice:

"I'm truly sorry, sir, to have caused you this distress and I thank you for all your kindness to me." He half turned. "As for you ladies, may I congratulate you on your charitable efforts, which have effectively destroyed my one chance to redeem and regenerate myself. The children in my class had nothing but good from me, and I believe they loved me."

He then turned and went out, closing the door quietly, then slowly and sadly set out for the house on the Quays. No longer could he think of it as home, so sickeningly was it identified with his misery and ruin.

When he reached the Quays it was almost eleven o'clock and the inevitable Mrs. Mullen, harbinger of good or, more frequently, of evil, was walking up and down in some distress outside the house.

"Oh, I'm glad to see you back, sir. The lady has gone out, all dolled up, and she's locked the door. Now I hear the baby crying pitiful and I can't get in."

"Thank you, Mrs. Mullen. I have the key. I'll go in and see to the child."

He opened the door and went in. When the child saw him it muted its cries to a little whimper. Quickly he set to and, since there was no milk in the cupboard, heated some of the prepared cereal that the baby seemed to prefer to the milk, and when it was ready he fed her with tiny spoonfuls until she was satisfied. Then he must change the diaper. He lifted her from her cot and carried her to the living room, where the better light from the large windows would enable him to see what he was doing in this complex operation.

He had barely removed the soiled diaper and begun to clean the little soiled bottom when the doorbell rang. He thought, with relief, that Mrs. Mullen had come to his aid, and called, "Come in!"

But it was not his friendly neighbor who entered. There in the doorway, stood Mrs. O'Brien and the Canon.

"May we come in, Desmonde? Mrs. O'B. and I are in town buying some fine linens for the church. And we couldn't go back without giving you a call."

"Please come in," Desmonde said faintly. "As you see, I'm rather busy at the moment."

"Enjoying the pleasures of a father," said the Canon, as the baby, naked and unattended, began to howl in misery.

"Let me, please, Desmonde. Please, where is the bathroom? Through there?" Quickly Mrs. O'Brien stepped forward, lifted the child, whipped the obscene napkin from the table, and

[231]

disappeared. The Canon then came in and closed the door, sat down, and in silence viewed the stale end of loaf, the half-empty pot of cheap jam, and the dirty teacup..

"Well, lad," he said at last, "I see you're not only in the headlines, all over Ireland, but at home, by the look of it, you're on the verge of starvation. You're pale, thin, hollow-cheeked, a miserable shadow of what ye were when I had the pleasure of knowing ye. But then ye have the recompense, and all the joys, of a faithful loving wife. We spotted her at the Hib on our way out, in the lounge at an early drink, lookin' like the Queen o' Sheba, with three of the flashiest young toughs ye'd ever meet at the Baldoyle Races."

Desmonde remained silent.

" 'Tis wonderful, of course, the true nobility of sacrifice for love. To abandon your religion, your vocation, your splendid standing and propriety in the Church, in fact, everything, all for the sake of some sexy little bitch that got round you in a weak moment in the dark. Are you still proud of it? Or, now, do you think it was folly?"

Desmonde did not raise his head.

"Not folly," he muttered. "Madness. And how savagely I have been punished."

"If only, when ye felt the need of a bit of lovin', why did ye not turn to Madame? She was completely gone on you, head over heels. Then, when the first flurry was over, ye could have settled down quietly, in loving friendship, and nobody a bit the wiser. After all, didn't some of our best Popes have their women, in the good old days? But no, you chose to play the gentleman, the hero, all for a worthless little bitch who has dragged you down to her own level, to the gutter, and will now, sure as God's in Heaven, give you the soldier's farewell." Desmonde remained silent. The Canon continued: "A true daughter of her mother, who left a decent husband to run off with a worthless scamp who had his will of her for a few months, all over Europe, then left her without a penny, in the middle of nowhere." He paused. "She threw herself under a train in Bregenz station."

A long silence followed, then the Canon exclaimed with a sigh so deep it was almost a groan:

"If only ye were back in Kilbarrack with me, lad. Just up from your own good Mass, or from teaching your little Communion class, and were sat down at the table and I was slashin' the carver into a lovely leg o' lamb, all crisp with cracklin', cooked to a turn by Mrs. O'B., and you were due for a quiet afternoon stroll to Mount Vernon for tea and music with Madame, and the archbishop had just sent me a letter full of your praises . . . making me as proud as if ye were my own son . . . Oh, God, it fair breaks my heart to think of it . . ."

He broke off. A long pained silence followed, broken only when Mrs. O'Brien came back into the room.

"Well now," she said cheerfully. "Baby's all cleaned up and washed and is cozy in her cot, almost asleep."

Abruptly the Canon stood up.

"Then we'll be off, Mrs. O'B. There's no more for us to do here. The mischief is done and canna' be undone. Goodbye Desmonde, dear, and God succor you." He made the Sign of the Cross over the bowed figure at the table and turned to the door.

"Goodbye, dear Desmonde," murmured Mrs. O'Brien. "I pray for you every night and will never forget you."

When they had gone Desmonde made an effort to throw off the misery into which the Canon's melancholy soliloquy had plunged him. He got up and went into the bedroom where the little one, freshly bathed and neatly tucked into her cot, was fast asleep. The room had been tidied and the bed properly made up, something of a novelty, since the sheets were unusually flung back in a tangled bunch. The bathroom, too, had been cleaned, the towels straightened out, the soap and sponge retrieved from the bottom of the bath, and correctly placed in the washbasin.

[233]

And there, on the little shelf above the basin, tucked in beneath a tube of toothpaste, was a brand-new five pound note.

This was the last straw, the final touch of loving pity and compassion that broke through Desmonde's self-imposed restraint. He returned to the living room, sat down at the table, put his head in his hands and wept — bitterly, bitterly, he wept.

At last he pulled himself together and forced himself to think of the future. The envelope from Dr. O'Hare contained twenty-five pounds. His reserve of fifty pounds, carefully preserved in his suitcase, and the five pounds from Mrs. O'Brien, made altogether a total of eighty pounds. The rent of the house was paid until the end of the year. At least he was not insolvent. He unlocked the suitcase, put the twenty-five pounds in the pocket of the lining with the original fifty, locked the case, and with the five pound note in his pocket went out, and along the street to pay the grocery bill.

"I was afraid ye had forgotten it, sir," remarked Kelly significantly, when the note was placed on the counter. "Let's see, now. You have seventeen and ninepence coming back to you. Shall I send the morning milk around to you again?"

"Please, Mr. Kelly. And some of those apples you have over there. I'm sorry for the delay."

"No harm done, sir. Whatever they may say of ye, the name o' Fitzgerald is good enough for me. Let me give you one of the apples, on the house. They're the first of the season's Coxes."

With the apple and seventeen and ninepence in his pocket, Desmonde left the shop and went home, relieved on his arrival to find Mrs. Mullen in the house.

"I thought you might be needing a bit of a hand, sir. You've had a lot of callers. Can I do anything?"

"If you would keep an eye on baby, Mrs. Mullen, I'd like to go out for a couple of hours. I'll give you the key of the house."

"Aye, sir, go and get some fresh air to yourself. For in God's truth ye're not lookin' at all well."

Desmonde handed over the key and went out, with a strange

sense of escape, as he slowly set out for his inevitable resort where, as a boy, he had so often walked with his father.

The afternoon was fresh and fair, the park deserted and, though he felt he should walk, he soon was seated in his usual secluded corner, with trees around and the songs of the birds to soothe him. He ate the apple, skin and all, threw the core to some friendly sparrows, sat back and closed his eyes. Soon he was asleep.

7

It was not a lazy sleep but, so poor was Desmonde's physical
state, a sleep of sheer exhaustion, a benign blackout that lasted
a full three hours. Twilight was falling as he awoke and hurried
to the park gates, lest he be shut in for the night. Then, at a
more moderate pace, he started on the return journey to the
Quays and reality. He felt better, and better able to face whatever lay in store for him.

As he approached his house he saw that Mrs. Mullen was
again on patrol, now always a presage of evil. She half ran to
meet him.

"Oh, God, sir, thank God you're back. I've been at my wits'
end. What's happened wouldn't bear repeating." She paused to
catch her breath. "Just after ye'd gone, your lady came back
in a flash little car, driven by a flash-lookin' man. Into the
house she swept and in no time at all she was out again with her
luggage, then in again for a longer time, then out with more
things, and baby, wrapped in a blanket. Into the car they
crowded, with everything in the boot o' the car or packed in the
seat behind them.

" 'Where are ye off to, madame?' I ventured to call.

" 'To Cobh Pier,' she called back, tipsylike. 'And to hell with
you, and the rest of you, old bloody Mullen.'

"So off they went with a blare o' the horn." Again she paused.
"I've had a look in the house, sir. It's like all the furies of hell
were let loose in it."

Desmonde entered the house. The living room looked a shambles — the table upset, chairs turned over, cutlery and china strewn on the floor. In the bedroom the crib was lying on its side, blankets and sheets in a twisted knot upon the floor and, on the chest of drawers, his two prized little pictures, the Bartolommeo *Annunciation* and the photograph of his mother, were totally destroyed, smashed, no doubt, on the hard edge of the chest, the glass broken, frames bent and twisted, the pictures pierced and torn beyond repair.

Desmonde sat down on the mattress and silently viewed the damage, such an expression of wanton rage and actual hatred that his heart sank within him, in bitterness and pain. Suddenly a thought struck him. He jumped up and ran into the living room, flung open the cupboard door.

His suitcase was still there, but the lock had been forced and hung limp and useless. He dropped to his knees and lifted the lid. His money was gone, gone to the last pound note. She had finished as she had begun, with unutterable selfishness and inherent unfaithfulness. She had cleaned him out.

He was still on his knees and motionless, a petrified figure, when Mrs. Mullen came into the room.

"Do get up, sir," she said soothingly. "I'll send Joe in to clear up the mess. He'll soon put things to right."

He permitted her to raise him, and to lead him to a chair, which she set back squarely on its four legs. There he sat, an acrid bitterness in his mouth and a chill sense of fear in his heart. No longer a priest, a schoolmaster sacked in disgrace, he had exactly seventeen shillings and ninepence between himself and starvation.

A voice roused him:

"Don't take on, sir. I'll have everything straight for you in no time."

Joe had come in and, in his shirt sleeves, had begun the work of restoring decency and order. Desmonde simply sat there in a state of dazed inertia. But when Joe had finished and both rooms had resumed their normal shape and form, he motioned Joe to sit near him.

"Thank you, Joe, from my heart. I can't understand why you and your grandmother are so kind to me. I'm not worth it."

"You are worth it, sir. And we're truly sorry for you. Besides, we remember that your father was very good to us. When my widowed mother died he bought our house for us so that Gran should always have a roof over her head."

Desmonde was silent. Always his father's virtue, distinction, and nobility returned to confound him, and now more so than ever.

"I would love to give you something myself, Joe. But I am absolutely and completely broke."

"I thought she would skin you to the bone, sir. We waiters at the Hib see and hear more than you would ever guess. We summed her up as a right bad lot!" He paused. "Now that you're up against it, have you any idea as to what you'll do?"

Desmonde shook his head slowly. "I'm down and out. With no way to pick myself up."

"I think you're wrong there, sir!" Joe exclaimed, then hesitated. "You forget about your gift in your voice — I read all about it in the *Chronicle,* and I believe I could get you a job."

Desmonde looked at him doubtfully.

"It's like this sir. Up at the Hib in the big lounge after dinner it's usually chock-full, and Mr. Maley, the manager, very often has an *artiste* in, to sing or play to the customers. Last winter we had Albert Sammons the violinist. So if you'd permit me to talk to Mr. Maley, he might give you an engagement."

Desmonde was silent. To sing in a pub — had he fallen so low? Better to sing in the streets. And why not? He had an impulse to degrade himself still further. Yet the reality was not quite so bad: the Hibernian was a first-class hotel, patronized by the best of Dublin society and by many distinguished visitors. Above all, he urgently needed work, not only because he was destitute, but as an escape from the brooding solitude that now hung over him.

"Joe, you are a real friend," he said at last. "I'll come to the hotel with you anytime you say, and take my chance with Mr. Maley."

"Right you are, sir. He's a fine man is Mr. Maley. I've a feeling he'll take to you in your distress." He paused. "Could you manage to come up around four o'clock tomorrow afternoon? Tog yourself up nice and quiet. Try and look your best."

Desmonde nodded and held out his hand. "I'll be there."

When Joe had gone Desmonde glanced at his watch. Almost eight o'clock. Exhausted, mentally and physically, he wanted only to rest. But first he forced himself to eat: a bowl of hot oatmeal and milk, followed by one of the apples sent earlier in the day, which Mrs. Mullen had stowed away in the cupboard. He then took a hot bath and lay down on the big bed, conscious immediately of the peace, the blessed quiet and roominess, the divine solitude of lying alone and unmolested, in the slow search for sleep.

8

At ten minutes to four o'clock next day Desmonde set out for the Royal Hibernian Hotel. He had shaved and groomed himself with more care than he had lately come to bestow on his appearance. He had brushed his sadly neglected shoes until they shone and put on his best Italian suit with a soft collar and dark tie. Let it be admitted: although frightfully pale, he was as handsome as ever, and still so young-looking he seemed little more than a stripling.

Outside the hotel the usual string of cars was lined up, some small and ordinary, others larger and of a more distinguished lineage. He went in and passed through the entrance hall to the lounge, directed thereto by the chatter and hum of many voices. The place was indeed crowded, mainly with women, for this was the fashionable hour for tea in Dublin, and the Hibernian the fashionable resort. Desmonde remained standing outside. Threading in and out of the tables he could see Joe who, obviously expecting Desmonde, soon caught sight of him and presently came over.

"You're looking grand, sir. And there's a lovely crowd here today. I'll send a word to Mr. Maley that you're here."

Desmonde waited, still standing, and presently Mr. Maley came toward him. The hotel manager was a well-set-up man of fifty or thereabouts, with a commanding presence and an expression firmly indicating that he would stand no nonsense. He looked Desmonde up and down; and finally:

"You have had your troubles. Joe tells me you are practically down and out."

"Your information is correct," Desmonde said.

A pause. The reply had created a favorable impression.

"Well, there's your audience. Get in and show me what you can do with them. I'll sit here to watch and listen."

Desmonde inclined his head and without a word walked firmly to the platform, no more than a foot high, on which stood the grand piano. His appearance had caused an immediate cessation of the chatter, followed by the murmur of many whisperings. Desmonde waited until this too had ceased. Then he bowed and, in complete silence, sat down at the piano.

His first choice, with an eye toward Mr. Maley, was that lovely little song of Schumann's, "Wenn ich in Deine Augen seh." He sang it in German, softly and sweetly, as befitted the words, then, without pausing, passed immediately into the most tender of all songs, "Jeannie with the Light Brown Hair." When this ended, in a silence of rapt attention, he was obliged to stop, so warm was the applause. Across all the upturned faces Desmonde could see that Maley was smiling and applauding vigorously.

Desmonde gave no sign whatsoever of gratification at his success, but continued with his program, wisely interpolating his Irish ballads with German lieder: "Der Lindenbaum" and "Frühlingstraum." How often he was obliged to stop for spontaneous and prolonged applause need not be recorded. But when he ended with his favorite "Tara" and immediately stepped from the platform, so demanding were the cries for an encore that he was obliged to return to sing the last verse again. Only then was he free to escape through the little side door at the rear of the platform that led him into the waiters' mess hall. And here he found himself face to face with Mr. Maley, who pulled two chairs forward from one of the tables.

"Sit down, Desmonde. Are you tired?"

"Slightly, sir. And rather hungry."

"All that will be attended to, my boy. Now listen to me. I

have the name of a fair and honest man and I will not, I say not, take advantage of your dire need. You gave a marvelous performance and I know what I'm talking about. I believe you could fill these rooms until people would be falling over themselves to get in!" He paused, looking Desmonde in the eye. "Now, what I propose is this. If you would sing at teatime for one hour and no more, for I don't want to kill you, then rest in a room I will reserve for you and be served there with our full a la carte dinner and an appropriate wine, then, after another little rest, sing again for just one hour for the after-dinner crowd, I would be prepared to pay you thirty pounds a week, provided you stay with me the entire season, right through Horse Show Week."

Desmonde had turned very pale. He murmured:

"You are noble, truly noble. You know my absolute need."

Maley smiled. "But yes, I could have swindled you. But that's not James Maley. Besides, I've a hunch you'll fill the hotel. Now," he stood up, "I'll send Joe in with a drop of tea. He'll show you to your room. And your dinner will come later."

He took Desmonde's limp hand in a firm clasp, turned, and was gone.

Alone, Desmonde felt torn between a rising tide of joyful relief and the nervous reaction of tears. The entry of Joe, smiling all over his face, saved him from giving way.

"I know how you feel, sir. You've made a smash hit and I'm delighted. Now drink up your tea, it's good and hot."

"Thank you, Joe. Thank you a thousand times." His voice broke. He could say no more.

Joe watched with a paternal air while Desmonde gratefully gulped the hot tea.

"There's a couple of ladies, Mrs. Boland and her sister from Ballsbridge, really nice people, ladies of quality, I know them well. They asked if you would favor them by coming to their table."

Desmonde shook his head.

"No, Joe. Please thank them, but let it be known that I have made a resolution never, never to accept such invitations."

"I understand, sir. And I respect you for it. Of course, these ladies, and others like them who come to us, are quite first class — real good people. Now, if you're finished I'll take you to your room."

The room, conveniently near on the ground floor, was small, with a washbasin, a neat single bed, and a window that looked out on the yard — completely quiet at this hour. Desmonde threw himself down on the bed and closed his eyes.

"You've a good hour and more before dinner, sir." Joe said as he closed the door.

Desmonde slept until seven o'clock, awakened by Joe bringing in his dinner.

"Mr. Maley chose it himself for you," Joe said, laying the well-equipped tray on a small table near the window. "He thought something light might be in order for your first night." He added, on his way to the door, "You should see the evening papers, sir. They're a fair treat!"

Desmonde had no interest in what the papers might say of him. Hardened by the scurrilous treatment he had already received, his mind was passive, his state of being in a cloak of total indifference, of curious nonreceptivity. Good or bad, everything was superficial, nothing important.

Yet he was perfectly able to enjoy his dinner: a cup of delicious beef bouillon, followed by a thick slice of turbot and string potatoes, suitably accompanied by two glasses of white wine. The dessert was chocolate soufflé with whipped cream.

Not for a very long time had he savored such a meal, and one which by its very excellence so revived and fortified him. He smiled faintly as he thought of what he would give his audience tonight, and how he would play upon it with careless skill. He was still planning when the door swung open, admitting none other than Maley himself, a smiling, hand-rubbing Maley, a warm, solicitous Maley.

"Was everything all right, Desmonde, the dinner to your taste?" And then, reassured: "You should see the evening papers. They're ecstatic. They say you're even better than John McCormack. We are absolutely booked out in the dining room and we've had to cram another thirty seats into the lounge. I hope the big crowd won't worry you."

"Not in the slightest. But if I should feel tired might I spend the night in this room?"

"Of course, of course, man. And tomorrow I'll find you a better one."

"Thank you, Mr. Maley, but I rather like it here. It reminds me of a little room I had in Spain during my novitiate."

"Well, well, just let me know. You know I want to please you." He paused. "You'll be all ready by eight o'clock?"

Desmonde merely smiled, a pleasant indifferent smile, symptomatic of his present mood. And at eight o'clock he was ready, brushed and freshened by a wash in cold water. He left the room impassively, with no thought of a little prayer for renewed success, calm and untroubled by the hum of many voices that came to him, resolved to maintain that calm, never to smile, but to use without stint or reserve the wonderful gift that was within him, to use it as a bitter answer to those who had so viciously abused him.

9

When Desmonde was well established at the Hibernian, an event occurred that could be regarded as unusual. It was Horse Show Week, the great Dublin festival that attracts many hundreds of visitors to the city. Maley was at his wits' end, not only to provide accommodation for his many wealthy patrons clamoring for the best rooms in the house but, in a word, to cope with the unbelievable demand for Desmonde. He had extended the lounge by throwing open two extra rooms and, wisely, had placed a cover charge of two guineas on the seats. He was, thereby, apart from preventing a riot, coining money hand over fist, and his attitude toward Desmonde had become more deferential than ever.

"Anything more I can do for you, Desmonde, just say the word. You know, of course, that I'll give you a bonus now that the Show is ending."

"Very well, Mr. Maley. You know, of course, that I shall be leaving you soon."

Maley started. "Good God, man! You can't do that! We're not near the peak yet!"

"Nevertheless, I shall go. You remember the terms of our agreement. You definitely said, till the end of Horse Show Week."

"But you see, Desmonde . . ."

"I do not see, Mr. Maley. And as you are, in your own words, an honest man, I hold you to your word."

"I'll pay you the double — and more."

"The answer is no. You cannot expect a singer of my quality to continue without some respite. In addition," Desmonde lowered his voice, "I have a personal reason for leaving."

"Then you'll come back, Desmonde, lad. You must come back."

"We shall see, Mr. Maley. We shall see."

That afternoon Desmonde was at his best, singing with a distant look, as though, oblivious of his audience, he envisaged a joy that was to come. At the end of the performance he found Joe in the waiters' room, apparently snatching a moment from the tearing rush of his job.

"Listen, sir. There's a fat little woman, sitting at the very corner of the platform, has ordered me to ask you to see her." Anxiously he exhibited a five-pound note. "I wish you would, sir, for my sake. She's far from beautiful, I assure you, and I could bet this fiver she's somebody important."

"I'll go, Joe. Just this once. For you."

When the crowd had thinned, Desmonde moved quickly across the platform and stepped down to the table Joe had indicated. The woman, rather as Joe had described her, was seated with a tumbler of whiskey and soda, barely touched, before her. She was wearing a low-necked Paris gown that emphasized her fat bosom and suited her ill.

Desmonde stood, silent, with an expression of distaste, awaiting her request, he assumed, for an autograph. She, too, studied him in silence. At last, in a vivid American southern accent, she threw out:

"So you're the little Fitzgerald priest they kicked out for adultery."

His face hardened. "As you say, madam."

"Was the fornication pleasant?"

"Excessively." He bit out the word and spat it at her.

"And you're a little bit of a singer too, it seems."

"As you say, madam."

A pause.

"Don't you use your bottom for sitting on?"

"I prefer to enjoy your pleasantries standing, madam. And now that you have exercised your wit, may I leave you. But before so doing, may I tell you that you are the most foul, fat, obscene, vulgarly got-up and, in a word, repulsive creature I have ever encountered in my entire life."

Surprisingly, she burst out laughing and, although he had begun to move away, she shot out a fat arm. Little podgy fingers, one adorned with a diamond the size of a hazelnut, gripped and swung him into the chair beside her.

"Don't run away, Desmonde. I think I like you, very much. I'm so used to people pandering to me, lying, licking my boots, trying desperately to win my favor, that it is refreshing, for once, to be told the truth." She paused. "You know, of course, who I am?"

"I have not the faintest notion, madame. And I have no wish to know."

"I am Bedelia Basset. Known all over the U.S.A. as Delia B. Now you know of me?"

Silently, Desmonde shook his head.

"My God! You *are* the original backwoods boy. Don't you know I am syndicated in sixty of America's best-selling newspapers, that top Hollywood directors tremble in my presence, that famous stars beg and beseech me for kind words that may make them more famous, or dread the words that may send them back on the streets selling candy bars?"

"Madam, I know, and care, nothing of this. My sole knowledge of your fabulous kingdom comes from my friend, my dear friend, the only one I have in the entire world. He is A. J. Cronin, now a novelist. He has been to Hollywood, and indeed sold his first two novels to the pictures."

"A. J. Cronin! I believe I know him. But novelists are two-a-penny in Hollywood. We regard them as keech! You say your only friend?"

"Yes. Except for big Joe, the waiter. I am cast off by all the others."

"What about your wife?"

"I hate her," said Desmonde simply. "Yes, as much as I love my darling little babe. I am going to see my baby soon. She is with my wife's aunt, Madame Donovan, whose whiskey you are now drinking."

"My God, Desmonde, I'm a hard case, yet you startle me. Madame Donovan must be worth millions. She donates cathedrals. Yet here you are . . ."

"Singing in a pub for a few quid a week." He paused. "It's my own choice. I don't care anymore. And of course I'm leaving Mr. Maley to visit my little one."

"He'll not let you go. You're manna from heaven to him. Unless . . . you've signed nothing?"

Desmonde shook his head.

"Thank God. That would have been a bad start. Now listen to me, Desmonde. I don't like often, but when I like . . . I like all the way. And what I must tell you is this. You're wasting your time and your talent here. Your magnificent talent! I know you've been hurt and you want to hide. But it's got to stop. I'm off tomorrow to the West Country, to look at a little village I believe my forebears came from, but I'll be back in about a week. Before I go will you do one little thing for me?"

Desmonde inclined his head.

"I'll be at this same table tonight. Don't sing those lovely little Irish songs. Sing something big, classical, out of the operas. Do this, and I know you're with me! Now go and get your dinner. I'll sit here awhile, send off some cables, and finish your auntie's whiskey."

Despite his habitual indifference, Desmonde was somewhat taken by this unusual little woman. When he had finished his dinner he felt compelled to write one of his periodic letters to his friend.

This afternoon I was accosted by a little fat weirdie of a woman, fearfully ornate and calling herself, with great éclat, Bedelia Basset. Believe it or not, she seems to have taken a fancy to me, or rather to my prospects. It's a joke of course, but she does know you, although despising all authors and dismissing them with one unprintable nasty word. You know I am chucking my job at the pub here. The delicious and nourishing food, supplied gratis by the good Maley, has quite put me on my feet again, and I am going to Vevey to see my little darling. I am terribly fond of her, A. J., although no doubt you will regard this as further evidence of my weakness. What has happened to my wife I neither know nor care. We are irreparably parted and I have no doubt she is finding her own kind of fun elsewhere. Are you by any chance in the mood to take a short vacation and to come with me to Vevey, just for two or three days? It's too long since we have met and the Swiss mountain air would do you no end of good . . ."

When the letter was finished, sealed and stamped, Desmonde gave it to Joe to post. He had just come in to remove the dinner things, looking particularly jubilant.

"You know that queer little fat Yank, sir?"

"Intimately, Joe!"

"Well, sir, she just gave me a tip to keep that same little corner table for her. Guess what?"

"Sixpence, Joe."

"No, sir, this . . ." Joe exhibited another five-pound note. "And she did ask me to remind you about them opera songs."

"She will be obeyed, Joe."

For perhaps the first time since his engagement at the Hibernian, Desmonde's mood was cheerful, as he stepped onto the familiar platform that night. He actually smiled as he faced his audience which, as large as ever, was somewhat different in nature from those immediately preceding it. The Horse Show was over, most of the wilder elements had departed, and here, tonight, were members of the Irish gentry who had stayed on, either to hear him or for purposes of their own.

"I hope I won't disappoint you tonight," Desmonde began, very quietly. "As you may know, I sing a great many Irish songs and ballads. Tonight, however, at the request of a very distinguished American visitor, I have consented to sing two numbers from the operas. The first will be from the beloved Puccini, from

Tosca, the last heartrending song sung by Mario before his execution. The second will be the Prize Song from *Meistersinger* which, you might care to know, I sang in Rome, when as a young priest I won the competition for the Golden Chalice." He paused, waiting for the hum that succeeded his announcement to subside, then said: "I shall sing the first in the original Italian, the second in German, exactly as Wagner wrote it."

He sat down at the piano and from memory, partly improvising, played the haunting melody of *Tosca,* the motif that runs throughout the opera. Then he stood and began to sing.

Tonight, perhaps because of his impending holiday, he was in superlative form. Into that last passionate, loving, despairing yet courageous cry from the condemned Mario, he put all the feeling that Puccini had therein ordained.

When he had finished, the applause, while orderly, was deafening, led by a series of Bravos from the corner table by the platform. Desmonde bowed repeatedly, then sat down at the piano to rest. He could not fail to see that the little American, her thin cigar discarded, was writing like mad on a pad of cable forms.

Fully rested, he was on his feet again. Dead silence. He waited, just for a moment, then threw back his head and began to sing, to give forth that sublime ascending volume of delicious and arresting melody, the finest ever written by Wagner, in whom the fatal Germanic mystique was so deeply rooted.

It is a long, and exhausting song, and Desmonde gave it everything within him. When it ended he felt spent, and instead of immediately leaving the stage he felt for the chair, sat down, and with bent head let wave after wave of the applause roll over him.

Everyone was standing up. Vaguely he saw his little American friend fighting her way to the door and he thought, I'll never see her again. At last he forced himself to his feet, bowed and bowed again, throwing out both arms and repeating, again and again: "Thank you, thank you, thank you." Then he turned, made his way to his room, and lay down on his bed.

Joe was longer than usual in coming to him, but at last he arrived, his hands crammed with cards and torn-off pieces of paper.

"You never saw such a commotion in your life, sir. At least I never have, in all my days at the Hibernian. More nor half the gentry o' Ireland, talking tegether about you, sending in their cards with all sorts of messages, beggin' ye to call on them, and to stay too. Shall I read them to you?"

"No, Joe. Drop them in the wastepaper basket."

Joe seemed stunned.

"God bless my soul, sir, you're not serious. Here's one from the Lord Lieutenant of Ireland and his lady. 'Do call on us, Desmonde, we do wish to meet you.' "

"Drop that one in first, Joe."

"And here is one, sir — " Joe dropped his voice to a reverential whisper — "which is actually from no less than His Lordship, Archbishop Murphy, that says: 'My son, now surely you have expiated your sin. Come to me, Desmonde, and I will see what might be done for you.' "

"Take that one, Joe," Desmonde said, bitterly, "tear it in little pieces, and flush it down the toilet."

"I will not, sir." Joe said, outraged. "That would be a mortal sin on me. Whether you like it or not, I'll tuck it in the pocket of your suitcase."

"Nothing from that nice, funny little Yank?"

"There is indeed, sir, scribbled on a cable form. Will ye be wantin' to put that one down the jakes also?"

"Stop teasing me, Joe. Read, read, read!"

Provokingly, Joe cleared his throat several times, then read:

" 'Darling, darling, Desmonde, you have given me the scoop of the year. Tomorrow your name will be splashed in the headlines of thirty newspapers all over the United States, announcing my discovery, young handsome ex-priest, Irish, new, better than Caruso, singing for coppers in pub, a story that would bring tears from a stone. Don't, don't, don't sign any contracts till I see you again. Till then I remain with love and kisses your most foul, fat, obscene, vulgarly got-up and in a word, repulsive creature you ever encountered in your entire life.' "

"That's a real person, Joe," Desmonde said.

"She is indeed, sir. Afore she dashed off she gave me another fiver and told me to take care of you."

"And so you have done, Joe, all along. Drop that message in the suitcase. At least it deserves keeping as a souvenir."

"And now, sir," Joe bent forward obsequiously. "What can I do for you in the way of something to eat?"

"Cut it, Joe! Bring me something good. I'm hungry and tired. And if you can, pinch me a half bottle of champagne."

"No need to pinch, sir, Mr. Maley will give you the pick of the cellar. I'll be along in half an hour."

Desmonde got up, took a hot bath and soaked in it, then had a rubdown, and got into slippers, pajamas and dressing gown. He did not know what to think and therefore decided not to think at all.

FIVE

1

The Irish Mail train was late, causing me to spend almost an hour in the dank beastliness of Euston Station. But at last it came in, the engine puffing and snorting as though it had climbed Snowdon en route. And there was Desmonde walking down the platform, carrying a limp suitcase. We both wanted to embrace, but refrained and shook hands.

"Is your luggage in the van?"

"No, I have it here."

"Splendid, then we can start from scratch."

"Give me your arm A. J. I'm still rocked in the cradle of the deep."

"It was rough? As usual?"

"Tempestuous."

I had come to the station by bus, unwilling to throw my possessions in Desmonde's face. We quickly found a taxi and sat looking at each other as we rattled off.

"You look terribly fit, A. J."

"You do too, Desmonde," I lied cheerfully. He was still entrancingly handsome as ever, but sad, and of course, tired.

"And your dear mother?"

"Well and happy. She has a nice little flat on the seafront at Hove, just three minutes from the church. Of course when my boys are home she is always with us."

"Where are you taking me?"

"Home. It's just a little house in Kensington, but nice, quiet, and within a few paces of the Gardens."

He wanted to know more but, as always, was too well-bred to ask. And presently we drew up at Number 3 Eldon Road, the little white house I loved so much, one of a quiet row, totally free of traffic noise. I got rid of the taxi and opened the front door with my key.

I took him upstairs to the guest room that looked out onto the garden of the house.

"You can park here; your bathrooom's just there. Now, how about some food?"

"Absolutely not, A. J. I'd love a good wash, then lots and lots of talk."

I smiled, put my hands on his shoulders, and gave him a good shake to break down the constraint that lay upon us. After all, it was a very long time since we had last been together. Then I went down to the kitchen to see Mrs. Palmer, my especially good "daily," who had consented to wait beyond her usual four o'clock departure.

"Everything ready for your dinner, sir . . . The chops on the grill, the spuds are peeled and ready, the salad made and in the fridge with the apple tart."

"Thank you, Mrs. Palmer. And it was kind of you to stay over."

"It's a pleasure sir, for the likes of you."

She picked up all her gear, thanked me again for the left-over joint of beef I had given her, and went off, saying:

"Your mail's on the hall table, sir."

Upstairs, I glanced at my letters, which seemed promising, then went into the drawing room. Desmonde was already there, standing, looking about him.

"Oh, come, Desmonde, stop looking and sit here beside me."

"I can't A. J. It's such a lovely room — everything, everything, and your pictures! Don't you remember my prediction in the Winton Art Gallery?"

I took his arm and drew him onto the settee beside me. But still he kept looking.

"That lovely Sisley, the early Utrillo, the Mary Cassatt, that lovely little violety conversation piece — is it a Vuillard?"

I nodded. "Madame Melo, the actress, and her daughter. But do stop, Desmonde, you're making me frightfully uncomfortable."

"I can't stop, A. J., I'm enjoying it so much and, my God! I believe that's a Gauguin over there! Pont Aven, just after he came back penniless from Tahiti."

"Good for you, Desmonde. Yes, he had not enough to buy a real canvas. That lovely thing is painted on burlap. Of course, I had it rebacked in New York, where I bought it. And it's housed in a genuine Louis Sixteenth frame, stripped, of course. Now about you, Desmonde, what . . ."

"Just one more, A. J., that lovely thing, of the Seine, I believe."

"I don't mind talking of that masterpiece, Desmonde, for it's my favorite. It's the Seine at Passy, the last scene painted by Christopher Wood. A letter from his mother is on the back."

"Just before . . . at Salisbury Station, wasn't it."

"Yes . . . What a loss!"

Desmonde was silent, then said:

"You seem to be alone here, A. J."

"Yes, I am. My dear little wife and my two brats, both boys, are down in Sussex."

"At a hotel?" Desmonde asked, studying the photograph on an adjoining table.

"Of course not. I have an old shack down there. We use it a lot."

Idly, Desmonde said, "That's a lovely old Georgian house, with heavenly old brick stables made over into a loggia, and with a view, it seems, of the Downs. Whose is that?"

"That's the Old Sullington Rectory, and of course it belongs to the Vicar. Very decent chap. And just up the road is the old Sullington Church. Genuine Norman, you can see the long and short brickwork. I can't tell you how lovely it is. One of these days I'll show you."

"Thank you, A. J. Perhaps the Vicar will let us stay at the Old Rectory." Then he said, "A. J., you are, as always, the best and dearest friend a man could ever hope to have. But for God's sake, because of the abysmal failure I've made of my life, don't try to minimize the success you've made of yours."

"Stop it, Desmonde! Your success is just ahead of you."

"I won't stop it. You put yourself through school and university on a shoestring. You've no money, so you have to find work as medical assistant in a ghastly mining district in Wales. It's hard work, often you're up at night, but three evenings a week, on your secondhand motorbike, you scorch down to Cardiff thirty miles there and back, for classes and experimental work. You go to London, take the hardest of all medical degrees, then your MD, your D.Ph., you buy a London practice on tick, in three years you're making seven thousand a year. You then sell out, take off for Scotland to write a novel and now, here you are, not so long after, with your town house, your country house, your heavenly pictures and furniture, and although you lied to me, your Rolls-Royce at the door. If I didn't know you'd worked this miracle I would not believe it. And I . . . I am a kicked-out priest, deserted, thank God, by my bitch of a wife, with no more than thirty quid in my pocket."

"Please be quiet Desmonde." I moved closer to him and put my arm around his shoulders. "I've been infernally lucky. And now we're going to work a miracle for you. Tell me, what did Bedelia B. say when she came back?"

"She said quite a lot, and once you get used to her, you rather like her. Well, here it is, straight. They are definitely committed to making a film based on the life of Enrico Caruso. It won't be called that, of course, but some bloody tripe like *The Golden Voice,* or *The Voice That Breathed O'er Eden.* Anyway, they have an excellent script all ready, but the original idea of using Caruso records has been ditched. All the old records are terrible, and besides, even if usable, the result would be transparently mechanical and feeble. So they're urgently looking for someone to act the part and sing, if possible, like Caruso. Little Bedelia thinks it's made for me, and mind you, she is no fool, and she knows Hollywood inside out. She seems to like me, why, God only knows, and is going to try to land me the job."

I took both Desmonde's hands and wrung them.

"There's *your* miracle Desmonde. What a heavenly opportunity. It's God-given. With a start like that nothing could stop you. Now I promise you this, Desmonde — I'll do everything to help. Of course I'm coming with you. I've some business of my own to do out there. We'll go shopping tomorrow. I'll take care of everything, tickets, reservations, accommodations, everything."

"I must first go to see my little one. She's with Madame, in Switzerland."

"We'll do that en route. Join the boat at Genoa."

I still held his hands. He raised mine and kissed them both. I saw with distress that he was fighting tears.

"A. J., you are so eternally kind to a washed-up bloody wreck of a fellow, and I love you for it as I always have."

"Enough, Desmonde. Come and help me get up the dinner."

We went downstairs to the kitchen where I switched on the electric grill and lit the gas under the pot of potatoes.

"I thought you'd rather eat in than out, tonight. Are you hungry?"

"Voracious, now I've ceased to rock and roll. I was in the vomitorium half the voyage." He was sitting at the kitchen table. I joined him.

"Wonderful ideas those old Romans had to regain their appetite."

"But painful, surely."

"Do you remember old Beauchamp and the cake? He had such an appetite he must surely still be alive."

Desmonde smiled. "He did nourish himself assiduously. But I'm afraid the dear old Mother Superior must be gone."

"Oh, yes. She's certainly in Heaven. Desmonde, I'll never forget the scene when you sang to her. From that moment you were destined for the movies."

"I'll never forget the stumpy little hockey player. What a sport she was. And what buttocks!"

When the potatoes were ready I poured them and turned off the grill.

"Let's feed here, A. J. Such a fag carrying everything upstairs."

"Wouldn't dream of it. Go up to the dining room. You'll find the table already laid."

He looked at me indecisively for a moment, then obeyed. Quickly, I put the food into the little dumbwaiter sunk into the wall, and joined him upstairs.

"Where's the grub, A. J.?"

I pressed the button on the wall. There came a faint whirring, immediately two paneled doors sprang open, and there was our dinner.

"What a topping idea."

"You won't get maids running up and down these Victorian stairs, nowadays. Our Mrs. Palmer is extremely good, but she would jib at that!"

We sat down to dinner, simple but good. Desmonde polished off two chops with commendable ease, and a good thick hunk of pie.

"I can't offer you wine, Desmonde. We don't go in for it here."

"This Perrier is awfully good."

"Another slice of pie?"

"Just a little bit. It's delicious."

When he had finished I said:

"Now the prescription is, hot bath and bed, so that you're all rested and fresh for tomorrow."

I put the dishes in the waiter and sent them down for Mrs. Palmer's attention in the morning. Then we went upstairs.

"Have you got everything you need? Pajamas, toothbrush, razor, et cetera?"

"Everything, thank you, A. J. And my room and bathroom are lovely."

"Good night then, Desmonde. Sleep well."

"Good night, my dear A. J."

2

Next morning I got up at my usual hour, seven o'clock, then took my cold bath and my usual half-walk, half-run up Victoria Road and across the Gardens to the Carmelite Church, just in time for the seven-thirty Mass.

On the way home I picked up the paper and fresh rolls. Mrs. Palmer, never failing, was already in and had my coffee ready, steaming hot.

"I think Mr. Fitzgerald would probably like his in his room. I'll take it up, Mrs. Palmer, in about ten minutes."

When I had glanced through the paper hoping, without success, for some mention of my new novel, I took the tray Mrs. Palmer had prepared, added a second cup of coffee for myself, and went up to Desmonde's room. He was awake, but still luxuriating. I placed the tray on the bedside table while he raised himself on an elbow.

"What a kind idea! I haven't had coffee in bed for at least a hundred years." He drank. "And such good coffee. Did I hear you go out?"

"My usual morning prowl. Up to the Carmelite for early Mass."

He seemed to shrink slightly, but forced the words out.

"And to Communion."

"Of course. That's routine too. And a jolly good start to the day."

He was silent, then said:

"I'm obliged to tell you, A. J., that I have broken completely with the Church. I never go. Never. I consider that the Almighty has given me a beastly rotten deal."

"Didn't you rather set it up for Him? Anyway, I'll bet you a new prayer book that you *will* go back one day. Now, it's a lovely morning and we're not going to waste it discussing theology. Get dressed and we'll get going on the town."

Within half an hour Desmonde came into my room, fully dressed. I had put on my West End togs, dark suit, black shoes and bowler hat.

"I say, A. J., are you something in the City?"

I laughed. "On my first visit to Hollywood, a very important woman, who had just written and produced *The Big House,* took me quietly aside. I was all tweedy, with colored shirt, flowing tie and suede shoes. 'A. J., don't for heaven's sake dress like an author — you'll get nowhere. Dress like a businessman.' I've taken her advice."

We went downstairs and out. The morning was delicious, fresh, lovely and sunny. The prunus in the little front gardens of the quiet road were already in heavenly bloom.

"Where's the big car?" Desmonde demanded.

"Damn it, man, didn't I tell you it wasn't mine." I had phoned the garage man earlier not to bring it around. "We're going in on the top of a bus. There's no better way to see London."

We walked to the end of Victoria Road and took the Number 9 bus at the stop outside Kensington Gardens.

The Gardens were green and lovely, some early nursemaids already abroad with their prams. Green too, and in fresh foliage, was the park. Then past the Marble Arch and into Piccadilly with its wonderful shops. What a lovely city London was in that era: uncluttered by traffic, the lively buses springing along, the pavements clean, uncrowded, the policeman on his beat, the milkman on his round, the whole enlivened by a sense of honest activity, beauty and order.

We got off at Burlington House and turned up left into Savile Row.

"Now your work really begins, Desmonde. All we're now going to do is frightful foppery, but all the people I know do it, so I've just fallen into line."

I did not take him to Poole's, since I knew they would refuse to make the suit available in time, but to Bluett's, a younger house I sometimes patronized.

"Ping" went the door as we entered, a delicious, reassuring, old-fashioned sound matching the rich smell and sight of good cloth, bales and bales, on the long, heavy mahogany table, and the deferential gentleman with the inchtape around his collar.

"I believe you know me as a customer?"

"Mr. Cronin, isn't it sir, the author?"

Impassive, but inwardly delighted by this hint of publicity, I said:

"We would like two suits if you could oblige us by making them within a week and sending them, without fail, to the offices of the Italian Line in Genoa."

He thought for a moment, then went through to the work-room, emerging with a smile.

"As you are a customer, sir, I am sure we can oblige you, without fail. I assume the suits are for the gentleman who accompanies you."

Then the fun began, the long, careful choosing, the equally protracted measuring, the tailor's plea for just one fitting, in two days' time. Then we were shown out with the utmost courtesy, Desmonde the potential owner of a lovely herringbone gray, and a dark, soft, blue-black merino suitable for evening wear.

Bond Street was near, always an interesting, though narrow, thoroughfare, and here, in Turnbull and Asher's, we bought half-sleeve sports shirts, six pairs of socks, and half a dozen conservatively hued Macclesfield silk neckties.

"I do badly need some ordinary shirts," Desmonde murmured.

"Not here, Desmonde. Hats first, then shirts."

Across the street we went to Hilhouse's where, very easily, we found a dark checked tweed hat, that Desmonde kept on, and a knockabout soft Panama.

"Shall I send your friend's hat with the Panama?" asked Mr. Hilhouse, gingerly holding the battered relic by the brim.

"Oh, no," Desmonde said, hurriedly. "Please throw it out."

"It's been a good hat in its day, sir. But now . . . I'll burn it."

"Are you tired?" I asked Desmonde, as we stepped out of the little shop. "There're two more measurings to be done. So I think we'll now have lunch."

"Good idea! I spotted a good-looking A.B.C. just up the street."

"Silence, Fitzgerald. Do you think I'm going to spoil our day by taking you for tea and buns?"

We recrossed the street and turned into Grosvenor Street. As Claridge's hove in sight, guarded by two uniformed giants, Desmonde faltered.

"I'm not going in there, A. J. Not in these rags. I'd eternally disgrace you."

"Come, child, take my hand, and stop howling."

We entered the magnificent portals and went downstairs. Seated outside the restaurant on one of the settees, and obviously awaiting a guest, was that wonderful woman, Lady Colefax.

"Well, A. J.," she greeted us. "I hear you're a marked man. This new book of yours that's due next week has half of Harley Street looking for your blood."

"They can't kill me, Sybil, I'm not a patient."

"Who is your handsome friend, in those atrocious clothes?"

"He is Desmonde Fitzgerald, and he's coming to Hollywood with me, next week. He's just come off the set and hasn't bothered to change."

"What are you making?"

"A modern version of *Hamlet*, madam," Desmonde supported

me, launching his marvelous smile. "I am the third gravedigger."

"Weren't there only two?"

"It's a dreadfully deep grave, madam."

"Well, do wipe your boots before you go in. I see my guest coming. And do take care of yourself, A. J. Send me an autographed copy of your book."

The headwaiter had seen us chatting with Sybil, so we had a first-class table, when otherwise we should have been shunted to a far corner of the long, lovely room. We studied our menus, gold-printed on double pages of embossed, tasseled cardboard.

"Shall we be simple and have the table d'hôte? It's usually awfully good."

Desmonde agreed. "And no wine, A. J., please. Perrier, if you wish. Who is your nice friend?"

"Sybil Colefax. She's been terribly kind to my wife and me. Inviting us to her parties and to lunch at her perfect little house in Westminster. Even when we were new in London, and painfully green."

The lunch, as might be expected, was extremely good. We did not talk much, since I had no wish to linger. More work lay ahead of us. Not long after two o'clock we had finished the *mousse au framboise à la crème,* drunk our coffee and, with the bill paid and the waiter tipped, we were on our way.

"Do let's take a taxi, A. J., and tip the head porter. I can't sneak out of this place in my broken-down shoes."

I obeyed, saying, as we rolled away:

"Apropos of tipping, there's a story that a fabulously rich Eastern potentate, who often stayed at Claridge's for months on end, never tipped the head porter, but repeatedly and affectionately promised him he would be remembered lavishly in his will. When Mahomet did take him to his bosom the will was read. Guess how much the head porter got?"

"Half a million."

"Absolutely nothing."

"What a sell," Desmonde murmured sympathetically. "But all rich people are not mean."

"I'm not rich, Desmonde," I laughed. "I enjoy spending money. And I can never, never forget how kind you were to me when *my* shoes were broken-down."

We were now at the far end of the Burlington Arcade, the driver having kindly taken us the long way around by Saint James's. But he duly received his tip. No Londoner ever has a row with his taxi driver — that fatal error is left to tourists.

At the Piccadilly end of the Arcade we entered a small shop which bore on its signboard the name Budd. Here we resumed our work : viewing, examining, feeling and finally selecting various materials, silk, poplin, cotton. And again Desmonde was subjected to various tapings and measurings.

"Now shoes, lad," I exclaimed as we emerged, again reassured that everything would be dispatched on time.

"For heaven's sake, stop, A. J. It's all far, far too much. You make me feel as if I were going to boarding school."

"You're going to Hollywood, you dear idiot. Do you want to arrive in your bloody bare feet? I know from my own experience that those things you're wearing won't last much longer."

Quite near, a few doors below Lobb's, shoemaker by royal appointment, to whom I had not aspired, we went into the Churchill shop, less famous but equally good.

My position as a customer immediately rectified the shock conveyed by Desmonde's horrifying feet. He was seated, the remnants removed, and the usual careful measuring begun. I was glad to observe he had only one small hole in the toe of one of his socks. Finally, after the order had been given for two pairs of black, two of dark brown, and one patent leather for evening wear, Churchill tactfully suggested :

"I am sure I have some shoes in stock, sir, that would serve the gentleman until his order arrives."

He went into the rear shop and came back with a brand-new pair of black shoes.

"The old gentleman who bespoke these, sir, a very old and

favored customer, we've had his last for almost fifty years, died before delivery. Of course we did not press the matter."

The shoes fitted Desmonde very well indeed, although Churchill said, disparagingly:

"Not bad, sir. Rather slack across the base of the meta-carpals, but they should do for the time being."

I thanked Churchill and said we'd take them and to put them on the bill.

"Those you've got on, your good self, sir, they seem to be wearing remarkably well. Don't tell me you've had them re-soled."

"Good heavens, no, Churchill," I lied. "I wouldn't dream of it."

"Then it's my good leather, sir," Churchill said, adding sadly, "It lasts forever."

When we got out of the shop I inquired:

"How do you feel standing in dead men's shoes, Desmonde?"

"Totally rejuvenated. I can't tell you what a blessing it is to have something solid on one's feet."

The office of the Italian Lines was our last port of call, and her we were fortunate. The flagship of the line, the *Cristoforo Colombo,* was due to sail from Genoa in ten days' time. I recognized the girl at the desk.

"Have you a double stateroom available, midships, on the port side?"

She examined the plan of the ship.

"You may have C19, if you wish, sir. It is the accommodation you and your wife occupied last year."

"That would be splendid."

"Shall I reserve you a table in the restaurant, sir?"

"Oh, please don't trouble. I'll see Giuseppe on board — I'm sure he'll know me again."

She smiled. "We all know, sir. Your books are much, much read in Italia."

With everything completed, I turned to Desmonde as we came out to the street.

"You see now who reads my books? All the little girl clerks, the stewardesses, the yearning housemaids, the fat, love-hungry cooks and heart-throbbing domestic servants in jolly old Italy. Now you're tired, so no more bussing, but home, James, and don't spare the petrol."

I hailed a taxi and presently we were back in the quiet of Eldon Road and thirsting for tea, which I asked Mrs. Palmer to bring up to the study, a cozy, book-lined little room, obviously an addition to the house, that opened off the first landing.

"Any messages, Mrs. Palmer?" I asked, when she appeared with a well-stocked tray.

"Miss Jennings called from Sullington, sir. Nothing important, she said, some contracts for you to sign. The little boys have gone back to Avisford, and madam, your wife, is well and hoping you'll be down soon."

"Thank you, Mrs. Palmer, and also for this very good-looking cake."

"I hadn't that much to do, sir, so I just baked one. It's quite plain, the way you like them."

"Thank you again, for your thoughtfulness."

She blushed and looked pleased.

We were silent, savoring the rapture of our first cup of tea. When I handed Desmonde his second cup he said:

"What a nice way you have with people, A. J. I've been noticing it all day. And how wonderfully fortunate and happy your life has become."

"Yes. I thank God for it on my knees every night."

Again I noticed that slight shrinking from the very mention of the Deity. But he persisted.

"You must really be very well-off now, A. J."

"I am not. I have a good income from my royalties and I spend every penny of it. People like to read my books, Desmonde. With some exceptions, I am not a favorite with the critics. Best-sellers are anathema to them, though God knows Dickens and Thackeray and even Walter Scott were all best-sellers. But I don't mind . . . much. In many countries I am read and liked. And I keep smiling, all the way to the bank."

He had been looking at the books, arranged in shelves against the wall.

"That is a vanity of mine. Absolute conceit. I keep one copy of each first edition, wherever I am published."

He stretched a long arm, picked out a book, and opened it.

"Good heavens, what's this? Arabic?"

"No, Japanese. I sell very well in Japan. The Arabic is on the next shelf."

He took up another book, a heavy, substantial volume.

"Blow me down, A. J. What's this?"

"The Russian edition of *The Stars Look Down*. I have reliable information that four million copies of that book were distributed last year. What royalties did I receive? Not one bloody ruble! Not even a pot of caviar. I'm still trying."

He went on to another, but this too-personal demonstration had gone far enough. I stood up and moved to the door.

"I must go and telephone my wife. And do keep your sweaty fingers off my books."

Downstairs in the hall I rang Sullington. It was Miss Jennings who answered.

"Mum there, Nan?"

"She's just gone out, around the garden. Shall I fetch her?"

"No, Nan, this is just to say I'll be down tomorrow."

"Oh, good. I've some good news for you."

"Can't believe it. Tell Mum I may have a friend with me. It will just be for the day. How is the garden?"

"Coming on lovely. The strawberries are almost ripe!"

"Have you been pinching?"

"Maister! You're the one with that delightful habit. Besides, Dougal has netted them."

"Nan, I'm bringing down the big car and will leave it. I'll take the Morris. Will you mind coming with us to drive it back?"

"Of course not, Maister. But . . . I hope you're not going away again."

"Just for three or four weeks, Nanno."

"Oh, dear. And it's so lovely down here in the early summer. I shall miss our walks on the Downs."

"I'll be back, Nanno. Do rest and take care of yourself. There'll be bagloads of work when I get home. Perhaps you'll tell Mum to have a nice, light, salad lunch for us tomorrow."

"I will, indeed, dear Maister."

I hung up, thinking what a splendid girl she was, so good, trustworthy, and hard-working. What on earth would I do without her?

At the foot of the stairs I yelled up, "Like to come with me to Sullington tomorrow?"

"Love it," he yelled back.

I did not go up. I knew he'd be fingering through all my books. I hoped he'd find the one in Hindustani. I went into my room, closed the door, and lay down on the bed. I still had my letters to go through. But first I'd have a nap.

3

Next morning after breakfast, coffee and fresh rolls for both, we set off for Sullington. As the car slid silently along the Great West Road before turning south toward Sussex, Desmonde said:

"This is supreme luxury, A. J. Don't you love it?"

"Desmonde, shall I be honest and admit that I prefer to drive my little Morris Oxford?"

"Good heavens, why?"

"Desmonde, last summer we, my wife and I, were touring in France. We had stopped at a little café in Avranches, on our way down to take another look at Mont-Saint-Michel, and were seated outside drinking coffee. The big Rolls was there, brand-new, simply glittering in its glory. Just then two fat peasant women came down from the market, their arms full of vegetables. Naturally they paused to look.

" '*Oh, là, là,*' rapturized one. '*Quelle splendeur!*'

" '*Ah, non,*' said the other, moving off in disgust. '*C'est trop grosse pour moi.*'

"That's the answer to your question, Desmonde. '*C'est trop grosse pour moi.*' "

"Yes, A. J., I know from our adventures yesterday that you have very modest tastes. Merely the best, nothing more."

The day was lovely and promised to continue so, with a warm sun and bluey-gray skies. Happy to be going home — Sullington was my home, the little London house no more than an outpost

— I felt like singing, but was restrained by the presence of the maestro beside me. How good to see my dear little wife, and Nanno, and to have news of my two sons, and to see, with Dougal, how my beloved garden grew. I could not resist the impulse.

"Sing, Desmonde. Something sweet, touching and home-coming."

Desmonde never resisted such an invitation. He loved to sing. And so we rolled through the Sussex lanes — I knew all the shortcuts — to the strains of "Loch Lomond," leaving behind us a trail of bemused villagers, gazing fearfully through our dust, puzzled as to whether they had glimpsed a mirage or the advance guard of Barnum & Bailey's Circus.

But all was quietly expectant as we finally turned up Sullington Lane and swung through the open white barred farm gateway, which I had insisted on preserving, and drew up before the rectory. Immediately there was an explosion from the house as Paddy, the Irish Setter, hurled himself upon me, almost knocking me down. Then came my wife, on Nan's arm, followed by Annie, the strong, plump little country maid, all smiles, and inquiring if there was luggage. Behind, peering from the shadow of the portico, stood Sophie, our Austrian cook, while at the corner of the barn I caught sight of Dougal, dramatically attacking the wallflower bed.

I embraced and kissed my dear little wife, who looked remarkably well, gave a hand to Nan, and said:

"Darling, here at last is Desmonde Fitzgerald."

She smiled. "My husband has spoken of you so often and so nicely, I almost know you already."

"Madame." Desmonde bent and kissed her free hand. "Your husband has spoken of you so continually and so lovingly that I am enchanted to meet you."

"Enchanted? I am no witch, Desmonde. So do keep your fine words and manners for Hollywood. Do you know of our dear Nan?"

Rather deflated, and deservedly so, Desmonde murmured, "I have certainly heard of Miss Jennings."

"Then let us go into the house. Would you like coffee? No? Then perhaps you'd rather go around the garden."

We went first to the old walled garden, my pride and joy, where, sheltered by the lovely eighteenth-century rose-pink wall, Dougal had tended and brought to perfection all our early plantings. The herbaceous border was in bloom; the vegetable garden was nobly productive with lettuce, trenched celery, radish, endive, runner beans, delicious fresh peas, and Dougal's pride, the marrow bed, bulging with green footballs which, no doubt, would shortly be culled to a single enormous globe for the village flower show. Then came the currant bushes, red, yellow, and white, dangling with variegated bunches; the gooseberries, amber globes, rather ravaged for a reason I suspected, but still thriving; next, the raspberries, safely caged, loaded with ripe berries; the espalier peaches with alas, few immature fruits, many nipped off by the Sussex blight, and finally the strawberry bed, a glorious huge spread of ripening Royal Sovereigns.

I turned to Dougal, who had quietly followed us.

"Congratulations, Dougal. Everything looks wonderful, especially the strawberries."

"Ay, they've done fine, sir. I kent ye like them. But I've had a bit of a struggle keepin' the wee laddies off them." He smiled. "I even caught Miss Jennin' putting a dainty wee finger through the net."

"She'll be suitably chastised. The raspberries are gorgeous too, Dougal."

"Ay, sir, they're splendid. Ever since ye gien me permission to put the cage up."

I glanced at Nan, who was trying not to laugh.

"You were right, dead right there, Dougal, and I was wrong. It's not at all unsightly."

He looked pleased, and I chose this moment to say coaxingly:

"Dougal, I ken how ye hate picking the fruit afore it's ready, but could you manage to find just a few ripe strawberries for our lunch. My guest here is a very important man from Hollywood."

"I jaloused he was important, sir, frae the terrible auld claes he has on. Verra well, sir, I'll dae my best to let ye have a nice wee punnet. And if ye've a moment, sir, I'd like to see ye by yoursel', out by the barn doors."

"Certainly, Dougal. I'll come with you now."

Out by the corner of the barn I gazed with rising anger at the ruin of my wallflower bed.

"Damn it to hell, man, who did this? Was it Paddy?"

"I thought, sir, ye'd be rightly angered, as was I. No, sir, 'twas not Paddy. He's a well trained animal. 'Twas these two wee sons of yours, at their football. I begged them to stop but they just laughed and wouldna'."

I was indeed very angry and I wisely exaggerated my rage.

"My beautiful wallflowers! I'll let them have it, I warrant you, Dougal. They'll play football in the far field and nowhere else, I promise you. Can you do something with the bed?"

"Verra easy, sir. I'll pick up a couple o' dozen new shoots at the nursery and have them charged to you." He smiled. "Maybe ye'll let me order a dozen for masel'. Like you, I love them wallflowers!"

"Certainly, Dougal," I said heartily. "Two dozen if you wish."

"Na, na, sir. The ane dozen will dae fine. And don't be too sore on the laddies. Boys will be boys, ye ken. And thank ye again."

I saw that he was not only appeased but pleased. I shook hands with him and saw him immediately depart for the strawberry bed. Dougal was a priceless gift from the neighboring big estate that also supplied me with its pheasants. A trained and skillful man and a hard worker, he had come to me after a violent quarrel with the head gardener, to whom he was second in a staff of six. I valued him and made every effort to appease his rather craggy nature. He liked me because I was obviously

Scottish, though masquerading under an Irish name. I felt sure now that he would stay with me. Half an hour later he handed to my wife a large punnet of delicious big ripe strawberries.

Meanwhile, I rejoined the others who were emerging from the path that wound through our little wood.

"Why do you call it the Canon's Walk, A. J.?"

"There's a story that a previous incumbent, Canon Herbert, walked here every day reading his breviary. My neighbor's pheasants are very fond of it. They usually find their way to our dinner table."

"These fields are yours, I suppose," Desmonde said, looking left.

"Fortunately, yes. The tennis court we put in ourselves."

We paused in the orchard. The two ladies had gone on to the house.

"Tell me, A. J., why does Miss Jennings address you as Maister?"

I laughed. "It's a silly story. When Dougal first came to us he wanted to put a cage over the raspberries. I said 'no.' There was an argument, rather hot, which I terminated by saying in broad Scots: 'Dinna' forget, Dougal, that I'm the Maister.' Nan, who was with us, thought this very funny and has adorned me with the name ever since. Of course, next year Dougal talked me into the cage, a great success. He's a splendid fellow."

"And what a splendid girl is Miss Jennings," said Desmonde wistfully.

Lunch was ready when we reached the house. Sunlight poured into the dining room as we sat down to one of Sophie's Emperor omelettes and a huge bowl of gorgeous salad fresh from the garden. Afterward came the strawberries, served with fresh cream from the neighboring farm. They were inexpressibly good. Then came coffee.

Oddly enough, conversation did not flow easily, and now it became apparent to me that neither my wife nor my secretary was well-disposed to Desmonde, a formality which he himself seemed to feel, since he became increasingly anxious to please.

When we rose from the table he looked engagingly at Nan.

"If you're in the mood for a walk, Miss Jennings, would you care to show me the Downs?"

She looked him straight in the eye.

"I am going to be very busy, Mr. Fitzgerald. But if you walk out of our gateway, turn left, and follow your nose, you will be on the Downs in exactly two minutes."

"Thank you," Desmonde said politely. "Can you spare me for an hour, A. J.?"

"Certainly, my dear fellow. Have a good walk, but be back before three."

When he had gone off alone, I said, "It's too bad. Everyone treats him as a pariah. Why must you?"

"He is not good, darling," my wife said. "There's something wrong with him inside."

I looked at Nan who said, apologetically, "I feel like Mum. And I can't stand his bowing and knee-bending and hand-kissing."

"That's because he's nervous. The poor devil has been kicked into the mud, has had his nose ground into it, is absolutely down and out. I can never forget our friendship when we were boys. I'm trying to help him make a comeback. And I hope I succeed."

"You are always so kind, dear," my wife said.

"Nonsense! Go and lie down for an hour. Then we'll run over to Avisford and see the boys, just for five minutes."

"Oh, do let's," she said. "And take the Rolls — the boys will love that."

I went upstairs with Nan to my little study that overlooked the garden and the outbuildings. Dougal was hard at work on the wallflowers. All the papers requiring attention were on the desk. I looked through them quickly and signed where necessary.

"Why do the Italians want four copies of every contract? I see there are a couple of less-than-bad early notices here."

"And some rude postcards from your ex-colleagues."

"Burn them, Nan. I only wrote the truth. I can't help it if they don't like it."

"It's too bad, Maister, that you're going off again. Mum doesn't like it. We're very lonely here when you're away."

"I promise I'll be back within two weeks. Perhaps sooner, if I sell the film rights. Then you'll have to put up with me for the next hundred years. I'm taking Mum for a quick run to Avisford. Want to come?"

At half-past two we set out for Avisford, a run of not more than six miles. Desmonde had just come back, looking fresh, but rather bored with the Downs. He sat in front with me. Mum and Nan were in the back. In no time at all we were gliding to the large country house converted to a school, with playing fields around, and a swimming pool at one side. Our two sons spotted us at once and rushed over from the cricket pavilion. A scratch match was in progress and they were not fielding.

"Had a good innings?" I asked.

Vincent answered, "Mine was short and completely uneventful."

"In other words," Patrick said, "he had a duck. I made twenty-seven."

"All flicked off the edge of the bat. Missed twice in the slips."

"Three jolly good boundaries and caught, at last, off a possible sixer."

"We can't stay, boys, but I did want to see you and to tell you, if you're out at the house before I come back, don't, don't, don't mutilate the wallflower bed. If you promise not to, Nan has something nice for you."

Both together: "We promise, Dad."

"Now first come and kiss Mum and tell her that you love her. Then shake hands with my friend Mr. Fitzgerald, who is taking me to Hollywood."

This was accomplished, and Nan was also kissed. She then produced a bag of gooseberries.

"I say, how lovely, Nan. Pat, I thought we'd cleared all the bushes."

"These must be new growth, ass."

"Don't eat them all over the car, boys. I'm sorry, but we must be off. You can sit under that tree and polish them off."

"Drive around past the pavilion, Dad, so that all the other chaps can dekko the Rolls."

"You see, Desmonde," I said, as we rolled off. "Public school snobbishness already. I'm glad we didn't go to that kind of school."

"I very much wish we had," Desmonde said sadly.

In no time at all we were back at Sullington. When I had put away the Rolls I went immediately to Douglas and told him I'd made a special journey to the school to admonish the boys.

"Och, ye shouldna' have done that, sir." But he smiled. "Ye may depend on me to look after the gairden weel while ye're away."

Then it was time to think of leaving if Nan were to drive back before dark. I brought the Morris Oxford to the front door and sought my wife, who was resting on the couch in her room. I knelt beside her.

"I'm sorry to be leaving so soon, darling. I'll be home again in about three weeks, and then we'll have a lovely long time together. You are looking so much better. Keep on taking care of yourself."

"Nan takes care of me. She's such a dear."

"You are a darling, darling. And I love you with all my heart."

I kissed her gently. Her lips were soft, passive, tender as a child's. Before I reached the door she had closed her eyes.

In five minutes we were off, Desmonde at ease in the back seat, Nan and I sitting up in front. I drove fast, very fast, not taking risks but cutting everything fine. I knew the road so well and it was practically free of traffic at this hour. None of us said anything, not a word. At four o'clock precisely we drew up outside Number 3 Eldon Road.

"I hope I didn't scare you," I said to Desmonde, as we stretched, then went into the house.

"Nothing scares me now, A. J." he answered, in that same note of sadness. "Anyway, you're a magnificent driver. You do that well, as you do everything else."

"Come, come, now, Desmonde, that won't do. You're needing your tea."

As we went slowly upstairs I told Nan to ask Mrs. Palmer to bring tea for three in the study.

"I'll just have a quick cup with Mrs. Palmer in the kitchen. I want to be off and home before the traffic. Shall I take your mail for filing?"

"Yes, dear Nan, and answer as you think best."

We looked at one another. I knew then that I loved her and that she loved me. I had the overwhelming desire to take her in my arms.

"Goodbye, dear Maister. Come back soon." She smiled faintly. She had seen love in my eyes.

"Goodbye, dear darling Nan." I touched her cheek lightly with my lips. Then I went upstairs to my room.

Only when I heard the sound of the departing car did I go to the study. Desmonde was already there, as was the tea tray. I poured his cup and gave it to him, then poured my own.

"Desmonde, I've a horrible feeling that my idea of giving you a breath of fresh air in the country has been a fiasco, a rush around in cars, simply a wasted day."

"Not at all, A. J. I've seen your beautiful estate and duly admired it."

"Good God, man, I did not take you for that beastly purpose."

"I've also seen your two fine boys and duly admired them."

"Oh, shut up, man. What's come over you?"

"I have also met your sweet wife, who loves you, and the good Miss Jennings, who also loves and respects you. And I have come to the sad conclusion that in the society of good, pure women, I am nothing more than a cheap, posturing, broken-down, unspeakable, lecherous, God-damned bastard."

I was about to remark that he would meet few pure good women in Hollywood, when I saw, with a start of pained surprise, that he had his hand across his eyes to hide the tears dropping into his cup. I immediately moved toward him and put my arm around his shoulders.

"Please, Desmonde, please don't, my dear old friend. You know that all that's finished and done with. You're on the very threshold of a new and brilliant career. Just cut out all the bowing, genuflecting, hand-kissing. Stop and be yourself again. Damn it all, man, think how I've set you up for a big success, all that I've done for you, all the trouble I've taken. Are you going to quit when we're in sight of the promised land? Are you that kind of a lousy quitter?"

He slowly uncovered his eyes, and handed me his cup.

"More tea, quickly, you Scotch-Irish, American best-selling, Roman Catholic, daily communicant, and unutterably decent fellow. My hurts will heal, vanish, when I have Hollywood at my feet."

"That's the spirit, Des. Keep it up."

"Then I will thank you for all the wonderful things you have done for your old friend who loves you."

"That's enough, Des. You've just got yourself back in the groove. Here's your tea, and I'll have mine. When do you want to go to Switzerland to see your wee lassie? We haven't much time before we board the *Cristoforo Colombo*."

"Let's go now."

"Don't be an ass, my newly restored and fortified friend. If you get up very early when I call you tomorrow morning, I'll have you in Geneva by tomorrow night."

"It's a deal, pal," he said, handing his cup for more tea.

4
=====

Next morning we were up with the dawn and left immediately for Victoria Station. I had paid Mrs. Palmer the night before and given her the keys of the house. She would forward all mail to Sullington.

The daily boat train left in time, as did the cross-Channel steamer when we pulled into Dover Pier Station to make the transfer with five minutes to spare. The crossing was not unduly rough, and at ten thirty we were on Calais Pier taking the long walk to the Paris train. Some delay here owing to the loading of baggage, but when we took off, to the accompaniment of shrill whistles, the train was nonstop all the way. At Gare du Nord it was of course necessary to change stations, but a slow taxi took us to Gare du Lyon where the Continental Express, steaming at its platform, was ready and waiting. At noon exactly we slid away in slow grandeur, merging gradually into the speed, remarkable for that age, of sixty-five miles an hour.

We had lunch in the restaurant car. Desmonde apparently had little appetite. He kept looking out of the window, occupied with his thoughts which were, undoubtedly, directed toward his little daughter. He had thanked me so often for my kindness in coming with him that I no longer answered, merely shook my head and smiled. After lunch we both nodded off into a nap that took us on to four o'clock and a pot of rather indifferent tea. At five thirty-four we drew up, in clouds of steam, at

Lausanne Station. Nowadays, of course, air transport makes fun of our journey — when the planes fly, are not delayed by strikes, crashed, or hijacked in transit. But for the day and age, it was a good performance.

So Desmonde seemed to think when we stood on Lausanne platform. He smiled.

"Can't believe we're here. What next, A. J.?"

"A taxi to Burier, just beyond Vevey. There's a hotel near Burier, not large, but good."

"If it's small and good it'll be full up."

"Well, we'll see." I did not wish to appear too perfect, so I did not mention that my wire for reservations had been confirmed.

We found a man who would take us to Burier for the modest sum of thirty francs. It was a beautiful drive, the lake on one side, and on the other, hillsides draped with vines, great extents of famous vineyards, where the grapes were already large as currants. The sun, not yet setting, was low, drenching the still water with a glittering radiance. We passed through lovely little Vevey, always so peaceful, spread out along the lake, then on to La Tour de Peilz, where Courbet lived and died, still a village, towered by its château — a gem in an antique setting. Here we turned off the main thoroughfare, moving uphill on a country road that took us past wide pastures to the little village of Burier, a handful of houses on a strip of high land, almost a cliff, overlooking the lake. On the other side of the road, the little village station, embowered in rambler roses, vast stretches of pastureland beyond.

"What a lovely spot," Desmonde murmured, as we drew up at the hotel.

This, though named Reine du Lac, was not a large or pretentious establishment, but as we entered, gave manifest evidence of class. Our rooms, separated by a bathroom, overlooked the lake, with a superb view of the Dents du Midi, still snow-capped and now bathed in a rose-red, empurpled sunset.

"And all that lovely open country behind," Desmonde continued. "Trust Madame Donovan to find it."

We were both hungry and decided on an early dinner. We had an admirable table for two by one of the windows. Most of the other early diners were rich old ladies for whom this hotel was obviously a choice resort. One had a tiny toy Pekinese, supremely well-behaved, on her lap, which she fed with minute snippets from her own plate.

The dinner was excellent, the fish unbelievably good, a grilled ferra, which the headwaiter described as "swimming in the lake only this afternoon." Then, inevitably, chicken, but tender and nicely cooked. The sweet, a well-made *crème caramel*. Finally, as we drank our coffee, the moon came up in slow grandeur over the distant Les Roches. Although slightly on the wane, visually the great white disk was as good as new.

"Let's spend the rest of our lives here," Desmonde said.

"That's what Madame Donovan seems to be doing. I gather she's in Ireland for no more than three months each year."

"Let's go out and see if we can spot her place."

Outside, in that soft light, it was almost clear as day. We walked across the road to the little red-tiled station which, on that single line, served perhaps three or four trains in a day. In the little garden the stationmaster, so distinguished by his official cap, was taking the air. We approached him and Desmonde greeted him in French. I wish I might record the conversation in the idiom of that tongue — it was extremely amusing — but the translation must serve.

"Master of the station, may I trouble you to answer a question?"

"You are not troubling me, sir. As you see, I am not occupied with my official duties, which have been fully and effectively completed for the day. I am regarding my artichokes, which, alas, do badly."

"I regret that your artichokes do badly, sir."

"I, too, sir. What is your question?"

"We are seeking a lady named Donovan."

"Ah, ha, the Irelander."

"Exactly! So you know her?"

"Who does not know Madame Donovan?"

"She is well-known here?"

"Have I not said so, sir?"

"For what is she well-known, stationmaster?"

"For everything, sir."

"Everything?"

"Everything that is good, sir."

Desmonde looked at me and said, aside, "Shall I go on?" I nodded.

"Stationmaster, what good exactly does Madame Donovan do?"

"Have I not said, sir, that she gives to all, to the village, the school, the home of old men there, at the end of the road — you observe it from here. Even in the smallest givings. There is a great oak tree where the old men used to gather to talk. Only this month she puts a good strong seat all around the tree, where now they sit with comfort."

We could have gone on pleasantly in the delicious cool air, but now Desmonde put the final question.

"Where does the good Irish lady live?"

The stationmaster removed his pipe and waved it widely, as he answered, "Look over the other side of my little station, sir. Look to the right, very far, and to the left, as far as the village. Look then to the distance, the tall wood on the left, the home farm with cows still in the fields, on the right. Look then to the large house in the center, upon the little walled eminence. You will then have seen the domain of Madame Donovan."

Desmonde looked at me in silence.

"Thank you profoundly, stationmaster."

"A pleasure, sir. Do you visit Madame?"

"Tomorrow, stationmaster. Good evening."

"Good evening to you, sir."

"Some domain," I remarked, as we turned away.

"We must breach it, A. J."

Back in the hotel we took turn about in the bathroom. The beds were excellent, the hand-washed linen sheets softly caressing. I fell asleep instantly.

At seven o'clock next morning I was awakened by a knock at my door. A maid entered silently with coffee in a thermos and fresh rolls, put the tray on the table with a murmured, *"Service, monsieur."* She seemed surprised, almost sad, when I said I would have my breakfast later. I felt sad, too. I knew the coffee was good, and burning hot, while the rolls, not the usual horrible *ballons,* were genuine croissants, sure sign of a first-class hotel.

When she had gone, I rolled out of bed, took a cold shower, and quickly dressed. I then went downstairs and, following directions received from the headwaiter on the previous evening, set off at a hard pace for La Tour de Peilz.

On the outskirts of that lovely village, I found the small convent toward which I had been directed. Those of my readers who still remain with me are, I fear, heartily sick of my early-morning devotions. However, this occasion of my piety must not be omitted, since on entering the little chapel in which the convent nuns, some twenty in all, were grouped at the back, I observed that another member of the laity, in addition to myself, had come for the eight o'clock Mass, which now began.

She was a woman of perhaps forty years, possibly more, quietly but most expensively dressed in black, a mink cape about her shoulders, an English prayer book in her hands. She was undoubtedly beautiful, yet her expression was so withdrawn, intent, and severe, that one was impressed more by her piety than by her beauty. As I had passed an antique but magnificently maintained Rolls-Royce in the courtyard with a uniformed chauffeur in the front seat, I guessed this to be hers, and also that she was probably English.

We ignored each other during the service, although once or twice I felt her glance upon me. But when all the nuns had communicated and we rose simultaneously to receive the Eucharist, she smiled faintly as I allowed her to precede me.

When Mass was over I left the chapel and set out at a good pace for Burier. The lady had remained behind to talk with the nuns. However, I had not gone far before the antique Rolls purred alongside me.

"May I give you a lift, young man? Where are you going?"

"To the hotel at Burier."

She opened the door. "Oh, do step in, then."

I would much rather have walked, but the opportunity was too good to miss. I stepped in.

"Are you English?" she asked.

"No, Madame. An Irish Scot."

"And what are you doing in this beautiful and still, mercifully, remote part of Switzerland?"

"I am on my way to Hollywood."

"Good heavens! Are you an actor?"

"No, Madame, merely an author. And I am sponsoring a friend who, in an admirable life, made one horrible mistake for which he has suffered atrociously. He now has a chance, quite literally, to pick himself out of the gutter."

"In Hollywood!"

"He is a singer. His one possession, his buried talent, is a superb voice."

Now I saw comprehension dawning in her eyes. I continued.

"He wants to see his child before he goes. I beg you to permit it. It is only for one day."

She drew back, with a sudden darkening of her face.

"He sent you specially to the chapel, in pretended piety, to get hold of me."

I looked at her steadily.

"If you think that, Madame, that I would so defile the Eucharist, I can only pity you."

Now she had turned pale. The car drew up at the hotel. I opened the door. As I stepped out she said, in a low voice, "He may come."

My adventures, which I had certainly not anticipated, were not yet over. As the ancient Rolls drew away, a voice hailed me from the far side of the hotel yard, where a man was cleaning the windshield of his car. Now, as he beckoned, I went over.

He was a big fellow, in a flashy expensive brown suit, and his car was rather different from the vehicle I had just quitted. It was an Alfa Romeo, low, rakish, and incredibly fast, the finest product of Italy.

"Good morning!" He spoke excellent English. "I see you know Madame Donovan."

"Oh, slightly. She gave me a lift from La Tour."

"I know her niece, more than slightly." He flashed his big teeth at me. "My name is Munzio. I hope to marry her when she gets her divorce."

"Congratulations," I said. Then, quickly, "I am admiring your car. Very fast, I suppose."

"That is the finest car in the world. And fast? Let me tell you. After breakfast, which I often take at the hotel, since I garage my car here, I leave for my office in Milano, pass around the lake, narrow twisting dangerous road, *over* the Gotthard, not by the tunnel, then across the frontier, again many bad roads, then to Milano, do my business, have lunch and am *back here in time for tea.*"

It sounded impossible. Yet I believed him.

"You must be a first-class driver."

"I am the best." Again he flashed his teeth. "I drive this car like I ride and master a good horse, a thoroughbred."

"You go now?"

"Of course."

"Then I'll look out for you at tea."

Again he flashed the smile.

"I see you then. I show you."

I went into the hotel, rather full of my recent experiences, which, after I'd had my coffee, I immediately related to Desmonde who, breakfasted and dressed, was sitting on the balcony of his bedroom.

"I believe I saw that fellow," he said calmly. "He must be from northern Italy, he's so big and powerful." Then: "It takes someone like that to keep Claire in order." Then again: "How fortunate you met Madame Donovan. Now we won't be turned away at the gate. Although I'm sure she won't receive me."

And so it was when, at ten o'clock, we strolled down the village street, past the old men seated around the oak tree, and presented ourselves at the heavy iron gates of the estate. These were immediately opened, but the lodge keeper said to Desmonde, in Italian:

"Madame does not receive today, sir. But you may proceed to the terrace."

We walked slowly toward the house, in bright sunshine, with rooks circling and cawing in the tall trees that bordered the entrance to the estate. The drive was freshly raked, the edges trimly clipped, the park stretching on either side, recently mown and in good heart. A large walled garden came into view on the left as we breasted the slight rise at the end of the drive. The house itself, of plain gray stone, was large and square, entirely unornamental, and surrounded by that invaluable protection against the Swiss winter, a covered terrace.

On the south side of this terrace, preparations had been made which caused Desmonde to hasten his pace. A rug had been spread on the clean tiles and on this stood a substantial playpen, beside which, seated erect on a hard chair, was an elderly, severe Schweizerdeutsch nurse, immaculately garbed in a fresh linen uniform, a small watch pinned to her breast and around her neck a high starched linen collar, the unendurable tightness and stiffness of which bespoke the wearer's implacable fortitude. And within the pen a little animated bit of life in petticoats was already cajoling Desmonde, on his knees beside the pen.

"She knows me, the darling," Desmonde murmured as I arrived, tears welling from his eyes, adding equally mistakenly: "The moment she saw me, she smiled with recognition all over her darling face."

Yet who knows? He had bathed and bedded the little one so often — he might indeed have touched a slender cord of recognition. He had brought a present for his child, a little silver and ivory rattle and wisely, oh, how wisely — for Desmonde knew women — he handed it to the nurse, who accepted it with a prim, gratified smile, looked it all over, wiped it carefully with a strip of clean linen, then gave it to the child. Immediately, rattles and delighted laughter filled the air. I thereupon left Desmonde to it, aware that he would presently win the approval, if not the sympathy, of the nurse, and be permitted guardedly to handle and to hold his own child. Already he had narrowed the breach by addressing her, with proper humility, in her own Schweizerdeutsch.

Back at the hotel, I asked at the desk for a picnic lunch, went upstairs and changed into shorts, sweater and sneakers. When I came downstairs the neat packet was already at the front desk — what a good hotel was the Reine du Lac!

I went back into the estate, parked the lunch on a seat in the park under one of the big trees, and set off at the double. I had not had my exercise for some time and was sadly missing it.

Around the grounds I went at scout's pace, fifty yards running, then fifty hard walking, an admirable method of progression in which you do not exhaust yourself and which you can keep up indefinitely. In my circling I made out that Desmonde was progressing in his own particular way. First he was given a cushion for his knees, then a chair on which he sat, actually with the child upon his knees. I also had a shrewd suspicion that I was being watched from behind the long curtains of one of the upper windows.

I was still going well when the noon bell tolled, not for the angelus in this canton, but to summon the old men to their dinner at the Home. I then felt it was time for another old man to lunch, the more so since Desmonde, nurse, and child, had disappeared from the terrace. I could have done with a shower. Instead I rubbed myself down with the napkin that enwrapped my lunch, put on my sweater, and sat down on the bench.

What a good lunch! Avoiding the usual unwanted surplus, the packet contained one delicious ham sandwich, a slice of Emmenthaler between two buttered digestive biscuits, then fruit: apple, orange, a huge, heavenly Comice pear. How I enjoyed it all, after my run! Then, having carefully tucked the fruit cores and other fragments into the napkin, I stretched out on my back on the tree-shaded bench. I would willingly have spent the entire summer in this lovely place. Let me confess that at moments such as this I felt rather tired of Desmonde. I had seen quite a lot of him lately, and in his present embittered mood he was not a stimulating companion. But I had given the poor devil my word and, come what may, I would keep it.

I must have fallen asleep; my watch showed half-past two when I awoke. And now a charming little cavalcade was in progress on the avenue that led to the walled garden: the nurse, Desmonde wheeling the child in a little open carriage, and two Kerry Blue terriers following obediently to heel.

I watched them for a few minutes, pleased that everything had been accomplished without open rage or rancor. Then, as I was no longer needed, I decided to take myself off. I had crossed the park and reached the main avenue when I saw a figure beckoning from the west terrace. Although I had no wish to meet Madame Donovan again, I could not well ignore that invitation.

"I could not let you go without apologizing for my atrocious remark to you this morning."

"Please do not worry, Madame. I am used to hard knocks in my profession."

She paused, leaning forward as though in propitiation.

"Won't you let me give you tea. Here, on the terrace."

Again, I could not refuse.

"Thank you, Madame."

She smiled. "I'm sure you are thirsty after all your running. Do sit a moment while I tell Maria."

She returned a few minutes later followed by a stout Italian maid bearing a well-equipped tray. As I accepted my first cup I asked myself: how should one open the conversation?

"You have a very beautiful place here, Madame. And very large, too."

"Yes. When I came here, prices were not high, and I thought it a pity to break up the estate. I even took over the farm and am very glad I did so." She paused. "I have Italian workers, and most excellent they are. You know, I suppose, that many Italians come to work in Switzerland, glad to find work and a decent wage."

"So you are really settled here, Madame?"

"I love Switzerland. Chiefly, of course, for its beauty. But in every way it is an admirable, contented country where the people work hard, the trains run on time — in fact, where everything is in order." She paused. "Naturally, I go home to Ireland for three or four months in the year."

"I am often tempted by Switzerland. But for a very base reason. Taxes."

"Yes, they are kind to us, and to their own people too." She smiled. "You would not settle in Hollywood?"

"Never, madame. Authors are not persona grata there. They are regarded with contempt. Mere scullions!"

"And yet you go there tomorrow."

"I am going for two reasons. Mainly for Desmonde. But also to try to sell my new novel."

There was a silence. Then she said:

"It is sad that Desmonde should not redeem himself more suitably, more nobly. I have been reading again today of a young man who spent all his life in the remote, empoverished interior of China, giving himself to relieving suffering, sickness, and famine."

"Yes, Madame. But for Desmonde to attempt a mission of redemption would be a complete negation of his character. He would get no further than Hong Kong, returning by the first boat with a splendid assortment of K'ang-Hsi china. No, Madame, he must sing his way to salvation!"

She barely smiled. "How do we know what lies ahead for us, or for anyone. The future is unpredictable." She added, "I can't understand why you are so good to him."

"We were great friends at school, and he was very decent to me when I had nothing. I owe it to Desmonde that I sat in the stalls of the Kings Theatre, enthralled by the wonderful performance of Geraldine Moore in *Tosca*." Her expression did not change. "Besides, he has had a very rough time since he got mixed up with your attractive niece."

"It was of his own choosing. You know that Claire is seeking a civil divorce. She is already living with Munzio."

"It makes no difference. We are leaving early tomorrow for Genoa. He will never see her again."

There was a silence. I felt drawn to this woman and, suddenly, immensely sorry for her. She was not made for a virginal life, yet willed herself to it. What could one say? I stood up.

"Now I must go, Madame. I expect Desmonde will stay to see his infant in her bath. Thank you again for your courtesy."

She smiled and said, "Don't fail to let me know if you settle in Switzerland. And come to see me in Ireland when I am there."

"And you, Madame. If you are in London, do visit us in Sussex. My wife would love to know you. She does not get about much, and would welcome you."

"I will come," she said. And in these three words was the beginning of a long and precious friendship.

We shook hands. Then I turned and went back to the hotel. And there, sure enough, outside the hotel garage, thoroughly spattered, awaiting a wash, was the Alfa Romeo. At the front desk I arranged for a car to take us to Genoa the next day, leaving at six thirty. I also asked to have my bill prepared at that hour.

I then went upstairs to my room, feeling unaccountably depressed, perhaps in the knowledge that I had spent a useless week. I therefore sat down and cheered myself up by writing a long letter home, inquiring tenderly, among other things, about the well-being of the new wallflower bed. What a God's blessing it was for a man to have a home and a wife and sons who loved him! Desmonde had none of this, so I must be tolerant of his unmanly rhapsodizing over his child.

He was late in coming to the hotel. I was halfway through dinner when he arrived. He seemed to have little appetite, and ate in absolute silence. Finally, he looked at me with misery in his eyes.

"I gather that my wife is about to divorce me and remarry. If she should claim the child, that would be the end."

What could one say in reply? Nothing. In view of our early start on the morrow we both turned in early.

6

The *Cristoforo Colombo* slid out of the wide harbor with flags flying, speeded away from her home port by the blare of sirens and the ringing of churchbells. We had arrived in Genoa with two hours to spare, ample time to collect the packages awaiting us at the offices of the Italian Line. All that we had ordered was there, everything, neatly packaged and awaiting transit through customs. What a triumph of London craftsmanship, skill, efficiency and integrity. Normal and expected features of that age, no doubt, but could they be duplicated in the present day? The mere question is absurd.

I had left Desmonde busily unwrapping in our stateroom while I went aft, on deck, to watch the receding coastline and to renew my acquaintance with this lovely ship in which I had voyaged once before. I was extremely fond of these Italian ships, not only because they followed the southern route, but for everything else: speed, comfort, and a typical Italian type of service, willing and friendly. Below, the head steward was already taking bookings for tables, and I reserved the side table on the port side where my wife and I had previously been seated. Then I looked in at the little chapel, a delightful feature of this line. Already an Italian padre was on his knees there, so I knew that we should have Mass every morning. One last trip to the sun deck, where I reserved two well-placed chairs. No covered promenade deck for me, on this perennially sunny voyage.

Back in the cabin I found Desmonde seated and steadily regarding his new clothes, all laid out on his bed. Ever since leaving Switzerland he had been in a queer, often morose, mood. I accordingly approached him with a guarded cheerfulness.

"Tried anything on yet, for fit, size, color and cut?"

"No! I'm just thinking what a popinjay I shall look in them. Do you know that this is the second time in my beastly life that I have been outfitted by charity?"

I laughed. "Keep on your old duds then, if you'll feel more comfortable."

"And waste all that you've done for me. It will be wasted anyway."

"Come now, Des! Pull yourself together. You haven't been at all yourself lately."

"Could you expect me to be!" Desmonde rarely used foul language, but now he did. "My child in charge of an old perpetual virgin who hates me. My wife in bed with a big Italian bastard, getting it hot and hard every night and loving it." He put his hand to his head. "Oh, God, I still love her, bitch though she was, still is, and ever will be. And here I am, bloody swine that I am, sponging, sponging on you, costing you the earth — and all for nothing. That publicity freak won't get me to sing. And even if she does I'll fall flat on my face."

There was only one thing to do and I did it. I went out of the cabin and quietly closed the door. Naturally I was worried. If he broke down now, how should I feel, backing a horse that refused to go to the post? Nevertheless, I was hungry, and at half-past twelve I went down to lunch, where my steward from the previous voyage greeted me with affection — I must therefore have tipped him handsomely.

"But are we alone, sir?" he inquired sadly, fitting me tenderly into my chair.

"Not at all. I have a friend . . ."

At that moment precisely Desmonde appeared, a new Desmonde, washed, shaved, brushed, attired in the smashing new gray suiting, the new soft-collared shirt and near-Old Etonian tie, the new brown handmade shoes, and silk hosiery. The steward, further overpowered by Desmonde's perfect Italian and his equally perfect knowledge of all Italian dishes on the menu, took our orders in an attitude almost of prayer, then retreated, backwards.

"I'm terribly sorry, A. J." Desmonde said, firmly unwrapping his napkin. "In fact, I'm damned sorry. But no more of it, I promise you."

He was as good as his word. Never again did he lapse into that abysmal mood during the voyage. Yet he was not the cheerful, lighthearted Desmonde I had once known. Moody and irritable, he seemed obsessed by an inward brooding.

The wind blew lightly, the sun shone, Desmonde did as he pleased, mainly on his back in his deck chair with his eyes closed, moodily avoiding all attempts at shipboard acquaintance. I followed my usual enjoyable routine: up fairly early for a run around the deck and some easy exercises in the gym, a plunge in the pool, then the short Mass and Communion in the chapel. I was then ready for a good breakfast and a lazy, lazy day in the sun. Unfortunately, the nice little padre latched on to me. He came from a most laudable institution in Rome, to which I had been enticed on a visit to that city some years before, and which was run by young priests who taught useful handicrafts to the homeless boys taken off the streets. The purpose of his visit to the United States was, inevitably, to collect money from the various Italian communities in New York and other large cities. I should have had him at my side all the voyage had I not given him a fifty with the whispered confession that my doctors had prescribed silence and complete rest for me, owing to an affliction of the liver. But before he left me I asked him about Desmonde, briefly explaining my friend's present situation. His answer was emphatic and immediate.

"He will never be at peace, never, never, never, until he returns to the Church. I have seen it before, many, many times. Once you quarrel with the Lord, you will never be happy till you make up and tell Him you are sorry."

Too soon we were across, the engines ceased their violent throbbing, and we glided past the Statue of Liberty into New York harbor. How pleasant to disembark when one has little luggage. Carrying each a light suitcase, we walked freely past crowds of passengers gathered in confusion around enormous piles of huge cabin trunks, baby carriages, golf bags, and other paraphernalia of travel *en famille*. Immigration had been passed on the ship. We simply took a taxi to Penn Station and the morning train to Chicago that connected with the Super Chief, on which I booked a double compartment.

Those who know only the utilitarian, strike-dislocated trains of today, or who simply travel by air, cannot conceive of the splendor and luxury of that magnificent train. We changed stations at Chicago and there, awaiting us, was the Super Chief, shining with the potential of speed, a great greyhound waiting to be unleashed. The red carpet was already unrolled and, to the sound of music — preamble of Hollywood, ridiculous, yet agreeable — we boarded the monster. Our double compartment was ready, indescribably immaculate, fresh antimacassars on the seats, the two bunks folded up against the partition, the bathroom spotless, and the car attendant, white teeth gleaming in a smile, asking if we wished breakfast. As we drank coffee the train pulled out silently on its flashing dash across America.

Twice before I had made this journey, but it was a novelty for Desmonde. Yet he was never interested or relaxed, gazing moodily through the window, and as we approached our destination he began to show signs of anxiety and tension only partly dispelled by a Western Union telegram handed to him at Albuquerque which said curtly:

GET OFF AT PASADENA. WILL MEET YOU THERE.

"At least she expects us," Desmonde muttered.

"Expects *you*," I corrected him. "I'll get the hoof!"

At Pasadena, where most of the Hollywood elite leave the train, we obeyed the telegram and got off. Our attendant had been wonderfully good all the way. I shall never forget his remark when I tipped him a ten-dollar bill. "Ain't seen one o' them in a long, long time!"

And there, on the platform, in full flesh, was the little Delia B. She reached up and embraced Desmonde. I heard the smack of the kiss.

"Glad to see you, darling. Everything's planned and ready. You're looking good." Then to me: "Why in hell are you here, Red?"

"I'm the valet."

"Then stay valet. I've only a single room booked for Desmonde at the Beverly Hills."

"In that case I'll make do with the four-room cottage I've reserved in the Beverly Hills garden."

She actually laughed. "You win, Red. You want to bunk in with him, Des?"

"Don't you think I'd better?" Desmonde said drily. "You see, I wouldn't be here but for A. J. He's paid cash for everything, even the clothes I'm wearing."

"Not bad, Red, not bad. You got anything of your own to do here?"

"Certainly. I'm here to sell my new book."

"I think I heard about that one. *The Cuticle,* ain't it?"

"That's the one, Delia B. The story of an ingrowing toenail."

We got into her car, not the opulence I had expected, but a knocked-about Ford which she drove with all the slapdash abandon of her nature. She parked at the hotel and, when we had registered, came through the garden to the cottage to make sure that I had not been lying.

"Not bad, not bad, Red. You got the doings. This will set you back plenty."

"My wife and I had it last year."

"Why didn't you let me know you were in town? Ah, well, this will suit nicely for you, Des. Just do nothing, rest up over the weekend. The big day is still uncertain but may come soon."

When she had gone, we unpacked and stretched out on long

chairs in the sun. At that period, before the increase in population, automobiles, and industries had darkened the light coastal mist into smog, Beverly Hills was one of the most enchanting resorts in Southern California, and the hotel at which we were staying one of the best.

We simply lay about that day, but after dinner in the hotel restaurant I rang my agent, Frank Vincent, at his home. He knew that we had arrived from a splash in the *Evening Sun*.

"How do you like your new job, A. J.?"

"It's a lot easier than writing best-sellers."

"Well, if you can stop pressing pants tomorrow morning, will you come out here for breakfast?"

"I'd love to, Frank. I'll get all the shoes brushed tonight. Say, how are you doing with that book of mine?"

"Great, A. J. I've got Metro hot as a five-dollar gun. You know I've refused one offer from Paramount."

"What about a bird in the hand, Frank?"

"The bird they offered hadn't enough feathers. A measly hundred thousand."

"That ain't hay, Frank. But you know best, only don't sell me short. Listen, I'd like to bring a new customer along with me tomorrow. At present he's only a prospect, but I think he might be big stuff."

"Bring him along, A. J. I gather he's got Bedelia B. behind him. Anyway, I'm looking forward to seeing you."

We both slept well that night. However one may laud the Super Chief, there is no escape from the symphony of the rails.

Next morning at nine o'clock we were in Frank Vincent's top-floor downtown apartment, I, at least, conscious of the esteem manifested by the invitation to Frank's home, rather than to his busy office. Frank, a clean-living man of the highest principles who never had a contract with his clients beyond his given word, was devoted to his health, an idiosyncrasy typically exemplified in his choice of breakfast. When he had asked us what we wanted he rang down to the kitchen, gave the order, and added: "The usual for me, please."

The "usual," which came up with our coffee and rolls, was an inviting assortment of prepared raw vegetables: cut radishes, spring onions, dainty little carrots, hearts of lettuce, choice pieces of cauliflower, and fragrant strips of celery, all fresh that morning from the Farmers' Market. We agreed afterward that we could well have forgone our excellent rolls and butter for such a mouth-watering spread.

Meanwhile, we talked, first of the chances of my book, then of Desmonde, whose dossier I reeled off while Frank listened intently.

"It's very apparent —" he smiled at Desmonde — "that Bedelia B. is absolutely sold on you. And that, incidentally, is a rare bit of luck, for when Bedelia B. backs anyone or anything she usually sees it through. Mind you, she's not the queen. That title belongs to Louella Parsons, a very different type and a great lady. But Bedelia is on the up-and-up, a sticker, who never lets a thing go, once she has her teeth in it. For days past she's been dropping hints, thick as a paper chase, mostly directed toward the young Caruso group. So the next move is up to her."

"What do you think this will be?" asked Desmonde.

"It's an easy guess. Bedelia has a terrific in with the really big movie people: Selznick, Sam Goldwyn, Mayer, particularly Sam. The next time one of them throws a big party, she'll have you there, Desmonde. My guess again is that she'll fix a real slam-bang opening for you. Take it, my boy, and you're in. And if you're in, don't sign any quick contracts or you'll bitterly regret it. I'll be here, waiting to help you make that first million."

When we left Frank some twenty minutes later, I felt that Desmonde had been impressed.

"You like him?"

"Who wouldn't?" He smiled drily. "And I rather fancied his breakfast."

"Frank has done me an awful lot of good. I don't mind what he eats."

[302]

Now there was nothing we could do but wait. And how pleasant, in that golden era, to idle in the garden of the Beverly Hills Hotel. The big blue pool was there for the early morning plunge, then the quick walk to the nearby resort of the faithful. How often, and always in vain, did I ask Desmonde to accompany me rather than watch me gloomily as I set off. He awaited me in the sun, studying me morosely when I returned.

"Got your sins forgiven?" he asked me sarcastically, one morning when I was later than usual.

"No, Desmonde! But I had a good, and I hope useful talk with Father Devis."

Fortunately, at that moment breakfast rolled in, crisp bread wrapped in a napkin, honey, coffee in the silver thermos pitcher and, best of all, the big pink grapefruit, halved and ready to be eaten.

Erich Remarque had a cottage next to ours, and most afternoons, when he was not entertaining a lady friend, he came down for tea and a chat. He was an interesting fellow, with one of the finest collections of Impressionist paintings I have ever known. Of course they were not with him, but on loan to the Metropolitan in New York, where I had often enviously drooled over them. When I teased Erich on the fabulous cost of these masterpieces he replied quite simply, and truthfully, that he had bought these treasures at ridiculously low prices when they were quite unrecognized.

On the fifth day of our stay, when I had begun to worry about the bill, we received a short yet momentous visit from Bedelia, who suddenly appeared as from thin air, pounced like an eagle upon Desmonde and, hooking him by the arm, walked him up and down, articulating rapidly into his ear. Intermittently Desmonde would nod in acquiescence. Finally, Bedelia returned him to the cottage where, with empressement, she produced a large and magnificently ornate card.

"Take care of this, Des, for although you'll wind up the star of the party, without it you'll never get in."

"What about my ticket, Delia B.?"

"Ah, Red," she said kindly. "You don't want no ticket. Abe's parties are big stuff. Authors definitely included out."

"Come on, D. B. Give. I'm entitled to see the fun. I'll sit like a mouse in one corner."

"Mice are out too, Red." Suddenly she laughed, handing over another ticket. "I guess you're due to be in on it. But see you clean yourself up nice, and don't even mention the word books, or you'll be chucked out on the spot."

On Delia B.'s departure, we examined the beautiful tickets: formal gold-edged, gold-engraved invitations to a party to be given by Abe Finkelstein at his home in Beverly Hills, on the evening of June 12th. I looked at Desmonde. "Only four more days to wait!" After our big trip out, it seemed a very short time.

"Have you decided what to sing?" I asked. "The set piece, I suppose — the Prize Song?"

"Good God! Am I a school kid who has just learned up one bloody song? I'll sing whatever comes up my bloody back." After a pause he added: "I'm tired of that damn aria and I'm sure you are too. Let's not talk about it, A. J. We'll just go and see what happens."

The rule of silence was strictly observed, although the imminence of that fateful night weighed upon us. When, finally, it was upon us, we got ourselves, in the words of Delia B., cleaned up nice. I could never, on any occasion, look soigné, but Desmonde, bathed, shaved, in his dark suit and other new accouterments, really looked smashing, a starlet's dream of delight. He was at his best a sensationally handsome young man, and rest, sunshine, and the Beverly Hills good living had put a bloom on him.

When we were both ready we sat looking at each other in silence, since Delia B. had strictly enjoined Desmonde to arrive late, extremely late. Desmonde was calm, with that expression of complete indifference, now almost habitual. This was his moment of truth, the crux of a checkered career that might bring dazzling success or abysmal failure. Even for me, who mattered not at all, this waiting was hell.

At half-past ten, after several earlier false starts, sternly repressed, we passed through the hotel to a waiting taxi. The drive was short, too short, before we drew up at the large, brightly illuminated house. Our humble taxi was clearly suspect by the posse of police on duty at the entrance, but our tickets were eventually validated and we passed into the house, where our hats were accepted by another detective, disguised as a butler, who showed us to the great drawing room of the house. On the threshold we looked at each other, took a deep breath, and went in.

The enormous room, brilliantly lit by two huge Venetian chandeliers, furnished and decorated, carpeted and draped with the taste and luxury that extreme wealth can command, and sporting two Steinway grand pianos, one at each end, was populated by perhaps forty human beings, the sexes separated according to American custom, so that the elegantly gowned women chattered in a gay group on one side, while the men, many immediately recognizable as international stars, were scattered around, self-consciously playing the role of he-men, on the other.

Between the two groups, on an elevated little platform, sat the inimitable Abe, master of all he surveyed, surrounded by intimates, among whom, beside a couple of hard-faced men, and in full battle array, with a scarlet ostrich feather in her hair, was Delia B. At one of the grand pianos sat Richard Tauber. At the other, much to my relief, John McCormack, and behind John on a little settee, John's wife. Both of these splendid people were my friends, so I immediately made tracks across the room and sat down beside Lily, who welcomed me with a smile. No finer or sweeter woman ever set foot in Hollywood.

Now she whispered, "John tells me there's something cooking."

Desmonde, alone in the doorway, was naturally a conspicuous figure, but after surveying the room with complete composure, he walked quietly to a deserted area of that magnificent chamber, sat down in a Louis XVII gilt armchair, crossed his legs, and with an air of remote interest, let his eyes rest on a stupendous Andrea del Sarto on the opposite wall depicting in some detail The Rape of the Sabine Women. Indeed, as Desmonde viewed it, a slight critical lift of his left eyebrow seemed to indicate that in his considered opinion it was not by the hand of the master, but rather by one of his pupils, possibly Jacopo Fellini.

Was it my imagination, or was there a lull in the feline chatter, almost a silence, as eyes were compelled toward this elegant, imperturbable, solitary figure? Nothing attracts women more in Hollywood than the attractive, when it is unknown, and a man. Naturally, all the lovelies had their beauteous optics trained on Desmonde. These were stars of the silver screen, world-famous. Some were without talent, but drilled by clever directors into some semblance of the histrionic art, performers who could be taught to mime the requisite emotions upon request — I shall leave them nameless. But others there were, with great, magnificent talent. I could see Grace Moore, Carole Lombard, Lila Lee and, sitting a little apart from the others, Ethel Barrymore and Norma Shearer.

There was, in fact, little else to attract. Tauber and John were playing little operatic snippets and tossing them across to one another, in a competitive kind of game. But the party had, in fact, dwindled to that midpoint in Hollywood parties when everyone is talked out, and waiting for something to happen before supper.

It was then that a woman detached herself from the group on the settee and, as every eye was turned upon her, slowly approached Desmonde. She was Grace Moore, slim, attractive, and already famous as a singer. She paused and held out her hand as she reached Desmonde, who immediately stood up. At that moment Puccini took over, skillfully led in by John at the

piano, and Grace, drawing near to Desmonde, began to sing
that incomparable Bridal Aria from *Butterfly*.

> *Quest obi pomposa*
> *Di scioglier mi tard*
> *Si vesta la sposa.*

Very beautifully she sang the first part of the love duet. Then
Desmonde broke in.

> *Con moti di scojattolo*
> *I nodi attenta e scaeglio !*
> *Pensar che quel gioca ttolo*
> *E mia mogli !* . . .

Let it be said, without further transcription, that this beautiful and touching love duet was continued with appropriate
amatory gestures. So unexpected, so gracefully accomplished,
and with such restrained perfection of the male voice — there
was immediate applause.

"Desmonde," said Grace, "that was delightful. I did enjoy
it. So kind of you to keep yourself in check, and not drown me
out. Now ! You must sing for your supper, alone."

With a smile Grace disengaged herself and sat down.

Desmonde smiled too, but with assumed modesty. He was
off to a good start and was taking no risks : I knew it would
be the set piece. He said :

"If it would not bore all the famous and distinguished people
here I would like to offer a great aria, which has been sung
by a voice infinitely greater than mine : the voice of Enrico
Caruso."

It was a brilliant move. At the outset he had set himself up
against the ultimate in perfection. A few suppressed female
titters, followed by dead silence. Then with complete composure
— that mood of uncaring unconcern that had lately possessed

him — Desmonde began to sing. I had hoped he would play it safe and sing the Prize Song, but he did not.

It was that last, wild, heartbreaking, aria of Mario in *Tosca*, as he was led to his execution.

> *Amaro sol per te m'era il morire*
> *Da te la vita prende ogni splendori . . .*

I had heard that aria several times before, but never, never as Desmonde sang it now, with all the feeling, the bitterness that was in his heart.

There were no titters now, no whispers, scarcely a movement. Desmonde was really giving them the works. And when that final cry, *"Avra solo da te voce e colore,"* hit the ceiling, the applause, for a party of this nature, was astounding. Everyone was standing. John stood up at the piano, roaring, "Bravo. Bravissimo!" Tauber joined the tumult on the bass keys of the piano. Delia B. with cupped hands was trying to make herself heard. I was doing my bit with the full force of my lungs, but at the same time stealing toward the door. Desmonde had done it! Now I was no longer needed, a mere accessory after the fact. As I stood for a moment in the doorway I heard Delia B.'s voice come through:

"Now sing the Prize Song, Des."

"Yes, do, Desmonde," cried John. "But first, now that Mario is gone, let's have something simple and tender for the ladies. Sing Purcell's 'Passing By.' "

A silence fell while Desmonde seemed to reflect. Then he smiled to John. I hoped it would be the Purcell, the sweetest and most tender of them all. And so it was. Half-turning to the ladies he raised his voice:

> *There is a lady sweet and kind,*
> *Was never face so pleased my mind,*
> *I did but see her passing by,*
> *And yet I love her till I die.*

Nothing could have been more captivating, more intimate. And so different from the *Tosca*. One glance at those rapt, listening faces assured me that it was a perfect choice.

Then, quietly, I took off.

7

I came away from that great beautiful brilliant room, my ears still resounding with the swelling acclamation of all within, and set out at a hard pace for Beverly Hills. I knew I ran the risk of being picked up — night walkers are criminally suspect in that choice district — yet it was only a short way to the hotel and I felt I must violently exorcise my inner turmoil.

Desmonde had done it. He had more than done it, he had justified himself at last, and how rosy would be his future from now on. And now, even as I exulted, I wanted only one thing: to get home, as urgently, as speedily as train and ship could take me. I had done what I set out to do, I had helped my friend at some inconvenience to myself — nothing more was demanded of me. And oh, how overpowering was the vision of my little country house and garden and of all the dear people within. The raspberries and currants would be in full swing, the Victoria plums and greengages coming along, the roses in all splendor, at their best.

I reached the hotel in record time, and at the desk made inquiry as to the method and means of sudden departure. I was not lucky enough to catch a returning Super Chief, but the ordinary Chicago train, nonsleeper, was due to leave at 6 A.M. that very morning — it was now past 4 A.M. I immediately paid the bill for the cottage till the end of the week, thus securing a fuller cooperation from the night clerk, who rang Los Angeles Station and booked me a first-class reservation on the Chicago train. We then studied the trans-Atlantic sailings from New York. With luck I might be aboard the *Queen Mary* leaving on the following Saturday. I then tipped the clerk, explaining that my friend would probably return later that day, and went through the hotel and garden to the cottage.

Here I packed my belongings, and sat down and wrote a note to Desmonde, which I left on the desk. I then rang Frank Vincent. Surprisingly, his voice came over the wire at once.

"Frank," I said. "I know you hate being wakened, but this is A. J. and I absolutely had to call you."

"Don't worry, A. J. I've already been called four times in the last hour."

"Then you know he's made it. In a big way."

"I know, A. J. I'm just waiting for the early editions."

"Frank, I rang you to let you know I'm bowing out by the six A.M. train. I've done my little bit and now I'm relying on you to take care of the new star."

"I'll do that. Say, A. J., now you've done everything, double plus, for the guy, don't you want to stay and cash in on it?"

"I guess not, Frank. I've had an awful lot of Desmonde lately. I need a little rest, back home."

"I get you, A. J. Say, your book hits the bookstores and libraries today. Rely on me to cash in on that."

"Thanks a lot, Frank. Good luck and goodbye."

"Same to you, A. J."

How easily one falls into the idiom of Hollywood. I hung up with a warm feeling around the pericardium and, as I was too bung-full of impetus to rest, I went back to the desk and asked the clerk to call a taxi. This he did, the night porter brought my suitcase from the cottage, and I was off.

At the station I picked up and paid for my ticket. My train was at Track 2, the engine, no Super Chief but a solid cross-country plodder, already with steam up. I hung around waiting for the morning papers to come in. Just before we pulled out I managed to grab a copy of the Hollywood *Star,* and there it was, splashed across the front page:

Last night at a splendid reception given by the King of Hollywood, our beloved Abe Finkelstein, in the presence of all
the top stars of his kingdom, Desmonde Fitzgerald, a young
man, admittedly of great personal attraction, one might even
say beauty, but completely unknown, rescued from menial toil
in Dublin, held his audience of stars, all experienced, worldly
wise, and talented in their own right, utterly spellbound for
more than an hour by the magic of his voice, while he sang his
way into their hearts with selections from grand opera, and
in their own languages, arias of Italy and Germany, and above
all, through repeated encores, the touching songs of his native
Ireland.

When at last, perforce, the recital was over, though all
would have wished it to continue, every living being in that
magnificent salon, not excepting our beloved Abe himself, stood
up and took Desmonde to their hearts with a prolonged standing ovation. Not since Caruso took the U.S.A. by storm has
such a voice been heard in America, the equal or, dare one
say — yes one dares — the superior of the great Italian
Maestro.

Lots more of this followed, lusher and lusher, and I read
every word of it, forced to confess that as one horrendous superlative followed another, so did the warmth around my heart
expand. Full credit to the little trumpeter, but I had helped, in
my own way, helped to rescue this splendid talent from despair
and hopelessness.

We were now pounding over the metals at a steady pace. I
wrapped myself in my coat and, as the seat in front of me was
empty, I put up my feet and went to sleep.

This train was, in reality, a penance after the luxury of the
Super Chief. But I have a strange masochistic streak which
makes me welcome sufferings and tribulations, provided I have
the ability to endure them: suffer in silence has, in my view,
always been an admirable admonition.

I shall therefore pass over my journey to Chicago with no
other comment than that I was delivered safely to the New

York express, which sped me to Penn Station with just enough time to board the *Queen Mary* within an hour of her departure, in which accomplishment I must again extol the virtue of traveling light.

My first action on board was to cleanse myself in a prolonged hot bath. I then asked the steward for the English papers. He brought me *The Times*, the *Daily Telegraph* and the *Daily Mail*. From this selection I must steel myself to endure the critiques of my new novel, just published in England and America. But first I was burning to find out whether news of Desmonde had percolated. And there, indeed, on the front page of the *Daily Mail* was a passable photograph of Desmonde, and the following embarrassing screed:

> Young Irish tenor, Desmonde Fitzgerald, who, under the auspices of his friend, *Citadel* author A. J. Cronin, hit Hollywood like a bomb last week, has now signed contracts to play the lead in *The Young Caruso* scheduled for immediate filming by Paramount. Only one slight snag: Fitzgerald reputedly sings better than Caruso!

This was good news, in that it put the final hard practical touch to our joint adventure. Frank Vincent would ensure that Desmonde's contract was gilt-edged — in Frank's terminology, a bonanza.

I did not feel like spoiling this good moment by turning directly to the literary pages. I thought, with despicable cowardice, that I would first take a little exercise. The windward side of the promenade deck was completely untenanted, the breeze blew fresh, and I set out to enjoy a fast walk. No ship was better fitted for such exercise than the beloved *Queen* — I cannot vouch for actual measurements, but the broad sweep of her promenade deck seemed almost as long as a football field.

The chief deck steward, in his cross-deck snuggery, had been watching me from time to time with some amusement, and when I finally drew up beside him he said:

"You're a great walker, Mr. Cronin, sir, I remember you well from a couple of years back, on the outward trip. My mate said you practically walked your way to New York."

"It's because I'm nervous, steward."

He laughed. "Never saw a fitter man. By the way, sir, I think it might interest you to take a slow walk down the port side."

"How so?"

"We're fairly light this trip and it's not a sunny morning. But there's exactly thirty-two passengers in the deck chairs, and believe it or not, every one of them is reading the same book."

"The Bible."

"Something more interesting, sir. When I went around with the bouillon, not one of them put it down. Why not take a look?"

I took a look, moving slowly along the deck, prolonging one of the best moments of my life, one which, alone, was worth my long journey. Every single passenger was reading — clearly distinguishable by its brand-new yellow jacket with the name splashed across — yes, *The Citadel*. I walked back, to enjoy it again.

To the steward, who was smiling, I said sadly:

"It's hell! They've started giving them away already!"

Then I went down and, seated alone at my usual table, enjoyed a very excellent lunch. When I returned to my cabin I again turned, though reluctantly, to the papers. Suddenly, my eye was caught and held by a paragraph that put all thought of literary criticism out of my head.

DOUBLE FATALITY ON THE GOTTHARD

Early yesterday morning, an Italian couple, Madame and Signor Munzio, traversing the Gotthard Pass in a sports Alfa Romeo, were hurled to their deaths by a sudden freak ice storm.

Signor Munzio, well-known on this route as a fast and

skillful driver, was warned of the danger on the Swiss side, and strongly advised to take the tunnel train. But as the barriers were not yet up he persisted in an attempt to beat the storm. Alas, without success. Both bodies have now been recovered. The car is a total wreck.

8

The news of Desmonde's meteoric career was fully conveyed to us through the public press. His first film, *The Young Caruso,* was a spectacular international success, followed almost immediately by an equally successful Hollywood adaptation of *Der Rosenkavalier.* Meanwhile came records, *Operatic Gems, Irish Songs, Love Songs,* sending Desmonde's voice over the air and into a multitude of homes.

From Desmonde himself we heard only in short infrequent snatches, hurriedly written on postcards: "Working hard, here on location, and hating it." And again, "After three retakes under kleig lights, how dark the world seems. I am worn-out, but resolved to stay the course."

I had begun to think that he had forgotten me and all that I had done for him when, one afternoon, almost a year later, a huge metal-bound packing case was delivered to me at Sullington, the markings indicating that it had come from New York. With Dougal's help I opened it in the barn and there, after innumerable wrappings had been removed, was a breathtaking Degas, at least five feet by four, *Après le Bain,* immediately recognizable as the master's late and best period, when he used color unreservedly to offset the lovely nude female form stepping gracefully from her bath, an arm extended for the towel handed by the maid.

Even Dougal was impressed as we both gazed at it in silence, my heart meanwhile beating like mad with joy.

"It must have cost a pretty penny, sir," he said, at last.

"The earth, Dougal. It's priceless, really. Far beyond my purse. And just the one picture I needed for my collection."

"It's a beautiful thing, sir. Even I can tell that. But," he looked at me slyly, "what will the wee laddies say when you hing it up?"

"They'll just have to be educated up to it, Dougal." I laughed, fully aware of the comments that would be made in regard to the lady's beautiful bottom.

When we got it to the house I sat down and wrote Desmonde a long rapturous letter, thanking him for his most wonderful gift and begging him to take time to write me fully. We had all heard of his successes, yet we knew nothing of him. I then gave him all the news I thought might interest him. I had recently had a visit from Madame Donovan, and could assure him that all was well with his little daughter. But Canon Daly had been ill and was on sick leave from Saint Teresa's. My sons had made another sortie on the wallflower bed. I had begun a new novel which Nan was busy typing. My wife was now better after a recent rather worrying attack.

I ended by again beseeching him to write to me unreservedly and soon.

I then sealed the letter and, summoning Nan, who liked nothing better than a walk, we set off to the village to post it.

"What do you think of the new masterpiece, Nanno?"

She thought for a moment, then said:

"Very beautiful. But frankly, Maister, for me, it's a little bit much."

"You would have preferred a view of Sleaford Parish Church?"

"Yes, if painted by Utrillo."

We both laughed. I took her arm and said, "Pictures apart, I'm terribly happy to have heard from Desmonde. Although I've a feeling that *he* is not happy."

"I'm sure he's not."

"Why not?"

"When he was a priest serving the Lord he *was* happy. Now

he's merely a servant of the American moving picture industry."

"What a pity he ever met and loved that girl. I can't speak ill of her, now she's dead."

"The pity is that he was weak enough to fall for her. Love is quite a different cup of tea, Maister."

"Would you care to expound on the nature of that tender emotion, professor?"

"Certainly. I love you, and I am happy to think that you love me. But we both have the virtue, the strength, and decency, quite apart from our love of dear Mum, to remain chaste. Desmonde, the weakling, did not have that. Now he's an outcast, blaming the Lord for what was entirely his own fault. He'll never find peace until he flings himself down on his pretty face and begs for forgiveness."

"That's exactly what an Italian padre said to me on the *Cristoforo Colombo,* when I spoke to him of Desmonde."

Now we were in the village. I stamped and posted the letter.

"How about a coffee at the Copper Kettle? And one of these jolly good homemade gingerbread squares?"

"Oh, good. And we'll bring Mum some. She's fond of that gingerbread."

We walked home by the Canon's Walk, holding hands in silence.

My hope of an early reply from Desmonde was gradually dulled. I gathered from the popular weeklies that he was busy beginning his third picture, and resigned myself to wait. And indeed, I heard nothing for a further three months, when I received the following long and extraordinary communication.

My dear A. J.,

I have withheld my letters for so long simply because I have had nothing to say. Indeed, my state of being has been so permanently depressed, troubled, and unhappy that I have refrained from inflicting it upon you.

You know, I suppose, that the popular romantic conception of Hollywood is a myth, fostered by those to whom glamour is the catchword for box office receipts. I can now assure you that the actual life in the studios is a hard, grinding, incomparably wearing business where, under blinding white lights, one repeats, often many times, a single piece of action or dialogue that forms a minute part of the completed film, or in the final analysis may even be cut out altogether. When not on the spot, under these blinding lights, one waits one's turn to be called, scanning the daily papers for news of the outside world. It is a dehumanizing existence which drives many of the actors, if I may so call the puppets controlled by a megaphoned director, to nightly excesses that hit the headlines, adding luster to the popular notion of a glorious, gilded existence.

But enough, all this was borne in on me when I started work on my first picture. I then decided that I would endure this unnatural life, an existence utterly barren of all that I had previously enjoyed and loved, for three years and no more. I would then have fulfilled my three-picture contract and acquired a large fortune that would enable me to disappear, suddenly and forever, from this hollow city of glittering make-believe.

So far I have succeeded in pursuing my intention, and Frank Vincent, one of my few friends in this wilderness, has advised me well, and most admirably managed my affairs. Frank keeps urging me to take up some form of relaxation, to play golf at Bel Air, or to join the Racquet Club at Palm Springs. He has even suggested that I pick myself a nice girl from the flock of lovely starlets, poor little playthings, who hang around me, hoping and hoping to be noticed and taken up for the "break" that would lead them to fame and fortune. Alas, they are out of luck with me. I have learned my lesson, and it was a bitter, bitter one. For this same reason I never, but never, go to parties.

How, then, do I spend such spare time as my overlords allow me? I live permanently in one of the Beverly Hills cottages, where everything is done for me and I am free of all housekeeping worries. On my free days, I drive out to Malibu in my unostentatious car, park, then walk, walk for miles on Malibu Beach, that great wide stretch of sand on which the waves of the Pacific thunder endlessly. Few people use this stretch, far from the swimming beach and bathing huts, and I encounter only two regulars: Charles Chaplin, too enwrapped in his own genius to be conscious of anyone but himself, and a tall, strongly built man who walks slowly, reading, but who occasionally nods and smiles to me as we pass. These apart, one can find solitude, and here I walk, struggling with myself and with my own unhappy thoughts.

You know, of course, that I have abandoned all my religious

beliefs, in the beginning from a sense of anger and resentment at the unjust punishment meted out to me for a fault not entirely my own. Anger fades after a time, so too does resentment, and I will now confess to you that I have several times, at first feebly and then more strongly, had the incentive to seek the quiet of the church in Beverly Hills which you yourself frequented — not for purposes of prayer, but from a kind of curiosity to see how it would affect me, or if indeed it would in some way alleviate the inner ferment that churns, like a live thing, in my breast.

Now mark this, A. J., and you know that I am not and never have been, a liar. On three separate occasions when I approached the church and climbed the steps with the intention of entering it, a frightful spasm took possession of me. I trembled, felt deathly sick and thought I must vomit but could not. Although unable to be physically sick, a stream of words issued from my lips. You know that I have never been addicted to the use of foul language. But these words were unbelievably foul, blasphemous and obscene. So violent were my spasms I thought I would have a fit. I turned and stumbled down the steps. Only when my feet were on the pavement of the public road did my agitation and vituperations cease. I felt the blood course back to my arms, my legs; in short, within a few moments I was myself again.

The first time this occurred I was not only alarmed, but so shaken that I made up my mind never to risk a repetition of the experience. Nevertheless, I was curious as to the nature of my attack and presently came to the conclusion that I had been the victim of a physical reaction, possibly cardiac in origin.

To test this theory I drove out to the summit of Bel Air. Here I parked the car, walked downhill for perhaps a hundred yards, turned, and set myself to climb this steep incline at top speed. When I reached my car I was slightly blown, but no more, than I would normally have expected.

I drove back to my cottage, thoughtful and indeed worried. I was certainly the victim of some strange phobia, connected with the church in Beverly Hills. You will remember that I refused to accompany you to this particular church.

For the next few weeks I was busy in the studio, faking my way through the love scenes in the Hollywood version of *Rosenkavalier*. But on my first free Saturday I drove through the city of Los Angeles to the big new Catholic Church off Sunset Boulevard. I parked the car and, calmly facing the church, assured myself that

I was sound in mind and body. I then set my teeth and began to walk up the steps of the great church.

My God, A. J., how can I write you of my experience — worse, much worse than before — so violent that I fell down in a fit, rolled down the steps, and came to myself in the center of a crowd, with a policeman supporting my head.

Fortunately he knew me and fully realized that I was cold sober.

"You took a nasty toss, sir. And not the first here. They built these steps far too steep."

I got to my feet, thanked him, and assured him that I was not hurt. But as I drove back to Beverly Hills I was deeply and profoundly worried.

In this mood I reported for work at the studio, where I went through some fatuous love scene retakes with the leading lady, who has for weeks been trying to get off with me.

On the following day, Sunday, I drove out to Malibu, walked far along the strand, and sat down to examine my situation. Without doubt I was, under certain conditions, no longer master of myself or of my actions. A phrase from a poem learned in childhood came to mind. "I am the captain of my soul." I was no longer master of my soul. And if so, what next was in store for me?

Alarmed, crushed by this thought, I put my head between my hands, striving for self-control. Without doubt I must seek advice. A doctor, a psychiatrist? I knew of no one.

At this moment I became aware that someone was speaking to me.

"Are you ill? Can I be of assistance to you?"

The tall man whom I had often passed was bending toward me.

"No . . . no, thank you. I'll be all right in a minute."

He looked at me doubtfully, then sat down beside me.

"You are Desmonde Fitzgerald, are you not? The film star?"

I nodded silently. This was no beastly autograph hunter. He had a strong, lined, intellectual face. Suddenly I had a premonition that this was no chance encounter.

"I enjoyed your first film. Partly because I had often heard Caruso sing, in Italy. I found it difficult to decide which voice was superior, his or yours." He paused. "I believe you also have sung in Italy."

Now there was no doubt whatsoever. This man knew me. And from my earliest beginnings. Suddenly I had an impulse to unburden myself. I was in trouble. Perhaps he might help me. Then came the counterthought: don't make an ass of yourself with a total stranger. I got to my feet.

"I'll walk back now," I said.

"I'll come with you, if I may. I have often wished to speak with you, so often — forgive me — so often have I seen sadness and unhappiness written upon your face."

"Are you a doctor?"

"Of sorts."

"You seem to know of me rather intimately."

"Yes, I do," he answered simply. "I am the pastor of Saint Bede's Church in Beverly Hills. Your friend, the author and doctor who brought you here, came to see me. He was anxious about you, worried by the complete change in your natural character and disposition. We had a long talk. Now, of course, I could not intervene. Our meeting has been purely fortuitous, or should I say providential. I often come here to read my Office and to get a breath of sea air. Now that we have met, come and sit with me, in my car, or yours, and let us have a little chat."

Resisting an impulse to tell him to go to hell, I sat with him in his old Ford and, compelled by the strength of his personality, I let him have the whole story. He heard me in silence.

"What's the matter with me? Am I possessed? Or merely going crazy?"

"Don't say another word," he commanded. "Get into your car and follow me."

I obeyed. Where was he taking me? To the yard of the presbytery of Saint Bede's. Here we both got out. He came toward me, took my hand, and literally dragged me to the steps leading to the church. Then, before I could protest or resist, he lifted me bodily, bore me up the steps, and then, with a final rush, into the church and up to the altar, where suddenly he relinquished me.

I fell flat on my face, literally writhing in a series of convulsions, endlessly, the sweat pouring from my brow. At last, with a final spasm, I was still.

"Don't move, Desmonde."

He had a towel with which he wiped my lips, my brow. Then he raised me to sit beside him.

We sat together in silence for perhaps five minutes.

Then he said, "Desmonde, you are still weak. Nevertheless, I command you to go out of the church, and down the steps. You will then turn, and return to me here."

I went out of the church and down the steps. Then, without hesitation and with complete ease, I came back up the steps, into the church, up to the altar, and knelt down beside him.

Here the narrative broke off. And beneath, Desmonde had written:

I have to stop now, to go to the studio. I hope this long screed did not bore you. I simply had to write it to you, my dear, dear friend. Later on, I will continue.

When I finished reading, we were silent, both impressed, both deeply moved. At last Nan said:

"What on earth? Was he really possessed?"

"Who can tell? Satan has many wiles. Yet it could be rationally explained. A long and powerful psychological buildup of hatred, following upon his unhappy marriage. Hatred and revulsion against the Church, against God."

"How terrible."

"Yes, but it can happen. I'm glad I spoke to Father Devis."

"That was a blessing."

"And now, we'll have to wait, and hope."

9

Once again I was waiting for Desmonde, not at Euston but on this occasion at Waterloo Station, and once again I was early. Rather than submit to the jostlings of porters and passengers already moving toward the P. & O. boat train, I went into the waiting room and began to reread the amazing letter, written with the old Desmonde sentimental and ebullient panache, which had brought me here and which, dated the week before, was headed, incredibly, Seminary of Saint Simeon Tarrijas, Spain.

My very dear A. J.,

I am on my knees to you, begging absolution for my neglect, my unpardonable delay in advising you of all that has been happening to your old friend, of his trials and tribulations, and finally the wonderful solution, or say rather the Heaven-inspired resolution, which has raised his bowed head, fired him with new incentive, vigor and inspiration. Desmonde is himself again, looking forward to a new beginning, to an adventurous future dedicated to the service of suffering humanity and to the Lord. How can I adequately thank you, dear A. J., for your wisdom and foresight in alerting Father Devis to the fact that I should have need of him. He has brought me back to myself, as I was before, and although I have irretrievably lost my priestly privileges I am once again a practicing and penitent member of the Church.

And how kindly and thoughtfully the good Father Devis has guided me into the channel that my life must now take, a course which, indeed, has been dormant within me ever since my arduous days at Saint Simeon's. Yet who would have believed Father

Hackett when he said, "I'll make a missionary of ye yet, Fitzgerald."

You must know that I could never be reinstated as a priest, and even if this were possible, what chance would I have of properly officiating in an Irish or an English parish, where my past would be a matter for scurrilous street-corner gossip. Father Devis was emphatic on this point and so perforce was I. We decided that any work of expiation or atonement which I might undertake must be in foreign fields. It was then that Father Devis pronounced those fateful words: "You must go to Father Hackett to see what he can do for you."

Of course, I agreed, for the same thought was in my mind.

I made my escape, with great difficulty, from the studios of Hollywood, in which I never knew a single moment of happiness. They tried hard to lasso me with a new contract, but with Father Devis's help I escaped the noose, under the pretext that my voice required rest. And so I went, as a penitent, to Saint Simeon's, bearing, as a gesture of propitiation and submission, an exact replica of the Golden Chalice which, for one short year, had been in the custody of the college.

I spare you, dear A. J., the moving sentiments and deep emotions of my return to my alma mater. Needless to tell you that I was profoundly affected, the more so since the little monastic cell which I had once inhabited had been prepared and allotted to me again.

Dear little Petitt, alas, is no more. I shed tears over his grave. My enemy, the execrable Duff, has proved himself a better man than I. He is now out in the Congo, not a particularly comfortable spot in which to lead the forces of Christian endeavor.

Father Hackett is little changed. For a man almost continuously afflicted by a recurrent fever, he is not only brave, but remarkably durable. He received me calmly, and was greatly pleased by my offering of the Chalice.

Once we got together on my problem he had little difficulty in coming to a decision. He said, calmly and seriously:

"I know exactly, Desmonde, what I shall do with you. Since you are no longer a priest you are useless in the general field of missionary endeavor. In any case, you are not physically fitted for the jungles of Central Africa. However —," here he paused, regarding me intently — "there is an opportunity awaiting you, one eminently suitable, in India." He went on: "You are aware, Desmonde, of the work I started in Madras, among the children of the Untouchables, those little half-naked beings who clutter the pavements, even the gutters, of the city, neglected, destitute and homeless. I had done something toward starting a dispensary and a school for them, and when I was obliged to leave, this work was wonderfully developed by an excellent American priest, Father Seeber. He has done well, and now has a school of considerable size where many, many of these human wastrels have been clothed, educated, and transformed into happy and useful members of society. Some have even gone on to be teachers, priests, doctors.

"Now Father Seeber is no longer young. I know from his corresponce with me that he finds the work rather too much for him. He would welcome an assistant, particularly one who is fond of children and capable of dealing with them. What a blessing it would be if he could find the right person, who would help him to expand and develop his school, one especially who might assist him financially, for I assure you he is always in need of money." Father Hackett paused and looked at me significantly. "Would you wish me to cable him on your behalf?"

How can I describe, A. J., the arrow of joy that pierced my heart.

What a Heaven-sent opportunity! You know that I have always loved teaching children, and it was said at Kilbarrack and at my old school in Dublin that I "had a way with them." Now to have this chance to exercise my talent and in a foreign land, spiced with the savor of novelty and adventure. I immediately begged Father Hackett to cable.

He did so, and for all that day and most of the next, I paced the grounds of the seminary in an agony of suspense. Then came the reply. I was accepted. I was to go at once! I went immediately to the church and offered up a prayer of gratitude.

Then came the business of preparations for my departure, no easy matter I assure you, A. J., since there was much demanding my attention. A P. & O. liner was due to leave Southampton for Bombay in six days' time and immediately, by cable, I booked my passage on this ship. In Madrid I would pick up some attire suitable for the tropics, and train direct to Paris, thence to London, where I hope to meet with you. I thought it wiser not to break my journey in Ireland, but I shall return there one day when I have redeemed myself. So, on to London where I shall be with you. And what a happy reunion this will be!

I should explain that my purgatorial period in Hollywood had not been entirely wasted, and under the judicious management of Frank Vincent, a substantial fortune is wisely invested which supplies me with an annual income, adequate not only for the charitable needs in the adventurous future ahead of me, but for those personal obligations which it is my duty and pleasure to discharge.

You should know that an annuity has been settled on my daughter which will make her future safe and secure. I have also sent Madame Donovan a gift which I hope she will appreciate. This is a most adorable little antique silver statue of the Virgin, pure fifteenth century, not Benvenuto Cellini, of course, but by a comparable artificer, which I found in 57th Street in New York, before taking ship for Europe. In the same street I chanced upon a delicious Mary Cassatt, a mother and child, of course, which I could not resist. This has been shipped to you, dear A. J., and I know you will love it. Nor did I forget Mrs. Mullen and Joe, who were so kind to me in Dublin. They have been well rewarded. Canon Daly was a more difficult proposition. I would have sent him "Dew" but I know he is well supplied with that commodity, so instead I sent him, with my love, some finely embroidered linens for his altar.

Oh, God, how it pains me to recollect these happy days at Kilbarrack, and the foretaste of Heaven that I threw away through my own folly. But I shall make reparation in the slums and stinking alleys of Madras. Already I have borrowed a Hindustani phrase book from Father Hackett and am coming to grips with the language!

But enough, A. J., I will cable you when I am due to arrive and where we may meet. Perhaps you will give shelter for a night to this happy pilgrim, your most loving friend.

I folded and pocketed this gushing, effusive, so typical screed, with the cable that had followed:

DELAYED A FULL DAY BY YELLOW FEVER SHOTS IN PARIS. PLEASE MEET ME WATERLOO STATION 10 A.M. FRIDAY FOR A FINAL FAREWELL DESMONDE.

Train time was perilously near. Surely he must show up soon. I rose and went out of the waiting room.

And there, suddenly, my eye was caught and held by a traveler, garbed in a pulled-down black sombrero that had something of the cleric, but more of the bandit, a short, black, full-skirted coat, formidably belted at the waist by a four-inch leather strap, black trousers narrowed to ankle length, soft leather boots, and striding with the serious air of a pioneer behind two porters, who staggered beneath a huge brass-studded cabin trunk. Yes, it was Desmonde, dressed up for his new part and playing it for all it was worth.

He saw me and immediately came toward me, holding out both his hands.

"My dear, dear A. J. How wonderful to see you again! And how sadly unfortunate that our meeting should be here. Those beastly yellow fever shots! He looked at his large wristwatch which, peppered with the signs of the zodiac, seemed also to be a compass. "Come! We have at least ten minutes." He drew me into the deserted waiting room. "I've paid my bearers, they'll put my luggage in the van."

We sat down, looking at each other.

"You're just the same, A. J. You don't look a day older. It's those appalling cold baths. How do you find me?"

I saw that he was the identical Desmonde who sent Father Beauchamp the birthday cake, but I answered:

"Vastly changed in the outward man."

He gave me a pleased smile. "I've been through the fires of hell, A. J., but now I'm a new man."

"You've had a great rush getting here. Have you had breakfast?"

"I had some *chota hazri* on the Dover train," he answered with affected indifference. "Breakfast, you know. By the way, did you get the Mary Cassatt?"

"I did, Desmonde, thank you immensely. It's lovely."

"I expect Miss Jennings likes it."

"She does. And my wife too. It quite cheered her up. She's been not too well lately."

"I'm sorry, A. J." He had partly opened his coat, revealing, to my surprise, a formidable sheath knife, snugly holstered on his hip.

"You're armed, Desmonde."

"*Dacoits*," he murmured laconically. "They're around in the Madras area. One must be prepared. It's beastly uncomfortable, hurts rather, but I want to get used to wearing it." He paused. "Have you news from Ireland for me?"

"Yes, Desmonde. We see quite a bit of Madame Donovan these days. She has followed up our meeting in Switzerland, and when she's in London she comes to see my wife. They like each other very much. Very kindly, she has had me over to fish when the salmon were running in the Blackwater. I can report that she is well, that your little daughter is growing up bright and beautiful. And that the dear old Canon is still going strong."

He was silent, then said, "Do let them know how you found me." He spoke with dramatic verve. "Sallying forth in my war paint, resolute and unafraid."

I found it difficult to repress a smile. This, indeed, was Desmonde, who would never, never grow up. How lucky he had been in Hollywood to have Frank Vincent, and Father Devis too. Otherwise, the wolves would have eaten him. He would do well, no doubt, in India, if there were an audience of sorts to watch and praise. Perhaps some youthful maharani might require enlightenment and instruction. But I cut the thought and said:

"You must go back to Ireland one day."

"Yes, A. J., when, like Clive, I have conquered India."

Now I looked at my wristwatch.

"Don't you think, Desmonde . . . your train."

"Ah, yes." He stood up. "Come with me to the barrier, dear A. J."

I complied, following as he strode on, like Mario to his execution. And there, under the startled eyes of a couple of ticket collectors, he embraced me on both cheeks before striding off, manfully, toward his compartment.

I felt I ought to play up to him by waiting to see his train pull out. But I was rather tired of waiting, my wife was ill, my new novel looked like being a flop, and, as I had come out without my *chota hazri*, I thought I would go home.

10

We had finished our usual Sunday lunch, quickly produced after church, green salad with toasted Gruyère cheese on *knäckebrot,* followed by fruit and coffee, and were seated at the big window of the sun-room, looking down the long garden at the distant Dents du Midi and Lake Leman far beneath. The sun shone in a blue sky; a cool wind flailed the light branches of the trees. And again I thought how blessed we had been five years ago to find this lovely little place: the low, beautifully designed house, almost new, the garden already planted with choice shrubs and trees. Madame Donovan had heard of it and had enticed me to Switzerland. Nor were we alone in our choice. Great names had contributed to our obscurity, since Noël Coward had settled in a chalet high across the valley and Charles Chaplin lower down on the left, in a great villa that comfortably housed his growing family.

"More coffee," Nan said. "Another cup, Maister, or you'll fall asleep."

"Quiet, child. You know I promised to trim the azaleas. If I don't, you'll get no blooms next year."

"I meant to tell you, Maister, I did them yesterday. But the peonies need weeding."

"My mind was firmly set on the azaleas, and you've done me out of them."

"Look! There's the darling little blue tit in my feeding box."

"Your darling will eat all the cherries, the little brute. And that fat blackbird you cherish, Mr. Pickwick, there he is, digging holes in the lawn."

Suddenly the front doorbell buzzed.

"Damn it."

"I'll go," Nan said. "Gina's gone off for her afternoon."

"No, don't. It'll be some beastly intruder wanting to see around the garden. Don't answer and they'll go away."

The bell buzzed again.

"Two rings," I said. "They'll go now."

But after a short silence the bell buzzed again, loud and prolonged.

"Now we must," said Nan, and rising, hurried to the door. Almost at once a dialogue began which I could not distinctly hear. Then Nan came back, looking troubled and uncertain.

"Maister," she said, in a low voice. "There's a strange little man out there, dressed in black, with a great bristling white beard. He wants to see you. I think he's a priest. His name is Father Keever."

"Keever?" Then I shot out of my chair and made for the door. "Could it be Seeber?"

And so it was! I would have known him anywhere, not only from Desmonde's frequent descriptions, but from the inset photo that always authenticated his delightfully amusing appeals for money.

"Do come in, Father," I said, offering my hand. "What a magnificent surprise!"

"I will, I will come in." He smiled. "But just to relieve your mind, I can't stay. I've been over in Cologne visiting my brother, but I couldn't go back without breaking my return journey to look you up."

"You simply must stay over with us."

"No, no, doctor, I cannot. My plane leaves Geneva at six thirty."

"Then let me get you some lunch."

"No, doctor. I had a fair good feed on the plane from Cologne. But if you offer me a cup of your coffee I'll not say no."

Nan immediately poured a cup from the thermos flask. As he accepted it, he smiled.

"Miss Jennings, is it not? I've heard of you from Desmonde. You don't like him?"

"Not him. Only his bowings, knee-bendings, and hand-kissing."

"You'll never shake him out of those." The little man laughed. "You haven't heard from him lately?"

"No. Not for ages. And we're thirsting for news."

"Well, you'll have it. But first, let's have news from you. You're both well?"

"Don't we look in fairly good form?"

"You do, you do. And your poor wife?"

"She is well too, physically. But . . . all else is gone. She does not know me now, nor her children. Yet she is happy and, I assure you, since she is prohibited from being at home, well cared-for, with two special nurses and her doctor in a beautiful country estate . . . the best clinic available for one in her condition."

"Oh dear, oh dear! What a pity!" He sighed, adding, "And what a fearful expense for you?"

This was an inquiry that required no answer. But it was my main reason for living in Switzerland.

There was a silence while our visitor studied us with wise, kind eyes.

"And you two dear people, now you are quite alone here . . . You've been to church, of course, this morning?"

"Naturally, Father. In Vevey. Our churches are within one hundred meters of each other . . . mine Saint Teresa's, and for Nan the nice little Church of England, All Saints."

"Good," he said. "So you are still keeping faith. The castle has not fallen."

"Well, Father, the battlements have suffered some crushing attacks, but the portcullis remains unbreached. Often when we have spent a long heavenly day together and at night must go to our separate rooms, I drool a little, and favor Nan with that atrocious line from Tosti's Goodbye:

" 'Adieu the last sad moment, the parting hour is nigh.' "

He smiled. "Yes, it is hard. But you will both be the better for it. And love the more. Besides, you have so much to be grateful for, this lovely garden and house. Such peace too: *domus parva, magna quies.*" He glanced appreciatively around the room, then exclaimed, "But where are your pictures? Desmonde speaks so often of your lovely Impressionists. I don't see them."

"They have been removed by the Swiss police."

"Good heavens!" He sat up, startled. "For your debts?"

"No! There have been so many robberies lately of valuable paintings that, as we go away often to visit my wife, I have been constrained, almost compelled, to remove them to a place of safety. They are now in the vaults of the Credit Suisse Bank, where we may visit and view them as often as we wish."

"Yes." After a moment's thought: "Undoubtedly a wise precaution. But what a sad indictment of the world of today. I must not tell Desmonde. He is proud of the picture he gave you."

"No, please don't tell him, Father. And certainly do not tell him that the Mary Cassatt he sent me is not genuine."

"What! A fake!"

"A clever copy. Unrecorded. And of no provenance whatsoever."

"No, I must not tell. Or he would in atonement immediately send you something extremely precious."

We both looked at him in surprise.

"You are joking, Father?"

He shook his head, then smiled, and said:

"I see that you are burning to have news of Desmonde. Well, I will tell you. So listen to what may be the grand finale of his varied and adventurous career." He paused, then began:

"When Desmonde came to me he was eager, ardent, overflowing with the resolution to prove himself in every way — in short, to redeem himself. He was tactfully persuaded to disarm himself — we assured him that his knife would not be needed, except in the kitchen where in fact it made an excellent ham slicer. Then we introduced him to his class. He immediately liked the little boys and it was evident that they were prepared to like him. Yet it was discouraging for him to discover that they were far from ready to be instructed, as he had hoped, in Greek and Latin. Instead, they must first be taught to spell, read and write. Another shock for Desmonde lay in our adequate yet admittedly plain diet, which depends largely on the two varieties of millet: *ragi* and *varagu,* both food staples, but far from titivating to the sophisticated palate." Here Father Seeber broke off to indulge in a little private chuckle. "It was amusing to observe Desmonde's face when presented with these platters. But determinedly he got them down, a resolution ameliorated by the fact that on the Saturday holiday he would, at lunchtime, be observed sidling off in the direction of the Commercial Hotel.

"Now, as you can imagine, Desmonde was not content to stop at 'c-a-t' spells 'cat,' and 'two and two make four.' What did he do? He began, of course, to teach his little boys to sing. And how they loved it! Soon he had them caroling away sweetly at hymns and nursery rhymes. Was this enough? Not at all. Selecting eight boys with the best voices, he collared them after school and, teaching in the church or in the empty classroom, he began to make a choir. And did he succeed? At our quarterly assembly in the big hall he produced his choir. It was, I assure you, a great, an immense success. God bless my soul! They even sang two of his favorite songs, 'Oft in the Stilly Night' and 'Passing By,' and were cheered to the echo. Even I was moved, deeply moved by those pure, lovely young voices ascending in perfect harmony."

Father Seeber paused. We were both listening intently, aware that there was more to come.

"Go on, do go on," Nan exclaimed. "More coffee? It's still piping hot."

Another cup of coffee was poured and gratefully accepted.

[335]

"Yes," Father Seeber resumed. "As you've guessed, nothing could stop Desmonde now. Madras is a great city, but news travels fast. Word of Desmonde's choir got around and before long an invitation came for the choir to sing at an afternoon charity concert to be held at the government's Art College. With my permission Desmonde accepted. Now, obviously, the little boys couldn't go in their poor, makeshift clothes. So Desmonde got busy, ordered and had made . . . you'll never guess what . . . eight little scarlet soutanes and eight red hats. His choir was now named the Little Cardinals."

One saw at once in this the expression of Desmonde's subconscious longing. We could scarcely wait till Father Seeber finished his coffee.

"Now, I'm not going to bore you with the success of the Little Cardinals. Early on, we decided we must accept only the few invitations that were absolutely impeccable and select. In Madras, third city of India, where indescribable poverty exists, there is also indescribable wealth, manifested mainly in the great houses and estates congregated in the aristocratic district of Adyar. Many of these rich people are Christians, and not infrequently, when a society luncheon or garden party was given, the Little Cardinals were invoked to entertain the guests. They went, and Desmonde, their teacher, cardinal *manqué,* went with them, not only to have them sing, but to look out that they were not spoiled with sweetmeats and caresses. Naturally, he stayed to lunch and was found to be charming, indeed even more beguiling than the little boys."

He paused, with a reminiscent air, half-smiling.

"Oh, do stop teasing us, Father," I implored. "You're doing it deliberately."

Still smiling, he resumed.

"One of the Adyar hostesses who manifested the greatest and most persistent interest in the Little Cardinals was a Eurasian lady, Madame Louise Pernambur, Christian, yet a veritable rani, widow of a puisne judge of the High Court of

Madras, who had inherited an enormous fortune from her father, whose cotton mills with many hundreds of looms had for years flourished in Calicut. Louise Pernambur, possessor of many things beyond her magnificent estate in Adyar and a house in Poona, whither she retired during the hot Madras summer, was at this time thirty-five years of age, admirably indolent, in figure tending slightly perhaps to a pleasing embonpoint and, as is often the way with Eurasian women, with her creamy complexion and dark languorous eyes, inordinately attractive. But, as many potential suitors had quickly discovered, those dreamy eyes could also be hard. Madame Pernambur knew her value and would never be bought cheap.

"How surprising then, how commendable that this tough, superbly rich and beautiful woman should be so tenderly interested in eight little choirboys. So much so, indeed, that when the Little Cardinals were not permitted to come, their teacher was bidden to luncheon, even to supper, delicious food served on the garden terrace under a huge, lustrous moon."

Suddenly Father Seeber paused and looked at his watch.

"Good heavens! Almost half past three. The car will be coming for me. In fact I think I hear it on your drive. Now I can't tease you anymore. There could be no doubt whatsoever. Louise had fallen deeply, extravagantly, in love.

"One Saturday afternoon when I was in Adyar visiting one of our patrons, I thought I would look in on Madame Pernambur. I knew that Desmonde had been invited there for tea and, as I was hot and thirsty, I hoped I might pick up a refreshing cup and a bun for myself.

"It was perhaps half past three o'clock, the day a real Madras blazer, very different from the persistent rains and heavy floods devastating Bihar up North. As I was now familiar with the house, almost persona grata, I slipped in by the terrace door, along the passage, and on to the great lounge. Here, I drew up, unobserved, in the shadow of the doorway.

"Seated side by side, on the great low settee, under the

[337]

punkah, rhythmically swung by one of the houseboys, were Desmonde and his hostess: madame in a lovely negligee of fine blue voile.

"Desmonde, to his credit, occupied the extreme end of the settee while madame, as though by some process of gravitation, had drawn quite close to him and was looking fondly into his eyes. Suddenly, softly, she murmured a few words in his ear. He responded with a polite smile which, however, barely concealed an air of fatigue, one might even say boredom, whereupon she stretched an arm, and pressed a switch.

"I knew what was coming, since recently an enormous record player had been imported from New York and, loaded with Desmonde's records, planted in a recess outside the lounge. And now, with a premonitory boom, it launched into:

> *You are my heart's delight,*
> *And where you are I long to be . . .*

"As this incomparable young voice swelled through the room she drew still nearer to him. And if ever I saw matrimony in a woman's eyes, it was there, at that moment — I knew Louise well, and with her it could never be anything else.

"So I turned and tiptoed out by the way I had come, then made the circuit to the main entrance where I left a polite message with the butler."

As Father Seeber concluded, we gazed at him in silence, partially stunned by his recital.

"Well," I said at last. "Trust Desmonde to make a soft landing. I hope he'll be happy."

"Wait, wait!" Father Seeber exclaimed. "Don't let us rush our fences. That evening, when Desmonde returned, rather earlier than usual, he went straight to his classroom. Here his little pupils had gathered to await him. Immediately he entered, he was greeted by a song which they had made up among themselves; childish rhymes of affection and praise, but which, sung by these sweet little voices, were really touching.

"Desmonde had moist eyes when he left the classroom, and I noted that he went into the chapel. I knew then that he would come to me and indeed, half an hour later, he knocked at my study door.

" 'Come in, Desmonde.'

"He entered and immediately knelt at my feet.

" 'Father, I have something to tell you.'

" 'Get up, you ass, and sit in that chair.'

"When, with reluctance, he obeyed, I went on. 'And you have no need to tell me. I already know, and you have only yourself to blame. With your hand-kissing and knee-bending, your long, lingering glances from those big blue adoring eyes, you have made the poor woman think that you are hopelessly in love with her and too shy, too humble to declare yourself. So —' I paused — 'she has done it for you. Am I correct?'

" 'Yes, Father,' he said miserably. 'She wishes to take me to Poona for a quiet wedding.'

" 'Do you wish to go?'

"He shook his head dolefully.

" 'I don't want to end my miserable life in her boudoir. Besides,' the poor fool mumbled, 'I really can't stand her smell.' "

Nan and I had an irresistible impulse to laugh, but a glance from Father Seeber restrained us.

"Desmonde was not quite himself. So very firmly I told him that if he wished to avoid further trouble he must clear out at once. They were yelling for helpers up in Bihar where the floods had created frightful havoc and the river had overflowed its banks, sweeping away an entire village. I told him to go and pack and to take a mattress, since it would be a long, slow journey up the coast to Calcutta.

" 'I don't want to leave my little boys, and you, Father.'

" 'Then Madame will never let you be.'

"After a long moment he rose, silently went to his room, packed his bag, and obediently brought down his mattress. At half past ten that night I saw him board the northbound mail at Madras station."

A silence followed this long, and for us, most interesting recital.

"Did he ever get to Bihar?" Nan asked.

"He did, and from reports coming back by wire, has conducted himself there with exceptional courage and resource."

"And Madame Pernambur?" Nan asked again.

"I have judged it expedient to pay a long-deferred visit to my brother," Father Seeber said mildly. "When I return she will be in Poona, to which lovely resort I shall direct a long, pleasingly adulatory, explanatory letter."

The car outside had now been hooting for some time. Father Seeber stood up.

"I wish I might stay longer. But now I must go. I'm glad to have found you both well and happy. And I shall tell Desmonde so."

As we escorted him to the door he took Nan's arm and, smiling, whispered in her ear. Then he shook hands, popped into the taxi, and was gone.

"What a nice, wonderful little man," Nan said. "A perfect darling."

"He is indeed," I agreed warmly. "I must send him a decent check. But, my goodness, that Desmonde! Can you beat it! He was fated to end a missionary in spite of himself. By the way, what did Father Seeber whisper to you?"

She lowered her eyes and murmured these words:

"Be good, dear girl, and you will both continue to be happy."